Latitudes Edge

PROLOGUE

By the final weeks of the year 1781, Lieutenant Nicholas Cruwys at twenty-one had travelled farther than most officers twice his age. He had left Devon a boy of fourteen—earnest, exact, and quietly yearning for the sea. Two years at the Royal Naval Academy in Portsmouth had sharpened his mind and instilled a competent foundation, but it was Captain James Cook and *Resolution* that truly set his course—and the storm that separated him from Cook's expedition late in 1777 which first made it truly his own.

In the Society Islands of the South Sea, he learned survival without command, and influence without rank. In Tahiti and Bora Bora, among people who had never heard of England, he was taught patience and a different view of life. He found and lost love—young, perhaps, but no less real for that. Determined to return to the Navy, he sailed to Samoa with the help of Polynesian navigation and skill. In Samoa, he came aboard a Portuguese trading brigantine and earned the esteem of its worldly captain, who instructed him as much in conduct as seamanship, over a circuitous voyage through the southwest Pacific ending in Macao—but only after Nicholas had survived hard fighting on a bloodied deck, and killed for the first time.

Reaching Calcutta as a passenger on a British East Indiaman in the early months of 1780, he was at last reunited with the Royal Navy and posted as acting lieutenant aboard *Lynx*, a small warship carrying dispatches to Bombay and home. His first temporary command came unexpectedly. *Lynx* was reassigned to escort a valuable convoy from Bombay, and in an attack by French forces from Mauritius (Isle de France), Nicholas played a major part in the capture of an enemy brig, later renamed *Growler*. He was given temporary command of *Growler* by *Lynx's* by his superior, Captain Walsh. As part of the escort, he brought *Growler* safely to the Cape, and then Angola, before standing aside as she was handed to another.

While in Bombay he had met Caroline Carlisle: brilliant, elegant, beautiful, and entirely unsuited to the limitations expected of her. Their understanding was unspoken but deepened across months and latitudes. In London, when they met again, she had accepted a marriage to Lord Ashton—not out of love, but from strategic necessity. The arrangement offered her freedom of a kind: social protection in exchange for silence about that which society would not permit. She chose it with clear eyes. Not easily, but deliberately.

He did not resent her choice. He could not. But the loss was raw and immediate, a wound not yet familiar enough to ignore. Each night brought the same moment of waking—that brief, cruel interval when sleep released him into a world where she had not yet walked away. The truth that followed was no easier for being expected.

The fading glow of Captain Cook's expeditions, which had captured the public's imagination in more settled times, ensured a respectful hearing at the Admiralty, but with the country now embroiled in war against both France and Spain—who had thrown their weight behind the revolting American colonies—it had not secured him the coveted appointment he had envisioned. Instead, for the better part of a year, he had endured service as second lieutenant aboard Walsh's new command, the 28-gun frigate *HMS Triton*, grinding through the thankless and bitter work of Channel patrols in seas made treacherous as much by enemy privateers as by winter gales.

But now, as Lord North's government teetered on the brink following the catastrophic news from Yorktown, the recollection of his skills—evident in his careful reports of Polynesian navigation techniques and surveys of Bora Bora, and indeed in his meetings at the highest levels of the Admiralty—had finally borne fruit. Orders had arrived directing him to join Rear Admiral Hood's staff aboard the flagship *HMS Barfleur* in the West Indies. *Triton* and Walsh were to sail with the reinforcements bound for Hood's squadron, and Nicholas would transfer to the admiral's staff upon arrival.

Nicholas Cruwys carried these orders in his dispatch case, and a harder-won knowledge in his person. He had learned what could be achieved without favour, and what could not. Merit alone might advance a man's career, but connections determined its ultimate reach. The war that had erupted with the colonial rebellion in 1775 now raged across three oceans. France had entered the fray in 1778, Spain a year later, and recently the Dutch Republic had joined the coalition. As 1782 dawned, Britain faced this ring of enemies in virtual isolation, with Parliament itself convulsed by recriminations over Cornwallis's surrender—a disaster precipitated in large measure by Admiral de Grasse's masterful control of the Chesapeake.

Now Nicholas Cruwys would serve under Rear Admiral Samuel Hood, whose tactical brilliance and fighting reputation commanded respect throughout the service—and whose ships along with those of Admiral Rodney might yet salvage something from the wreckage of Britain's fortunes.

CHAPTER ONE

The morning sky stretched azure and cloudless over English Harbour, the early sun already promising another balmy day as Nicholas approached *Barfleur* in the ship's cutter. After a fast passage of four weeks across the Atlantic, *Triton* had reached Antigua's sheltered anchorage only hours before dawn on the 17th of January 1782, and Nicholas felt his spirits lift with the blessed warmth on his face—a welcome reprieve from the bone-deep chill of Channel patrols. The farewells to Walsh had been brief—a firm handshake and words of mutual respect between officers who had endured those bitter winter watches together. Now the great three-decker loomed before him, her massive hull rising from the crystalline turquoise water like a floating fortress, dwarfing the smaller vessels anchored nearby. At 98-guns, she was one of the largest ships in Britain's fleet—a second-rate ship of the line. Only the six first-rate ships, each carrying 100 guns or more, were larger. She had been built to serve as a flagship and ship of the line in the truest sense, designed to stand in formation and deliver devastating broadsides that could shatter enemy vessels at close quarters.

Word had reached the West Indies that Admiral Rodney was expected to depart England any day with substantial reinforcements—if he had not sailed already. The fleet desperately needed every gun and experienced officer, for Hood's situation here remained precarious despite his tactical brilliance in the recent actions off St. Kitts.

Nicholas had served aboard ships of various sizes—from Cook's *Resolution* to the nimble ship sloop *Lynx*, the captured brig *Growler*, and most recently, the small frigate *Triton*—but *Barfleur* was his first experience with a true three-decker. Only *Thunderer*, a modern 74-gun two-decker he had toured at Gibraltar as the guest of his distant relation, Captain Matthew Trevenen, came close to this leviathan.

He studied her with professional interest as the boat approached. Her hull measured nearly one hundred and eighty feet from stem to stern, with a beam of fifty feet, providing the stable gun platform necessary for her extensive armament: 28 thirty-two-pounders on her lower gun deck, 30 eighteen-pounders on her middle deck, 30 twelve-pounders on her upper deck, and 10 six-pounders on her quarterdeck and forecastle. When fully manned, she carried upwards of seven hundred and fifty officers, men, and marines—a floating community larger than many English villages.

The cutter pulled alongside the starboard accommodation ladder, where a midshipman and side party awaited to receive him with the formality due an officer joining the admiral's staff. Nicholas ascended with practiced ease, despite the gentle swell that caused the massive vessel to roll slightly at her anchorage.

"Lieutenant Cruwys reporting for duty," he announced as he gained the deck, returning the midshipman's salute.

"Mr. Midshipman Everett, sir," the young officer replied. "Captain Simpson's compliments, and he requests you report to the admiral's secretary in the great cabin at your earliest convenience. I'll have your effects taken to your quarters."

Nicholas thanked him and paused to gain his bearings before proceeding aft. *Barfleur's* weather deck stretched before him, its expanse accentuating the vessel's enormous size compared to the ships he had known. The quarterdeck bustled with activity despite the ship being at anchor—officers and midshipmen supervising the stowage of supplies, marines at their posts, and topmen aloft checking the complex web of rigging that supported three towering masts. The methodical precision of a three-decker in preparation for deployment was a testament to naval discipline at its most refined.

He made his way aft, noting how the men moved with quiet efficiency under the watchful eyes of their officers. Despite her size, *Barfleur* ran with the same naval routines that governed all King's ships, though on a grander scale than most others. As he approached the companion ladder leading to the admiral's quarters, a marine sentry came to attention, scrutinizing his uniform and appearance before standing aside to allow him passage.

The layout of *Barfleur* followed the arrangement typical of all three-deckers with their rows of stern windows, and in the case of *Barfleur* and her sisters, ornate stern galleries aft of the captain's and admiral's quarters. Captain Simpson occupied the stern cabin on the upper deck, his quarters spacious and well-appointed as befitted the commander of such a vessel. Rear Admiral Hood's flag quarters occupied the stern of the middle deck immediately below. The gunroom, where the ship's officers messed together, was situated below the admiral's accommodations, its windows without a gallery but still spanning the width of the stern.

Nicholas descended to the admiral's quarters on the middle deck, where another marine stood guard at the entrance. The great cabin itself was a revelation in size and appointment—considerably larger than those Nicholas had seen on smaller vessels. Tall stern windows admitted gray daylight, illuminating a space that combined military function with the dignified comfort appropriate to an admiral's rank. The aft cabin served as a council chamber and study, dominated by a substantial mahogany table surrounded by chairs for the admiral's councils of war. Charts in leather cases were stowed in purpose-built lockers, while others lay spread across a side table, weighted with brass navigation instruments. The bulkheads were paneled in polished oak, lending warmth to the space despite its military purpose, and adorned with several fine maritime paintings of naval actions from previous conflicts, a reminder of Britain's seagoing heritage.

A man of perhaps forty looked up from a desk positioned to catch the best light from the stern windows. His civilian attire, a well-cut coat of bottle green superfine wool and cream waistcoat, marked him as a secretary rather than a naval officer, though his bearing suggested familiarity with the service.

"Lieutenant Cruwys, I presume?" he said, rising and extending his hand. "Martin Thornhill, secretary to Rear Admiral Hood. We've been expecting you."

Nicholas shook the offered hand, noting the secretary's firm grip and assessing gaze. Thornhill had the smooth manner of a man who moved effortlessly between naval and political spheres, his speech carrying the refined accent of good education.

"The admiral is ashore in conference with the Port Admiral this morning," Thornhill continued, "but wishes to meet with his staff officers at four bells in the afternoon watch. In the meantime, I'll acquaint you with your duties and accommodations."

He led Nicholas through a door into an adjacent compartment that served as the secretary's office and working space for the admiral's staff. Here, several desks were arranged to maximize the available space while providing each officer with sufficient room for his work. Charts, signal books, and correspondence were organized with meticulous care, the administrative machinery of naval command evident in every detail.

"As you're aware, Lieutenant, a flag officer's staff serves as an extension of his command function," Thornhill explained. "Rear Admiral Hood maintains a small but efficient staff. You'll join as junior staff lieutenant alongside Flag Lieutenant Craddock, with specific responsibility for signals and fleet communications, in addition to matters related to navigation, coastal intelligence, and convoy protection. The admiral values precision and brevity in reports, with particular emphasis on actionable intelligence rather than speculation."

Thornhill conducted Nicholas through the intricacies of staff protocol—how reports should be formatted, the chain of communication for different classes of information, and the specific expectations Hood held for his officers. Throughout, Nicholas was struck by the secretary's methodical approach and evident competence. Though not a naval officer himself, Thornhill clearly understood the service's requirements and the particular demands of fleet operations.

"Lieutenant Craddock, as flag lieutenant, handles the admiral's personal communications, fleet discipline matters, and serves as Admiral Hood's direct representative when required," Thornhill continued. "You'll work closely with him on the signals system, though you'll report directly to the admiral when circumstances warrant. Mr. Craddock has served with Admiral Hood for three years and knows his methods well."

As if summoned by the mention of his name, the inner door opened to admit a stocky officer perhaps five years Nicholas' senior. Lieutenant William Craddock carried himself with the quiet confidence of a man secure in his position, his uniform immaculate, his movements economical without seeming rigid. Though of only medium height, his square shoulders and precise bearing gave him a commanding presence that belied his physical stature. Nicholas immediately noted the distinctive features that marked Craddock as a flag lieutenant, including most notably, the elegant aiguillette hanging from his right shoulder that signified his direct attachment to the admiral rather than to the ship itself. His bicorne hat, tucked precisely under his left arm, bore Hood's family crest discreetly embroidered on its cockade—another subtle indicator of his special position.

"Ah, Craddock," Thornhill said. "Allow me to present Lieutenant Nicholas Cruwys, the new staff officer."

Craddock studied Nicholas with cool assessment, his gray eyes missing nothing. "Captain Cook's expedition, then *Lynx* under Captain Walsh, followed by temporary command of the captured *Growler*, and most recently service in the Channel as second lieutenant aboard *Triton*, also under Captain Walsh" he said without preamble, summarizing Nicholas's recent service. "I've reviewed your service record. The Admiral expects his staff to anticipate requirements rather than merely respond to them. I trust you've developed such foresight during your somewhat unusual career."

"I endeavor to, sir," Nicholas replied, matching Craddock's formality while noting that the flag lieutenant's tone carried neither warmth nor hostility, merely professional evaluation.

"Good. The Admiral detests wasted time and redundant questions. If you're uncertain about a matter, consult me before approaching him. If I'm unavailable, refer to Mr. Thornhill." Craddock glanced at a pocket watch. "The morning signal conference begins in twenty minutes. You'll attend as observer today, then assume your duties fully tomorrow. I suggest you use the interim to familiarize yourself with our current signals book and fleet orders."

He indicated a desk in the corner that would be Nicholas's workspace, smaller than his own but positioned near a lantern providing good light for chart work. A stack of documents awaited Nicholas's attention, topped by the leather-bound signal book used by Hood's squadron.

"Your sleeping quarters are just forward," Craddock added. "Small but adequate. The Admiral dines at five bells with Captain Simpson and selected officers. You'll join them this evening." With a nod that acknowledged Nicholas's position without suggesting particular welcome, Craddock returned to his own desk, clearly expecting Nicholas to begin work immediately.

Thornhill gave Nicholas a faint smile that suggested he was accustomed to Craddock's brusque manner. "The lieutenant is thorough in his duties, as you'll discover. His attention to detail has saved the admiral considerable trouble on more than one occasion."

Nicholas settled at his desk, opening the signal book to begin memorizing the particular flags and combinations used by Hood's squadron. The system, while based on the standard Admiralty patterns, included additional signals developed by Hood himself to facilitate more complex fleet maneuvers. Some had been adapted from those used by various admirals in previous conflicts, while others reflected Hood's own tactical innovation—the product of decades of experience.

As he worked, Nicholas became increasingly aware of the subtle rhythms of the admiral's quarters: the quiet efficiency of the servants who maintained the space, the regular reports from the ship's officers, the constant flow of communications between the flagship and other vessels in the harbour. Even at anchor, a ship like *Barfleur* operated as a nerve center of naval power, coordinating the complex logistics required to manage a large squadron of fourteen ships of the line and lesser vessels. As junior staff lieutenant with responsibility for signals, Nicholas would play a critical role in this system of communication once they were at sea, transmitting Hood's tactical orders to the fleet through the language of flags.

Shortly before the appointed time, Craddock rose and gestured for Nicholas to follow him. They made their way to the outer cabin, where several officers had gathered around the large table. Captain Simpson, a solid, square-built man, acknowledged Nicholas with a brief nod before returning to his discussion with the ship's first lieutenant. Other staff officers, the fleet surgeon, chaplain, and several midshipmen, took their accustomed places with the practiced ease of men who had attended such conferences many times before.

The signal conference proceeded with brisk efficiency, covering the day's communications with the Admiralty, preparations for the squadron's departure, and updates on the readiness of individual vessels. Craddock conducted much of the session, his precise questions and clear directives revealing why Hood valued his services. Nicholas observed carefully, noting not just the content but the methods, how information was prioritized, which matters were escalated for the admiral's attention, and which were handled at lower levels of command.

Following the conference, Nicholas was shown to his quarters, a small but private cabin. The space was modest by shore standards, barely eight feet by six, with a cot, a small writing desk, a sea chest, and hooks for hanging his uniforms. Yet it offered the precious luxury of privacy, something rare aboard even the largest warships. Unlike the ship's lieutenants who had cabins off to the sides of the gunroom one deck below, staff officers' quarters were on the same level of as the admiral's. Nicholas returned to his desk to continue familiarizing himself with his new position. As he worked through the documents Craddock had provided, he gained a clearer picture of the West Indies campaign that lay ahead. Hood would join Admiral Sir George Rodney, the overall commander in the Caribbean theater, bringing reinforcements that would significantly strengthen the British position against the French. The strategic objective was threefold: protect Britain's valuable sugar islands, disrupt French commerce, and if possible, engage and defeat the French fleet in a decisive action.

At four bells precisely, the muted noises of the ceremony of a flag officer's arrival came from the deck above, and shortly after the marine sentry announced Rear Admiral Hood. Nicholas rose alongside Craddock and Thornhill, and moved to stand at attention in the main stern cabin as the door opened to admit their commander.

Samuel Hood, Rear Admiral of the Red, entered with the confident stride of a man accustomed to authority. At fifty-seven, he retained the vigor that had characterized his long naval career, though silver now dominated his hair and lines of command marked his face. Of medium height and spare build, Hood nonetheless possessed a physical presence that commanded attention without theatrical effort. His uniform, while immaculate, showed signs of practical wear that suggested a commander who valued function over ostentation.

Hood's gaze swept the cabin, taking in his staff with swift assessment before settling on Nicholas. The same sharp, intelligent, and deeply set eyes beneath heavy brows Nicholas remembered from the Admiralty meetings studied the new lieutenant with penetrating intensity.

"Lieutenant Cruwys," he said, his voice clear and measured. "You've arrived as instructed. Good. Punctuality is the foundation of naval efficiency. Have you reviewed the squadron orders and signal book?"

"Yes, sir," Nicholas replied. "Lieutenant Craddock provided them this morning."

Hood nodded, apparently satisfied with this brief response. "You'll join the tactical planning conference tomorrow at nine bells. Tonight you'll dine with Captain Simpson and myself to discuss your specific duties regarding coastal intelligence. No doubt you've already begun familiarizing yourself with our system."

It was not a question, but Nicholas recognized the implied invitation to demonstrate his preparation. "Yes, sir. I've noted the additional signals your lordship has developed for close-order maneuvers in restricted waters. They seem particularly relevant to operations among the islands of the Caribbean."

Something approximating approval flickered briefly across Hood's features. "Indeed. The West Indies campaign presents unique challenges, restricted sea room, treacherous shoals, and complex wind patterns created by the islands themselves. Your experience in the Pacific archipelagos may prove valuable, though the scale differs considerably."

He glanced around at the others and gestured to a chart of the Leeward Islands spread on the side table. "We'll rendezvous with Rodney off Barbados, then establish our primary base here at Antigua. The French maintain their main squadron at Martinique, with supporting elements at Guadeloupe. Fort Royal harbour offers them excellent protection, but limits their freedom of movement. We must be prepared to blockade effectively while maintaining our own mobility."

For the next half hour, Hood outlined his preliminary thinking on the campaign to his staff, moving markers representing ships across the chart with the precision of a chess master. Nicholas observed that the admiral's strategic approach balanced aggression with calculation—he sought decisive engagement but would not sacrifice strategic advantage for temporary tactical success. Throughout, Hood displayed the comprehensive grasp of both strategic principles and practical seamanship that had earned him his reputation as one of the Navy's most capable commanders.

"The French have capable officers," Hood concluded, "particularly the Comte de Grasse—who distinguished himself at the Chesapeake and was, in effect, the architect of our defeat at Yorktown. We may expect skilful opposition. But their ships are often short of hands, their lines of supply overextended, and their strategic aims divided between the Caribbean and the American coast. These are weaknesses, and we must be prepared to exploit them."

He straightened. "Carry on, gentlemen."

With that, Hood withdrew to his private cabin, leaving Nicholas with the distinct impression of a commander who favoured competence and initiative above formality or deference.

Dinner that evening in the admiral's dining cabin provided further insight into Hood's character and methods. The space, situated forward of the great cabin, was furnished with the refined simplicity that characterised Hood's approach to command—quality pieces chosen for durability rather than ornate craftsmanship. The meal itself followed the same principle: excellent but not extravagant, served on the admiral's personal silver and porcelain by servants who moved with practised efficiency.

Captain Simpson proved more genial in this setting than his more public manner had suggested, sharing anecdotes from previous campaigns with dry humour that occasionally drew forth a smile from Hood. Nicholas noted the easy rapport between admiral and captain.

"Sir George Rodney, like many of us, has served extensively in the West Indies," Hood observed as the cloth was removed after dinner, "but fresh perspectives may prove valuable. You'll compile a briefing document on approaches to the French and other islands, Lieutenant Cruwys. Though you've not sailed these waters yourself, I understand you have exceptional skill in interpreting charts and currents."

"Aye, sir," Nicholas replied, recognising both the responsibility and the opportunity such an assignment represented. "I'll consult with the sailing masters who have direct experience in these waters."

Hood nodded with evident satisfaction at the initiative and suggestion. "Good. Begin with Mr. Harlow, *Barfleur*'s master. In addition to his many years in the Navy, he has served in the Caribbean trade before joining the service. Then visit each ship in the squadron; speak with any officer or master with regional knowledge. Craddock will arrange a boat for you to-morrow."

Nicholas immersed himself in the assignment. He spent mornings poring over the detailed Admiralty charts of the Windward and Leeward Islands, noting how the prevailing winds and currents would affect fleet movements among the islands. Afternoons found him visiting the other ships of the squadron in turn, consulting with sailing masters, lieutenants, and even veteran quartermasters who had navigated these waters in previous campaigns or merchant service. The knowledge he gathered proved invaluable. He learned of hidden anchorages not marked on official charts, of treacherous currents that shifted with the seasons, of passages between reefs that local traders used to bypass the main shipping lanes. Though he lacked personal experience in the Caribbean, Nicholas found that his background in Pacific navigation gave him a framework for understanding the complex interaction of wind, tide, and island geography that shaped naval operations in archipelagos.

Craddock, while never warm, gradually displayed a grudging professional respect as Nicholas demonstrated his competence and willingness to learn the staff's particular methods.

Three days after joining Hood's command, Nicholas received an unexpected letter forwarded from Coutts & Co., his London bankers. Opening it in the privacy of his cabin, he discovered a formal notification that his full prize money for the capture of the French vessels in the Indian Ocean more than a year before had been adjudicated and deposited to his account—a sum considerably larger than the advance he had received in London. The total, just over £200, represented nearly four years' worth of a lieutenant's pay. While not a fortune by aristocratic standards, together with the nearly £170 already in the account, it provided a welcome financial cushion that freed him from the immediate monetary concerns that plagued many officers of his rank.

The letter included a brief personal note from Mr. Lawrence, the bank partner who had established his account:

> *"This total sum of £370, prudently managed, might serve as the foundation for future security. The bank stands ready to advise on suitable investments should you wish to provide for eventual retirement from active service."*

Nicholas smiled at the banker's assumption that a lieutenant bound for a war zone would be contemplating retirement, yet recognised the practical wisdom in the suggestion. Many naval officers, even those who survived combat, found themselves destitute in later years when age or injury forced them ashore. With a small but secure financial foundation, his own future now seemed marginally less precarious—a rare luxury for an officer without family wealth to sustain him.

His first dinner in the gunroom on his second evening aboard had proved illuminating. Unlike the compact wardrooms of smaller vessels, *Barfleur*'s gunroom was expansive—a long compartment across the stern of the lower deck, with multiple windows providing both light and ventilation. A massive oak table dominated the space, surrounded by chairs, with a sailor acting as servant standing behind each officer. Oil lamps swung in gimbals overhead, casting a warm glow over the assembled company.

The gunroom mess operated as its own society within the larger ship's community, with the first lieutenant serving as president at the head of the table. Lieutenant Grady, a solid professional in his thirties, greeted Nicholas with proper formality but genuine welcome.

"Lieutenant Cruwys—Admiral's staff, if I'm not mistaken? Welcome to our humble establishment. We observe certain traditions here that may differ from smaller vessels, but nothing too burdensome. The mess subscription is three guineas per month, which covers wine and extras beyond the purser's standard fare. Our steward will add you to the accounts."

Nicholas found himself seated between Lieutenant Barnes, *Barfleur*'s third lieutenant, and the Master, Mr. Harlow—the experienced Caribbean navigator Hood had mentioned. The conversation during dinner ranged widely, from professional matters of seamanship and navigation to the inevitable speculation about their upcoming operations against the French. Unlike the formal discussions in the admiral's quarters, here the officers spoke more freely, offering candid assessments of both their own capabilities and those of their potential opponents.

"De Grasse is no fool," observed the Master, running his hand through his salt-and-pepper hair and refilling his glass as the cloth was removed after the main course. "I observed his operations off the Chesapeake last year. He understands these waters and how to use the islands to tactical advantage. Some believe the French may be inferior sailors on the whole, but their officers are well-trained in formal tactics."

"And their ships usually are faster," added Barnes. "They can outsail us in light airs, though they can't stand up to close combat like *Barfleur* and her sisters." The Master grunted at this last comment and shook his head.

"Perhaps so, but in any event I believe it will come down to gunnery more than manoeuvre."

Nicholas listened attentively, absorbing these perspectives from officers who had faced the French in recent actions. The conversation eventually turned to his own background, with several officers expressing interest in his Pacific experiences and subsequent journey.

"Cook's expedition, was it?" inquired the purser, another older man who had served in multiple theatres. "I met him once in Portsmouth before his second voyage. Remarkable navigator. A great loss to the service."

"Indeed," Nicholas agreed. "His methods transformed our understanding of oceanic navigation and charting. And he was a fine commander."

"And now you find yourself in quite different waters," Harlow remarked. "The Caribbean is a treacherous mistress compared to the open Pacific—more islands, reefs, contrary currents, and hurricane seasons. Though I understand from a remark of the admiral that you are to begin collecting information on alternative passages among the islands?"

"Indeed," Nicholas acknowledged. "I believe the patterns of wind and current around volcanic islands may follow certain principles whether in the Pacific or Caribbean, though the scale differs. We shall see."

The evening continued in this vein—professional discussion interspersed with naval anecdotes and the occasional ribald joke. Nicholas found himself appreciating the camaraderie of the gunroom, a space where rank remained important but where shared professional identity created bonds that transcended immediate hierarchy. By the time he retired to his cabin, he had begun to feel integrated into *Barfleur*'s company in a way that complemented his position on Hood's staff.

In just a few days life aboard settled into a rhythm characterised by the blending of naval routine with the particular demands of a flagship. Nicholas typically spent his mornings in the admiral's quarters, working with Craddock on planning and correspondence, while afternoons often involved consultations with various officers or focused work on specific assignments. Most evenings, unless specifically invited to dine with Hood, he took his meals in the gunroom with the ship's regular officers.

Six days after Nicholas had joined *Barfleur*, and was still mastering the protocols of a flag lieutenant's duties, news arrived on the morning of 23rd of January.

A schooner from St. Kitts reached English Harbour under press of sail, bringing urgent intelligence: the Comte de Grasse, with a fleet of over thirty ships of the line, had landed a substantial French force at Basseterre. Siege works had commenced against Brimstone Hill, where the British garrison held position with limited supplies.

Hood's response was immediate. The captains of the squadron were ordered aboard *Barfleur*. Signals were issued for sailing within the day. The force then assembled at Antigua numbered twenty-two ships of the line, including a division under Rear Admiral of the Blue Sir Francis Samuel Drake. Hood, though of equal rank, held seniority and overall command of the fleet.

In the great cabin, the captains stood about the chart table while Hood laid out his plan: he intended to sail immediately for St. Kitts, approach under cover of darkness, and attempt to occupy the anchorage to the leeward of the island—placing the fleet between the enemy and the sea.

Nicholas, standing ready at the clerk's table, recorded the notes and took down Hood's operational points for signal preparation. There was little discussion. Hood spoke precisely, ensuring that each captain understood the timing, sail order, and anchoring formation.

Boats were despatched back to their ships, signal flags were raised, and by mid-afternoon the fleet stood out from English Harbour in formation—*Barfleur* leading, followed by *Alfred*, *Valiant*, and the rest in close order. The weather was fair, the wind at northeast.

By late afternoon, the cabin had assumed its characteristic discipline. The great table, cleared of personal correspondence and laid out with the squadron's night signals, reflected the shift from deliberation to execution. Overhead, the timbers creaked gently as *Barfleur* continued a northwesterly course.

Nicholas sat opposite Thornhill at one of the smaller desks, reviewing the lantern hoists and sail configurations for the evening approach. Signal intervals had been adjusted twice in the last hour, each time to account for timing between divisions and changes in the wind. Lanterns were to be used in strict economy—two abaft, shielded; a third permitted only on the rear ships of each line for station-keeping once they were committed inside Frigate Bay.

Thornhill read aloud from the master list while Nicholas cross-checked the entries against the flag lieutenant's notations. No discussion passed beyond the immediate necessity of the task. The room, for all its furnishings and comfort, had taken on the character of a gundeck just before action: focused, quiet, exact.

Lieutenant Craddock entered without announcement, having come from the quarterdeck. His boots were clean, uniform crisp despite the tropical heat, and he carried the confidence of a man who understood not only the plan but its likely execution. He surveyed the table, eyes moving quickly between the orders and Nicholas's notes.

"Time from head of column to anchoring?" he asked.

"Thirty-eight minutes, assuming steady wind and no drift, sir," Nicholas replied, not looking up.

Craddock nodded. "It will be less. Hood intends to press the centre in tight. *Alfred* will be late if her topsail crew aren't up to it."

He took up the final draft of the instructions, scanning it with practiced economy. "This will serve."

Thornhill affixed the sealing wafer to the copy bound for *Belliqueux*, then handed it to a waiting midshipman for dispatch. "The admiral will review the final orders shortly."

Nicholas glanced toward the tall stern windows, now shrouded in the violet haze that preceded true nightfall. The fleet was already drawing close to the southern tip of Saint Kitts. Lights would be doused soon. Conversation would give way to pacing feet, whispered corrections, the tension of sailing in darkness toward a hostile anchorage.

Craddock turned to Nicholas. "The admiral will want your signal hoists laid out in order of execution—no improvisation. You'll be on deck beside me once we round the point. Stay within arm's reach."

"Aye, sir."

He made no comment about Nicholas's short tenure aboard, nor did he need to. The implication was clear: the margin for error was none.

The sky began to pale behind the high ridgeline of Brimstone Hill, casting the anchored fleet in a hush of soft gold and pearl-grey. Light filtered across the anchorage in layers—first catching the topgallants, then warming the curves of the upper yards—until the hulls of *Barfleur*, *Alfred*, *Belliqueux* and the other eighteen British ships of the line emerged clearly against the bay's rippling calm. The

Caribbean dawn came on without fanfare: humid, radiant, utterly still.

Nicholas stood to windward on the quarterdeck, glass in hand. Beyond the curve of the land, the French fleet remained at anchor, strung across the mouth of the bay in deliberate array. Thirty large ships, perhaps more—distinct now in the rising light. They had not yet stirred.

"Not bad, for a night's work," Craddock said beside him, voice even, almost wry.

Nicholas lowered the glass. "Either their watch was inattentive, or they didn't believe it possible."

"They believed we'd wait," Craddock replied. "They thought the admiral would stand off and signal. Instead he anchored under their nose. Classic Hood—cool as a surgeon and twice as quick."

He scanned the horizon again, eyes narrowing. "Still, they'll not let it lie. Not with this much iron at our backs."

Below them, boats were already being hoisted out and signal halyards double-checked. The gun crews lingered nearby, loose-limbed but alert. The call to quarters had not sounded, but every man aboard knew it was a matter of minutes.

"The admiral?" Nicholas asked quietly.

"Waiting. Wants a full sighting before he commits. Doesn't bluff."

Craddock paused, then added without affect, "He saw you correct our bearing last night. Didn't say anything—but he saw."

Nicholas inclined his head slightly, acknowledging without presuming.

A breeze stirred the flags on the leeward ships, carrying the faint smell of smoke. Ash drifted down from Brimstone Hill like pollen. French mortars had begun again—slow, probing shots against the hilltop batteries. The sound reached them after a pause: a low, deliberate rumble.

Craddock's voice dropped. "If they mean to dislodge us, it'll be today."

Nicholas said nothing. The air aboard *Barfleur* was perfectly still, like canvas before the wind. The fleet held its breath.

Shortly after the sun cleared the heights, a runner came aft from the admiral's quarters with a curt instruction: the flag lieutenants were to attend immediately.

Nicholas followed Craddock below without a word. The great cabin had been stripped of most furniture save the long central table, now strewn with charts and signal books. Hood stood at its head, his posture as still and assured as if at a formal audience. Thornhill stood by the sideboard, ink still wet on the copies before him.

"They are beginning to weigh," Hood said without preamble, gesturing toward the chart of the bay. "Two columns forming off the anchorage. De Grasse intends to press the southern end of the line, likely to break our formation or push us off station."

He looked from Craddock to Nicholas. "They must be made to believe we are prepared to receive them at anchor—no running, no slack gunnery. I want the signal flags laid out for defensive engagement and readiness. If they attempt a cutting action, the inner ships are to fire chain and aim to dismast."

Craddock nodded once. Nicholas bent over the chart, noting positions already updated with greased pencil. *Prudent* and *Valiant* held the southern flank, while *Barfleur* and *Shrewsbury* anchored near the centre.

Thornhill stepped forward. "Reinforcing signals drafted, sir—general order to stand fast, and readiness to deploy kedge anchors if repositioning becomes necessary."

"Very good. Deliver them," Hood said. "We'll hold this line."

Craddock turned on his heel, Nicholas following him out. Within moments the quarterdeck was a storm of activity: flags unfurled, orders shouted, midshipmen sprinting to the halyards. In the distance, sails blossomed among the French masts—broad pennants snapping as the wind caught them. Their lead ships had cleared the anchorage and were now standing in.

Nicholas took his station near the signal locker, hoists in hand. The horizon filled with the enemy line, sun glinting off their gunports like flints struck in succession.

Behind him, Craddock's voice rang clear. "Make signal: all ships engage from current position. No manoeuvre."

A flurry of colour shot upward on *Barfleur*'s main.

Then, like a vast inhalation reversed, the sound of the first broadside rolled across the water—heavy, deliberate, and astonishingly near.

The battle had begun.

The engagement settled into a rhythm as the morning wore on—not the chaos of boarding or close quarters, but a deadly exchange at range, where the line held steady and the enemy circled like wolves. The French advanced in partial divisions, testing the flanks, then drawing off when met by concentrated fire. It was a trial of nerves as much as arms.

From the quarterdeck, Nicholas watched the enemy ships stand in, one after another, their broadsides breaking against the anchored British line with little effect. Smoke drifted thick across the water, clinging to the gunports and settling in eddies along the deck like fog. At intervals, *Barfleur* returned fire with her lower battery, the reports shuddering through the hull.

Twice, messages arrived from *Shrewsbury* and *Alfred*—minor damage, no casualties. Hood read each one, gave a single nod, and returned to his glass.

Craddock stood a pace behind him, his arms folded. Nicholas worked quietly between the signal halyards and the ready slate, noting orders, tracking movement, ready to relay a new disposition should the admiral signal it.

But no such order came.

By noon, the French had ceased their advance. Their heaviest ships had found no opening and taken more damage than expected. A single dismasting aboard the *Zélé*—her main top snapped clean away—was enough to dissuade a second pass.

A breeze shifted. The sound of firing slackened, then stopped altogether.

Hood lowered his glass and turned to Craddock. "They will not try again today."

"No, sir."

"They'll fall back to Basseterre. Let them."

The admiral turned to go below. "Make no signal."

Nicholas remained a moment longer at the rail. The anchorage held. The fleet was intact. Smoke drifted toward the hills, its scent acrid and sharp on the Caribbean air.

Somewhere inland, Brimstone Hill still held. But they knew now that no reinforcements would come in time.

And yet, against the odds, Hood had done what he had set out to do: confronted a superior force, held ground, and left the enemy to puzzle how a British fleet had anchored under their guns in the night and faced them down in daylight.

As Nicholas looked out over the battered but unbroken line, he understood it in his bones. This was not victory in the official sense—not yet. But it was the kind that made reputations.

The anchorage at Frigate Bay held for three more days. Hood's line remained at readiness, though the enemy made no further move to force the anchorage. Ashore, however, the matter had run its course. On the morning of the 28th, a flag was raised over Brimstone Hill— the French Bourbon white, motionless in the windless air.

There was no ceremony in departure. By mid-afternoon the fleet was underway again, standing off under easy sail. The battered *Zélé* remained at anchor in the French lines, her splintered mast a mute reminder of their failure to carry the anchorage by force. Hood's fleet moved in disciplined silence, neither routed nor triumphant, but undeniably intact.

By the 29th of January they had anchored again in English Harbour, Antigua. The familiar green ridges, the rows of low warehouses and the sweltering dockyard air—all of it received them like the end of a held breath.

Barfleur was among the first to warp into the inner harbour. Her rigging had been scorched in places, sails torn, though her hull bore only surface wounds. Nicholas stood once more upon the quarterdeck, watching the harbour bustle to life at their arrival: tenders dispatched, repair lists unfurled, captains rowed ashore in white-topped surf.

Craddock passed behind him with a bundle of folded papers. "Dispatches to the Governor. Thornhill has three copies already aboard the cutter."

Nicholas nodded. There was no need for words. The meaning of the action would now be weighed—not by the enemy, who had failed to dislodge them, but by ministers, admirals, and secretaries far away.

The fleet had not saved St. Kitts.

But neither had it yielded.

Nicholas found his role expanding gradually as Hood came to recognise his particular capabilities. Beyond the coastal intelligence that formed his primary responsibility, he was increasingly consulted on matters requiring the kind of adaptability he had developed during his unusual career. The admiral, while demanding absolute precision in routine matters, valued creative thinking when confronting novel challenges.

By the 14th of February, signals from a fast cutter off the southern headland brought electrifying news: Admiral Rodney's squadron had been sighted off Barbados, bearing down from the eastward with a fresh wind and twelve ships of the line in company. The long-anticipated reinforcement—dispatched from England after the shock of Yorktown reached Whitehall in November—had arrived at last.

Rodney's command included several new-built seventy-fours and the three decker *Formidable*, a ninety-gun ship newly refitted to serve as his flagship. His orders were explicit: assume overall command of His Majesty's naval forces in the Leeward Islands, neutralise the French fleet under de Grasse, and recover Britain's initiative in the Caribbean theatre.

Five days later, on the 19th of February, Rodney's fleet stood into English Harbour under full sail, their arrival a calculated demonstration of restored British strength. From *Barfleur*'s quarterdeck, Nicholas watched as the newcomers entered the anchorage—gunports dressed, canvas drawing clean—each ship taking station with stately precision until the waters of the bay filled with masts and yards.

The effect was not lost on any man aboard. Hood's twenty-two sail, seasoned from the action at St. Kitts, now joined with Rodney's twelve brought the fleet to thirty-five ships of the line—the greatest British naval force yet assembled in the West Indies.

What followed was not rest but methodical preparation. The newly unified command moved with deliberate speed: victuallers worked round the clock, gunners replenished powder and shot, and staff officers met daily to chart probable French movements. All eyes turned toward Martinique, where de Grasse was reported to be concentrating his fleet and convoy for an expected thrust northward.

On deck and below, the talk was of when the French would move, where they might be intercepted, and whether the next battle would bring final decision. There was no mistaking it now: the balance had shifted. The blow Yorktown had struck was being answered at sea.

CHAPTER TWO

Several days after arriving at English Harbour, signals from *Formidable* summoned Hood and his principal officers to dinner aboard Rodney's flagship. Nicholas found himself included among the invited staff—a recognition of his position despite his junior rank.

"Admiral Rodney maintains formal dinner traditions aboard his flagship," Craddock advised as they prepared to board the barge that would transport them to *Formidable*. "He appreciates proper etiquette and expects his officers to maintain standards regardless of being at sea."

The company from *Barfleur* was received aboard *Formidable* with full ceremony—side boys, boatswain's calls, and marine guards presenting arms as Rear Admiral Hood came aboard, followed by the other officers in order of seniority. *Formidable*, like *Barfleur*, was a second-rate three-decker ship of the line. Though rated at 90 guns, she was in fact a sister to Hood's 98-gun flagship, which—like others of her class—had her original armament augmented by eight smaller pieces.

As they were escorted below into the flag quarters, Nicholas noted the rich appointments of Rodney's accommodations, more elaborate than Hood's more functional spaces, with fine carpets, silver sconces holding beeswax candles, and several paintings of naval actions that appeared to be original works rather than copies.

Admiral Sir George Brydges Rodney awaited them in the great cabin, seated in a chair that resembled a throne more than a naval officer's seat. At sixty-four, Rodney was considerably older than Hood, and his physical appearance reflected both age and the toll of illness. Thin to the point of gauntness, with deeply lined features and noticeably swollen joints that betrayed his struggle with gout, he nonetheless projected an unmistakable aura of command. His uniform, adorned with the insignia of his rank and decorations from earlier campaigns, was immaculate, and despite his physical frailty, his posture remained rigidly upright.

"Ah, Hood! Welcome aboard *Formidable*," Rodney greeted, not rising but extending his hand. His pale blue eyes—still sharp despite his years—moved beyond Hood to assess the officers who accompanied him. His voice had the authoritative timbre of a man accustomed to immediate obedience. "I look forward to meeting your officers. Introduce them, if you please."

Hood presented each in turn, beginning with Craddock and proceeding through the hierarchy. When Nicholas's turn came, Rodney studied him with particular interest.

"Cruwys... not familiar with the name. Devon family, perhaps?"

"Yes, sir," Nicholas confirmed. "From near Exeter."

"Ah, the West Country produces fine seamen," Rodney remarked. "Though I understand you've had a most unusual career path. Cook's expedition, then the Pacific islands, and now Hood's signals officer? An eclectic progression."

"Fortune has provided diverse opportunities for service, sir," Nicholas replied carefully.

Something resembling amusement flickered briefly across Rodney's austere features. He turned back to Hood. "Your young lieutenant appears to have benefited from his unconventional experiences. We shall see if they prove advantageous in our coming operations."

Dinner was served with a formality that would not have been out of place in a London mansion. Rodney's table settings were elaborate—fine porcelain, silver service, crystal glassware, all presumably captured in various prize actions over his long career. Nicholas had heard many tales of the admiral's keen eye for valuable prizes and his relentless pursuit of enemy merchant vessels that might augment his personal fortune. Rodney's reputation for prize-hunting was matched only by the stories of his earlier years as a notorious womanizer and gambler whose debts had once forced him to flee to France to escape his creditors—a colorful past now somewhat tempered by age, illness, and the dignity of high command. The food reflected the admiral's reputation for maintaining luxury despite the limitations of naval service: fresh turtle soup, tropical fish prepared with French sauces, island fruits preserved in brandy, and wines of exceptional quality.

Throughout the meal, Nicholas observed the complex dynamic between the two admirals. Rodney dominated the conversation, expounding on strategic considerations, political developments in Europe, and his previous campaigns in the Caribbean with the certainty of a man unaccustomed to contradiction. Hood listened attentively, offering occasional observations that were invariably precise and germane, yet phrased with careful deference to Rodney's seniority.

Yet beneath the formal courtesy, Nicholas detected significant differences in their approaches. When discussion turned to the French fleet at Martinique, these distinctions became more evident.

"De Grasse must not be permitted to join the Spanish at Santo Domingo," Rodney declared. "We shall establish our base at St. Lucia and maintain a blockade of Fort Royal that will prevent his sortie. Should he attempt to break out, we will bring him to decisive action according to established tactics."

"A sound approach, sir," Hood acknowledged. "Though I would respectfully suggest that positioning part of our force to windward might offer greater flexibility should de Grasse attempt to slip past our main body."

Rodney's thin lips compressed slightly. "The fleet operates as a unified command, Admiral Hood. Division of force introduces unnecessary complications and risks. We shall maintain the traditional line of battle, which has served the Royal Navy well for generations."

"Of course, sir," Hood replied, his tone neutral while his eyes revealed a carefully contained disagreement.

As the dinner progressed to dessert and port, Rodney turned the conversation to the officers' experiences in various theaters. When he directed a question to Nicholas regarding Pacific navigation techniques, Hood tensed slightly, clearly concerned that his junior officer might inadvertently challenge Rodney's professional opinions.

"The islanders navigate primarily by wave patterns, star positions, and the flight of birds, sir," Nicholas explained carefully. "Without instruments or charts as we know them, they've developed remarkable methods for position-finding that rely on sensory observation."

"Fascinating," Rodney commented, though his tone suggested limited interest. "Primitive yet effective for their purposes, I suppose. However, I doubt such methods would serve in coordinating a fleet action against the French. Precision instruments and established navigational science remain the foundation of naval operations."

"Indeed, sir," Nicholas agreed diplomatically. "Though I've found that understanding alternative approaches sometimes suggests refinements to conventional methods."

Rodney's eyebrows rose slightly. "An interesting perspective from so junior an officer. Admiral Hood, your staff lieutenant shows promise, a certain intellectual curiosity that, properly disciplined, might serve the fleet well."

This qualified approval, coming from the Caribbean commander-in-chief, represented a significant endorsement, particularly given Rodney's reputation for critical assessment of subordinates. Hood acknowledged it with a brief nod, while Nicholas maintained a carefully neutral expression despite his inner satisfaction.

As they departed *Formidable* later that evening, Hood offered his own assessment. "You navigated that encounter well, Mr. Cruwys.

Rodney does not suffer contradiction gladly, yet you managed to impress him without challenging his authority. A valuable skill in fleet politics."

"Thank you, sir," Nicholas replied. "Admiral Rodney seems to value traditional approaches."

"He does," Hood agreed, his voice lowered as they were rowed back to *Barfleur*. "And those traditions have served the Navy well in many respects. Yet warfare evolves, and with it, the tactics required for victory. Remember that in the coming campaign—principles endure while methods adapt to circumstances."

Nicholas found his signals expertise increasingly vital as the fleet conducted exercises to perfect their coordination before the inevitable clash. When not directly engaged with Hood's operational planning, he spent countless hours studying the intricate geography of the Lesser Antilles, consulting with local pilots and naval officers who knew these waters intimately. The channels between islands, the treacherous reefs, the daily patterns of wind and tide—all became elements in a complex strategic puzzle that might determine the outcome of battle.

During these weeks of preparation, Nicholas found an unexpected outlet for both physical exercise and social connection in the sword and small arms exercise during the afternoon watch sessions organized by the marine officers. The initial invitation came after Hood had instructed his officers to maintain their physical readiness for the coming campaign. Major Thomas Elliot, commander of *Barfleur*'s marine contingent, had established a regular practice session on the gun deck during the afternoon watch, when space could be cleared among the great guns.

"Lieutenant Cruwys," Elliot had said, approaching him one morning after the signal conference, "I understand from the wardroom that you acquired some unusual sword techniques during your time in the Pacific. We could use some fresh perspectives in our practice sessions. Would you care to join us this afternoon?"

Elliot cut an impressive figure, even among the generally fit marine officers. Tall and broad-shouldered, with the straight-backed posture that characterized the corps, he carried himself with the quiet confidence of a professional soldier. His face bore a thin scar along his right jaw—evidence of combat experience that commanded respect among both marines and naval officers.

"I'd be honored, Major," Nicholas had replied, sensing an opportunity to maintain the fighting skills that had served him well against the French privateers in the Indian Ocean. "Though I should warn you, my methods are somewhat unorthodox."

Elliot's blue eyes had shown genuine interest. "Unorthodox methods that prove effective in combat are precisely what interests me, Lieutenant. I look forward to it extremely."

That first session established a pattern that would continue throughout their time in the Caribbean. Nicholas arrived to find a space cleared on the upper gun deck, just forward of the quarterdeck, with wooden practice swords laid out and several marine officers already engaged in preliminary exercises. Major Elliot introduced him to the participants—two marine lieutenants, the sergeant-major, and two other naval officers who valued the practice.

"Gentlemen, Lieutenant Cruwys joins us today," Elliot announced. "He brings experience from beyond the usual naval circles. Lieutenant, perhaps you'd demonstrate your approach against Second Lieutenant Morris here?"

Morris, a young compact, muscular marine officer with a perpetual half-smile, took up position opposite Nicholas. They saluted with the wooden practice swords, then began a cautious exchange of techniques, Morris employing the standard military style taught at the Marine training establishment, Nicholas initially responding in kind before gradually introducing elements of Silva's pragmatic methods.

The contrast became immediately apparent. Where Morris attacked with textbook precision, Nicholas countered with fluid movements he had learned from Silva, techniques designed for the unstable footing of shipboard combat rather than the formal dueling floor. After several exchanges, Nicholas executed a subtle shift of weight combined with a sweeping cut that bypassed Morris's guard entirely, stopping just short of his ribs.

A momentary silence fell, broken by Elliot. "Interesting technique. Not taught in any manual I've encountered." He stepped forward, practice sword in hand. "Would you demonstrate that movement again, Lieutenant? Against me this time."

What followed was less a contest than a mutual exploration of methods. Elliot proved to be an exceptional swordsman, his formal training enhanced by practical experience in boarding actions during previous campaigns. He adapted quickly to Nicholas's unorthodox style, integrating elements even as he tested their effectiveness.

"The Portuguese trader who taught you these methods understood something many European masters forget," Elliot observed after their third exchange. "In actual combat, one fights on uneven ground, in confined spaces, against opponents who aren't following the rules of engagement."

"Silva would have appreciated that assessment," Nicholas replied, lowering his practice blade. "He considered classical fencing a useful foundation, but insufficient for survival in the waters he traversed."

Elliot nodded, genuine respect in his expression. "These sessions could benefit us all, Lieutenant. Would you consider joining us regularly? Perhaps demonstrate some specific techniques for the officers and senior marines?"

This initial encounter developed into a regular practice routine that provided Nicholas with both physical conditioning and valuable connections beyond Hood's immediate staff. Three afternoons each week, weather and duties permitting, he joined Elliot and a rotating group of officers, sharing techniques and engaging in spirited practice bouts that gradually attracted an audience of off-duty sailors and marines.

Major Elliot, in particular, became a friend as well as a practice partner. The marine officer's background—son of a country clergyman who had entered the corps through merit rather than purchase, gave him a perspective different from both the aristocratic naval officers and the common seamen. Like Nicholas, he had advanced through capability rather than connection, creating a natural affinity between them.

"You maintain a curious balance, Cruwys," Elliot remarked one evening as they shared a glass of wine in the gunroom after practice. "The scientific perspective from your time with Cook, practical seamanship, and something else—a philosophical quality I've not often encountered in naval officers."

Nicholas considered this assessment. "The Pacific islands teach one to question assumptions," he replied after a moment. "Ways of thinking we consider universal prove to be merely cultural, effective within their context but not absolute."

"Precisely what makes your sword techniques so effective," Elliot observed. "You're not bound by the expectation that combat must follow established forms." He studied Nicholas with genuine curiosity. "I wonder how that perspective might apply to our coming engagement with the French. Their tactics are as formalized as their fencing, perhaps vulnerable to similar disruption."

These conversations, continuing over weeks of preparation, gave Nicholas insights into the marine perspective that complemented his naval training. Elliot's experience in amphibious operations and ship-to-ship actions provided practical knowledge that might prove valuable in the coming campaign, while his thoughtful approach to command reflected a mind that considered broader implications beyond immediate military objectives.

"De Grasse is no conventional opponent," Elliot observed during one of their discussions. "His success at Yorktown demonstrated tactical flexibility unusual among French commanders. We would be unwise to expect him to follow predictable patterns in the coming engagement."

By late March, intelligence reports confirmed that the French fleet at Martinique was preparing for a major operation, likely in support of a planned Spanish invasion of Jamaica. The strategic stakes had never been higher; Jamaica represented Britain's most valuable Caribbean possession, its loss potentially devastating to both imperial prestige and economic interests. Rodney positioned the fleet at St. Lucia, perfectly situated to intercept de Grasse should he attempt to sail north to rendezvous with the Spanish forces.

Life aboard *Barfleur* during this period of heightened tension followed the disciplined rhythms of a fleet preparing for combat. Hood and the ship's captain drove their officers and men relentlessly, conducting daily signal drills, gunnery practice, and tactical exercises. Nicholas often found himself working eighteen-hour days, collapsing into his cot for brief periods of rest before returning to duty. Yet despite the grinding schedule, he felt a growing sense of professional accomplishment as his contributions to the fleet's signal system earned Rear Admiral Hood's increasing approval.

The relationship between Rodney and Hood fascinated Nicholas. Both were commanders of exceptional ability, yet their approaches to naval warfare differed significantly. Rodney, the senior admiral, favored traditional line-of-battle tactics, though he was not afraid to innovate when conditions warranted. Hood, by contrast, advocated more aggressive maneuvering to secure the weather gauge and tactical advantage. Their professional discussions—occasionally verging on heated disagreement in conferences aboard *Formidable*, provided Nicholas with an education in high-level naval strategy that no textbook could match.

"Rodney believes in overwhelming force delivered at the right moment," Craddock explained during one of their rare moments of relaxed conversation in the gunroom. "Hood prefers decisive manoeuvring to place the enemy at maximum disadvantage before engaging. Both approaches have merit, though reconciling them in a single battle plan can prove... challenging."

On the 8th of April, 1782, the strategic game of cat and mouse reached its critical phase. Lookouts spotted the French fleet under de Grasse departing Fort Royal, Martinique, clearly bound northward toward its rendezvous with the Spanish. Rodney immediately ordered the British fleet to pursue, determined to bring the French to battle before they could complete their objective.

What followed was a complex naval dance. For four days, the two fleets manoeuvred for advantage among the islands, with periodic skirmishes between vanguard ships but no general engagement. The British struggled to close with the French, who seemed determined to avoid a decisive battle until they could join their Spanish allies.

During this period, Nicholas worked almost without rest, his signals responsibilities critical as Hood and Rodney attempted to coordinate their divisions through frequent changes of wind and tactical situation. Sleep became a luxury measured in minutes rather than hours, meals reduced to hasty mouthfuls taken while bent over charts or signal books. Yet amid the exhaustion, Nicholas found a strange exhilaration—the sense of participating in events that might shape the course of empire, of applying everything he had learned throughout his extraordinary journey to this moment of historical consequence.

By the evening of the eleventh of April, the fleets were approaching the passage between Dominica and the small islands known as the Saints. Intelligence indicated that de Grasse planned to pass through this channel the following morning, hoping to use the islands' disruption of wind patterns to slip away from the pursuing British. Rodney, conferring with Hood and his other flag officers aboard *Formidable*, developed a plan to intercept the French as they emerged from the passage.

As he left the gunroom after dinner that night, Major Elliot followed him and stopped him on the companion ladder.

"Ah, Nicholas," Elliot greeted him with the casual familiarity their practice sessions had established. "I wonder if you would do me the favour of holding certain letters, in case..."

Nicholas understood immediately. It was a usual practice before battle. "I'd be honoured. How are your marines?"

Elliot's expression turned serious. "As ready as discipline and training can make them. We've been drilling boarding parties all week. If it comes to close action, they'll perform their duty." He paused. "And you, any letters or papers you'd like me to hold?"

Nicholas shook his head. For a moment, both men stood in silent recognition of what the following day might bring. Naval battles were chaotic, destructive affairs whose outcomes often hinged on factors beyond any officer's control—a sudden shift of wind, a lucky shot, the timing of a crucial signal.

"I've something for you," Elliot said at last, reaching into the inner pocket of his coat and drawing out a narrow bundle wrapped in oilcloth. "A small token, for your good humour and steady edge these past weeks."

Nicholas unwrapped it to reveal a finely woven sword knot—dark marine crimson and gold thread braided over a stiffened loop, the tassel tightly knotted and capped in polished brass.

"Not Navy issue," Elliot added. "Made up by a Maltese cordwainer for one of our sergeants, who then lost the use of his sword arm at Martinique. I remembered you carry a Portuguese blade—neatly kept, fine work—but no knot. That's a liability in a boarding action."

Nicholas turned the piece in his hands, the weight of the tassel surprisingly solid.

"It's beautiful," he said. Then, more quietly: "And useful. Thank you."

"Just see you don't lose the sword it's tied to," Elliot said, rising. "That one's not so easily replaced." Then with characteristic directness: "Good officers deserve proper tools, and this could be the difference in a close fight." He extended his hand. "Fair winds tomorrow, Nicholas. May we both see the other side of whatever comes."

"And you," Nicholas responded, clasping the offered hand firmly. "Your marines will do England proud, I have no doubt."

As he prepared his equipment for the coming day—checking his signal book, telescope, log sheets, and personal weapons—on the eve of what promised to be a decisive battle, Nicholas steeled his mind for what was to come. He had heard stories about what a fleet action was like, but only the event would tell. Sleep proved elusive that night, as it did for most aboard the British fleet. The tension of imminent battle, combined with the practical preparations that continued throughout the darkness, kept the ships humming with subdued activity. During his brief rest periods, Nicholas found his thoughts drifting to faces from his past—Cook's calm assurance, Atea's loving wisdom, Silva's practical cynicism, and Walsh's demanding precision. He tried not to think of Caroline.

Dawn broke clear and brilliant over the Caribbean on the 12th of April, 1782, revealing the French fleet struggling to form their line of battle in the confused winds between Dominica and the Saintes islands. Nicholas stood motionless on *Barfleur*'s quarterdeck, telescope trained on the enemy vessels, counting methodically as he identified each ship. The French order of battle had been studied obsessively during the preceding weeks, and he recognised the 104-gun *Ville de Paris* flying de Grasse's flag, followed by the 74-gun *Diadème*, *Réfléchi*, and *Scipion*.

"Let's be at it, Captain Simpson," Hood ordered, and Simpson turned to his first lieutenant, who gave the command. The beat of drums echoed across the ship as the men took their battle stations.

Nicholas felt the familiar tightening in his chest that preceded action—not fear exactly, but an acute, almost physical awareness of what lay ahead. He checked his weapons reflexively: the lightly curved cavalry sabre at his hip, and his fine Henry Nock duelling pistol tucked in his belt—one of a matched pair, and indeed the same he had used in defence of Edward Carlisle during the French attack on the East Indiamen convoy. The second remained below in his cabin; to appear with both, he felt, would draw comment.

Major Elliot appeared on the quarterdeck, his marines formed up in precise ranks behind him, their red coats vivid against the weathered planking.

"A good day for it, Lieutenant," he remarked with the peculiar calm that characterised veterans before action.

The sight before Nicholas was nothing short of magnificent—nearly sixty ships of the line spread across the azure Caribbean waters, their towering masts creating a forest of spars against the cloudless sky. It was a spectacle few men ever witnessed: much of the combined naval might of the world's greatest maritime powers assembled for decisive battle. White sails billowed against the blue backdrop, gilded figureheads caught the morning light, gunports opened like rows of dark eyes along wooden walls that rose like floating fortresses from the sea. Nicholas understood he was observing history unfolding before him—a tableau of imperial power projected thousands of miles from Europe that would determine the fate of nations.

"Twenty-nine sail, sir," he reported to Hood, who stood nearby conferring with Captain Simpson. "Their formation appears disrupted by the lee currents off Dominica."

Hood nodded without shifting his gaze from his own telescope. "Indeed. The island's wind shadow has scattered their line. Note how their rear division labours to maintain position."

The British fleet, by contrast, had emerged from the passage between Dominica and Guadeloupe in reasonably good order—thirty ships of the line formed into three divisions. Rodney commanded the centre from *Formidable*, while Hood led the rear division from *Barfleur*. The van division, under Rear Admiral Sir Francis Drake, had already begun to close with the leading French ships as the fleets converged on parallel courses.

At half after seven, the crack of gunfire echoed across the water as *HMS Marlborough* from Drake's division exchanged initial broadsides with the leading French vessels. The pattern of battle was establishing itself: the traditional line-ahead formation, with ships firing in sequence as they came within range of their opposite numbers.

"Prepare the standard battle signals," Hood instructed calmly. "Admiral Rodney will expect us to maintain formation and engage when the line extends sufficiently."

Nicholas moved to the signal locker where Lieutenant Craddock was already preparing the flag combinations that would soon be crucial to coordinating the fleet's movements. Unlike smaller actions, where individual captains might exercise considerable discretion, fleet battles demanded precise coordination through a complex visual language of flags and pennants. As signal lieutenant, Nicholas would be responsible for ensuring Hood's commands were properly transmitted not just to *Barfleur*'s consorts, but often to Rodney's flagship itself.

The breeze stiffened favourably, allowing the British line to bear down on the French with increasing momentum. Through his telescope, Nicholas observed the enemy ships more clearly as the distance closed—their distinctive black hulls with yellow decorative elements, the red gunport lids standing out vividly when open, the glint of morning sunlight on gun barrels run out through those ports, and the colourful signals flying from their mastheads. Despite their scattered formation, the French commanders were clearly striving to establish their traditional battle line.

By a quarter past eight, the battle was fully joined in the van and centre divisions, with the thunder of broadsides creating a continuous roar that carried across miles of ocean. Dense banks of powder smoke obscured portions of the engagement, though the morning breeze occasionally cleared sightlines, revealing the devastating exchange of fire between the massive ships.

"Signal from *Formidable*, sir," Craddock called out. "Admiral Rodney orders the fleet to close the enemy and engage."

Hood nodded. "Acknowledge. Mr. Cruwys, ensure our division signals are prepared for close action. I anticipate we'll be engaged within the hour as the lines extend."

As he worked alongside Craddock, Nicholas observed a curious development in the French line. The wind shift that had initially scattered their formation was now creating gaps between their ships—significant breaches that widened as the vessels struggled against contrary currents and fickle breezes.

Rodney, commanding the centre division from *Formidable*, appeared to notice the same opportunity. At seven minutes past nine, a fresh series of signals appeared from the flagship.

"*Formidable* signals a change of course," Nicholas reported, translating the flag combination instantly. "Two points to larboard, directly toward the gap in the French line."

Hood's expression remained composed, though his eyes narrowed slightly. "So Rodney means to break their line. Bold, very bold indeed." He turned to Captain Simpson. "Prepare to follow *Formidable*'s movements precisely. This manoeuvre, if successful, could prove decisive."

What followed would later be recognised as one of the most significant tactical innovations in naval warfare—the deliberate breaking of the enemy's line of battle—later brought to perfection by Vice Admiral Horatio Nelson. For generations, naval engagements had been conducted with opposing fleets passing each other in parallel lines, exchanging broadsides at close range. Rodney's decision to cut through the French line would allow his ships to rake the enemy fore and aft while disrupting their formation beyond recovery.

Formidable led the way, sailing through the gap between the French *Glorieux* and *Diadème*, followed by five more British ships. The manoeuvre split the French fleet, isolating their rear from their van and creating chaos in their formation. By half past ten, Hood's division was approaching its own point of engagement. *Barfleur*, ninth in the British line, would soon face the concentrated fire of multiple French vessels.

Barfleur shuddered as a French thirty-six-pound shot struck her bow, sending splinters flying across the forecastle. The battle had found them.

"Maintain station on *Bedford*," Hood called, referring to the 74-gun ship immediately ahead of them in line. "We shall follow her through the breach in the French line."

What followed was the controlled chaos of a ship of the line entering combat. *Barfleur*'s gun crews worked with mechanical precision—running out their weapons, firing in disciplined sequence, then swabbing, reloading, and repeating the deadly cycle. The noise was unlike anything in human experience—a physical force rather than mere sound. Each broadside created a concussive wall that pounded the chest and rattled the teeth, while the continuous roar of hundreds of cannon from nearby ships firing in sequence created an unrelenting thunder that made normal speech impossible. Above this foundation rose other noises at intervals: orders bellowed until voices grew raw, the crack of splintering wood, the screech of shot passing through rigging, and, occasionally, the screams of the wounded.

Acrid smoke stung his eyes and throat despite the freshening breeze. From his position on the quarterdeck, Nicholas maintained a constant flow of signals between Hood and the other captains of the rear division, even as French fire began to concentrate on *Barfleur* once they recognised the admiral's flag.

At twenty minutes past eleven, they approached the gap in the French line, following *HMS Bedford* as she cut between the French 74-gun *Scipion* and the 64-gun *Ardent*. As they penetrated the enemy formation, Nicholas witnessed the devastating effect of the manoeuvre. *Barfleur*'s broadside smashed into *Scipion*'s stern, raking her from end to end with catastrophic effect. Through gaps in the smoke, he glimpsed the carnage aboard the French vessel—gun crews decimated, rigging shredded, her quarterdeck a slaughterhouse.

Hood remained impassive, directing *Barfleur*'s movements with calm authority despite the storm of iron that now converged on his flagship. Shot screamed through the rigging, severing ropes and puncturing sails. A twenty-four-pound ball smashed into the bulwark just yards from where Nicholas stood, sending lethal wooden splinters scything across the deck. Three marines fell, one clutching his throat where a jagged fragment had pierced it.

"Signal *Alfred* to close up," Hood ordered, referring to the 74-gun ship that followed *Barfleur*. "We mustn't allow the line to stretch as we cut through."

Nicholas prepared the appropriate flags, but as he supervised their hoisting, a disturbing development caught his eye. *HMS Bedford*, immediately ahead, had taken serious damage to her rigging. Several of her mainmast shrouds had been shot away, and her courses were in tatters. More critically, the signal lieutenant on her quarterdeck appeared to have fallen, and no one had replaced him at the signals station.

"Sir," Nicholas reported to Hood, "*Bedford* appears unable to acknowledge signals. Her lieutenant has fallen, and her flag halliards are damaged."

Hood studied the situation with his telescope. "Most concerning. *Bedford* occupies a critical position in our line. If she cannot receive tactical signals..." He fell silent, considering options as *Barfleur* continued to exchange fire with the French ships to starboard.

At that moment, the overall battle situation was transforming dramatically. Rodney's breaking of the French line had thrown their formation into disarray. The isolation of their rear division created an opportunity for the British to concentrate overwhelming force against individual enemy vessels. Yet this advantage would be lost if ships like *Bedford* couldn't coordinate their movements with the rest of the fleet. Hood lowered his glass, decision made.

"Mr. Cruwys, you will take a boat to *Bedford*. Inform Captain Affleck of our next manoeuvres and ensure he understands Rodney's intentions to isolate the French rear. Their signals officer is down, and they must have someone competent to interpret the flag commands that will follow."

Nicholas understood immediately the danger and necessity of the mission. Small boats were desperately vulnerable during fleet actions. Yet without functioning communications, *Bedford* might operate independently, reducing the effectiveness of the British concentration against the French rear.

"Aye, sir," he replied, already calculating the safest approach to the embattled 74-gun ship, now approximately a quarter mile ahead and exchanging heavy fire with *Scipion*. His hand unconsciously adjusted the cavalry sabre at his side, ensuring it would not hinder his climb aboard the other vessel.

"Take four men from the marine contingent," Hood added. "Major Elliot will select reliable marksmen. They may be needed if the French recognise your purpose."

Within minutes, a boat was lowered from *Barfleur*'s lee side, relatively sheltered from enemy fire. Elliot personally selected four of his best marines to accompany Nicholas, all of whom would board *Bedford* with him. Four experienced sailors were also assigned to row the boat, along with a quartermaster's mate to steer—men chosen for their strength and steadiness under fire.

As Nicholas descended into the boat, Craddock handed him a leather dispatch case containing written orders and signal instructions. "*Bedford*'s captain may be wounded as well," he said quietly. "Be prepared to take initiative if necessary."

The small boat pushed away from *Barfleur*'s massive hull, immediately encountering the confused swell created by dozens of ships of the line ploughing through the waters. The four sailors bent to their oars with practised efficiency, while Quartermaster's Mate

Jeffries manned the tiller, his experienced hands guiding them toward *Bedford*, now partially obscured by gun smoke. The marines positioned themselves with loaded muskets ready, eyes vigilantly scanning for threats of sharpshooters from nearby French ships, Sergeant Miller at their head.

The scene that greeted Nicholas as they pulled away from *Barfleur*'s sheltering bulk was both magnificent and terrifying. The organised lines of battle had disintegrated into pockets of savage combat. To port, *Formidable* and her consorts hammered the isolated French ships with methodical broadsides. Ahead, *Bedford* exchanged fire with *Scipion*, both ships showing significant damage. Further ahead, the French flagship *Ville de Paris* stood defiantly against multiple British attackers, her massive hull absorbing punishment that would have sunk smaller vessels.

It was a terrible spectacle of human destruction on a scale that defied comprehension. Ships that had been marvels of engineering and craftsmanship just hours before now burned fiercely or listed with shattered hulls. Through gaps in the smoke, Nicholas could see decks slick with blood, gun crews decimated by chain shot, masts toppling in slow-motion grandeur to crush men below. The pristine blue Caribbean waters were littered with debris—spars, planking, personal effects, and occasionally bodies, some still moving among the flotsam. The acrid stench of powder smoke mixed with the metallic tang of blood and the sickly-sweet odour of torn flesh. It was war at its most primeval and horrific, man's technological ingenuity harnessed for the singular purpose of destruction.

Their journey across that quarter mile of churning water became an exercise in determination. A random French twelve-pound shot plunged into the water just yards away, drenching them with spray. Throughout, the sailors rowed strongly, their faces set in expressions of focused determination.

As they approached *Bedford*, Nicholas observed the extent of her damage more clearly. Her rigging hung in tangled festoons, her hull showed multiple shot holes along the waterline, and several gunports had been smashed into splintered ruins. Nevertheless, her gun crews continued working, sending broadside after broadside into the nearby French vessels.

"Pull for her starboard quarter," Nicholas instructed Miller. "She's engaged to port—we'll have better shelter on her lee side."

Miller nodded grimly, adjusting their course to approach the relative safety of *Bedford*'s unengaged side. As they drew alongside, Nicholas saw that a section of her main deck bulwark had been carried away by enemy fire, creating an impromptu entry point that would save them from the more exposed climb up her accommodation ladder.

"Secure the boat," Nicholas ordered as they bumped against the ship's hull. "Sergeant Miller, you and your marines will accompany me to the quarterdeck."

With the agility born of years at sea, Nicholas caught a dangling rope and hauled himself up through the shattered bulwark onto *Bedford*'s main deck. The marines followed closely, their practised movements belying the difficulty of boarding a ship of the line in the midst of battle.

The scene aboard *Bedford* was one of controlled chaos. Gun crews worked mechanically despite casualties lying nearby. Officers moved between stations, maintaining discipline through the storm of iron that continued to assail the vessel. The deck was slippery with blood in places, and the air thick with powder smoke despite the breeze.

Nicholas headed aft toward the quarterdeck, Sergeant Miller close behind. As they climbed the ladder, a broadside from *Scipion* struck *Bedford*'s quarter, sending wooden splinters scything across the deck. Both men instinctively ducked, then continued upward.

The quarterdeck presented a grim tableau. The fallen signal lieutenant lay where he had fallen, half his head carried away by a French ball. Nearby, two midshipmen worked desperately to maintain communications with signal flags, though their efforts were hampered by damaged halliards and their own limited experience.

More troubling, Captain Affleck was nowhere to be seen. The deck was commanded by a lieutenant whose blood-stained uniform and pale face suggested he had already been wounded but remained at his post.

"Lieutenant Nicholas Cruwys, Admiral Hood's staff," Nicholas announced as he approached. "I bring orders and signal instructions. Where is Captain Affleck?"

The lieutenant turned, revealing a makeshift bandage around his left arm, already soaked through with blood. "Lieutenant William Foster, first lieutenant. The captain lies below, severely wounded twenty minutes past. Ball took his foot clean off." He gestured toward the two struggling midshipmen. "Our signals officer killed outright."

Nicholas assessed the situation rapidly. *Bedford* occupied a crucial position between Hood's and Rodney's divisions. Without proper coordination, she risked becoming isolated—a dangerous position with so many French ships nearby seeking targets of opportunity.

"Admiral Hood sends these instructions: the fleet is to concentrate on isolating the French rear division now that their line is broken. Rodney intends to focus particular attention on de Grasse's flagship."

Foster nodded, understanding the strategic importance. "We've lost our master as well—shot through the chest when we passed through the French line." This was worse than Nicholas had anticipated. *Bedford* was effectively blind, both tactically and navigationally. With her captain incapacitated and her first lieutenant wounded, the ship lacked the experienced leadership needed in the midst of a chaotic fleet action.

"Who commands your signals section now?" Nicholas asked, eyeing the struggling midshipmen.

"Mr. Holloway there—fifteen years old and three years at sea," Foster replied with grim irony. "Brave lad, but hardly experienced in fleet signals during general action."

Nicholas made his decision instantly. "Lieutenant Foster, I shall remain aboard temporarily to establish proper signals communication with the flagship. These marines will stay to assist as needed." He turned to the quartermaster's mate who had come aboard with him. "Jeffries, return to inform Admiral Hood. Tell him *Bedford* has lost her captain, master, and signals officer, but remains in fighting condition. I will stay until the immediate tactical situation clarifies."

Nicholas moved to the signals station, where young Midshipman Holloway looked simultaneously terrified and relieved to see someone take charge.

"Mr. Holloway, we must repair these halliards immediately. Have two men from the afterguard assist you. I need clear communication with both *Barfleur* and *Formidable* within five minutes."

Over the next half hour, as *Bedford* continued exchanging fire with the nearest French vessels, Nicholas established a functioning signals system, training Holloway and another midshipman in the essential flag combinations needed for the kind of fluid, mobile battle unfolding around them.

The battle itself had entered a new phase. Rodney's breaking of the line had completely disrupted the French formation, allowing the British to isolate and concentrate on individual enemy ships. From *Bedford*'s quarterdeck, Nicholas could see the French 74-gun *Glorieux* dismasted and drifting helplessly under the combined fire of three British ships. Further north, the *César* fought desperately against *Centaur*, both ships locked together in a deadly embrace.

Most significantly, the French flagship *Ville de Paris* had become the focus of concentrated British attention. The massive 104-gun ship, largest in the French navy, stood like a fortress amidst the chaos, de Grasse apparently determined to fight rather than withdraw.

At half past one, Nicholas observed a critical signal from *Formidable* that would shape the battle's conclusion. Rodney ordered a general concentration against the French flagship—the classic "general chase" that released captains from strict line formation to pursue and engage the enemy at their discretion.

"Signal acknowledged," Nicholas told Lieutenant Foster, who had maintained command of *Bedford* despite his worsening wound. "Admiral Rodney orders us to close with *Ville de Paris* as part of the general concentration."

Foster nodded grimly. "Our standing rigging is severely damaged. We cannot carry much sail. Nevertheless, we shall comply as best we can." He turned to the master's mate now supervising the helm.

"Bring us about two points to larboard. We'll approach the French flagship from her quarter."

As *Bedford* adjusted her course to join the gathering British concentration around *Ville de Paris*, a boat approached from *Barfleur*. Hood had evidently received Miller's report and sent fresh instructions.

The message was delivered by Midshipman Wilson. "Admiral Hood's compliments, sir, and he commends your initiative," he informed Nicholas. "You are to return to *Barfleur* if you consider communications sufficiently restored aboard *Bedford* to ensure proper coordination with the flagship." He glanced at Foster's blood-soaked bandage. "The admiral also sends his compliments to Lieutenant Foster and acknowledges his gallant continuation of command despite being wounded."

Nicholas quickly briefed Mr. Holloway on the essential signals he would need to maintain coordination with the fleet. "Keep close watch on both *Formidable* and *Barfleur*. If you have any doubt about a signal's meaning, consult Lieutenant Foster immediately."

The midshipman nodded, his young face set in determined lines. "I understand, sir. I won't fail."

Nicholas turned to Lieutenant Foster. "I'm ordered back to *Barfleur*, sir. Your communications with the flagship should be restored sufficiently now."

Foster extended his good hand. "Godspeed, Lieutenant. *Bedford* is in your debt."

Leaving Sergeant Miller and his marines to continue supporting *Bedford*'s crew, Nicholas descended to the waiting boat. The return journey to *Barfleur* was even more perilous than the outbound trip had been. The battle had intensified, with ships manoeuvring at close quarters throughout the engagement area. Twice they needed to alter course drastically to avoid collision with drifting wreckage, and once they sheltered in the lee of a damaged British frigate as a French 74-gun ship passed nearby, her lower deck guns still firing steadily.

When they finally reached *Barfleur*, Nicholas found her in the midst of preparation for close engagement. Her gun crews stood ready, powder monkeys positioned at regular intervals, and the quarterdeck crowded with officers and marines. Most significantly, *Barfleur* was on a direct intercept course with the French flagship *Ville de Paris*, now increasingly isolated as other French vessels withdrew or struck their colours.

Upon reporting to the quarterdeck, Nicholas immediately noticed Lieutenant Craddock's absence. A marine officer informed him that Craddock had been taken below to the surgeon, having suffered a serious wound from a flying splinter that had torn into his shoulder and lacerated his face.

"Mr. Cruwys," Hood said as Nicholas approached. "Lieutenant Craddock's injury leaves us without a flag lieutenant at this crucial juncture. You will assume his duties immediately. We are about to engage the French admiral directly."

Nicholas moved quickly to the signals station, taking command from the midshipman who had been handling these duties in Craddock's absence. From this elevated position, he had a clear view of the developing action. *Ville de Paris* had already suffered significant damage from multiple British ships, including *Formidable*, but remained a formidable opponent. Her massive hull bristled with guns, many still firing defiantly despite the increasingly hopeless French position.

At a quarter past four, *Barfleur* came alongside the French flagship at less than fifty yards' distance. What followed was an artillery duel of stunning violence. *Barfleur*'s disciplined gun crews maintained a rate of fire nearly double that of their French counterparts, pouring broadside after broadside into *Ville de Paris*. From his position, Nicholas could see French gunners falling at their stations, replaced by others who continued the increasingly desperate defence of their admiral's ship.

By half past five, the outcome was no longer in doubt. *Ville de Paris* had lost her mizzenmast entirely, her mainmast was severely damaged, and many of her gunports had been silenced. *Barfleur*, though also damaged, with shot holes along her hull and tattered rigging, maintained steady fire into the increasingly defenceless French flagship.

At a quarter to six, the unimaginable occurred. The French flagship—de Grasse's mighty *Ville de Paris*—slowly lowered her colours in surrender. The admiral of France had struck to Hood's *Barfleur* in a decisive defeat that would alter the strategic balance in the Caribbean. A cheer erupted from *Barfleur*'s crew, quickly echoed across nearby British ships as the news spread visually from vessel to vessel. Hood, maintaining his characteristic composure despite the historic moment, ordered a boat prepared immediately.

"Captain Simpson, you will accompany me to receive Admiral de Grasse's formal surrender," he directed. Then, turning to Nicholas, he added, "Mr. Cruwys, in Lieutenant Craddock's absence, you will serve as my flag lieutenant. Join us to record the proceedings and act as interpreter if necessary."

Minutes later, Nicholas found himself in a boat approaching the shattered hulk of what had been the pride of the French navy. Alongside him sat Admiral Hood, Captain Simpson, and a small detachment of marines in their dress uniforms. As they pulled alongside *Ville de Paris*, the extent of the damage became shockingly apparent. Her once-magnificent hull was splintered and pierced in dozens of places. Blood streamed from her scuppers, and the moans of wounded men carried across the water. Her decks, visible as they approached, were a charnel house of broken bodies, shattered equipment, and the debris of destroyed rigging.

They were received aboard with the strange formality that military courtesy maintained even in the aftermath of slaughter. A French officer, his uniform stained but his bearing impeccable, escorted them across the scarred quarterdeck to where Admiral François Joseph Paul de Grasse awaited. The French commander stood tall despite the devastation around him. His uniform was torn and smoke-stained, but he maintained the dignified bearing expected of his rank and lineage. Around him lay dead and wounded officers, testament to his determination to fight to the last extremity before surrendering.

"Admiral de Grasse," Hood said in formal tones, "I receive your surrender in the name of His Majesty King George."

De Grasse bowed slightly, then reached for his sword. With formal dignity, he presented it hilt-first to Hood. "I surrender myself and my ship to you, monsieur. My officers and men have done all that courage could accomplish."

Hood accepted the sword with equal formality. "Your defence has been gallant beyond question, Admiral. You and your officers will be treated with all the respect due to brave men who have done their utmost for their king and country."

Nicholas, standing slightly behind Hood, understood he was witnessing a moment that would be recorded in naval histories for generations. The surrender of a full admiral, commanding the finest ship in the French navy, represented not just a tactical victory but a strategic turning point in the global struggle between Britain and France.

The boat carried the party across waters now calming as evening approached, back toward *Barfleur* with Admiral de Grasse and several of his senior officers aboard. British flags now flew above French ensigns on seven captured vessels.

Aboard *Barfleur*, Hood personally escorted the captured French admiral to his great cabin, with Nicholas attending in his temporary capacity as flag lieutenant. For nearly two hours, the details of capitulation were arranged with the practiced formality of professional naval officers. Nicholas was tasked with recording every detail of the negotiations, taking particular care to document the inventories of *Ville de Paris* and the terms of surrender for her officers and crew. Throughout, de Grasse maintained a dignified demeanour, though Nicholas observed the deep pain in the French admiral's eyes as reports of casualties aboard *Ville de Paris* continued to arrive—over four hundred dead and wounded from her complement of nearly one thousand three hundred men.

When Hood finally emerged on the quarterdeck after the formalities concluded, the sun was setting over a battlefield strewn with the wreckage of what had been one of history's most significant naval engagements. The admiral paused beside Nicholas, who was completing the formal documentation of the surrender.

"Lieutenant Cruwys. Your contributions today have been remarkable—first aboard *Bedford* ensuring her continued effectiveness, and then stepping into Craddock's duties with such competence during Admiral de Grasse's surrender." Hood's voice remained measured, but a certain warmth had entered it that Nicholas had rarely heard before. "I shall mention your name particularly in my dispatches to the Admiralty."

As darkness fell over waters still littered with the debris of battle, Nicholas finally allowed himself to feel the full weight of the day's events. From *Barfleur*'s quarterdeck that morning, through the perilous small boat journey, to his unexpected temporary duty aboard *Bedford*, then his return to witness the historic surrender of Admiral de Grasse himself.

Major Richard Elliot found him at the rail an hour later, offering a small silver flask without ceremony.

"Your marines performed admirably," Nicholas said after taking a grateful swallow, the raw rum setting a glow in his stomach. "Sergeant Miller organised them effectively aboard *Bedford*. I left them there to assist. They'll likely return to-morrow."

"Marines generally do perform admirably," Elliot replied with the hint of a smile. "Though I understand you did rather more than deliver a message. Acting as Hood's flag lieutenant during de Grasse's surrender after poor Craddock was wounded? Few officers of your rank ever witness such a moment, let alone participate officially."

Nicholas shrugged. "Circumstances required adaptation. *Bedford* needed functioning signals to remain effective, and Craddock's injury created an unexpected vacancy at a crucial moment."

"Indeed." Elliot took back the flask. "Word spreads quickly aboard a flagship." He paused, glancing around to ensure they weren't overheard. "Between us, Hood is furious that Rodney declined to pursue the French through the night. He believes we could have taken their entire fleet rather than the seven we captured. But the old man has his victory and his peerage secured, so perhaps caution seemed the wiser course to him."

"We've both survived another day, Richard," Nicholas said finally. "Many good men didn't. And I saw firsthand the cost aboard *Ville de Paris*—their casualties were severe."

"The fortune of war," Elliot replied simply. "We honour them by continuing to perform our duty as they would have done." He straightened, his marine's posture returning as emotion was put aside. "Dawn will bring much work—securing prizes, repairs, tending wounded. Best get what rest you can."

Nicholas finally reached his cabin in the predawn hours, having spent much of the night finalising Hood's preliminary battle report and the official documentation of de Grasse's surrender in Craddock's absence. Tomorrow—or rather, later in this day—would bring new challenges as the fleet consolidated its victory and prepared for the strategic opportunities it created. Jamaica had been saved, French naval power in the Caribbean crippled, and Britain's position in the ongoing global war significantly strengthened.

Within this larger historical canvas, Lieutenant Nicholas Cruwys had found his place, contributing in ways both small and significant to events that would eventually fill the pages of history books.

Sleep came quickly despite the day's tumult, bringing dreams not of battle but, strangely, of Bora Bora—its peaceful lagoon and sheltering mountains so different from the smoke-filled chaos he had just experienced. Perhaps, he thought as consciousness faded, the mind seeks balance through contrast, finding tranquillity in memory when reality offers only the controlled violence of naval warfare.

CHAPTER THREE

The morning sun of the 2nd of May, 1782, cast a golden light across Kingston Harbour, where the victorious British fleet had anchored barely a week earlier, fresh from their triumph at what was already being called the Battle of the Saintes. The harbour teemed with vessels of every description—from the towering ships of the line that had secured the Royal Navy's momentous victory, to the coastal traders and local fishing craft that sustained Jamaica's commerce.

HMS Formidable, Admiral Rodney's 90-gun flagship, dominated the inner anchorage, her massive hull rising from the water like a floating fortress. Further out but nearby, *HMS Barfleur,* Hood's 98-gun flagship during the battle, rode at anchor with equal majesty. *The Duke, Bedford, Prince George,* and other ships of the line that had participated in the historic engagement were distributed throughout the harbour, the worst battle damage now mostly repaired by Kingston's naval yard.

Nicholas Cruwys stood on the weathered dock at Kingston, waiting for his boat to *Barfleur*. His gaze lingered on the forest of masts that filled the harbour—the ships of the line, frigates like *Resource* and *Nymphe*, and the smaller support vessels that attended them. Among them, something unusual caught his eye—a sleek vessel with lines unlike any Royal Navy ship, her raked masts and narrow hull hinting at exceptional speed. He wondered idly about her story as his attention returned to more immediate matters.

The rich aroma of sugar, rum, and coffee from nearby warehouses mingled with the salt tang of the harbour and the pervasive scent of tar that seemed to cling to any port that serviced warships. Here and there, the pungent smell of roasting meat from street vendors cut through the maritime odours, tempting sailors on shore leave.

Kingston itself presented a curious mixture of English provincial town and tropical outpost. Along the waterfront, substantial warehouses constructed of local limestone stood shoulder to shoulder, their façades weathered by tropical storms and bleached by the relentless Caribbean sun. Behind them rose the more refined buildings of the colonial administration and the grand homes of merchants who had made fortunes in sugar, slaves, and trade.

The streets nearest the harbour bustled with activity—sailors from the fleet on brief shore leave, merchants and their clerks tallying goods, slaves loading and unloading cargo under the watchful eyes of overseers, free black and mixed-race traders selling produce and trinkets from small stalls. Taverns and grog shops did brisk business despite the early hour, their doors open to catch any breeze that might provide relief from the growing heat.

Nicholas had spent the previous night in one such establishment— *The King's Arms*, a tavern frequented by naval officers and wealthy merchants rather than common seamen. He had celebrated his recent temporary role as acting flag lieutenant after Craddock's wounding. The celebration had included more than merely rum, as the daughter of the tavern keeper had shared his bed until dawn. She had been eager and skilled, if mercenary in her attentions, making it clear that officers were welcome as long as their pockets remained deep. Nicholas had paid generously, recognising the transaction for what it was—a brief respite from the tensions of naval life, but satisfying nonetheless for what it was. He wondered again if his capacity to ever feel as he had with Atea had left him forever after the wrench of Caroline Carlisle.

Now, nursing the mild after-effects of Jamaican rum, Nicholas's attention returned to the harbour as a ship's boat pulled away from *Barfleur*, making for the dock where he waited. In the sternsheets sat Lieutenant Craddock, Hood's flag lieutenant, his rigid posture unmistakable even at a distance.

As the boat neared, Nicholas could see how the battle had changed the once-handsome officer. Craddock's face now bore a prominent wound whose stitches ran from his right temple down across his cheek to the corner of his mouth—the result of the flying wooden splinter that had torn into him during the battle. The wound had begun to heal, but it had left its permanent mark, pulling slightly at his upper lip and giving his face an asymmetrical quality that drew the eye.

The boat bumped gently against the dock. Craddock rose and climbed the steps with measured precision, each movement controlled and deliberate. His uniform was immaculate, the gold aiguillette of a flag lieutenant gleaming on his right shoulder.

"Lieutenant Cruwys," he said, his voice carefully neutral. "Admiral Hood requests your immediate presence aboard *Barfleur*."

"Of course," Nicholas replied, noting how Craddock's eyes never quite met his own. "Is there any indication of what the admiral wishes to discuss?"

A slight tightening at the corner of Craddock's scarred mouth suggested irritation at the question. "It is not my place to speculate on the admiral's intentions, as I'm sure you appreciate."

The rebuke—subtle but unmistakable—confirmed what Nicholas had suspected. During the period when he had temporarily served as acting flag lieutenant while Craddock recovered, he had worked even more closely with Hood, gaining the admiral's trust. Hood had mentioned Nicholas in his dispatches to the Admiralty, praising his actions during the battle and his subsequent service. It seemed Craddock now viewed him as a potential rival for the admiral's favour.

They made the journey to *Barfleur* in uncomfortable silence. Once aboard, Craddock led Nicholas directly to the admiral's day cabin, where a marine sentry stood at attention. The sentry knocked, announced them, and opened the door to admit them to Hood's presence.

Rear Admiral Hood stood by the stern windows, examining a chart spread on the table before him. He glanced up as they entered, his keen eyes taking in both officers with a single sweeping glance.

"Ah, Lieutenant Cruwys. Thank you for coming so promptly." Hood gestured to the chart. "And Lieutenant Craddock, I'll need the dispatches for London prepared immediately. The packet sails with the evening tide."

Craddock's expression remained perfectly composed, though Nicholas detected a momentary hesitation. "Of course, sir. I'll see to it directly." He turned and left the cabin, closing the door with careful precision.

Hood watched him go, then sighed softly. "A fine officer, Craddock. His wound troubles him still, I think, though he would never admit as much."

"Yes, sir," Nicholas agreed, uncertain how else to respond to this unusual confidence.

Hood waved a hand toward the chart. "Come, look at this. The waters between Jamaica and Hispaniola. You've made a study of local navigation since the battle, I believe?"

Nicholas stepped forward to examine the chart, which showed the Windward Passage between Jamaica and the western end of Hispaniola. "Yes, sir. The sailing masters of both *Barfleur* and *Bedford* were kind enough to share their knowledge."

"Good. And what would you say is the primary challenge in patrolling these waters?"

Nicholas considered the question carefully, aware that Hood was testing him. "The currents are treacherous, sir, particularly around the eastern tip of Jamaica and through the passage itself. Combined with the variable winds caused by the mountainous terrain of both islands, navigation requires constant vigilance. Additionally, there are numerous small coves and inlets where smaller vessels might shelter, invisible from the main shipping lanes."

Hood nodded, apparently satisfied. "Precisely. Our ships of the line and frigates maintain control of the major sea lanes, but they lack the agility to pursue smaller vessels into shallow waters or narrow passages—and we are short of smaller craft. The enemy knows this and exploits it. French and colonial rebel privateers and smugglers slip through our patrols. Spanish *guardacostas* harass our merchants. And intelligence moves between Martinique and Havana without our knowledge."

He straightened, fixing Nicholas with a penetrating gaze. "This brings me to the purpose of our meeting. Walk with me."

Hood led the way out of the cabin and onto the stern gallery, a covered balcony-like structure that extended from the great cabin, offering a panoramic view of the harbour and surrounding sea. Here, sheltered from both the tropical sun and prying ears, admirals could converse in private while enjoying the open air.

"I trust you noticed an unusual vessel newly arrived in the harbour this morning," Hood said, leaning against the polished rail. "A sleek craft with distinctive lines, anchored apart from the main fleet?"

"I did, sir," Nicholas replied, curious now about the connection between this vessel and his summons.

"Three days past," Hood continued, his voice pitched for Nicholas's ear alone, "*Cornwall* came upon an American privateer in a narrow cove east of Montego Bay. A fast vessel—unusual in her lines, what the Americans are calling a 'Baltimore clipper,' though this one was built, we believe, in Virginia. Shallow in the draught, built for speed—particularly to windward."

Nicholas followed the admiral's gaze to where the sleek vessel lay at anchor, a little apart from the fleet. Even from this remove, her lines were unmistakable—longer, lower, and far finer drawn than those of her British counterparts. Her sharply raked masts bespoke a design devoted wholly to speed.

"She was taken without a shot fired," Hood continued. "The vessel had run gently aground on an uncharted shoal while seeking refuge from our patrols. When *Cornwall*'s boats were sighted bearing down, her captain struck his colours at once, seeing little profit in defiance with a seventy-four's trained upon him. The dispatches she carried for the French at Cap-François were taken intact—a rare and valuable stroke of intelligence."

Nicholas studied the vessel with growing interest. "She looks swift, sir."

"Indeed. Our master shipwrights have examined her and report that her design incorporates principles our own builders might well study. She is thought to be extremely fast, highly weatherly, capable of operations in shallow coastal waters yet sturdy enough for ocean passages." Hood turned to face Nicholas directly. "The Admiralty most likely will want her for study in home waters eventually, but I have convinced Admiral Rodney that she might serve an immediate practical purpose here in the Caribbean—and indeed the North American coast—before being sent to England."

Understanding began to dawn. "What sort of purpose did you have in mind, sir?"

"Intelligence gathering. Interception of enemy communications. Rapid transport of diplomatic correspondence between our scattered possessions. Missions that require speed, discretion, and the ability to operate where our larger ships cannot go." Hood's eyes held Nicholas's steadily. "Missions that require a commander with... unusual qualifications."

Nicholas felt a surge of excitement tempered by caution but said nothing.

Hood went on, "Your record speaks for itself. Your experiences with Cook taught you navigation and scientific observation. Your time in the Pacific islands gave you insights into operating in unfamiliar waters with limited resources. Your voyage with the Portuguese trader Silva taught you the practical aspects of commerce raiding and unconventional tactics. You demonstrated independent command ability in *Growler*'s voyage from the Indian Ocean around the Cape to Luanda."

Hood gestured toward the distant vessel again. "She is to go into dock to-morrow to be refitted to our requirements, with heavier guns unavailable to the Americans. Six six-pounders to a side, with nine-pounder bow and stern chasers planned—though I fear acquiring suitable pieces may prove challenging. The ordnance masters are reluctant to part with their best brass guns, particularly for a vessel of her size. But that will be for her commander to negotiate. Her crew complement will be ninety, including a small detachment of marines. But more important than guns is a commander who can think beyond traditional naval tactics—someone comfortable with unconventional approaches."

"The vessel will be renamed *HMS Alert*," Hood continued. "She should be ready to commission in a fortnight."

Nicholas felt his pulse quicken. "Sir, are you offering me command?"

"I am offering you an opportunity, Lieutenant Cruwys—or should I say, Commander Cruwys." Hood allowed himself a small smile at Nicholas's expression. "Your promotion to Master and Commander has been approved, effective to-day. By a rather remarkable coincidence, I understand to-day is your birthday—perhaps an auspicious sign. The paperwork will be finalised this afternoon."

Nicholas stood momentarily speechless. The jump from lieutenant to commander was significant. Though not unprecedented in wartime, particularly after a major engagement like the Battle of the Saintes, such rapid advancement usually required powerful patrons or exceptional circumstances.

"Sir, I don't know what to say."

"Say nothing yet," Hood advised. "This assignment carries significant responsibilities and risks. *Alert* is not a standard vessel, and your duties will not be those of a typical captain. You'll operate independently much of the time, making decisions without the ability to consult higher authority. You'll need to be diplomat, intelligence officer, and fighting captain by turns. The position requires discretion, initiative, and sound judgment."

He paused, his expression becoming more severe. "I should add that not everyone approves of this appointment. Some feel that a more...

conventional officer would be appropriate, regardless of the unconventional nature of the vessel and her missions."

Nicholas understood the unspoken message. His rapid rise would inevitably create resentment among officers who had waited years for similar advancement. Craddock's barely concealed hostility was likely just the first example he would encounter.

"I understand, sir. If you believe I'm suitable for the command, I will endeavour to justify your faith."

"Good. Report to the naval yard tomorrow morning at eight bells. The prize agent and master shipwright will meet you there to discuss the refit." Hood turned back toward the harbour view, then added, "One more thing, Commander. Select your officers with care. You'll need men who can adapt to *Alert*'s unique requirements. I've granted you unusual latitude in this regard. Draw from the fleet as needed, with the understanding that I must approve your final selections."

"Thank you, sir. I already have some thoughts on suitable candidates."

"Very well. I understand your former quartermaster Markham is serving aboard *Nymphe* as master's mate since your return from the Pacific. He might be worth considering for a position appropriate to his experience."

Nicholas felt a jolt of surprise. "You're aware of Markham, sir?"

"I make it my business to know the capable men in this fleet, regardless of their rank," Hood replied. "And in your case, I took a particular interest in the man who survived your remarkable journey from the Society Islands. The master of *Nymphe* speaks highly of him."

"Markham would be an excellent choice for master of *Alert*, sir—if he's willing."

"See to it, then. You have my permission to approach him." Hood's expression softened almost imperceptibly. "Craddock requested this command for himself. I judged him unsuitable, despite his seniority. I tell you this not to create division, but so you understand the... complexity of the situation."

"I understand, sir."

Hood studied him a moment longer. "Nicholas," he said—using his first name, an astonishing moment of informality—"this is a rare opportunity. What we accomplish in these waters may determine the outcome of the war. I believe you have the qualities needed for this command, but be warned—you will face scepticism from traditional officers. They will watch for any misstep, any excuse to question my judgment in appointing you."

The use of his given name, unprecedented in their professional relationship, emphasised the gravity of the moment. Hood was speaking not merely as his commanding admiral, but almost as a mentor.

"I won't disappoint you, sir," Nicholas replied simply.

"Good. Now, I have matters to attend to. You have my permission to withdraw." Hood straightened, the brief moment of personal connection giving way again to proper naval formality. "Good day, Commander Cruwys."

Nicholas saluted and departed, his mind racing with all that had transpired. As he made his way across the deck, he encountered Craddock, who was overseeing some administrative matter with a midshipman.

"Ah, Lieutenant..." Craddock caught himself. "Commander Cruwys. I understand congratulations are in order."

"Thank you, Lieutenant," Nicholas replied evenly. "The admiral's decision was unexpected."

"Indeed." Craddock's damaged face twitched slightly. "*Alert* is an unusual vessel. I'm sure your... unique experiences will serve you well in her command."

The words were correct, but the tone conveyed their true meaning clearly enough. In Craddock's view, Nicholas had been given an opportunity he had not earned through traditional naval service, bypassing more deserving officers like himself. That his disfigurement from a wound received in battle had coincided with Nicholas's advancement only added to the perceived injustice.

"I hope to make her a credit to the squadron," Nicholas said simply.

Craddock nodded stiffly. "I'm sure you'll do your utmost. If you'll excuse me, the admiral's dispatches require my attention."

The ship's boat returned Nicholas to Kingston's waterfront, where the bustle of colonial commerce continued unabated. His mind raced with plans and considerations. First, he would need to find Markham aboard *Nymphe* and offer him the position of master. Then there was the matter of the bow and stern chasers. Hood had mentioned that acquiring suitable nine-pounders might prove challenging, and Nicholas understood why.

"Brass" guns (which were in fact bronze) were rare and expensive—often reserved for the larger ships of the line or specialised vessels. The naval yard at Kingston would have few to spare, and those would likely be earmarked for more established commanders. If he wanted quality chase guns for *Alert*, he would need to secure them through less conventional channels.

Nicholas recalled a merchant he had met at *The King's Arms*—a man named Abernathy who dealt in surplus naval stores and had hinted at connections to more irregular commerce. If anyone in Kingston could procure brass nine-pounders without excessive questions, it would be Abernathy. Such an arrangement would skirt the edges of proper naval procedure—perhaps even regulations—but Nicholas had learned from Silva that results sometimes justified unconventional methods.

Nicholas's first priority was his uniform. A commander's rank required distinctive insignia, and he would need to appear the part before visiting *Nymphe* to find Markham. Fortunately, Kingston boasted several tailors and outfitters catering to naval officers, the presence of the fleet ensuring brisk business for such establishments.

He made his way to *Clifton & Sons*, a shop known among officers as the most reputable in Kingston for naval attire. The establishment occupied the ground floor of a substantial building on one of the better streets leading away from the harbour, its windows displaying bolts of fine blue wool and brass buttons arranged in neat rows.

A bell tinkled softly as Nicholas entered. The interior was cool and dim after the bright Caribbean sunlight, the air scented with the distinctive smell of new cloth and beeswax polish. Racks of uniforms in various stages of completion lined one wall, while shelves held stacks of neatly folded white breeches, waistcoats, and shirts.

Mr. Clifton came forward from behind the cutting table—a lean man in his late fifties with neatly combed grey hair, a plain cravat, and the brisk, assessing manner of one long accustomed to the demands of naval clientele.

"Good afternoon, sir," he said, giving Nicholas a quick but thorough look. "How may I be of service?"

"Commander Cruwys," Nicholas replied, returning the nod. "As of to-day. I'm here to be fitted accordingly."

Clifton's eyebrows rose slightly, but his professional demeanour betrayed no further surprise. "My congratulations, sir. A well-deserved advancement, I'm sure." He gestured toward a private fitting area at the rear of the shop. "If you'll come this way, we can discuss the requirements for your new rank."

In the fitting room, Clifton took Nicholas's measurements with practised efficiency. "The 1782 uniform regulations for a Master and Commander are quite specific, sir," he explained. "Blue coat with white lapels and cuffs—similar to a lieutenant's, but with distinctive differences. Silver lace at the buttonholes, more generous trim at the cuffs and collar."

Back in the main shop, Clifton ran his hand over a bolt of deep blue wool. "This superfine from Yorkshire would be most suitable—takes gold lace well and holds its shape in this climate better than most."

"How quickly can they be ready?" Nicholas asked. "I'll need at least one uniform for immediate use."

Clifton considered. "I have a commander's coat that was commissioned by an officer who unfortunately did not survive to collect it. If you could wait a quarter hour, with minor alterations, it could be made to serve. For a complete set—three coats, waistcoats, breeches, and appropriate accessories—I would require a week."

"Very well. The altered coat will serve for now, along with my existing breeches and waistcoats," Nicholas decided. "I'll commission the full set as well."

They discussed other details of style and materials, Nicholas selecting options that balanced proper appearance with practical considerations for tropical service. The price was considerable—nearly thirty guineas for the complete set—but unavoidable. A naval officer's uniform was not merely clothing but a symbol of authority and station.

As Clifton made notes of the order, he said casually, "I don't suppose you're to command the American prize, sir. *Alert*, I believe she's to be called?"

Nicholas wasn't surprised that the tailor knew of the ship's new name. In Kingston's naval community, such information spread rapidly. "That's correct. Do you have some interest in her?"

"Merely professional curiosity, sir. My son serves as midshipman aboard *Resource*. He mentioned the vessel's unusual lines when they brought her in." Clifton hesitated, then added, "He also mentioned that Lieutenant Hawkins of *Cornwall* was disappointed not to receive her command himself."

"I imagine he was," Nicholas replied neutrally. "Though I understand the prize money should provide some consolation."

Clifton nodded, a hint of a smile touching his lips. "Indeed, sir. Prize money soothes many disappointments in naval service." He made a final notation in his ledger. "The remainder of your order within the week, as promised, sir."

Nicholas left the tailor's shop with conscious pride and proceeded to his next task—finding Markham aboard *Nymphe*.

The 36-gun frigate had been anchored at the outer edge of the fleet, her clean lines and newly repaired rigging marking her as one of the faster vessels in the squadron. As Nicholas's hired boat approached, he noted the signs of recent battle: freshly replaced planking visible along her starboard side where French shot had struck home, new canvas among her sails, and the distinctive smell of new paint and pitch that indicated recent repairs.

Captain Ford had received Nicholas in his cabin—more compact in a frigate than the more spacious accommodations of a ship of the line, but still a beautiful space. The captain, a lean man with the weathered features of a career sailor, had skimmed Hood's letter with raised eyebrows.

"Master's mate to master, is it?" Ford had remarked, glancing up at Nicholas. "Quite a leap. Though I suppose no more remarkable than lieutenant to commander." There had been a trace of irony in his tone, but no overt hostility. "Markham's a good man—knows his business better than most certified masters I've sailed with. You're fortunate to claim him, Commander Cruwys."

Nicholas had acknowledged the compliment with a nod. "I served with him under Cook, sir, and again during our journey back from the Pacific. There's no one I'd rather have as sailing master."

Ford had nodded. "I'll have him sent for. You're taking the American privateer, I understand?"

"Yes, sir. Being renamed *HMS Alert*."

"Unique vessel. Captured without a shot fired, I hear. Lucky for us, unlucky for her captain." Ford had shaken his head. "These American designs have merit, though I'd not admit as much in certain company. Fast, weatherly, shallow-drafted. Good choice for the type of operations Hood has in mind."

That Ford knew of Hood's intentions for *Alert* had surprised Nicholas momentarily, but he'd quickly realised that little remained secret in the close confines of a fleet at anchor. News travelled rapidly between ships, carried by boat crews, visiting officers, and the constant exchange of signals and orders.

When Markham had appeared at the cabin door, Nicholas had felt a surge of genuine pleasure. The quartermaster—now master's mate—looked much as he had when they'd served together, though his face was perhaps more deeply lined, his hair showing touches of grey at the temples. His sturdy frame remained powerful, his hands still bearing the calluses of a working sailor despite his warrant rank.

Recognition had flashed in Markham's eyes, followed immediately by a broad smile that transformed his usually serious features.

"Mr. Cruwys!" he'd exclaimed, before catching himself. Markham's eyebrows had risen nearly to his hairline. "Begging your pardon, sir.

I should say, Commander Cruwys. You've come up in the world since we parted ways in Calcutta, sir."

Captain Ford had excused himself tactfully, leaving them to speak privately. Nicholas had quickly explained his new command and the offer of the master's position aboard *Alert*.

Markham had listened attentively, his expression growing more thoughtful as Nicholas outlined Hood's intentions for the vessel. When Nicholas finished, the older man had remained silent for a moment, considering.

"It's a considerable opportunity, sir," he'd said at last. "Master of a King's ship, even a small one, is no small thing for a man who started before the mast. But I should know what I'm signing on for. This won't be conventional service, will it?"

"No," Nicholas had admitted. "Hood wants *Alert* for special operations—intelligence gathering, courier duties, interception of enemy communications. We'll operate independently much of the time, often in waters where larger vessels can't follow."

A slow smile had spread across Markham's weathered face. "In other words, the sort of unorthodox business we got up to with Silva—but with the King's commission to back it."

"Something like that," Nicholas had agreed. "Though hopefully with less risk of being hanged as a pirate."

Markham had laughed, a deep rumble that seemed to come from his very core. "When do we begin?"

Early the next morning, Nicholas and Markham arrived at the naval dockyard where *Alert* had been towed the previous afternoon to be refitted. The yard was a hive of activity—carpenters, riggers, caulkers, and sailmakers swarmed over vessels in various states of repair. The air rang with the sounds of industry: the sharp crack of mallets, the rasp of saws, the shouts of foremen directing gangs of workers, and beneath it all, the constant rhythm of pumps keeping dry docks clear of seawater.

A sandy-haired man in the practical garb of a master shipwright stood at the edge of the dry dock where *Alert* rested, consulting a sheaf of papers while directing workers with sharp gestures. He looked up as Nicholas and Markham approached, his expression suggesting he had been expecting them.

"Commander Cruwys?" he inquired, setting aside his papers. "James Thornton, master shipwright. Admiral Hood informed me you'd be coming." His accent marked him as a Londoner, probably from the Deptford yards originally.

"Mr. Thornton," Nicholas acknowledged with a nod. "This is Thomas Markham, who will serve as *Alert*'s master. What can you tell us about her condition?"

Thornton gestured for them to follow him down the wooden steps into the dry dock itself, where they could examine the vessel more closely.

"She's American-built, as you likely know," Thornton began as they descended. "Constructed in Virginia, we believe—though she's registered out of Baltimore. Not more than two years old, by my assessment. Hull is primarily white oak with some live oak at key stress points—excellent materials, I must admit. Copper-bottomed, which is unusual for an American vessel, suggesting she was built specifically for sustained operations in these waters."

They reached the bottom of the dry dock, where Thornton led them beneath the vessel's keel. Nicholas noted how dramatically different her underwater profile was from typical British naval vessels. Where most Royal Navy ships had a relatively full midsection and substantial draught to provide stability as gun platforms, *Alert* was lean throughout, with a shallow draught and an almost knife-like forefoot.

"She's designed for speed above all else," Thornton continued, patting the wooden hull with something like professional admiration. "Her builders sacrificed cargo capacity and gun-carrying capability to achieve it. But the construction is sound—done by shipwrights who knew their business, even if they were colonials."

Nicholas ran his hand along the copper sheathing that protected the hull below the waterline. "Any damage from her grounding?"

"Minimal," Thornton replied. "She went aground on sand, fortunately. There's some minor scraping of the copper and a few loose fastenings we're replacing, but nothing structural. Remarkably lucky—hit a coral head instead, and we'd be looking at substantial rebuilding."

They continued their inspection, moving up to the main deck where carpenters were already at work modifying the vessel for Royal Navy service. Thornton explained the changes being made: reinforcement of the deck to support the weight of heavier guns, installation of improved pumps, modification of the captain's quarters and officers' accommodation, and adjustment of the rigging to suit British naval practices.

"How soon can she be ready for commissioning?" Nicholas asked, watching as workers measured for new gunports.

Thornton scratched his chin thoughtfully. "Three weeks at the earliest, I'd say. There's considerable work still to be done, and we've other vessels with higher priority."

Nicholas frowned. "Admiral Hood indicated a fortnight. I understand there are many demands on the yard, but *Alert*'s mission is of considerable importance to the fleet."

"A fortnight?" Thornton's expression suggested this was nearly impossible. "With all respect, Commander, I've limited men and materials. The ships of the line take precedence, and there are frigates awaiting repairs as well."

Nicholas exchanged a glance with Markham, who gave an almost imperceptible nod. This was the first test of command—securing the resources needed for his vessel despite competing priorities.

"Mr. Thornton," Nicholas said, lowering his voice, "I appreciate the challenges you face. However, Admiral Hood has emphasised the urgency of *Alert*'s commissioning. Perhaps there might be a way to allocate additional resources to her refit?"

Thornton's eyes narrowed slightly, understanding the unspoken suggestion. "Additional resources would certainly help, Commander. But such things are... difficult to arrange."

Nicholas reached into his pocket and withdrew a small purse, feeling its weight in his palm. It contained ten guineas—a significant sum, particularly for a newly promoted commander with modest means. But he recognised the investment for what it was: not merely a bribe, but an establishment of priorities in a system where such unofficial payments were expected.

"I believe this might assist in overcoming the difficulties," Nicholas said quietly, passing the purse to Thornton with a handshake that concealed the transaction from casual observers.

The shipwright's fingers closed around the coins, and he gave a slight nod. "I see you understand how things work in Kingston, Commander. I believe I can rearrange some priorities. A fortnight is still ambitious, but we'll do our utmost."

"Excellent. I'll check on progress regularly," Nicholas said. "Now, there's the matter of armament. I understand she's to be fitted with twelve six-pounders on the main deck?"

"Yes—six to a side," Thornton confirmed. "The ordnance master has already allocated the guns—good pieces, though not the newest. Assuming you agree, he suggests ten six-pounders and a pair of twelve-pounder carronades in the forward ports, which will help keep her bows light. They'll be installed once we've completed the gunport modifications and strengthened the deck beams."

Nicholas nodded. "That seems sensible. And what of the bow and stern chasers? Admiral Hood mentioned nine-pounders."

Thornton's expression became guarded. "Ah, that's more problematic. The ordnance master has allocated two iron nine-pounders, but they're older pieces—rather worn. Brass guns of that calibre are in short supply, and those we have are reserved for the larger warships."

Nicholas had expected this. Hood had warned him that securing proper chase guns would be challenging. "I see. And who might I speak with regarding this allocation?"

"That would be Captain Wilcox, the ordnance master," Thornton replied. "Though I should warn you, Commander—he's not a man easily swayed. Particularly not when it comes to brass ordnance."

"Nevertheless, I should like to meet with him," Nicholas said firmly. "When might that be arranged?"

"He inspects the yard each morning at ten o'clock," Thornton said. "You could speak with him then, though I wouldn't be overly optimistic about changing his mind."

Nicholas nodded, already considering alternative approaches. "Thank you, Mr. Thornton. We'll leave you to your work now, but expect me again to-morrow."

After leaving the dockyard, Nicholas decided their next priority was to visit the marine barracks. Sergeant Miller, who had fought alongside Nicholas during the Battle of the Saintes, would be an ideal choice to lead *Alert*'s marine detachment. Miller had distinguished himself during the battle, showing both courage and initiative. His experience and proven capabilities would be invaluable for the type of operations Hood envisioned for *Alert*.

"You're thinking of the Sergeant Miller you mentioned for our marines?" Markham asked as they walked toward the barracks.

"Yes," Nicholas confirmed.

"Poaching marines from the flagship?" Markham raised an eyebrow. "That's bold—even for you."

"Hood granted me unusual latitude in selecting my crew," Nicholas replied. "And Miller proved himself capable of the kind of adaptable thinking we'll need. Besides, I've found that having men who have already faced fire at your side creates a certain bond of trust."

They reached the marine headquarters—a substantial stone building flying the Royal Marines' flag alongside the Union Jack. After speaking with the duty officer, they were directed to the training ground behind the main building, where Sergeant Miller was supervising a drill with a squad of marines.

Miller was a compact, powerful man with the weathered complexion of a career soldier who had served in tropical climates for years. The three chevrons on his sleeve and the straight-backed posture spoke of his rank and discipline, while the quick, assessing glance he gave Nicholas and Markham as they approached revealed the alertness that had likely kept him alive through numerous engagements.

"Commander Cruwys, sir," Miller said, snapping to attention and saluting when he recognised Nicholas. His eyes widened slightly at the new rank, but he maintained his professional demeanour. "Congratulations on your promotion."

"Thank you, Sergeant," Nicholas replied, returning the salute. "I see news travels quickly."

"The fleet's worse than an old wives' market for gossip, sir," Miller said with the faintest hint of a smile. "Word is you've been given command of the American prize."

"That's correct. She's being renamed *HMS Alert*." Nicholas gestured to his companion. "This is Mr. Markham, who will serve as her master. I'm here because I'd like you to consider a position aboard her—leading her marine detachment."

Miller's expression remained carefully neutral, though his eyes showed interest. "How many marines would the vessel carry, sir?"

"Twelve—including a corporal. A small complement, but important given the special nature of our operations. We'll be conducting intelligence gathering, courier duties, and likely intercepting enemy communications. Situations may arise requiring a landing party of marines who can operate independently but with discipline. I need marines who can adapt to unconventional situations—not simply stand in line and fire volleys."

Miller nodded slowly.

"With your permission, sir, I'd like to bring Corporal Jenkins and ten men who served with me during the action. They're proven fighters, and I know their capabilities."

Nicholas smiled. "That was exactly my hope, Sergeant. I have Admiral Hood's authorisation to draw personnel from the fleet. I'll speak with Major Elliot regarding the formal transfer."

"Very good, sir." Miller hesitated, then added, "If I might ask, sir, when would we be expected to report for duty?"

Alert should be ready for commissioning in a fortnight. I'd like you and your men aboard three days prior to familiarise yourselves with the vessel. She's different from anything in the Royal Navy—fast, manoeuvrable, but with her own peculiarities."

"We'll be ready, sir," Miller assured him. "The men will be pleased to serve under your command. Your actions during the battle... made an impression."

This was high praise indeed from a veteran marine non-commissioned officer. Nicholas nodded his acknowledgment. "I'll send word when the official transfer is approved. Until then, carry on, Sergeant."

As they left the marine barracks, Markham gave Nicholas an approving look. "That's a significant piece of our complement secured. Twelve good marines under a reliable sergeant will be invaluable."

"Indeed," Nicholas agreed. "Now we need to tackle the matter of those brass nine-pounders. I doubt Captain Wilcox will be persuaded to part with his best pieces."

"You have something in mind?" Markham asked.

Nicholas nodded. "There's a merchant I met at *The King's Arms*—Abernathy. Deals in naval surplus and other goods of... ambiguous origin. If anyone in Kingston can procure what we need, it would be him."

Markham frowned slightly. "Sounds like risky business, sir. Acquiring naval ordnance through unofficial sources could be seen as highly irregular."

"So it could," Nicholas agreed. "But *Alert*'s success may depend on having the best equipment available. Silva taught me that sometimes one must operate in grey areas to achieve the necessary result."

"Silva was a smuggler and occasional privateer," Markham pointed out dryly. "Not the best model for a King's officer."

Nicholas smiled. "And yet, his ship was always well-armed and well-equipped, regardless of shortages. I'm not suggesting outright theft or piracy, Markham—merely... creative procurement."

As evening approached, they made their way to *The King's Arms*, where Abernathy held court at his usual table. The merchant was not difficult to spot—a corpulent figure in an expensive but slightly outdated bottle-green coat, surrounded by ship's officers and local merchants. His florid face and expansive gestures marked him as a man comfortable in his role as a nexus of commerce, both official and otherwise.

Nicholas and Markham watched patiently, waiting for Abernathy to conclude his current business before approaching. When the merchant's companions finally departed, Nicholas caught his eye and gave a slight nod of recognition. Abernathy hesitated briefly, then returned the gesture with a small wave of invitation.

"Mr. Abernathy," Nicholas said as they approached his table. "I trust your business proceeds profitably?"

"Commander Cruwys," Abernathy replied, his eyes taking in the details of Nicholas's uniform with the practised assessment of a man who judged others by their appearance and apparent means. "Word of your promotion travels quickly. Please, join me. And your companion...?"

"This is Mr. Markham, master of *HMS Alert*, my new command."

"Ah, the American prize. A fine vessel from what I hear. Unusual, but swift." Abernathy gestured for them to sit. "How may I be of service to the Royal Navy this evening?"

Nicholas settled into a chair, choosing his words carefully. "I find myself in need of certain... specialised equipment that seems to be in short supply through official channels."

Abernathy's eyes gleamed with interest. "The naval yard can be frustratingly rigid in its allocations. Many captains find themselves similarly constrained."

"I require two brass nine-pounder guns for bow and stern chasers," Nicholas said directly. "I'm told that all such pieces are currently reserved for larger vessels."

Abernathy took a thoughtful sip of his punch. "Brass nine-pounders. That's a particular request. Iron would be easier to come by—and cheaper by half."

"Iron won't serve," Nicholas said. "She's a fine-lined hull and lightly sparred. I need the weight savings, and brass runs truer. *Alert*'s not meant to stand and batter—she'll strike fast and be gone."

"I see." Abernathy leaned back in his chair, studying Nicholas with new interest. "Such pieces are indeed rare in these waters. When the fleet sailed from England, brass ordnance was in short supply even there, with the foundries struggling to meet wartime demands."

Nicholas waited, sensing that Abernathy was circling toward a price rather than an outright refusal.

"However," the merchant continued after a calculated pause, "I may be able to help. Through various... commercial arrangements, I occasionally acquire items that naval officers find useful. There is a privateer currently in port—a Colonial loyalist from New York operating with a letter of marque. Her captain may be persuaded to part with two brass nine-pounders of Spanish manufacture, captured off Cuba."

"Spanish guns?" Markham interjected, scepticism evident in his tone.

"Cast at the royal foundry in Seville," Abernathy clarified. "Excellent workmanship, I assure you. The Spanish may be our enemies, but they cast fine bronze cannon. These pieces are nearly new and well maintained."

"And the price?" Nicholas asked.

Abernathy named a sum that made Nicholas wince inwardly—one hundred guineas for the pair, nearly a third of his personal funds.

"That seems excessive," Nicholas said calmly. "Particularly for guns that were, shall we say, irregularly acquired."

Abernathy smiled thinly. "The privateer captain took them as legitimate prize goods. His letter of marque entitles him to such captures. That he is willing to sell them rather than keep them for his own vessel is fortunate for you, Commander. However, I might be able to negotiate him down to eighty guineas, with ten as my commission for arranging the transaction."

Nicholas considered this. The price remained steep, but he recognised the value of having superior chase guns on a vessel designed for speed and pursuit. After a moment's deliberation, he made his decision.

"Seventy guineas total, including your commission," he countered. "And I'll require proof of their quality before payment is made. I won't purchase guns that might burst upon firing."

Abernathy stroked his double chin thoughtfully. "Seventy-five, and you may inspect them thoroughly before the transaction is completed. I'll arrange for a demonstration firing if you wish."

"Agreed," Nicholas said, extending his hand to seal the bargain. "When can you have them available for inspection?"

"The day after to-morrow, at the small battery near Fort Charles," Abernathy replied, shaking Nicholas's hand. "Shall we say ten o'clock in the morning?"

"We'll be there." Nicholas rose from the table. "A pleasure doing business with you, Mr. Abernathy."

As they left the tavern and stepped into the warm Caribbean night, Markham gave Nicholas a sidelong glance. "Seventy-five guineas is a considerable sum, sir. Are you certain this is wise?"

"Not entirely," Nicholas admitted. "But *Alert* will often need to fight and run rather than stand and engage. Having superior chase guns could make the difference between success and failure—or life and death."

Markham nodded slowly. "I suppose you're right. And if these Spanish guns are as good as Abernathy claims, they'd be worth every guinea. Still, there's something not quite proper about purchasing naval ordnance from a privateer through a merchant of questionable reputation."

Nicholas smiled slightly. "We're operating in the grey area between strict naval regulations and practical necessity, Markham. I suspect this won't be the last time we find ourselves there. *Alert* is not a conventional vessel, and her missions will often require unconventional solutions."

They walked in companionable silence through Kingston's darkening streets toward the waterfront, where a boat would return them to the fleet anchorage. To-morrow would bring new challenges—meeting with the ordnance master, checking on *Alert*'s refit progress, and beginning the search for a suitable lieutenant and midshipman.

Nicholas still needed to complete his officer complement and recruit the remainder of his crew—ninety men all told, including the twelve marines, a surgeon, a purser, and the usual complement of able and ordinary seamen. For his lieutenant, he needed someone competent but flexible—not so hidebound by tradition that he couldn't adapt to *Alert*'s unconventional role. Perhaps a younger officer who had seen enough action to be seasoned, but not so established that he resented serving under a newly promoted commander.

But that night, Nicholas felt a growing sense of accomplishment. The pieces of his command were falling into place: his own uniforms ordered, Markham secured as master, Sergeant Miller and his marines ready to transfer, and arrangements made for the crucial chase guns. *Alert* would soon be ready to play her role in the complex naval chess game unfolding across the Caribbean, and Nicholas Cruwys, newly minted commander, would have his first opportunity to prove Hood's faith in him had not been misplaced.

The Battle of the Saintes had altered the strategic landscape of the Caribbean like a hurricane reshaping a coastline. Yet despite this triumph, the broader war continued with undiminished intensity. As May of 1782 progressed, dispatches from London made clear that the loss of the American colonies was now accepted as inevitable in most political circles. Peace negotiations had begun in Paris, with the independence of the thirteen colonies the presumed starting point rather than a matter for debate. Britain's strategic focus had shifted toward preserving its valuable West Indian possessions and protecting vital trade routes from French and Spanish interference.

Against this backdrop of military success amid political accommodation, Kingston buzzed with activity. Prizes were being adjudicated, ships repaired, supplies gathered, and new strategies formulated. The naval yard worked through the night, lanterns illuminating the relentless industry of carpenters, sailmakers, and riggers as they prepared the fleet for continued operations.

It was in this atmosphere of urgent transition that *HMS Alert* was commissioned on the 14th of May, 1782, exactly a fortnight after Nicholas had first laid eyes on the sleek American prize vessel—a testament to the effectiveness of his arrangement with the master shipwright. There was no ceremony to mark the occasion, merely the quiet delivery of the vessel's commissioning warrant by a harried clerk from the Port Admiral's office.

Nicholas signed the necessary documents, acknowledging receipt of both ship and warrant with a brief stroke of the pen. No senior officers attended, no speeches were made, no formalities observed beyond the absolute minimum required by naval regulation. Most of the squadron was at sea, and those officials remaining in port had more pressing concerns than the commissioning of a small converted prize vessel, regardless of her unusual role or commander.

Still, as the White Ensign rose from *Alert*'s stern staff for the first time, Nicholas felt an undeniable surge of pride. The vessel might be small by Royal Navy standards—barely a sixth the size of *Barfleur*—but she was his first command, and she was extraordinary in her own way.

"She's a beauty, sir," said Lieutenant Michael Forester, stepping forward to stand beside Nicholas as the small assembly of crew and dockyard officials dispersed. "Nothing like her in the fleet."

Nicholas studied his newly appointed first lieutenant with appreciation. Despite his twenty-seven years, Forester had a youthful appearance that belied his experience. He was probably four inches shorter than Nicholas's six feet, but broader and with fair hair pulled back in a queue tied with a black ribbon. His grey-blue eyes and whole manner exuded quiet competence.

Forester had come highly recommended by Captain Ford of *Nymphe*, who had been forceful in describing him as "uncommonly capable and criminally overlooked for advancement. A good seaman and has a real feel for gunnery." Coming from Ford—who had also mentioned that Captain Walsh had once served under him as first lieutenant—that was high praise indeed. Ford had added that Forester's entrance to the service had been as a midshipman at fourteen, supported by a stepfather who had been eager to remove the boy from his household. With no family wealth or significant connections to support him after that initial placement, his advancement had depended entirely on his abilities.

"Indeed she is, Mr. Forester," Nicholas agreed. "Though I suspect the yard hasn't finished complaining about the gun carriage slide you suggested."

Forester's face creased in a brief smile. "The slide mechanism for the bow chaser was worth arguing over, sir—though it's taken some work. Being able to run it back to the foremast when not in use should significantly improve her trim in heavy seas, while allowing it to be trained through either bow port."

"I'll defer to your expertise on such matters," Nicholas replied. "Your gunnery experience serves us well, and gunnery is something I value and enjoy as well."

Forester acknowledged this with a nod, his broad shoulders straightening slightly at the recognition. "Aye, sir—and those long nines of yours"—he was aware of Nicholas's private purchase—"are beautiful guns. I have every hope for their accuracy."

They moved forward along *Alert*'s deck, inspecting the results of the hasty but thorough refit. The vessel retained her original hull lines—the distinctive shape of a fine entry with a narrow beam and sharply raked masts. She embodied speed and weatherliness rather than the gun-carrying stability favoured by traditional naval architects.

Nevertheless, the refit had adapted her for service consistent with the Royal Navy's practices without sacrificing her essential qualities. Her armament had been upgraded, with five of the six-pounder guns on each broadside. Additionally, as had been suggested, the sixth, most forward gunports on each side were now filled with one of the new twelve-pounder carronades—whose lighter weight and devastating firepower at shorter ranges Nicholas was eager to try. Finally, the bow and stern had been reinforced to accommodate the nine-pounder chase guns. Their existence had been quietly accepted by the naval authorities, who had asked no questions about their provenance. Although heavier by more than three tons than her previous cannons, Nicholas and the yard master believed she would carry it well—and that the old armament was more likely due to American shortages than her true capability.

In the matter of appearance, he had kept her low hull painted with fresh black topsides, including the gunports to better hide her ability, with only a thin unbroken line of white paint just below the bulwarks accenting her lovely sheer. He had paid out of his own pocket to have her scrollwork around the bowsprit and her newly carved name board on the stern picked out in gold leaf. All in all she was absolutely striking, and many sailors and officers were seen to pause and look her over with approving nods as boats passed in the anchorage.

"Ninety men aboard, sir, our full complement," Forester reported as they continued their inspection. "Admiral Hood's authority allowed us to draw experienced hands from throughout the squadron, and nearly all were volunteers. We've been fortunate in the quality."

"Excellent," Nicholas replied. "The type of service *Alert* will perform requires capable men."

"Agreed, sir. Sergeant Miller has his twelve marines transferred from *Barfleur*. The ship's boys have been aboard since yesterday, and Mr. Markham has been drilling them mercilessly in *Alert*'s particular requirements."

They descended to the lower deck, where the differences between *Alert* and conventional naval vessels became even more apparent. The hull, optimised almost entirely for speed rather than capacity, created spaces that felt cramped even by naval standards. Nicholas's cabin occupied the stern but lacked the traditional stern windows found on British warships, with only a skylight admitting natural light. The officers' gunroom was equally spartan, while the crew clearly would be watch and watch, even with a generous interpretation of whether the minimum space for the hammocks had been met.

"It's rather cosy," Forester observed diplomatically.

They went below to Nicholas's cabin, where Markham joined them to review the ship's particulars before their departure. Nicholas spread out the vessel's plans on his small table.

"A topsail schooner," Markham observed, tracing the distinctive rig with his finger. "The Americans have refined the design considerably over the past decade."

"For those of us more familiar with traditional square-riggers, perhaps you could explain the advantages," Nicholas suggested, aware that Forester might benefit from Markham's practical knowledge.

Markham nodded, plainly gratified to be asked. "Unlike the smaller schooners that carry only fore-and-aft canvas, a topsail schooner gives you the best of both rigs. She sets fore-and-aft sails on both main and foremast—good for working to windward with her heads'ls drawing clean—but she also carries square topsails and t'gallants on the foremast, and in fair weather, may even set stuns'ls. It's a handy combination: spry in stays, yet still able to run before it like a square-rigger."

"So she's fast off the wind, but can still point high," Forester said, leaning over the plans.

"Exactly. The square sails give her power on a broad reach or running free, and the schooner rig lets her tack and wear with far more precision than a square-rigged brig. For a vessel that may need to chase or disappear, it's near ideal."

"And these raked masts?" Forester inquired, indicating the distinctive aft rake of *Alert*'s masts on the drawing.

"American innovation," Markham explained. "The rake reduces the tendency to bury the bow in heavy seas and improves her balance on a close reach. Combined with her narrow beam and sharp entry, it makes her remarkably fast—especially to windward."

Nicholas observed the exchange with satisfaction. The three of them—commander, lieutenant, and master—would need to work in close coordination for *Alert* to reach her full potential. This early sharing of knowledge boded well for their future operations. Nicholas was pleased to see how quickly Markham had adapted to his new role, applying the same thoroughness that had served them well during their Pacific journey. He excused himself and went on deck, leaving his officers to continue the discussion.

After a few moments, Forester said, "May I ask if you know of our orders, sir?"

Nicholas thought for a moment. Some captains kept their orders to themselves and ran their ships with a rigid formality, even with their senior officers. While he had learned enough from Cook, Walsh, and his experiences commanding *Growler* to know the importance of discipline with no undue familiarity, he also was aware that in a small ship like *Alert*, with far more nuanced missions than convoy escort, he would need the confidence and close understanding of his first lieutenant to be most effective.

"Already received," Nicholas replied. "A sealed packet from Admiral Hood sent just before the flagship sailed a few days ago, with instructions not to open until we're at sea." He patted the inside pocket of his coat. "We sail with the morning tide. Hood has been quite specific about that much."

"Mysterious," Forester commented. "Though not unexpected given what I've heard of *Alert's* intended role, sir."

"Indeed. We've been granted considerable latitude in how we operate. Admiral Hood expects results but understands we may need to employ...unconventional methods at times."

Forester nodded, his experienced eyes assessing Nicholas with new interest. "May I speak frankly, sir?"

"Please do, Mr. Forester. I will always value your counsel within the limits of naval discipline."

"Thank you, sir. Your reputation precedes you, Commander. Your experiences in the Pacific, your journey with a Portuguese trader, your actions during the battle—they're widely known. Some officers question your rapid advancement, but others see the value in a commander with your particular background."

"And your own assessment?" Nicholas asked, curious about his first lieutenant's perspective, though normally a junior officer would not be so forthcoming, especially with a new captain.

"I believe standard approaches produce standard results, sir," Forester replied carefully. "The war has reached a stage where standard results may not be sufficient. *Alert* is an unconventional vessel. She deserves an unconventional commander, and I'm bound to say I look forward to serving with you and this ship, and only wanted to add that I am properly thankful of your selecting me."

Nicholas appreciated the honest evaluation, and the candid but not overly deferential manner in which it was delivered. Looking Forester in the eye, he said, "And I need officers who understand that unconventional doesn't mean undisciplined."

"Precisely so, sir." Forester's gaze was steady. "I may lack family connections, but I've learned that practical seamanship and adaptability often count for more, and hope to continue to make my way in the service."

"We share that philosophy, Mr. Forester. I think we'll work well together. Please see that all preparations are complete for departure at first light."

"Aye, sir," Forester replied with new confidence. "*Alert* will be ready."

As Forester left the cabin, Nicholas reflected on how quickly his command was taking shape. In Markham, he had a master he trusted with his life and whose abilities he knew intimately from their shared Pacific experiences. Indeed, Markham within the limits of naval life and rank was a friend, and the only other person who knew of Atea. In Forester, he appeared to have found a first lieutenant whose practical background and lack of rigid adherence to naval orthodoxy might make him particularly suitable for *Alert's* unique requirements. And in the vessel herself, Nicholas had been given a tool of remarkable potential, small but swift, nimble but capable, perfectly suited for the specialized tasks Hood had hinted would be their focus. Tomorrow they would sail, and Nicholas would begin to discover whether the promise of this unusual command could be fulfilled. They had not even sailed her yet, but he was already smitten by his command.

The morning dawned clear and bright, with a steady easterly breeze that rippled the waters of Kingston Harbour. *Alert* stood out to sea, her sleek black hull cutting through the water with an ease that confirmed all Nicholas had hoped about her performance. Designed for speed rather than stability, she heeled noticeably even in the moderate breeze, but there was nothing concerning in her motion— merely the eager response of a vessel built to run. Nicholas stood near the helm, feeling *Alert's* particular rhythm through the soles of his feet. Every ship had its own character, its unique way of responding to wind and wave. *Alert's* was immediately distinctive— lighter, more responsive, and somehow more alive than the heavier vessels he had served aboard previously.

"She balances beautifully, sir," Markham commented. "Hardly any weather helm at all, even close-hauled like this, and she doesn't pitch."

"Credit to Mr. Forester's modifications to the bow chaser slide, and the lighter carronades in place of long guns forward," Nicholas replied, nodding at his first lieutenant and noting how the vessel maintained course with minimal adjustment to the wheel. "The yard thought him presumptuous, but he understood what *Alert* required."

They cleared the headland and entered the open Caribbean, where the true test of Alert's capabilities would begin. Nicholas ordered the course adjusted to east south-east, as they felt the northeast trades, to begin the long sail to windward, following Hood's initial directive to rendezvous with the fleet in the vicinity of Barbados. She buried her starboard rail and sheets of fine spray swept across the foc'sle. Nicholas, Forester, and Markham exchanged nods of approval as she came further and further into the wind. The nods changed to delighted grins and even laughter, quickly muted, including among the experienced hands on deck, as she continued up, lying closer than any ship in their experience as *Alert* showed her paces.

The crew seemed to be adapting well. Many were experienced seamen transferred from other ships in the squadron, drawn by curiosity about the American prize and her unorthodox commander. All had volunteered. The twelve marines under Sergeant Miller maintained the disciplined professionalism Nicholas had observed during the Battle of the Saints, even as they leant their weight to the sheets as she trimmed into the wind. Overall, they appeared to be a promising company, though only time would reveal how they would mesh as a crew.

"Mr. Forester," Nicholas called to his first lieutenant, who was supervising the trimming of the foresails. "Once we're settled on course, I'll brief you and Mr. Markham on our orders. My cabin in thirty minutes."

"Aye, sir," Forester acknowledged.

Later, with their one midshipman on deck as officer of the watch, Nicholas spread Hood's sealed orders on the small table in his cabin. He had include Markham consciously from the beginning, given his role as master in the small ship, and more importantly the value of his judgment and experience.

"Our initial task is straightforward but critical," Nicholas began. "We're to intercept a French dispatch vessel believed to be carrying important communications between Martinique and Cap Français on Saint-Domingue."

He indicated the likely route on the chart. "Intelligence suggests she's a small schooner, lightly armed but fast. She's to depart Fort Royal the first week in June and will likely follow the island chain northward, pausing at Guadalupe before making the crossing to Saint-Domingue."

"Do we know what information she carries?" Forester asked.

"Admiral Hood indicates only that it relates to French diplomatic communications that may impact the ongoing peace negotiations. Our orders are to intercept, capture the dispatches intact if possible, and return them directly to Admiral Hood, who will have rejoined the main fleet near Barbados by then."

Markham studied the chart with practiced attention to detail. "Given our sailing qualities, I'd estimate ten days to the area, and if she follows the usual route, we might intercept her near Guadeloupe or Montserrat."

"That's my assessment as well," Nicholas agreed. "We'll take position to west of Basse-Terre on Guadeloupe and patrol the likely sea lanes."

"A straightforward commerce raiding mission, then," Forester observed. "Though diplomatic dispatches rather than trade goods. But why not patrol nearer her destination, and pick her up there?"

"I believe there is a question of timelines in getting the information to the Admiral, though in fact," Nicholas hesitated, "Admiral Hood has granted us considerable discretion in how we accomplish it. The dispatches are our priority, but any additional intelligence we might gather would be valuable."

Markham and Forester exchanged a brief glance, clearly sensing there was more to the mission than Nicholas had explicitly stated.

Neither pressed for details, however, understanding the nature of such assignments.

"We should have the advantage of speed over any French schooner," Forester said"

"Let's hope so," Nicholas replied. "Because I intend to put that speed to the test once we've accomplished our primary objective."

The following days provided ample opportunity to assess *Alert's* capabilities as they sailed across the Caribbean towards the Leward Islands. She proved remarkably fast in the steady trade winds, maintaining eight to nine knots with minimal effort, even as she cut through the swells of the northeast trades.

The crew quickly adapted to her particular characteristics. *Alert's* motion was different from the heavier naval vessels most had served aboard—quicker, more responsive to the sea, with a tendency to accelerate rapidly when struck by stronger gusts. This required adjustments in sail handling and general seamanship, but the men responded well to Forester and Markham's practical instruction.

By the evening of the ninth day, they had reached their designated patrol area west of Guadeloupe, just over the horizon from the main port of Basse-Terre, where the French dispatch vessel was likely to appear after her stopover before she began the run downwind. Nicholas established a methodical search pattern, taking advantage of *Alert's* speed to cover the most probable routes while remaining vigilant for any sail on the horizon.

It was shortly after dawn on their third day of patrol when the lookout's call echoed from the masthead.

"Deck there! Sail ho! Two points off the starboard bow!"

Nicholas raised his glass, focusing on the distant speck that had appeared on the horizon. As the morning light strengthened, the vessel's profile gradually resolved—a small schooner running downwind with the trades on a course for the island of Hispaniola, with its French, divided between French Saint-Domingue in the west and Spanish Santo Domingo on the east, both hostile to the British.

"French by the cut of her sails, sir" Foreseter observed, studying the distant vessel through his own glass. "And making good speed."

"Precisely where our intelligence suggested she would be," Nicholas said with satisfaction. "Mr. Forester, clear for action but keep the gun ports closed for now. I want to close the distance before she recognizes us as a threat."

Nicholas considered his approach carefully. *Alert*'s distinctive profile with her raked masts might be recognized as American. The French vessel was still several miles distant, but if her captain was vigilant, he might alter course at the first sign of pursuit.

"Mr. Markham, let's adjust course a point to starboard," Nicholas decided. "We'll appear to be on a slowly converging course rather than directly intercepting."

"Aye, sir," Markham acknowledged, giving the necessary orders to the helmsman.

The tactical dance that followed demonstrated *Alert's* remarkable qualities. As they gradually converged with the French schooner, Nicholas observed the moment when the other vessel's captain finally recognized the potential threat. The French ship abruptly altered course, turning northeastward up wind to open the distance between them.

"She's seen us," Forester commented unnecessarily.

"Indeed," Nicholas replied. "And now we'll see what *Alert* can really do. Mr. Markham, come up three points and set the outer jib."

Alert responded magnificently, as the additional sail filled and was sheeted home, heeling further and accelerating noticeably as her sails were trimmed to perfection. While the French schooner was clearly fast—her captain skillfully extracting maximum speed from the available wind—*Alert* proved faster. Gradually, the distance between the vessels diminished. *Alert* sliced through the waves with remarkable efficiency.

"We're outsailing her smartly close-hauled," Forester observed with professional appreciation. "I've never seen anything like it."

"American designers understand the value of weatherliness," Nicholas replied.

Within an hour, they had closed to within half a mile of the French vessel. Close enough now for Nicholas to confirm it matched the description of the dispatch vessel they sought. He could see activity on her deck as her crew presumably prepared for the inevitable confrontation.

"Run out the bow chaser," Nicholas ordered. "Let's encourage her to reconsider her situation."

The gleaming brass nine-pounder was promptly prepared, its Spanish craftsmanship evident in the elegant lines of the weapon. With Forester watching, and indeed hardly able to keep from interfering as Nicholas noted with a wry smile, the gun captain took careful aim, compensating for *Alert's* motion.

"Fire."

The shot landed precisely where intended, across the French vessel's bow, close enough to nearly spray her foc'sle with water but not so close as to risk damage. It was remarkable accuracy at this range, and what he had expected after their practice of the last several days. Clearly, the guns were exceptionally accurate. The message was clear: heave to or face more direct fire.

For a moment, the French schooner maintained her course, her captain perhaps calculating whether continued flight might succeed. But as *Alert* continued to close the distance, the reality of the situation apparently became clear. The French vessel gradually turned fully into the wind, her sails luffing as she hove to.

"Well done, Mr. Forester," Nicholas said. "Prepare a boarding party. I'll lead it myself."

"Aye, sir," Forester replied, though his expression suggested he questioned the wisdom of the commander personally leading such an operation.

Nicholas understood the unspoken concern but had his reasons. If the captured schooner carried the sensitive diplomatic dispatches Hood believed it did, he wanted to secure them personally rather than risking mishandling by others. As *Alert* hove to astern of the French vessel—which they could now see was named *La Mouette*, Nicholas evaluated the situation. She appeared to carry a crew of perhaps twenty men, with four small guns visible on her deck. Most significantly, he observed several men in civilian attire among the crew, suggesting she indeed carried passengers of some importance.

The boat splashed down and the boarding proceeded without resistance. The French captain, a weathered man named Durand, surrendered his sword to Nicholas with the resigned dignity of a professional seaman who recognized when further resistance would be futile.

"Your vessel sails remarkably well, Capitan," Durand commented in accented English as Nicholas accepted his surrender. "We have outrun British frigates before, but your ship..." He shook his head in reluctant admiration.

"She's a special vessel," Nicholas acknowledged, his gaze sharp and calculating. He glanced toward the handful of passengers assembled on the deck, noting a young woman who bore a striking resemblance to Durand—likely a daughter or niece.

A moment of recognition flickered in Nicholas's eyes. "Captain Durand," he said quietly, "shall we discuss this matter more privately? Below, in your cabin."

It was not a request.

The subtle change in Nicholas's tone caused Durand to stiffen imperceptibly. He nodded, following Nicholas down the narrow companionway to his own cabin, the young woman's anxious gaze trailing them.

Once inside, Nicholas closed the door with deliberate care.

"The dispatches?" Durand said, a carefully modulated tremble in his voice. "They were put overboard the moment we hove to. Standard procedure when capture seems imminent. Diplomatic protocols demand their destruction."

Nicholas's eyes narrowed. They had been tracking the French ship from the instant she altered course, and no such disposal had been observed. The claim was a fabrication—transparent, yet deliberate.

"An interesting claim," Nicholas replied, his tone cutting as a blade's edge. "I propose a simple arrangement. Produce the dispatches, and I guarantee safe passage for your passengers. Specifically, Mademoiselle—" he paused, "—your daughter, I presume?"

Durand's composure fractured momentarily. A subtle fear flickered in his eyes.

"When we search the vessel," Nicholas continued, his voice low and precise, "I will ensure it appears the papers were discovered during our standard maritime inspection. No blame will attach to you personally. Your daughter will be put ashore under a flag of truce, along with any others who wish to disembark."

The threat was implicit. Those who remained would be subject to the full conditions of naval warfare—imprisonment, potential exchange, uncertain futures.

Durand understood immediately. Naval officers like himself knew the unwritten rules of maritime conflict. Nicholas was offering a humanitarian option, but the underlying message was clear: cooperation would be rewarded with mercy, resistance with consequences.

"As a naval officer, I must protest—" Durand began.

"Your protest is noted," Nicholas interrupted smoothly. "But your vessel is a legitimate prize. Our nations remain at war."

What followed was a careful negotiation. Nicholas did not raise his voice. He did not make explicit threats. Instead, he outlined potential scenarios with clinical precision—the treatment of prisoners, the uncertain fate of those captured, the potential separation of families.

After what seemed an interminable several minutes, Durand's resistance crumbled. From a cunningly concealed compartment behind a side locker, he extracted a leather dispatch case. The seals were French diplomatic—untouched, undamaged.

"They were never put overboard," Durand said quietly, the admission dragged from him like a confession.

Nicholas accepted the case, not showing any sense of triumph. "A wise decision," he said. "Your family will be treated with full consideration."

With a prize crew left aboard *La Mouette* under the command of Midshipman James Wells, Nicholas ordered *Alert* to resume her course toward the rendezvous with Hood's fleet, the captured French vessel staying in company. The dispatches were now secured in his cabin, though he had not broken the diplomatic seals to examine their contents. Hood's orders had specified that the dispatches should be delivered intact if possible, and Nicholas intended to comply—at least for the moment.

That evening, as *Alert* sailed southeastward toward Barbados with her prize following in her wake, Nicholas sat alone in his cabin contemplating the leather dispatch case. The other documents found aboard *La Mouette* had proven interesting but not immediately significant—routine communications regarding supply shipments, personnel transfers, and similar administrative matters. It was the sealed diplomatic pouch that likely contained the intelligence Hood sought.

A knock at his cabin door interrupted his contemplation.

"Enter," he called, setting the dispatch case aside.

Markham appeared in the doorway, his expression suggesting he brought significant news. "Begging your pardon, sir, but the lookout reports multiple sails on the horizon to the southeast. A substantial force by the spread of canvas."

Nicholas rose immediately. "British or French?"

"Too distant to determine with certainty, sir, but their position suggests it might be Admiral Hood's squadron returning from Barbados as planned."

"Very good. I'll come up directly."

On deck, Nicholas trained his glass toward the distant sails, which appeared as little more than specks on the horizon in the fading evening light. The number of vessels and their apparent formation clearly were a naval squadron rather than merchant shipping, and therefore almost certainly British.

"We should have confirmation of their identity by morning," Forester observed, joining Nicholas at the rail. "Assuming they maintain their current course."

"Indeed," Nicholas agreed. "Maintain our heading for now, but have the watch keep close observation. If it proves to be Hood's squadron, we'll adjust course to intercept."

Throughout the night, *Alert* continued southeastward while the distant vessels maintained their own course, gradually resolving into a substantial naval force as dawn approached. By first light, there was little doubt they were observing a Royal Navy squadron—the distinctive silhouettes of ships of the line becoming visible through the morning haze.

"That's Hood's squadron, sir," Markham confirmed as the sun rose fully. "I recognize *Barfleur's* profile leading the line."

"Signal our identity," Nicholas ordered. "And adjust course to rendezvous."

By mid-morning, *Alert* was closing rapidly with the British squadron, *La Mouette* following at a distance, limited by her lesser speed. The line of powerful warships presented an impressive sight—ships of the line formed in a disciplined column with attendant frigates flanking the formation. In the lead sailed HMS *Barfleur*, Hood's 98-gun flagship.

From a slightly different angle, HMS *Pylades*, a nimble 28-gun sixth-rate frigate, also returning from some detached duty, was converging on a similar course to the squadron that would bring her parallel to *Alert*. The two vessels seemed locked in an unspoken race as they slowly converged to a point that would be within a quarter mile of the flagship.

As they drew nearer, Nicholas studied the frigate. She was a beautiful ship and he knew from Jamaica she had a reputation for being an excellent sailor. On the *Pylades's* quarterdeck stood a figure that seemed vaguely familiar, though Nicholas couldn't immediately place him at this distance.

"Signal from , *Pylades* sir," reported Midshipman Wells. "She requests we identify ourselves and state our business with the fleet."

Nicholas considered the request briefly. Hood had granted *Alert* special status to operate independently, including the privilege of direct communication with the flagship rather than adhering to normal protocol with intermediate vessels. The dispatch pennant now flying from *Alert's* masthead should have made this clear to any officer familiar with the squadron's operations.

"Acknowledge the signal," Nicholas decided, "but maintain course for the flagship. Lower and raise the 'dispatches aboard' pennant."

As *Alert* continued toward *Barfleur*, *Pylades* adjusted her own course to intercept more directly, her captain apparently dissatisfied with *Alert's* response. The schooner and frigate were now drawing closer, their hulls cutting parallel lines through the choppy waters, each vessel seeming to challenge the other's right of way.

As the distance closed between the vessels, Nicholas finally recognized the figure on *Pylades's* quarterdeck – Edward Fanshawe, a former classmate from his Naval Academy days, and now clearly a post captain though only two years older than Nicholas. The recognition brought a slight tension to Nicholas's stance, a subtle tightening around his eyes that suggested their history was not entirely amicable.

The recognition was apparently mutual. *Pylades* signaled again, more insistently, repeating it with a signal gun, now ordering that *Alert* heave to. Again, Nicholas acknowledged the signal without complying, exercising the discretion Hood had granted him for situations exactly like this.

"He seems rather determined, sir," Forester observed dryly.

"Captain Fanshawe and I have history," Nicholas explained briefly. "We attended the Academy together, though he was two years my senior. His family connections apparently secured him early promotion."

"Ah," Forester replied, the single syllable conveying complete understanding of the dynamics at play. "And now you're unexpectedly a commander not just a lieutenant as he probably assumed."

"Something like that," Nicholas agreed. "Though I suspect his interest has more to do with protocol than personal history."

Pylades altered course again, more aggressively this time, clearly intending to position herself directly in Alert's path and force acknowledgment. It was a technically legitimate exercise of a senior captain's authority, though one that disregarded the special status indicated by *Alert's* dispatch pennant.

Nicholas studied the developing situation. The two ships were now only a mile or so from the squadron, and he was somewhat surprised that Hood had not intervened with a signal of his own as even from

89

this distance he could see more hands than usual on the flagship, and indeed down the line, watching the impromptu race. He could, of course, simply heave to as Fanshawe demanded, but doing so would establish a precedent undermining *Alert's* operational independence, and that was not acceptable. Besides he was technically in the right of it as strictly speaking no other ship was permitted to interfere with a dispatch vessel absent an emergency, though indeed that rule was not always strictly followed. The more he considered it, Fanshawe was acting like a fool, and he determined teach him a lesson, just as he had years ago in their fencing encounter. *Pylades* was hard on the wind on the starboard tack windward under top'sls and courses, leaning well over in the strong trade wind. *Alert* pointing just slightly higher and therefore converging at about the same speed or slightly faster and therefore staying even.

"Mr. Markham," he said calmly, "adjust course half a point to starboard."

"Sir?" Markham questioned, clearly surprised by the order that would bring them even closer to the wind, higher than the square rigger could steer and therefore closer to Pylades's approaching position.

"You heard me. Mr Forester, all hands prepare to make more sail sharply when I give the word."

Markham nodded with dawning understanding. "Aye, sir. Half a point to starboard."

Alert adjusted her heading, now appearing to be on a collision course with the approaching frigate. Through his glass, Nicholas could see activity on *Pylades's* deck as her crew responded to the apparent danger. Fanshawe himself could be seen gesturing emphatically.

"Steady as she goes," Nicholas instructed calmly. "Wait for it..."

The two vessels continued to converge, *Alert's* superior speed rapidly closing the distance. Just as collision began to seem inevitable, Nicholas gave the order:

"Luff up another point!"

Alert responded with remarkable agility, her bow swinging to starboard and her great fore and aft sails beginning to shiver. The maneuver brought her across *Pylades's* stern not 100 feet clear. Fanshawe screamed angrily, "What the devil do you think your playing at, Cruwys! By, God I'll have you before the Admiral!"

"Fall off a point and a half, Mr. Markham. Set the outer jib and top'sle, Mr. Forrester," Nicholas snapped. "Let's demonstrate *Alert's* qualities for Captain Fanshawe's benefit."

As *Alert* accelerated on her new heading, now positioned to windward of *Pylades* and sailing just slightly upwind of her course, the difference in the vessels' capabilities became immediately apparent as the outer jib and top'sl were sheeted home. Despite *Pylades's* larger sail area, *Alert* began to pull alongside from astern, for indeed unlike the frigate she was sailing a bit free due to her higher pointing ability. Fanshawe's yelling continued. And now distant cheering can be heard from some of the squadron's ships.

"We're stealing her wind, sir," Forester observed with professional appreciation, as they continued to pull ahead and began to overlap the other ship directly to leeward. Indeed, *Alert* was not merely passing *Pylades* but doing so to windward so close that her sails, began to block and disrupted the frigate's access to the full force of the wind, at least on her lower sails, which began to waiver and lose thrust. As *Alert* shot ahead, Nicholas could see Fanshawe's reaction on Pylades's quarterdeck. The captain's face had flushed deep red, his expression a mixture of surprise and fury as he yelled orders to his crew. Nicholas lifted his hat in mock salute. There was a banging of canvas as the frigate tried to set her royals, but as they watched, her main royal yard snapped in a welter of rigging, and she fell further behind. The bosun muttered, "God almighty" in a low voice.

Within twenty minutes, they had drawn level with *Barfleur* herself, the massive flagship now flying signals instructing Nicholas to come aboard immediately with his dispatches. A quick glance astern showed *Pylades* now a half mile astern, still sorting out her broken main royal rigging. *Alert* came about and turned smoothly into the wind just under the flagship's lee as *Barfleur* turned and backed her topsail.

"A most effective demonstration, sir," Forester commented as Nicholas prepared to drop into the boat. "The entire fleet has now witnessed *Alert's* capabilities."

"Along with Captain Fanshawe's discomfiture," Nicholas acknowledged. "Though that was merely a secondary effect. Carry on."

Forester's expression suggested he wasn't entirely convinced by this claim of innocent motivation, but he made no further comment.

As Nicholas boarded the flagship, dispatches and reports of *Alert's* condition securely in hand, he was immediately escorted to the admiral's day cabin. There he found not only Hood but also the admiral's secretary, Martin Thornhill, waiting with evident interest.

"Commander Cruwys," Hood greeted him. "I see you've already made quite an impression on the squadron. Captain Fanshawe has been signaling most energetically about your disregard for protocol."

"I exercised the discretion you granted *Alert* regarding direct communication with the flagship, sir," Nicholas replied carefully. "Captain Fanshawe seemed determined to assert his authority despite our dispatch pennant."

"Indeed." Hood's expression revealed nothing of his thoughts on the matter. "In any event I was observing your "race", and *Alert* seems to be in excellent condition. All we had hoped. And these are the dispatches you were sent to intercept?"

Nicholas handed over the leather case. "Yes, sir. Captured from the French vessel *La Mouette* yesterday morning northeast of Guadeloupe. The seals remain intact as instructed. We also secured these additional documents, which were concealed aboard." He presented the supplementary papers found during their search.

Hood nodded to Thornhill, who accepted both sets of documents with careful attention. "Excellent work, Commander. The vessel itself?"

"Following probably three leagues or so behind at this point, I imagine, sir. I left Midshipman Wells with a prize crew. She's a fine schooner, very fast, though of course not quite *Alert's* equal."

"Good. We'll determine her disposition later." Hood studied Nicholas thoughtfully. "You completed your primary mission efficiently and effectively. *Alert's* performance seems to justify my confidence in both vessel and commander."

"Thank you, sir."

"However," Hood continued, "your instructions were simple and straightforward. Intercept, capture the dispatches, return. I'm curious why you felt it necessary to exceed those parameters."

Nicholas felt a momentary chill. "Sir?"

"Securing the French vessel should have been sufficient," Hood clarified. "Why did you feel it necessary to search for additional concealed documents?"

"Experience with Silva taught me that official dispatches often tell only part of the story, sir. Private communications, intelligence concealed from casual discovery, these often provide context that official papers and logs lack. I judged a thorough search to be within the spirit of our mission."

Hood exchanged a glance with Thornhill before responding. "A reasonable assessment, Commander. In this case, your initiative was appropriate."

Thornhill spoke for the first time, his voice measured and precise. "The supplementary documents may prove particularly valuable, Commander. They appear to contain information not included in the official dispatches."

Nicholas recognized this as significant praise from Hood's reticent secretary, though he couldn't help wondering what information the documents contained that warranted such interest.

"There is one more thing, Commander," Hood said, his tone shifting subtly. "Among the papers you discovered, did you happen to find any references to a woman associated with the British official Sir William Chambers?"

The question caught Nicholas by surprise. His orders had mentioned nothing about Chambers or any woman connected to him. "No, sir. Though I should note that we did not translate all the French correspondence, merely secured it for delivery. I thought that as with the dispatches, I should not disturb any sealed papers."

There was a knock and Craddock, the flag lieutenant came in, glancing at Nicholas. "Admiral, *Pylades* is hove to just beyond *Alert.*"

Hood responded without turning, his eyes still on Nicholas, who stood expressionless, "Signal Captain Fanshawe to report to Flag. Commander Cruwys, let's fill the time before he arrives discussing the changes to *Alert* in more detail, and how you find she handles."

Ten or so minutes later, Nicholas could faintly hear Fanshawe being piped aboard, and soon after the marine sentry reported "Flag Lieutenant and Captain Fanshawe to see the Admiral, sir!"

"Send him in," Hood ordered.

Captain Fanshawe entered the cabin with the precise formality of an officer acutely aware of naval protocol, accompanied by Craddock, whose scarred face remained impassive as he took position slightly behind Fanshawe, a red leather portfolio tucked under his arm. As flag lieutenant, Craddock would naturally be present for any formal complaint between captains, responsible for recording the proceedings and providing any relevant information.

Fanshawe's uniform was immaculate, every button polished to a high shine. At twenty-four, he matched Nicholas in height but had already developed the beginnings of a paunch that strained slightly against his waistcoat, the result, Nicholas suspected, of too many comfortable dinners in port, or indeed for that matter, at sea. His features were regular and might have been handsome were it not for the perpetual tight set of his mouth and the coldness in his gray eyes.

Those eyes flickered briefly to Nicholas before focusing on Hood with calculated respect. "Admiral Hood," he said, bowing slightly. "You requested my presence, sir."

"Indeed, Captain Fanshawe," Hood replied evenly. "I understand you have some concerns regarding Commander Cruwys's approach to the fleet."

Fanshawe straightened, clearly pleased to have his complaint acknowledged so promptly. "Yes, sir. *HMS Alert* disregarded proper signals and failed to heave to when instructed. Further, Commander Cruwys's maneuvers when approaching the squadron showed a disregard for established protocols that borders on insubordination."

Nicholas remained silent, studying his former classmate with detached interest. He noted the deliberate emphasis on his rank, a reminder that despite commanding a vessel, he held the intermediate rank of commander rather than post-captain like Fanshawe. The years had done little to temper Fanshawe's nature, it seemed, though in their school days it had been expressed through constant bullying of the younger and smaller boys.

Hood glanced toward Nicholas, then back to Fanshawe. "I see. And were you aware, Captain, that *Alert* was flying the dispatch pennant indicating priority communications for the flag?"

"I was, Admiral," Fanshawe replied without hesitation. "However, being the senior officer present outside the main body of the fleet, I judged it my duty to verify her identity and intentions before permitting any approach to the flagship. These are standard precautions, particularly given the vessel's... irregular appearance. She might easily have been a captured prize turned by the enemy for deception."

Hood gave a measured nod. "A reasonable concern, in principle. But *Alert* sails under special instructions in matters of communication. When bearing dispatches, she is authorised to approach the flagship directly, without passing through the usual chain of signals."

"With respect, sir," Fanshawe said, still firm, "such authorisation does not exempt a vessel from acknowledging signals from a King's ship, especially when fleet security is in question."

Thornhill, who had been silently examining the captured French documents at a side table, looked up briefly, his expression revealing nothing.

"Tell me, Captain Fanshawe," Hood said, his tone turning dry, "in your judgement, what danger did *Alert* pose to our squadron of seventeen ships of the line? Did you imagine this single schooner might threaten the combined firepower of nearly fifteen hundred guns?"

Fanshawe stiffened, visibly caught off balance. "It... it was the principle, sir. An unidentified vessel—"

"*Alert* was flying her colours, had made her number, and displayed the private signal and the dispatch pennant," Hood interrupted. "Hardly unidentified. And while your attention to protocol is noted, there are occasions when rigid observance must give way to necessity. Commander Cruwys was under orders to deliver those dispatches with all possible speed. Had he delayed to satisfy your curiosity, valuable time would have been lost."

"I was unaware of the urgency of his mission, sir," Fanshawe said stiffly.

"Just so," Hood replied. "You were unaware of many things, yet proceeded as though fully informed. In future, Captain, I suggest you allow for the possibility that not all matters lie within your immediate purview before pressing your interpretation of procedure."

"I observed the encounter from the quarterdeck. A remarkable display of sailing. *Alert* appears to be everything we had hoped for in terms of performance."

A dull flush rose along Fanshawe's neck.

"She may be capable, sir, but *Alert* crossed our wake in an unsafe manner and then placed herself to windward, seemingly as a deliberate show."

"Indeed. A demonstration of what, I wonder?" Hood raised an eyebrow, glancing toward Nicholas. "Commander Cruwys?"

Nicholas chose his words with care.

"Sir, on approach, I judged that continuing to close on *Pylades* might be misread as hostile. I therefore ordered *Alert* to luff across her stern, keeping what I believed a safe distance. Our subsequent course toward the flagship naturally carried us to windward."

"Naturally," Hood echoed, a flicker of amusement in his eye before his expression settled.
"Still, Commander, you cut it rather fine. While I appreciate a display of *Alert*'s qualities, I cannot permit manoeuvres liable to provoke misunderstanding between His Majesty's ships."

"Aye, sir," Nicholas said evenly. "It will not happen again."

Turning to Fanshawe, Hood continued, "And indeed aside from anything else attempting to set royals in such a breeze has cost damage to one of His Majesty's ships."

Fanshawe turned pale, then beet red.

Hood looked between them, his tone sharpening.

"Let me be perfectly clear. I will not have discord among my captains. The business ahead is hard enough without internal quarrels drawing our focus. Is that understood?"

"Yes, Admiral," they replied together.

"Good." He gave a short nod. "Captain Fanshawe, you are dismissed."

Fanshawe hesitated—just a fraction. Hood continued:

"Dwelling on perceived breaches of protocol serves no one. We have real work before us. I expect every officer in this squadron to attend to his duty and nothing else."

"Of course, Admiral," Fanshawe said, voice tight. "My only concern is the good order of the fleet."

"As is mine," Hood said crisply. "You are dismissed."

Fanshawe bowed, gave Nicholas a cool look, and withdrew with stiff formality. The door had scarcely latched behind him when Hood turned to Nicholas.

"An interesting history between you two, I gather?"

Nicholas hesitated, uncertain how much Hood already knew or had surmised. "We were at the Academy together briefly, sir. Captain Fanshawe was two years my senior, and unfortunately we were not on good terms, perhaps due to the results of several fencing matches, and indeed the Prize Contest in Arms."

"And now you command a vessel that can outsail his frigate," Hood observed. He waved a hand dismissively, "In any case, to more important matters."

He gestured toward the documents Thornhill had been examining, and Thornhill spoke up. "Your initiative in searching for hidden correspondence has proven valuable, Commander. The official dispatches contain diplomatic communications of interest but expected in nature. These supplementary papers, however, include something altogether more significant."

Thornhill stepped forward, holding several pages of closely written French text. "References to a network of informants in British ports and naval bases," he said, his voice clinical and precise. "Including a key operative with access to Admiralty dispatches who appears to be reporting fleet movements directly to French intelligence." Turning to Hood, "It's as we believed."

Nicholas felt a chill at the implications. A well-placed spy could cause incalculable damage to British naval operations. "A traitor, sir?"

"So it would appear, and what's worse within Government." Hood confirmed grimly. "Though the information is incomplete. The woman I asked about, Miss Catherine Holloway, is known to be the mistress of a senior Treasury official with extensive Admiralty connections who is currently stationed in Barbados. Confidentially, his name is Sir William Chambers, but you are to repeat that to no one."

Hood moved to the stern windows, gazing out at the fleet spread across the water. After a moment's contemplation, he turned back to Nicholas.

"Commander, I have a new assignment for *Alert*. One that requires immediate action."

Nicholas straightened, attentive. "Sir?"

"Intelligence suggests that a woman carrying sensitive information has departed St. Eustatius aboard an American merchant vessel bound for Charleston. The timing and description align with Miss Holloway, who was last seen in Barbados two weeks ago, though she's traveling under an assumed name." Hood's expression was grave. "If our suspicions are correct, she has been passing naval intelligence to the French for over a year. Critical information about fleet movements, convoy schedules, operational plans. From what Mr. Thornhill has said, I believe the documents you've recovered suggest she may be aware of our suspicions and is now fleeing with additional intelligence that could severely compromise our position in the Caribbean. She must be intercepted before she reaches American territory."

Thornhill nodded, "I agree with that assessment, Admiral. The situation requires discretion, Commander. Sir William Chambers is a powerful figure with connections throughout government. Any accusation against his mistress would inevitably reflect upon him and could create political complications."

Nicholas understood the delicacy of the assignment. "You wish me to intercept the vessel and detain Miss Holloway, along with any documents she may be carrying?"

"Precisely," Hood replied. "Your dealings with that Portuguese trader—Silva, was it?—suggest a certain... adaptability. The American vessel is *Liberty*, a merchant brig out of Boston. She departed St. Eustatius three days past."

Thornhill spoke from beside the chart table. "*Liberty* is a typical merchantman in rig, but larger than most—well manned, and armed with ten six-pounders. Based on prevailing winds and customary routing, she will likely make this course toward Charleston." He drew a line with his forefinger, tracing northwest from the Leeward Islands toward the American coast.

"Until your arrival, we judged her too far ahead to intercept," Hood added. "But *Alert*'s speed alters the equation. You may yet catch her before she makes landfall."

Nicholas leaned in, eyeing the chart, measuring distances against known speeds. "Even with a two-knot advantage, sir, it will be close work. She has near three days' lead."

"I know," Hood said. He straightened. "You will sail within the hour. Mr. Thornhill will furnish the particulars—description of the vessel, Miss Holloway's likeness, and all intelligence we've gathered. There is little time."

Nicholas nodded, his mind already turning to the practical aspects of the mission. "And if we apprehend her, sir?"

Hood exchanged a glance with Thornhill before answering. "Secure any documents in her possession and return directly to the fleet with both the evidence and Miss Holloway herself. Under no circumstances are you to take her to a port or transfer her to another vessel. This matter requires the utmost discretion."

"Understood, sir."

As Nicholas prepared to depart, Hood added one final instruction. "Commander, while Miss Holloway should be treated with appropriate decorum, do not allow her feminine appearance to cloud your judgment. If our intelligence is correct, her actions have cost British lives. She is to be considered dangerous despite her sex and apparent gentility."

"Aye, sir," Nicholas replied, recalling Silva's warnings about underestimating opponents based on appearance or status.

Ten minutes later Thornhill handed him a sealed packet. "Additional intelligence that may prove useful, Commander. Good hunting."

As he stepped into the boat waiting alongside *Barfleur*, Nicholas glanced across the water toward *Pylades*, sailing to her position ahead of the main line. He could see the figure of Fanshawe on her quarterdeck, his telescope trained over the taffrail on *Alert*. Nicholas allowed himself a brief smile as the boat pulled away from the flagship. He had an enemy there, but Captain Fanshawe's wounded pride would have to wait. *Alert* had more significant prey to pursue.

CHAPTER FOUR

Fourteen days of relentless pursuit had taken their toll on both ship and crew. *Alert* sliced through the gray swells off the Carolina coast, her hull straining as she beat against a stiff northwesterly wind. Her rigging, once impeccably taut, now showed signs of wear from the constant strain of carrying maximum sail through changing weather. Backstays had been reinforced with preventer lines, running rigging replaced where chafing, and sails patched where salt spray and wind had begun to erode the fabric.

Nicholas studied the charts spread across his small table. Their pursuit had taken them along a northwesterly course from the Leeward Islands, following the most likely route for a vessel bound for Charleston. They had sighted several merchant ships but none matching *Liberty's* description. If their intelligence was accurate, the American vessel had begun the chase with a lead of three days head start, perhaps 500 miles, plus the shorter distance from St. Eustatius compared to *Alert's* starting position northwest of Barbados, perhaps another 300 miles, or 800 miles total. Nicholas estimated that with an average two knot advantage, assuming no other factors, they would not catch her, but if it was anything more, they would, at least in theory.

The appearance of the French frigate *Insurgente* two days earlier had nearly compromised their mission. Only their knowledge of the Bahama Banks gleaned from one of Nicholas' talks with a quartermaster in the squadron whose "brother" used to be a smuggler, and later marked on their chart, had allowed them to slip between two small cays that the deeper-drafted French vessel couldn't follow. The temporary deviation had cost them valuable hours but preserved their pursuit.

Going on deck Nicholas joined Markham by the rail.

The master's normally immaculate appearance had likewise suffered from the rigors of the voyage. His eyes were bloodshot from constant vigilance, his uniform salt-stained. "I make us about seven leagues due south of Charleston, Captain."

"How much longer can we maintain this pace?" Nicholas asked quietly, pitching his voice for Markham's ears alone.

The master considered the question with characteristic thoroughness before answering. "The fore top'sle yard shows signs of springing. It might hold another day, perhaps two if we're fortunate, but it will need attention before we attempt the return voyage. Several blocks need replacement, and the mainsail is developing a weakness along the leech." He paused. "The men are in better condition than the rigging, though fatigue is becoming a factor."

Nicholas nodded, unsurprised by the assessment. They had driven *Alert* mercilessly since departing Hood's squadron. Even during the brief tropical squall three days earlier, they had carried more canvas than prudence dictated, heeling so severely that water had cascaded across the leeward deck.

"Mr. Forester," Nicholas called to his first lieutenant, who was supervising the morning watch on the forecastle. "We'll run the gun drill at six bells."

"Aye, sir," Forester acknowledged, his fair hair whipping in the wind. Despite the strain of the voyage, the first lieutenant had proven his worth repeatedly, organizing the watch system to maximize crew efficiency, supervising repairs even in heavy seas, and maintaining discipline without resorting to the harsh measures many officers deemed necessary. In the two weeks since leaving Hood's squadron, Nicholas had come to even more appreciate Forester's quiet competence and ability to anticipate needs before they were voiced. The lieutenant's longer time in service had given him a practical understanding of seamanship that only experience could provide.

"Mr. Wells," Nicholas said as the young midshipman approached with the morning report. "Join me in my cabin."

Midshipman James Wells, barely seventeen years old, followed Nicholas below with the eager attentiveness that had characterized his service since joining *Alert*. The youngest of three sons from a Hampshire clergy family, Wells combined a scholar's mind with a sailor's natural instinct for wind and wave. He had shown particular aptitude for navigation, often working alongside Markham to calculate their position with remarkable precision.

In Nicholas's small cabin, Wells presented the report with appropriate formality. "All watches accounted for, sir. Two men on the sick list with minor injuries. Water consumption remains within allocation. Mr. Davidson reports the forward magazine in good order."

"Thank you, Mr. Wells," Nicholas said, accepting the report. "I'd like your assessment of the coastline. You've been studying the charts of this region, I believe?"

Wells stood a bit straighter, clearly pleased to be consulted. "Yes, sir. The coast trends northeast of Charleston towards Cape Fear, a difficult spot characterized by shifting sandbanks that extend up to five miles offshore in places. He hesitated, then added with the confidence of youth, "However, *Alert's* shallow draft should allow us to navigate closer to shore than most naval vessels, if need be, particularly if we maintain careful soundings."

Nicholas nodded, pleased by the analysis. "Precisely. And that advantage may prove crucial if we make the entrances to Charleston ahead of our quarry, and she seeks the shelter of American waters further up the coast."

"Permission to speak freely, sir?"

"Granted."

"The men have been speculating about our mission," Wells said carefully. "They understand we're pursuing an American vessel, but the urgency has prompted questions."

Nicholas considered his response. The nature of their mission—intercepting Miss Holloway and her intelligence—remained known only to himself, Forester, and Markham.

"You may tell them this much," Nicholas decided. "We seek a specific vessel carrying information vital to British interests. The successful completion of our mission could save many lives across the fleet."

Wells nodded, accepting the limited explanation. "They'll appreciate knowing the purpose behind the hardship, sir."

"A crew performs best when they understand the stakes," Nicholas agreed. "Carry on."

"Signal from the masthead, sir," called Midshipman Wells. "Holcomb reports sails to the west."

Nicholas hastened on deck and immediately moved to the main shrouds. "I'll see for myself. "Mr. Forester, see to things here."

"Aye, sir," Forester acknowledged, taking position on the quarterdeck.

Nicholas climbed swiftly. In the Royal Navy, most commanders would have sent a midshipman aloft rather than going themselves, but Nicholas's time with Cook and later with Silva had taught him the value of seeing crucial details firsthand. Thankfully he had never suffered from a fear of heights, at least not extremely, as some did, just as he was unaffected by sea sickness.

Reaching the main cross trees, he found Holcomb, a former smuggler whose remarkable eyesight made him a prized lookout.

"There, sir," Holcomb said, pointing toward the northwest horizon. "Two masts, square-rigged. About twelve miles distant by my estimation, steering northeast."

Nicholas trained his glass in the indicated direction. After several minutes of careful observation through the intermittent sea haze, he could make out the vessel—square topsails visible above the horizon, moving on a northeasterly course that would eventually intersect with *Alert's* northerly course if both ships maintained their headings. He studied the distant ship with focused intensity, noting details that would be missed from deck level—the particular set of her sails, the angle of her yards, the way she moved through the water.

"She appears to be making up the coast towards Charleston, perhaps after making landfall further south," Nicholas observed. "What do you make of her?"

Holcomb's weathered face creased in thought. "Not likely a typical merchant crew, sir. Her sail trimming has been too precise—naval training or experienced privateer, I'd wager. Heavy crew."

This confirmed Nicholas's growing suspicion. The vessel they pursued was likely more than a simple merchant ship carrying a spy. He continued his observation for several more minutes, cataloging every visible detail before descending to the deck.

Mr. Quinn, what's your assessment of her likely course?"

Masters mate Patrick Quinn stepped forward, his weathered face creased with experience earned in decades at sea. Before joining the Navy, Quinn had worked the Atlantic coastal trade for fifteen years, developing an intimate familiarity with the American coastline.

"If she's bound for Charleston as we suspect, sir, she'd typically stand well offshore until reaching the latitude of the town, then approach from the east," Quinn said, "These waters have treacherous shoals, and most masters prefer the safety of deep water unless they know the coast intimately."

The information aligned with Nicholas's instincts. "Thank you, Mr. Quinn. Mr. Forester, we'll come up to larboard and get to windward of her. Set the fore stays'l."

As *Alert* altered course towards the other ship and increased sail, the atmosphere aboard ship subtly shifted. Men moved with greater purpose, conversations reduced to essential communication, eyes frequently turning toward the distant sails that might be their quarry. Nicholas observed the crew's preparation with approval. *Alert's* people had melded into a remarkably cohesive unit since leaving Jamaica. Daily gun drills had honed their skills with the six-pounders, the carronades, and the nine-pounder chasers. The latter had been a particular focus, with Nicholas emphasizing precision targeting of an enemy vessel's rigging rather than her hull. If they encountered *Liberty*, their objective was to disable rather than destroy—Miss Holloway and her intelligence needed to be captured intact.

The gun captain for the bow chaser, a barrel-chested Irishman named Sullivan, had proven exceptional at his task. A former privateer gunner who had joined the Royal Navy after being captured, Sullivan increased the weapon's already inherent accuracy through meticulous attention to the exact amount of powder used and careful maintenance of the barrel. He had his crew constantly tending to the smoothness of the shot. His precision in aiming had become legendary among the crew after fourteen days of daily practice.

"We'll need Sullivan's skills today," Forester remarked quietly as he rejoined Nicholas. "If that's indeed our quarry, we'll want to disable her quickly before she can reach American waters."

Nicholas nodded. "Agreed. Though I suspect our task may prove more challenging than Hood's intelligence suggested. Miss Holloway's value to the French would warrant significant protection."

"You think *Liberty* may be more heavily armed than reported?"

"I think we should prepare for that possibility," Nicholas replied. "Have the marines stand ready with their muskets. If we're forced to board, I want covering fire from the tops."

As the morning progressed, the distance between *Alert* and the unknown vessel gradually decreased. The other ship had altered course to the north, and was now close hauled, potentially making for shallow water.

"She's seen us," Markham observed as the vessel's change of heading became more pronounced. "Making for the shoals."

At four bells in the afternoon watch, Holcomb's voice rang down from the maintop. "Deck there! I can make her out clearly now! Two-masted brig, American colors! Matches the description of *Liberty*, sir!"

Nicholas studied the vessel through his glass, now visible in considerable detail. The brig flew American colors as reported, and her general appearance matched their intelligence—the figurehead of a woman with a torch, the distinctive profile, the repaired section on her port quarter. However, several concerning details emerged as they closed the distance.

"Gun ports," Nicholas said to Forester, who stood beside him with his own glass. "I count six on her visible side. More than the eight total we were told to expect."

"And she's riding lower in the water than a merchant vessel of her size should," Forester added. "Either heavily laden or carrying considerably more weight in guns and men."

Nicholas lowered his glass, decision made. "Beat to quarters, Mr. Forester. Open the gun ports and run out the guns. We'll approach and order her to heave to."

"Aye, sir."

The discipline of *Alert's* crew showed in the measured efficiency of their preparation. Gun crews took positions, weapons were distributed, ammunition brought up from the magazine, and the deck cleared of unnecessary items—all without the chaotic scramble that characterized less practiced vessels. Sergeant Miller positioned his twelve marines with careful attention to fields of fire, stationing four in the tops with muskets and the remainder amidships where they could support either a defense against boarders or launch their own boarding action if required.

"Two thousand yards, sir," Markham reported as they continued to close with the American vessel. Then, "She's tacking around to the southwest. She may believe she has the advantage of speed on this point of sail."

Nicholas nodded. *Alert's* superior performance was most evident when sailing close to the wind. On their current course, with both vessels running before the wind, *Liberty* might actually hold the advantage. A change of tactics was required.

"Mr. Markham, bring us about and hard on the wind on the starboard tack. We'll use our weatherliness to gain the advantage of position."

"Aye, sir."

Alert responded beautifully, her bow swinging smoothly through the wind and settling on nearly a due westerly course. Though this course initially took them at an angle away from *Liberty* as she reached down wind, Nicholas knew it would ultimately provide a superior tactical position.

"She's increasing sail, sir," Midshipman Wells reported from his position near the foremast. "Setting her topgallants and flying jib."

"So our quarry recognizes the chase has begun in earnest," Nicholas observed. "Mr. Forester, run up the ensign and signal her to heave to."

The red ensign of the Royal Navy broke out from *Alert's* staff, followed by the signal flags demanding the American vessel heave to. As expected, *Liberty* made no response except to set additional sail, confirming her intent to flee.

Nicholas had anticipated this reaction. "Mr. Markham, continue our course to windward. Once we've gained sufficient weather gauge, we'll bear down on her."

For the next hour, the tactical chess match continued. *Alert* worked steadily to windward, gradually gaining the advantageous position that would allow her to dictate the terms of engagement. *Liberty* attempted to maintain her distance, but the American captain eventually recognized the inevitable mathematics of his position, for *Alert's* superior windward performance meant she would ultimately be able to choose the moment and angle of interception.

By late afternoon, they had achieved the desired position—approximately a mile upwind of *Liberty*, with the option to bear down on the American vessel whenever Nicholas chose.

"She's cleared for action, sir," Forester reported after studying *Liberty* through his glass. "Gun ports open on both sides. I count six ports per side."

"Twelve guns total," Nicholas said grimly. "And likely twelve-pounders rather than the six-pounders we expected. Sullivan, prepare the bow chaser. Target her fore-topmast when we close to effective range."

"Aye, sir," Sullivan replied with professional enthusiasm. The gun captain moved to his position at the nine-pounder mounted on *Alert's* foc'sle, checking the precise adjustments to the elevation screw that would determine the shot's trajectory.

Nicholas turned to Midshipman Wells, who waited nearby for orders. "Mr. Wells, you'll serve as my messenger during the engagement. Remain close."

"Aye, sir," Wells replied, his youthful face flushed with excitement at his first real action.

"Mr. Forester, we'll commence our approach. I want to engage at a distance that maximizes the accuracy of our nine-pounder while targeting their rigging."

"Understood, sir."

Alert fell off to larboard smoothly, turning downwind toward the American vessel with controlled precision. The gap between the ships closed rapidly as they approached on convergent courses.

At approximately 1200 hundred yards—where the exceptional accuracy of their nine-pounder could be brought to bear most effectively—Nicholas gave the order.

"Sullivan, you may fire when ready."

Sullivan made a final adjustment to the gun's elevation, compensating for *Alert's* motion, then stepped back to pull the lanyard. "Fire!"

The nine-pounder leapt against its restraining tackles, its report cracking across the water. Through his glass, Nicholas watched the shot arc through the air, falling just short of *Liberty's* bow, sending up a splash that drenched her figurehead.

"Reload," Nicholas ordered calmly. "Adjust elevation, Sullivan."

Liberty responded as expected, altering course slightly upwind to bring her starboard broadside to bear. At this new angle, Nicholas could clearly see additional details that confirmed his suspicions about the vessel's true nature. More men were visible on her decks than a typical merchant crew would account for, and her gun ports revealed cannon that appeared to be twelve-pounders.

"She's a privateer, sir," Forester concluded, observing the same details. "Masquerading as a merchant vessel but armed and crewed for war."

"Indeed," Nicholas agreed. "Which makes our task considerably more challenging."

Liberty fired her first broadside at a range that demonstrated their guns were well-handled, even if the American gunners were optimistic about the distance. The shots fell short of *Alert*, sending up harmless splashes several hundred yards away. The display, however, confirmed the American's willingness to fight rather than surrender.

"She's trying to intimidate us, sir" Forester observed.

"And revealing her armament in the process," Nicholas replied. "Those are twelve-pounders without question. She outguns us considerably."

Sullivan's second shot from the bow chaser flew true, striking *Liberty's* foremast just above the cap. Splinters flew, but the mast held. The gun crew immediately began reloading with the practiced efficiency of men who had drilled for precisely this scenario.

Nicholas studied the developing situation with cold calculation. *Alert* carried five six-pounders, two twelve-pounder carronades plus the two nine-pound chase guns, while *Liberty* appeared to mount twelve twelve-pounders—a substantial advantage in weight of metal. Their best hope lay in using *Alert's* superior maneuverability and the accuracy of their bow chaser to disable the American vessel without coming under her full broadside.

"Maintain this distance, Mr. Markham. We'll continue working to windward between shots, forcing her to choose between keeping her broadside to us or making for the coast."

"Aye, sir. Maintain distance."

For the next thirty minutes, they executed this strategy with clinical precision. Sullivan fired the bow chaser eleven times, scoring three significant hits on *Liberty's* rigging. The foretopmast backstay parted, followed by damage to the main topsail yard. The American captain responded with determination, attempting repeatedly to close the distance by sailing higher into the wind, but *Alert's* superior weatherliness allowed her to maintain separation.

"She's making for shoal water, sir," Quinn warned as *Liberty* altered course toward the coast. "Trying to draw us into the shallows where she may have local knowledge."

Just as Sullivan prepared to fire again, *Liberty* executed a sudden maneuver, throwing her helm over and turning directly toward *Alert* in a bid to close the distance and bring her superior broadside to bear.

"Hard to starboard!" Nicholas ordered immediately.

Alert responded with the agility that justified her name, coming about rapidly to maintain the separation. As they completed the turn, however, *Liberty* fired her broadside. Most shots fell short, but two solid hits thumped into *Alert's* hull, sending splinters flying across the deck.

"Damage report!" Nicholas called out.

"Two men wounded, sir," Forester replied after a quick assessment. "Shot penetrated the hull at the waterline, but we're making no significant water. Carpenter's mate is already addressing it."

Liberty's aggressive turn had created an unexpected opportunity. As she came about, her stern momentarily presented a vulnerable target. Sullivan, showing the initiative that characterized experienced gun captains, had already adjusted the bow chaser's aim.

"Permission to fire, sir?" he called.

"Fire!"

The long nine roared, its shot striking *Liberty's* stern quarter with devastating accuracy. The impact shattered her rudder assembly, sending fragments of wood spinning into the air. The effect was immediately apparent as the American vessel's movements became erratic, her control compromised. A cheer went up from *Alert's* crew, quickly silenced by Forester's command for discipline.

"Well shot, Sullivan," Nicholas acknowledged. "Mr. Markham, bring us about again and close the distance. We'll pass across her stern at seven hundred yards and rake her with our starboard battery."

Alert executed the maneuver perfectly, positioning herself where *Liberty's* guns couldn't bear effectively. As they crossed her stern, Nicholas gave the order to fire. *Alert's* starboard six-pounders delivered a synchronized volley, and at least three balls swept *Liberty's* quarterdeck and stern, visibly damaging her already compromised steering and causing havoc among her crew.

The American captain, however, proved resourceful even with limited control of his vessel. Using sails alone, he managed to bring *Liberty* around enough to fire a partial broadside as *Alert* completed her pass. Four twelve pound balls slammed into *Alert's* hull, one passing directly through the officers' wardroom while another shattered a gun carriage, killing one seaman and wounding three others.

"Stern chaser, fire when you bear!" Nicholas ordered as they pulled away. The long nine mounted on *Alert's* stern spoke in response, its shot severing *Liberty's* foretopmast stay. The spar wavered, then crashed down in a tangle of rigging and canvas.

The battle settled into a deadly rhythm over the next hour. *Alert* used her superior handling to strike repeatedly from positions where *Liberty* couldn't bring her full firepower to bear, while the American vessel sought desperately to land the crushing broadside that could turn the tide. Both vessels sustained damage, though *Alert's* more grievous hits came not from the planned exchanges but from the occasional lucky shot during transitional movements.

"Four dead, nine wounded, sir," Forester reported during a momentary lull. "The foremast is holding but weakened. We've lost fore topsail yard entirely, and the carpenter reports two shots below the waterline that are admitting water. The pumps are containing it for now."

Nicholas nodded grimly. The engagement was proving costlier than he had hoped. "And *Liberty*?"

"Severely damaged aloft, sir. Her foretopmast is gone, mainmast damaged, and her steering remains compromised. However, most of her guns appear intact, and she has a substantial crew. I estimate at least seventy men."

The number matched Nicholas's own observation—far more than the twenty-four their intelligence had indicated. *Liberty* was clearly no ordinary merchant vessel but a well-armed, heavily crewed privateer. The presence of Miss Holloway aboard such a vessel suggested her importance to the French and Americans.

As the sun began to lower toward the western horizon, casting long shadows across the water, Nicholas recognized that a decision point was approaching. They had damaged *Liberty* significantly but not decisively. Night would soon complicate their tactics, and the American coastline loomed just fifteen miles distant.

"Sullivan," Nicholas called to the gun captain. "Can you target the base of her mainmast?"

Sullivan studied the target through narrowed eyes. "Aye, sir, with the right opportunity. We'd need to close to three hundred yards or less for certainty."

Nicholas weighed the risk. Closing to that distance would be risky, perhaps even fatal, if it resulted in multiple broadsides from *Liberty's* entire six gun battery. Yet the potential reward—dismasting the American vessel entirely—might be their only path to swift victory.

"Mr. Forester, prepare the starboard battery and double shot with grape, including the carronade. We'll execute one decisive pass at close range."

"Aye, sir."

Nicholas turned to Midshipman Wells, "Mr. Wells, inform Sergeant Miller to prepare his marines for boarding action if our next pass succeeds in dismasting her."

"Yes, sir!" Wells replied, his youthful face smudged with powder residue but alight with determination.

As Wells hurried toward the marines' position, a sudden cry came from the lookout. "Deck there! Shot from the enemy!"

Nicholas turned to see a puff of smoke from one of *Liberty's* bow chasers.

"Down!" Nicholas shouted, but the warning came too late.

The twelve pound ball struck Wells squarely, the impact horrific in its finality as blood and body parts sprayed across the deck. For an instant, Nicholas found himself unable to process what he had seen. Then training reasserted itself, the responsibility of command pushing personal reaction aside.

"Mr. Markham, execute our approach," he ordered, his voice steady despite the hollow feeling in his chest. "Mr. Forester, you will point the starboard carronade yourself. Target the quarterdeck. We end this now."

"Aye, sir," Forester replied, his own expression grim as he glanced at what remained of Midshipman Wells.

Alert came about with deadly purpose, driving directly toward *Liberty* on an intercept course that would bring her across the American's bow. Sullivan stood ready at the nine-pounder, his focus absolute as he calculated the approaching shot.

At precisely four hundred yards, with *Liberty's* broadside beginning to bear as the angle changed, Nicholas gave the order. "Sullivan, fire when ready!"

The bow chaser roared, its shot flying true to strike *Liberty's* mainmast exactly at the partners where it entered the deck. The already damaged mast shuddered under the impact, wood splintering as the giant spar began to topple. Simultaneously, *Liberty* fired her broadside, most shots passing harmlessly overhead as *Alert* heeled into a turn, though one ball smashed into her bulwark, sending splinters scything across the deck.

Liberty's mainmast crashed down in a catastrophic tangle of rigging, yards, and canvas. The fallen spar dragged across her deck, crushing men beneath its weight and sweeping others overboard. With both her fore and main masts now compromised, the American vessel lay helpless in the water, unable to maneuver effectively.

"Bring us alongside to windward," Nicholas ordered. "Prepare to board. Marines to the foredeck."

As *Alert* closed with the wallowing American vessel, her crew armed themselves for the coming confrontation. Boarding axes, cutlasses, and pistols were distributed, while Sergeant Miller positioned his marines for the initial assault.

Liberty, however, showed no signs of surrender despite her crippled condition. Men swarmed her deck, armed and clearly preparing to resist boarders. Her remaining operational guns were being trained on *Alert's* approaching hull.

"They mean to fight to the last," Forester observed grimly.

"So be it," Nicholas replied. The death of Wells had hardened his resolve. "Starboard battery, target their main deck. Fire as you bear."

Alert's guns spoke in sequence as they came alongside, the carronade forward sweeping *Liberty's* quarterdeck with a blast of grape shot that caused a huge red swath of wriggling bodies, and the other guns followed. At the same time *Liberty's* twelve-pounders smashed into the hull at close range. A gun was overturned and several men were down. Nicholas felt a tug on his left arm and gasped with pain as a splinter opened a deep red gash across his upper arm. As the vessels came together with a shuddering impact, grappling hooks flew across the gap, binding the ships together.

"Boarders away!" Nicholas ordered, drawing his sword. "Marines, covering fire!"

Miller's marines delivered a disciplined volley into *Liberty's* defenders, dropping several men and creating momentary confusion that *Alert's* boarding party exploited. Nicholas led from the front, leaping across the narrow gap between the vessels with Forester close behind.

What followed was the controlled chaos of close combat at sea. The Americans fought with desperate courage, while *Alert's* crew pressed forward with disciplined determination. Steel rang against steel, pistols cracked in the confined space, and men grappled in deadly embrace on decks slick with blood and seawater.

Nicholas found himself confronted by a burly American wielding a boarding axe. He parried the first swing with his sword, the impact numbing his arm, then stepped inside the man's guard to deliver a killing thrust. As that opponent fell, another took his place—a younger man in what appeared to be a French naval coat, confirming Nicholas's suspicion about *Liberty's* true allegiance.

The French officer was skilled with his blade, forcing Nicholas to give ground momentarily. A thrust narrowly missed Nicholas's ribs, tearing his coat but drawing no blood. He countered with a combination of attacks, the unorthodox pattern confusing his opponent long enough for Nicholas to land a disabling cut to the man's sword arm.

Across the deck, Forester fought with cold efficiency, his swordplay reflecting formal training tempered by practical experience. Sergeant Miller and his marines had established a position amidships, their disciplined musket fire controlling sections of the deck and preventing the Americans from organizing an effective counterattack.

Gradually, inevitably, the superior discipline of *Alert's* crew began to prevail against the more numerous but less organized defenders. Fifteen minutes into the boarding action, the American captain, a tough looking broad shouldered man, his coat torn and bloody and limping heavily, stepped forward with raised hands.

"Enough!" he shouted above the din of combat. "We yield!"

Nicholas raised his sword. "Cease fire! Quarter is given!"

The fighting subsided in stages, men disengaging with wary caution born of combat's intensity. Nicholas approached the American captain, sword still ready.

"Your vessel is taken in the name of His Majesty," Nicholas stated formally. "I require the immediate surrender of all arms and the mustering of your crew on the main deck."

The man nodded grimly. "Captain Josiah Hatfield. My men will cooperate."

As the Americans began laying down their weapons, Nicholas turned to Forester. "Secure the vessel. I want guards on the magazine and all access to the lower decks. And find Miss Holloway immediately."

"Aye, sir," Forester replied, already organizing teams to search below.

The human cost of the victory became apparent as the immediate tension of combat dissipated. On *Alert's* deck, fifteen men lay dead, including midshipman Wells, with another eleven wounded to varying degrees. *Liberty's* losses were even more severe—at least twenty dead and more than twenty wounded.

Nicholas supervised the securing of prisoners while *Alert's* surgeon, Maxwell, began treating the wounded of both vessels according to severity, working alongside the *Liberty's* surgeon. Maxwell paused as he walked past, whipped out a cloth bandage, and wrapped it tightly around Nicholas' arm, saying "I'll patch that for you properly a bit later, sir," and moved on. The carpenter and his mates assessed damage, reporting that while both vessels remained seaworthy, significant repairs would be required before either could undertake an extended voyage.

"Sir," Forester called from the companion ladder. "I believe we've found her."

He led Nicholas below to a small cabin near the stern, where two of *Alert's* crew stood guard outside a locked door. At Nicholas's nod, they broke the lock and swung the door open.

The woman inside matched the description perfectly, late twenties, dark hair, striking green eyes, and delicate features now set in an expression of cold defiance. She wore a simple traveling dress of blue wool, her hair arranged practically rather than fashionably. A small writing desk had been bolted to the deck before her, covered with papers she had evidently been destroying when interrupted by the sounds of combat.

"Miss Catherine Holloway, I presume," Nicholas said, surveying the scene with careful attention. "Or do you prefer Margaret Wilson for the duration of your journey?"

A flash of surprise crossed her face before the mask of composure returned. "You have me at a disadvantage, sir."

"Commander Nicholas Cruwys, Royal Navy. You are being detained on suspicion of espionage against the British Crown."

She lifted her chin slightly. "I am an American citizen traveling to Charleston on legitimate business. You have no right to seize me."

"Your true identity and purpose are known to us, Miss Holloway," Nicholas replied calmly. "As are your activities on behalf of French intelligence."

Something flickered in her eyes—calculation, perhaps, or the first hint of genuine concern. She glanced at the papers on her desk, many partially burned or torn.

"Mr. Forester, secure all documents in this cabin," Nicholas ordered. "Every scrap of paper, regardless of condition. And search her belongings and the cabin thoroughly for hidden compartments or enciphered communications."

"You'll find nothing of consequence," Holloway stated, though the tension in her voice suggested otherwise.

Nicholas studied her with professional detachment. "In any case, ma'am, you will be transferred to *Alert* immediately. Mr. Forester, please escort Miss Holloway to the gunroom once you've secured the documents. Post a marine as guard."

Returning to *Alert's* quarterdeck, Nicholas found Markham waiting with urgent news. "Sails on the horizon to the north, sir."

Nicholas raised his glass to scan the distance. Three distinct sets of sails were visible, their approach suggesting coordinated movement rather than coincidental routing.

"American?" he asked, though he suspected the answer already.

"Most likely, sir," Markham confirmed. "Their bearing suggests they've come from Charleston. Perhaps alerted by signals we haven't observed, or simply responding to the sound of gunfire."

Nicholas calculated rapidly. *Alert* was damaged but operational. *Liberty* was essentially crippled, capable of limited movement at best. The approaching vessels would reach them within three hours at most, potentially sooner if the wind held.

"Identify those ships," Nicholas ordered, handing his glass to Quinn.

Quinn studied the approaching vessels with practiced eyes. "Difficult to be certain at this distance, sir, but their profile suggests at least one substantial vessel—possibly a Continental Navy frigate, accompanied by smaller craft. Likely a response force based in Charleston."

The tactical situation was clear. While *Alert* might outrun the approaching Americans in her normal condition, her current damage made escape with a prize vessel impossible. Attempting to defend both ships against superior forces would certainly result in the loss of both *Alert* and *Liberty*, along with their crews and the crucial intelligence they had secured.

"Mr. Forester," Nicholas called as his lieutenant returned to the deck. "Prepare to fire the *Liberty*. Bring all captured documentation and Miss Holloway's personal effects. We have perhaps two hours before those vessels are upon us."

Forester grasped the situation immediately. "Aye, sir. What of the American prisoners and wounded? The most serious cases shouldn't be moved."

Nicholas faced the moral dilemma squarely. *Alert* could not accommodate even forty additional men, particularly with her own damage and casualties. Yet leaving prisoners and wounded men to drown was unthinkable.

"We'll leave them the ship's boats," he decided after a moment's consideration. "The approaching vessels will reach them before nightfall. Transfer the wounded into those, and any overflow will have to take turns in the water hanging onto the boats until rescue arrives."

"And Captain Hatfield, sir?"

Nicholas considered this. Naval protocol typically required the capture of enemy commanders as valuable prisoners. However, leaving wounded men without leadership could endanger their survival.

"Inform Captain Hatfield that he may remain with his crew."

The next 40 minutes passed in controlled urgency. The ships remained lashed together, *Alert's* crew transferring prisoners, documents, and provisioning the boats with essential supplies. Dr. Maxwell organized the care of wounded on both ships, ensuring the Americans left behind had proper medical attention until rescue arrived. Forester supervised the placement of combustibles designed to cause a rapid fire.

On what would be his final visit to *Liberty*, Nicholas found Captain Hatfield on deck helping his wounded into the boats alongside. The American looked up as Nicholas approached.

"Your lieutenant has explained the situation, Commander," Hatfield said quietly. "I appreciate your humanity in not abandoning my wounded men."

Nicholas nodded. "War does not require unnecessary cruelty, Captain. I trust you'll explain to the approaching vessels that we treated your men with appropriate care."

"I will convey that truth," Hatfield confirmed. "Though I cannot promise it will temper their pursuit. The lady you've taken is considered valuable by certain influential parties."

"So we've gathered," Nicholas replied. "The boats are provisioned with water and food sufficient for a day. Your rescuers should reach you soon after our departure."

As Nicholas prepared to depart, Hatfield spoke again. "One question, if I may. How did you know to look for us specifically? Our mission was supposedly known only to a select few."

Nicholas considered. "I couldn't say Captain, I'm just a sea officer. Good day, Captain."

Nicholas went below to *Liberty*'s main cabin with Markham. The space was a shambles—bulkheads scorched and splintered from the cannonade—but they located the log and a sheaf of documents in a scorched but intact desk. Rummaging through the lockers, they uncovered several small chests, unexpectedly heavy, which proved to contain gold specie. Nicholas ordered them sent aboard *Alert*, under marine guard, and secured in his cabin.

Back aboard, he found Miss Holloway already installed under guard in the gunroom, a space hardly designed for comfort, but at least dry and secure. Out on the horizon, the American vessels were now plainly visible, their sails taut with the favourable wind—perhaps an hour off.

"All essential personnel and materials transferred, sir," Forester reported crisply.

"Very good, Mr. Forester. Cast off those boats and fire the prize. Then make all sail. Course south-southeast. We'll use the coming darkness to our advantage."

Alert gathered way, pulling steadily away from the wallowing hulk of *Liberty*, where thick smoke was already pouring from the hatches. Nicholas watched through his glass as the American captain organized his men in the boats rowing slowly away from the ship with some uninjured men in the water clinging to the gunnels. It was the action of a professional seaman, and Nicholas found himself respecting Hatfield's competence despite their opposing allegiances.

They were perhaps two miles away twenty minutes later when *Liberty* disintegrated in an explosion as the fire reached her magazine, leaving only floating debris and the boats containing her surviving crew, which fortunately had rowed a sufficient distance to be safe from the blast. The pursuing American vessels adjusted course slightly toward the boats, confirming they had spotted their countrymen.

"They'll be rescued within the hour, sir" Forrester observed, joining Nicholas at the rail. "And then they'll resume pursuit."

"Yes," Nicholas agreed. "But by then we'll have darkness on our side, and they'll be burdened with additional men to accommodate. Make best speed on our current course until sunset, then we'll alter to east-southeast under reduced sail. With luck, they'll continue searching southward while we make for Antigua."

As *Alert* drove onward, her damaged rigging straining under full sail, Nicholas finally allowed himself a moment to process the day's events. They had achieved their primary objective—Catherine Holloway was in custody, along with whatever intelligence she carried. But the cost had been substantial: fifteen men dead, including young Wells, eleven wounded, some with small chance of survival, and *Alert* herself significantly damaged.

That evening, as the sun set behind them and the first stars appeared in the eastern sky, Nicholas stood silently at the rail, watching as the flowing wake gradually carried them farther from American waters. Tomorrow would bring the challenges of interrogating their prisoner, caring for the wounded, and repairing their vessel sufficiently for the long voyage back to Hood's squadron. But for this moment, in the gathering darkness, Nicholas allowed himself to remember James Wells—his eager intelligence, his dedication, his promise now forever unfulfilled.

In the naval tradition, there was no time for extended mourning, no pause in operations to honor the fallen. There was only the quiet understanding among those who commanded that each order might result in such losses. It was the burden of command that Nicholas had accepted upon taking *Alert*, a weight that now settled more heavily upon his shoulders with each passing mile.

CHAPTER FIVE

At first light on the 2nd of July 1782, *Alert* limped into English Harbour, Antigua, her battle-scarred profile testament to the encounter off the Carolina coast fourteen days earlier. The morning sun illuminated her patched sails and jury-rigged foremast, casting long shadows across a deck that still bore the dark stains of combat despite daily scrubbing. As they passed the narrow entrance guarded by Fort Berkeley, Nicholas observed the bustle of activity throughout the harbour—Britain's primary naval base in the Leeward Islands fully engaged in the business of war.

English Harbour presented a scene of ordered maritime industry. Within the sheltered confines of this natural anchorage, several vessels underwent repairs at the careening wharf, their hulls heeled over to expose damaged planking to the skilled hands of the dockyard's shipwrights. The naval yard itself—established nearly fifty years earlier and expanded steadily since—comprised substantial stone buildings housing sail lofts, cooperages, smithies, and storehouses. The Commissioner's House stood prominent on the hillside, overlooking the entire complex, its Georgian architecture a reminder of English authority in these distant waters.

Nicholas scanned the harbour as they proceeded toward their assigned mooring. The powerful presence of *HMS Barfleur*, Hood's 98-gun flagship, dominated the western side of the harbour, her imposing three decks rising majestically above the smaller vessels nearby. Not far from her lay *HMS Formidable*, Admiral Rodney's 90-gun flagship, her distinctive profile instantly recognizable to any officer in the fleet. The presence of both flagships confirmed the intelligence they had received from a passing British sloop three days earlier—the fleet's senior command remained concentrated at Antigua following their decisive victory over de Grasse at the Battle of the Saintes nearly three months prior.

"Signal from *Barfleur*, sir," Forester reported, glass trained on the flagship. "We're ordered to anchor in the inner harbour and report aboard immediately upon securing."

"Acknowledge the signal, Mr. Forester," Nicholas replied. "Mr. Markham, bring us to our designated berth."

"Aye, sir," Markham responded, issuing precise orders that guided *Alert* through the crowded harbour. Despite her damage and the fatigue of her crew, the sloop anchored with commendable precision in the appointed location, a testament to the seamanship Nicholas had fostered during their time together.

As the anchor splashed into the warm Caribbean waters, Nicholas surveyed his command with mixed emotions. *Alert* and her crew had performed admirably, but the cost had been substantial. They had buried five more men at sea during the voyage south, bringing their total losses to twenty dead and six still under Maxwell's care in the cramped confines below.

"The ship is secured, sir," Forester reported, approaching the quarterdeck. The first lieutenant's uniform hung looser on his frame than it had two weeks earlier, his features sharpened by the rigors of their mission. The superficial wound on his temple from a splinter during the battle had healed to a pink line partially hidden by his hair.

"Very good, Mr. Forester. "See to our water and victuals. I'll submit requisitions for repairs once I've reported to Admiral Hood." Nicholas paused, then added more quietly, "And ensure our guest remains secured. Double the marine guard and allow no communication with shore until I return."

"Aye, sir," Forester acknowledged, and nodded understanding. Throughout their fourteen-day passage, Catherine Holloway had remained confined to the small gunroom, under constant guard and with minimal interaction beyond essential needs. The documents seized from her cabin aboard *Liberty* had been secured in Nicholas's sea chest, unopened since their initial inventory. Hood's orders had been explicit on this point—the intelligence was for his eyes alone.

After changing into his best uniform, its gilt buttons and blue fabric a sharp contrast to the salt-stained working garb he had worn continuously since the battle, Nicholas made his way carefully into the boat. His left arm remained secured in a linen sling, the wound from the splinter still healing despite Maxwell's careful attention. As he was rowed toward *Barfleur*, Nicholas observed the harbour with professional interest. Beyond the two flagships, he counted three 74-gun ships of the line, four frigates, and numerous smaller vessels—a substantial force, though far fewer than the full fleet that had achieved victory at the Saintes. The remainder, he presumed, were dispersed on patrol or convoy duty throughout the Caribbean.

The tropical heat pressed down with oppressive intensity as they approached *Barfleur's* towering hull. They were piped aboard with the ceremony due Nicholas's rank, the bosun's calls shrilling across the water. A marine lieutenant received him at the entry port, directing them immediately to the admiral's day cabin.

Rear Admiral Hood and his secretary, Mr. Thornhill, awaited him in the spacious day cabin, standing before a table spread with charts and documents.

"Commander Cruwys," Hood acknowledged with a nod. "You appear to have encountered difficulties in your mission." The observation, delivered in Hood's characteristic clipped tones, contained neither criticism nor sympathy, merely assessment.

"Yes, sir," Nicholas replied formally. "*Alert* engaged and captured the American vessel *Liberty* off Cape Fear on the 18th. We confirmed the presence of the individual described in our orders and secured both the lady and associated documents. However, *Liberty* proved more heavily armed than intelligence suggested, twelve twelve-pounders rather than eight six-pounders. We sustained significant damage and casualties before securing our objective. I have my full report and the reports of *Alert's* condition here."

Hood's expression remained impassive. "Very well, I'll read your report later. You were pursued?"

"Yes, sir. Three American vessels, including what appeared to be a Continental Navy frigate, approached from Charleston. Given *Alert's* condition, we were compelled to burn *Liberty* after transferring the prisoner and intelligence materials. We evaded pursuit and made directly for Antigua as ordered."

"Casualties?"

"Twenty dead, including I'm very sorry to say Midshipman Wells, a promising lad, and six wounded still under care."

Hood nodded, "Nearly a quarter of your crew. I wish our intelligence on the *Liberty* had prepared you better." he glanced at Thornhill, who nodded grimly. Hood moved to a sideboard and poured three glasses of Madeira, offering one to Nicholas. The gesture signaled a transition to a less formal conversation.

"Sit, Commander," Hood directed, taking his own seat behind the desk. "Now tell us about Miss Holloway and what you observed before destroying the brig."

Nicholas gave a detailed account of Catherine Holloway's demeanor, and her attempts to destroy documentation prior to capture. He then described the vessel's crew composition, noting the presence of men in French naval attire among the American complement, none, however who had survived. He then said, "And finally, sir we secured approximately £2,000 in gold specie, sir. By my calculation, it amounts to nearly half the value of the brig itself."

Thornhill looked surprised and remarked, "Another layer to the story, Admiral."

Hood nodded thoughtfully, "And the documents?"

"Secured in my sea chest, sir, as per your orders. We conducted a preliminary inventory—correspondence in cipher, nautical charts of Caribbean approaches with annotations, and several journals containing what appear to be observations of British naval movements. All materials remained sealed afterward."

Hood nodded approval. "You exercised good judgment under difficult circumstances. The loss of so many men is regrettable, but the intelligence you've secured may save far more." He paused, taking a measured sip of his wine. "The prize money for the specie will be distributed according to standard practice forthwith. As commander of the capturing vessel, your share would normally be three-eighths, though I will, of course, claim my flag officer's eighth as is customary."

Nicholas inclined his head in acknowledgment. The admiral's share of prize money was a well-established practice, though the sum, approximately £250, would still leave Nicholas with a substantial windfall of over £700, far more money than he had ever had, nearly four years pay.

"Your prisoner, the papers and the gold must be transferred to *Barfleur* immediately," Hood continued. "I'll send marines within the hour. You will send the documents and specie over in the custody of your first lieutenant."

"Understood, sir."

"As for *Alert*, from what you've said and I'm sure as further detailed in your reports, she requires substantial repairs. Submit your formal assessment by tomorrow morning to the dockyard master. You'll be granted priority for repairs. Mr. Thornhill will also provide orders to make up your crew from that of *Formidable*."

"Thank you, sir," Nicholas said looking surprised. It was not usual to draft crew out of another ship, particularly a flagship.

Hood's expression tightened slightly. "Admiral Rodney departs for England tomorrow aboard *HMS Gibraltar*. His health has deteriorated since the Saintes, and the Admiralty has granted him leave to return home. He sails with considerable acclaim for his victory, despite—" Hood checked himself, the momentary flash of something like resentment quickly suppressed. Nicholas remained silent, aware of the delicate politics between the two admirals. Naval gossip had circulated extensively about Hood's disagreement with Rodney's tactical decisions before and during the Battle of the Saintes.

Hood's expression softened marginally. "You've done well, Commander. The Admiralty will be informed of *Alert's* performance under your command. Is there anything else?"

Nicholas hesitated, "Miss Holloway, sir, may I asks what will become of her?"

Hood didn't respond immediately, Thornhill said, "She will be questioned – in a civilized manner I should add," seeing Nicholas expression which he failed to keep entirely impassive, "and perhaps offered a chance to cooperate in exchange for clemency. However, I fear it is more likely she will be hanged as a traitor. She has caused immense damage to her country."

After Nicholas had left the cabin, Hood turned to his secretary, "Commander Cruwys continues to fulfill our hopes, but he is yet young. You were right to salve his thoughts with the possibility of clemency, though we both know there is none. I will give some more thought to his future, particularly in light of the latest news from London." Thornhill bowed.

Back aboard *Alert*, Nicholas had Forester join him in his cabin. "Our guest will be transferred to *Barfleur* within the hour. You will escort her in a boat of marines from the flagship, along with the captured documents and the specie, which will remain in your custody until handed directly to the admiral or his secretary. The admiral indicated there would be immediate distribution of prize money."

Forester nodded understanding. "The prize money will be welcome news for the crew, sir. And repairs to *Alert*?"

"Priority at the dockyard. We'll submit the full assessment tomorrow." Nicholas adjusted his sling carefully, wincing slightly as the movement disturbed his healing wound. "And we will receive a draft for replacement crew from the *Formidable*. You'll have to handle that with her first lieutenant."

As the boat full of marines pulled away towards *Barfleur* thirty minutes later, Nicholas reflected on his last meeting with Miss Holloway as she prepared to depart. She had said nothing, but looked at him with a kind of contempt. He knew she was a traitor and a spy who had caused loss and death, yet he felt a kind of shame. As the boat disappeared around the stern of *Barfleur*, he forcibly put her out of his mind and shifted his gaze across the harbour toward *Formidable*. Admiral George Brydges Rodney, recently elevated to the peerage as Baron Rodney of Rodney Stoke for his victory at the Saintes, was a formidable figure in more than name. His decades of naval service had established him as one of Britain's premier fighting admirals, and his defeat of de Grasse had potentially altered the course of the American war.

Yet Rodney's reputation extended beyond tactical brilliance. Known for his ambition and political connections, he had weathered multiple controversies throughout his career. His aggressive prize-taking during earlier commands had prompted accusations of profit-seeking at the expense of strategic objectives. He had feuded with various officials and fellow officers, including Hood, whose more methodical approach to naval operations contrasted with Rodney's temperament.

HMS Gibraltar, an 80-gun ship of the line preparing for transatlantic passage, lay near *Formidable*. Her yards were alive with activity as supplies and personal effects were loaded for the journey to England.

The sun climbed higher as the boat returned Forester to *Alert*, intensifying the already oppressive heat. Nicholas's thoughts turned again to Catherine Holloway. Hood's, or rather Thornhill's interrogation techniques would prove more than effective, he felt sure of that. It had become clear that the admiral's secretary was deeply involved in intelligence matters, and in that area as others it seemed likely the admiral's reputation for thoroughness extended to the questioning of such a significant intelligence asset with characteristic methodical precision.

Nicholas carefully tested the mobility of his injured arm within the sling. The wound was healing well according to Maxwell, but would require at least another week before he could resume full duties without restriction. The dull ache had become a constant companion, though far preferable to the fate that had befallen twenty of his men, or indeed to Catherine Holloway, he thought.

He walked over at Markham who was overseeing the initial assessment of repairs. The master looked up from his notes as Nicholas approached.

"We received word while you were on the flag, sir. The dockyard master will send his people tomorrow morning, sir," Markham reported. "Initial estimate suggests we'll need at least three weeks for proper repairs to the hull and foremast."

"Very good, Mr. Markham. Admiral Hood has granted us priority at the dockyard."

By late July, *Alert* had been hauled out at the careening wharf, her hull scraped clean of marine growth and repairs well underway. The dockyard's carpenters had replaced damaged planking below the waterline, while the ship's carpenter and his mates addressed the less critical repairs to her upper works. A new foretopmast had been stepped, fresh spars fitted, and her rigging progressively renewed by teams of skilled hands working in the relentless Caribbean heat.

Nicholas's arm had healed sufficiently to remove the sling, though a prominent scar remained where the splinter had torn through muscle and skin. Dr. Maxwell had pronounced him fit for full duty during their last meeting, adding that Nicholas had been fortunate—the wound had come dangerously close to severing a major blood vessel.

On this particular morning, Nicholas sat at his desk in temporary quarters ashore, reviewing correspondence that had arrived with the packet from England. The prize court had rendered its decision with unusual speed—likely due to Admiral Hood's influence—awarding the full value of the captured specie to *Alert's* crew according to the established distribution formula. Nicholas' £700 had been credited to his account with Coutts Bank in London, with similar arrangements made for the other officers. The crew's shares would be distributed before they sailed again, a prospect that had significantly improved morale despite the losses they had sustained.

A knock at the door interrupted his thoughts.

"Enter," Nicholas called, setting aside the financial documents.

Lieutenant Forester appeared, accompanied by a young man in a newly made midshipman's uniform that still showed the stiffness of unworn fabric.

"Good morning, sir," Forester greeted him. "May I present Mr. Thomas Parker? He's been assigned to *Alert* by Admiral Hood's order."

Nicholas rose to greet the newcomer, studying him with a professional eye. Parker appeared to be approximately sixteen, with the rangy build of a youth not yet grown into his full height. His fair complexion had already begun to redden under the tropical sun, but he met Nicholas's gaze steadily, suggesting a confidence that boded well for service.

"Welcome aboard, Mr. Parker," Nicholas said, gesturing for the young man to be seated. "Though technically we remain ashore for the moment."

"Thank you, sir," Parker replied with a crisp bow. "I'm honored to join *Alert*. Her recent action against the American privateer is still being discussed throughout the fleet."

Nicholas exchanged a brief glance with Forester, noting the lieutenant's subtle approval of the midshipman's preparation. The boy had clearly made an effort to learn about his new assignment.

"You've had previous sea service?" Nicholas inquired.

"Two years aboard *Monarch*, sir, under Captain Reynolds. I was rated midshipman six months ago."

"Reynolds is a fine officer," Nicholas commented, recalling the capable post-captain he had met briefly during Hood's campaign earlier that year. "And *Monarch* saw action at the Saintes, did she not?"

"Yes, sir. Third in the line. I was stationed in the maintop during the engagement."

Nicholas nodded, pleased with what he saw. Parker had combat experience, valuable training under a respected captain, and appeared to possess the proper demeanor for an officer.

"Mr. Forester will acquaint you with your duties and introduce you to our other midshipman, Mr. Parker. I expect you to continue your studies in navigation and mathematics while we complete our repairs.

"Yes, sir. Thank you, sir."

After Forester had escorted the new midshipman out, Nicholas returned to his correspondence. Among the official dispatches was a sealed letter bearing Admiral Hood's personal insignia. Breaking the wax, Nicholas found a brief message requesting his presence at the Commissioner's House that afternoon at four bells of the afternoon watch. The note offered no explanation for the summons, but its formal tone suggested matters of significance would be discussed.

As he sorted through the remaining correspondence received that day, a letter with a familiar feminine hand caught his attention. The direction was clearly written in Caroline's neat script, the letter having been forwarded from England to the Leeward Islands station. Nicholas broke the seal with a mixture of anticipation and trepidation, unfolding the single sheet of paper covered in Caroline's elegant handwriting. The contents were brief and measured, conveying news that Nicholas had long expected but which nonetheless struck with unexpected force. Caroline wrote of her formal engagement to Lord Ashton, announced at a summer ball hosted by his family. Her words were kind but distant, wishing Nicholas well in his naval career and expressing hope that their friendship might endure despite the changed circumstances.

Nicholas refolded the letter carefully, placing it in his desk drawer. The news was hardly surprising—Lord Ashton's pursuit of Caroline had been evident before Nicholas's departure, and her father had made his preference for the match clear. Yet knowing that the last tenuous connection to a life he might have had in England had been severed left a hollow sensation in his chest.

He had little time to dwell on personal matters, however. At the appointed hour, Nicholas presented himself at the Commissioner's House, an imposing Georgian structure that overlooked English Harbour from its hillside position. The building served as both the principal administrative center for the naval yard and occasional residence for senior officers requiring accommodations more spacious than those available aboard ship.

A marine lieutenant escorted Nicholas to a private study where Admiral Hood sat with Thornhillbefore a chart table, various papers spread before him. There was no sign of the flag lieutenant. The admiral looked up as Nicholas entered, his expression giving no indication of his mood or purpose.

"Commander Cruwys," Hood acknowledged, rising briefly. Then unexpectedly, "Please, be seated."

Nicholas took the offered chair, noticing that the papers before Hood and Thornhill included nautical charts of the waters between Puerto Rico and Santo Domingo.

"*Alert* is progressing well in her repairs," Hood began. "The master shipwright informs me she should be ready for sea within the week."

"Yes, sir. We've benefited greatly from the priority you assigned us."

Hood nodded, studying Nicholas with calculating eyes. "*Alert* has proven her value under your command," he stated. "The Admiralty will receive my commendation regarding your conduct during the Holloway affair. The intelligence she carried has already proven most illuminating regarding French intentions in these waters."

"I'm pleased to hear it, sir."

"However," Hood continued, his tone shifting slightly, "the strategic situation is evolving. As you no doubt are aware, Lord North's government has fallen, and the new ministry under Rockingham has begun peace negotiations with the Americans. The political appetite for continued aggressive action is waning, despite our recent successes at sea."

Nicholas remained silent, sensing that Hood was building toward something significant.

"I've received orders from the Admiralty," the admiral continued after a pause. "With Admiral Hugh Pigot's arrival in Jamaica last month and assumption of command of the Leeward Islands station. I am to return to England for consultation."

The news was unexpected. The replacement of Hood suggested a major shift in naval strategy for the region, likely driven by the significant changes in Admiralty leadership. With Lord Sandwich's departure as First Lord of the Admiralty after twelve years of service, and his replacement by the Whig Admiral Keppel, the entire approach to naval operations was being reconsidered. Keppel, a vocal critic of North's government and the prior conduct of the war, had wasted no time in implementing changes throughout the senior command structure.

"Admiral Pigot brings considerable experience to the station," Hood stated, his tone perfectly neutral though his careful phrasing suggested volumes left unsaid. "The Admiralty's instructions regarding operational priorities will naturally reflect the shifting diplomatic situation. The new First Lord's approaches differ considerably from his predecessor's."

Hood pushed forward a chart of the waters around Puerto Rico, nodding to his secretary.

"Commander, notwithstanding future policies, at this time, there remains a matter requiring attention from our squadron," Thornhill began. "Our intelligence indicates that a Spanish aviso, the *San Isidro*, will be anchored at Aguadilla on the northwest coast of Puerto Rico approximately ten days hence. She carries dispatches and a quantity of gold and silver specie bound for Havana, where the funds will support Spanish naval operations."

Nicholas studied the chart, noting the small bay on Puerto Rico's coast where the vessel would reportedly anchor.

"The *San Isidro* is a fast sailing vessel of perhaps one hundred and fifty tons," Thornhill went on. "She carries eight guns, though reportedly undermanned with a crew of approximately thirty. What makes her significant is not merely her cargo of specie—estimated at between £10,000 abd £15,000—but the dispatches she carries regarding Spanish and French intentions in these waters."

"A substantial prize, sir," Nicholas observed.

"Indeed, Commander Cruwys. And one that *Alert* is uniquely suited to pursue. Should you succeed in capturing the aviso," Hood added, "the prize would be substantial. Even after deductions for the Crown's share and other claimants, your portion as commanding officer would likely exceed £3,000. Such a sum provides a measure of security not often available to officers of your rank."

Nicholas nodded, understanding the significance. Such a sum would indeed provide financial independence for many years with care, allowing him to live as a gentleman during periods between commands.

Hood traced a finger along the coastline. "The vessel will reportedly anchor for two days while taking on fresh water and provisions. The bay provides reasonable protection, with two batteries as you see marked on the chart. But a well-executed night operation with ships' boats could allow for her capture, if she is not forewarned by an indiscreet approach, particularly of a large warship."

Nicholas understood immediately. A cutting-out expedition, using ships' boats to capture an enemy vessel at anchor, was a high-risk but potentially high-reward tactic that the Royal Navy had employed successfully throughout the war. And a fast approach at night by *Alert* with her speed and smaller size was less likely to be noticed by either the aviso, the batteries or any coastal watch station.

"Your orders, Commander Cruwys," Hood continued, sliding forward a sealed packet, "are to proceed to the coordinates provided under the pretext of delivering dispatches to Jamaica. Upon reaching the vicinity of Aguadilla, you will conduct a reconnaissance and, if circumstances permit, execute a boat action to cut out the *San Isidro*."

Nicholas accepted the packet. "And if we are successful, sir?"

"You will secure any dispatches or documentation immediately and deliver them, along with any captured specie, to Port Royal, Jamaica. The prize vessel, if seaworthy, should be sent under a prize crew to the same destination." Hood paused. "Following this action, regardless of outcome, your secondary orders direct *Alert* to proceed directly to England.

Nicholas was surprised by that, and said "May I ask why we're to return to England, sir?"

Hood's expression revealed nothing, and after a moment he nodded. "In his wisdom Admiral Pigot has taken the main body of the fleet north in consideration of hurricanes, though it is early in the season." Hood said, his tone neutral. "Vice-Admiral Sir Joshua Rowley now commands the Jamaica Station. You will report to him aboard

Princess Royal. He is a careful and experienced officer, and I have indicated my wishes in my letter to him in alignment with your orders: *Alert* is to proceed directly to England. With peace talks progressing, the Admiralty is shifting its priorities. There will be no shortage of employment for vessels of *Alert's* class in home waters."

Nicholas detected the careful phrasing. Hood clearly disagreed with Pigot's decision to take the fleet north so early, and perhaps of his appointment altogether by the Admiralty, but would only imply as much to even a trusted junior commander. It seemed clear though that he was arranging *Alert's* departure before Pigot's awareness of her whereabouts could result in other orders, or perhaps something else.

Hood seemed to hesitate, then continued, "There is one additional matter, Commander Cruwys," he said, his tone formal but carrying an undercurrent of personal concern. "I understand that Admiral Pigot has brought with him several officers expected to receive commands. One of these, Commander Edward Whiting, is the nephew of Lord Hartwell, who holds considerable influence with the new ministry."

Nicholas waited, sensing the warning behind Hood's words.

"Whiting has been seeking a vessel of *Alert's* class. His previous command, a brig sloop, was lost. Though he was cleared of negligence and fault in the mandatory courts martial, questions remained regarding his judgment. Were *Alert* to remain in Jamaica, or indeed be ordered to join the main fleet, it could lead to changes. Politics frequently influence naval appointments, Commander Cruwys. By sending *Alert* to England before the formal transfer of command, I ensure proper continuity of operations during a critical transition period."

Again, Hood's carefully chosen words conveyed his concern while maintaining proper decorum regarding his and Rodney's successor. The warning was clear—Nicholas might have earned Hood's respect, but potential political complications awaited in England.

"You're to depart as soon as *Alert* is certified seaworthy," Hood concluded. "I've arranged for a full complement of stores and provisions to be loaded beginning tomorrow."

"Thank you, sir. I appreciate your guidance and understand the importance of discretion in this matter."

Hood extended his hand, an unusual gesture from a senior officer to a junior. "You have conducted yourself with distinction, Commander Cruwys. Continue to do so and navigate the complexities of Admiralty politics with the same skill you bring to your seamanship."

Two days later, *Alert* slipped her moorings before dawn, catching the morning land breeze to carry her out of English Harbour. Fully repaired, new canvas gleaming white in the early light, she moved with the responsive grace that had first endeared her to Nicholas upon taking command.

The crew, their ranks replenished with men transferred from *Formidable*, though notably not until after Admiral Rodney's departure, worked with practiced efficiency. The prize money from the *Liberty* action had been distributed the previous day, creating a general atmosphere of satisfaction despite the lingering sadness for lost comrades. Midshipman Parker had quickly integrated into the ship's routine, demonstrating a natural aptitude that impressed even the more experienced petty officers.

As they cleared the headland and set course west-southwest, Nicholas stood on the quarterdeck beside Forester, watching the coast of Antigua recede behind them.

"Special orders, sir?" Forester inquired quietly, having recognized the unusual nature of their hasty departure and the sealed packets Nicholas kept secured in his sea chest.

"We sail with Admiral Hood's confidence, Mr. Forester," Nicholas replied carefully. "Beyond that, I can say only that our course may alter depending on circumstances we encounter."

Forester nodded, accepting the discretion required by their mission. "The men are in good spirits. The prize money has done wonders for morale."

"Indeed. And perhaps fortune will continue to favor us before we see England again."

As *Alert* gathered speed, cutting cleanly through the azure waters of the Caribbean, Nicholas contemplated the mission ahead. The cutting-out operation Hood had described would be dangerous but well within the capabilities of *Alert's* crew if properly executed. Success would bring both professional distinction and financial security at a time when the shifting political winds made naval careers increasingly uncertain.

The letter from Caroline lingered in his thoughts. Her engagement to Ashton closed a chapter of Nicholas's life, removing one of the few anchors that had connected him to the landed society he had left behind. Perhaps it was fitting that this news arrived as he embarked on a mission that might secure his independence in that world, should he choose to inhabit it between periods of naval service. For now, however, his focus remained on *Alert* and the challenges that lay ahead. The Spanish aviso, the boat action, the uncertain reception that awaited them in England—all would require his complete attention and skill to navigate successfully.

Ten days later, on the 7th of August, *Alert* approached the northwest coast of Puerto Rico under cover of darkness, her lights doused and her crew at battle stations. The reconnaissance conducted earlier that day as they had sailed along the coast under American colours had confirmed Hood's intelligence, the *San Isidro* lay at anchor in the small bay near Aguadilla. She was a handsome vessel built in the Spanish royal shipyards at Havana, typical of the specialized avisos that carried dispatches throughout the Spanish Empire. Approximately 90 feet on deck with a beam of 24 feet, giving her the fine entry and clean run that marked vessels built for speed rather than cargo capacity.

Her rig was that of a schooner-brig (also known as a hermaphrodite brig), with square sails on her foremast and fore-and-aft sails on her mainmast: a hybrid arrangement that provided both speed running before the wind and excellent handling when close-hauled or tacking upwind. In some sense she was in fact a somewhat smaller Spanish version of the concept inherent in *Alert's* design. The relatively low profile of her hull, combined with her raked masts and the elegant sweep of her stern, identified her as a purpose-built government dispatch vessel. Even at anchor, there was something elegant in her appearance, a swift messenger designed to outrun rather than outfight potential enemies.

Careful observation through the glass had revealed minimal activity aboard, suggesting the Spanish crew had grown complacent in what they perceived as safe waters.

Nicholas had spent the days since their departure meticulously planning the cutting-out expedition. Three boats would participate: the launch under Nicholas's direct command, the cutter led by Lieutenant Forester, and the gig commanded by Midshipman Parker. Each boat carried a carefully selected team of seamen and marines, armed with cutlasses, pistols, and boarding pikes—fifty men in total, representing nearly half of *Alert's* complement. They had rehearsed their approach and boarding tactics repeatedly, addressing contingencies and establishing clear chains of command.

"The boats are ready, sir," Forester reported quietly as midnight approached. *Alert* lay hove-to approximately two miles offshore, invisible against the dark horizon.

"Very good, Mr. Forester. Signal the boat crews to assemble." Nicholas studied the distant shoreline one final time through his glass. No warning beacons or signals suggested they had been detected. "We proceed as planned. Mr. Markham has his instructions should we fail to return by dawn."

The fifty men selected for the operation gathered silently amidships, their faces darkened with ash to reduce visibility, weapons secured to prevent telltale noise. Nicholas addressed them briefly, emphasizing the importance of silence, coordinated action, and discipline once aboard the target. The potential prize money associated with success required no elaboration—every man understood the substantial reward that awaited them if they succeeded.

As they lowered the boats and took their positions, Nicholas felt the familiar focused clarity that accompanied imminent action. The personal concerns and political complications that had occupied his thoughts in recent days receded, replaced by the immediate tactical considerations of the mission at hand. He checked his weapons one final time: the sword at his hip, and the two pistols, carefully primed and loaded, tucked into his belt.

The boats pushed off from *Alert's* side, the muffled oars dipping into the dark water with practiced precision. Nicholas sat in the stern of the launch, mentally reviewing the approach route and boarding plan. The distant lights of Aguadilla glimmered to their right, but the small bay where *San Isidro* lay remained shrouded in darkness.

Their approach took nearly an hour, the boats moving in tight formation through the calm waters. As they drew within five hundred yards of their target, Nicholas could make out the aviso's silhouette against the faint starlight.

No challenge came as they closed the final distance. Either the Spanish watch was negligent or, more likely, the boats remained undetected against the dark water. At one hundred yards, Nicholas raised his arm, signaling the three boats to separate according to their assigned approach vectors: the launch to the starboard quarter, Forester's cutter to the port bow, and Parker's gig directly to the stern.

The final approach proceeded with practiced stealth, oars now barely disturbing the surface as they glided toward their target. At thirty yards, a sudden shout from the *San Isidro's* deck shattered the silence—they had been spotted. Nicholas instantly gave the signal, and the three boats surged forward with renewed urgency, oars digging deep as the element of surprise transformed into the advantage of momentum.

Nicholas's launch reached the vessel's side first. Grappling hooks flew upward, securing the boat to the aviso's railings as the Spanish crew belatedly responded to the alarm. The boarding party swarmed up the side with practiced agility, Nicholas among the first to vault over the rail onto the deck, sword drawn and pistol in his left hand.

The scene immediately dissolved into the brutal reality of close-quarters combat. The Spanish crew, caught unprepared, grabbed whatever weapons lay at hand, belaying pins, knives, a few pistols hastily retrieved from the racks. A bearded Spanish seaman lunged at Nicholas with a boarding pike, the steel tip narrowly missing his chest as he twisted aside. Nicholas responded instinctively, raising his pistol and firing directly into the man's face at point-blank range. The Spaniard collapsed backwards in a spray of blood and bone fragments, the boarding pike clattering to the deck.

Without pausing, Nicholas drew his second pistol and led his party aft, stepping over the fallen sailor toward the quarterdeck where the vessel's officers would be emerging from their quarters. A Spanish officer appeared at the companionway, sword in hand, rallying several armed men to his side. Nicholas leveled his remaining pistol and fired, striking one of the men in the chest. The man staggered backward with a strangled cry, knocking into his companions and creating momentary confusion.

Nicholas seized the advantage, driving forward with his sword leading. The Spanish officer met his attack with skill, their blades clashing in a brief but fierce exchange. The man was clearly trained in swordplay, but Nicholas fought with the cold determination born of experience. After parrying a thrust, Nicholas stepped inside the Spaniard's guard and delivered a killing stroke to the neck, opening the carotid artery. Arterial blood pulsed in a dark fountain as the officer collapsed to his knees, clutching vainly at the mortal wound.

Around him, the boarding party had engaged the Spanish crew throughout the vessel. The harsh sounds of combat filled the night— steel on steel, the crack of pistol shots, cries of pain and shouted orders in English and Spanish. The air grew thick with the acrid smell of gunpowder and the metallic tang of blood.

Forester's team simultaneously secured the forecastle, overwhelming the watch stationed there before they could organize effective resistance. Parker's men came aboard at the stern, catching the Spanish from behind.

The fighting was brief but savage, and in less than ten minutes the Spanish threw down their arms. Nicholas wiped his bloodied sword blade on the fallen officer's coat as Sergeant Miller and his marines secured the main hatchway, bayonets fixed and ready, preventing reinforcements from reaching the deck from below.

"The deck is ours, sir!" Forester called from forward, where his party had subdued the remaining resistance. Blood darkened his sleeve where a Spanish blade had found its mark, but the wound appeared superficial.

Before Nicholas could respond, a flash of light from the shore caught his attention, followed by the distant boom of a cannon. A waterspout erupted fifty yards off the *San Isidro's* port bow.

"Shore batteries!" Nicholas shouted. "They've seen us. Mr. Parker, take your men forward and cut the anchor cable. Mr. Forester, get these sails loose immediately. We're sailing her out!"

The disciplined boarding party transformed instantly into a makeshift crew, men racing aloft to loose the tops'ls while Midshipman Parker and two of his party ran to cut the cable. A second shot from shore fell closer, sending spray across the deck.

"Cable cut, sir!" Parker reported from the bow.

"Make fast the boats for towing," Nicholas ordered. "Set the fore course and top'sle, and both jibs. We'll tow our boats out rather than risk men transferring back under fire."

The three boats were quickly secured with long towlines, trailing behind the aviso as she gathered way. The *San Isidro* responded beautifully to the offshore breeze, her Havana-built hull slipping easily through the water despite the drag of the boats. With the offshore breeze filling the square sails on her foremast and inner and outer jibs, she began to pull steadily away from the shore batteries.

Two more shots from the shore battery fell astern, the Spanish gunners struggling to find their range against the moving target in the darkness. Within fifteen minutes, they had drawn beyond effective range, the sleek aviso slicing through the calm waters toward the waiting *Alert* two miles offshore.

"We can recover the boats now, sir," Forester suggested as the immediate danger receded.

"Agreed. Heave to and get the men aboard. Then we'll make all possible sail to rejoin *Alert*."

The maneuver was executed efficiently, the boarding party transferring back to the ship while maintaining a skeleton crew aboard the prize to handle her sails. As they approached *Alert*,

Nicholas could see her crew had cleared for action, ready to provide covering fire had it proven necessary.

By first light, both vessels were safely away from the Puerto Rican coast, sailing in company on a southwesterly course through the Mona Passage, and Nicholas was back aboard *Alert*. With the immediate danger past, Nicholas ordered a more thorough search of the captured vessel and proper securing of the prisoners.

"Fifty-two crew in total, sir," Forester called across from the other ship after completing a count of the Spanish sailors now confined to the *San Isidro's* forward hold. "Plus three passengers—a Spanish official, his niece, and her maid."

"Lieutenant Forester, have the passengers brought aboard *Alert*," Nicholas ordered.

As the small boat shuttled between the two vessels, Nicholas supervised the transfer of the valuable cargo. The six chests of specie were brought aboard *Alert* for safekeeping, along with the ship's documents and official dispatches found in the captain's quarters. Early examination suggested they contained valuable intelligence regarding Spanish naval movements and possibly details of France's continued support for the American revolutionaries despite the ongoing peace negotiations.

When the Spanish passengers were escorted aboard, Nicholas walked over and made his introduction. The official, Don Francisco Valdés, appeared to be in his fifties, his formal bearing maintained despite the indignity of capture. His niece, Doña Elena Maria Valdés y Castellano, stood beside him with remarkable composure.

Nicholas had no more than a glimpse of any of the passengers the night before, but now in the clear morning light he could fully appreciate her striking beauty. Indeed he found it hard to not stare, as he admitted to himself this was one of the most beautiful woman he had ever seen, even after all his travels and time in London and even, with a twinge of guilt, of his memory of Atea, and with something other than guilt, of Caroline. He guessed her to be about his age, tall for a woman at perhaps seven inches over five feet, with clear very light olive skin unmarred by cosmetics or artificial pallor. Her features were classic Spanish aristocracy—high cheekbones, a straight, patrician nose, and full lips that suggested both passion and determination. Dark eyes, almost black in their intensity, regarded Nicholas with an unsettling directness that few men, let alone women, would dare display to a naval officer who had just seized their ship.

Her figure, even partially concealed by a hastily donned traveling dress of rich blue silk, was slender but unmistakably feminine, her narrow waist drawing the eye upward to the generous swell of her bosom, which the modest cut of the gown sought to soften but could not fully disguise. Her carriage was impeccable, shoulders squared and head held high with the natural dignity of someone accustomed to command rather than obedience. Her long dark hair, gathered in a simple arrangement that spoke of practicality rather than fashion, framed her face in a way that emphasized its natural symmetry.

The maid, a middle-aged woman named Luisa, hovered protectively at her side, fussing with her mistress's shawl and casting suspicious glances at the English sailors who surrounded them.

"Captain," Doña Elena addressed him in her accented but fluent English. "I must thank you for the restraint shown by your men. Though this capture is most unwelcome, your sailors have conducted themselves with unexpected discipline."

Nicholas bowed slightly.

"May I inquire as to our destination?" she asked, her voice carrying the melodic inflections of her native Castilian Spanish despite her excellent command of English.

"We sail for Port Royal, Jamaica, where your vessel will be processed through the prize court. As for your eventual disposition, that will be determined by the proper authorities there."

Don Francisco, who had been silent until now, spoke rapidly in Spanish to his niece, his expression concerned.

"My uncle wishes to know if we are to be treated as prisoners of war or as civilian detainees," Doña Elena translated, her eyes never leaving Nicholas's face.

"You are neither combatants nor contraband, Don Francisco," Nicholas replied, addressing the older man directly while Doña

Elena translated. "You are protected persons under the customs of civilized warfare. Your comfort and safety will be ensured to the best of our ability, and in time, arrangements will likely be made for your repatriation to Spanish territory."

As the translator conveyed his words, Nicholas observed a subtle shift in Don Francisco's demeanor—a slight relaxation of his rigid posture. Doña Elena, however, maintained her careful scrutiny of Nicholas, her expression revealing nothing of her thoughts.

"Captain," she said after a moment, "I appreciate your courtesies. However, I must inform you that my father and I are traveling to Spain on matters of some urgency regarding my family's affairs. This delay may have serious consequences."

"I regret any inconvenience, Doña Elena, but the circumstances of war often disrupt personal plans. I assure you that once we reach Jamaica, your case will be presented to the appropriate authorities with my recommendation for prompt resolution."

Their conversation was interrupted by Forester, who approached with a formal report on the prize. "She's sound in all respects, sir. Fast and weatherly based on our brief handling. Her armament is modest—eight six-pounders, Spanish naval pattern, mounted on well-maintained carriages. The magazine is well-stocked with powder and shot. She's built for speed rather than combat, as we suspected. Beyond the specie, she carries primarily official dispatches and a small cargo of luxury goods. All three of her officers were killed in the attack, along with five others and six injured."

"Excellent, Mr. Forester. You'll continue in command of her as we make for Jamaica. Select fifteen of our best hands for your prize crew."

"Aye, sir."

As Forester departed to make the arrangements, Nicholas turned back to Doña Elena. "You and your companions will be treated with all due consideration during our voyage. I've had my cabin prepared for you and your maid, please consider it your private domain for the duration of our voyage. Your uncle will be provided suitable accommodation in the gunroom. I've instructed the cook to prepare the best fare our stores allow. If there is anything else you require for your comfort, you need only ask."

Doña Elena regarded him thoughtfully, a slight tilt of her head causing a wayward strand of dark hair to fall across her cheek. With an unconscious grace that momentarily caught Nicholas's attention, she tucked it back into place.

"You are most courteous for a captor, Captain Cruwys. Perhaps if our personal luggage could be transferred as well?"

"Of course, madam. I prefer to think of myself as your host under unusual circumstances." Nicholas replied with a slight smile.

Something in her expression suggested she was reassessing her initial judgment of him. "Then as your guest, I shall endeavor to adapt to these unexpected circumstances with grace. Though I must warn you, Captain—a Spanish lady is not always an easy passenger."

"And the Royal Navy is not known for its luxurious accommodations, particularly in its smaller ships" Nicholas replied. "Perhaps we shall both make discoveries that challenge our preconceptions during this voyage."

After six days of fair winds and following seas, *Alert* made her landfall off Port Royal in early morning as the rising sun turned the waters of the Caribbean a deep blue. She stood in with the breeze filling her new canvas in proud curves, cleaving through the gentle swell. The *San Isidro* followed in her wake two cables astern, the prize crew having mastered her particular qualities in the way natural to experienced seamen.

As the sound of her salute to Admiral Rawley's flag aboard the *Princess Royal* died away and was returned by the flagship, *Alert* dropped her anchor in nine fathoms with a disciplined precision that gave Nicholas quiet satisfaction. The splash of the anchor was accompanied by the practiced movements of his crew stowing the sails, each man working with the coordinated harmony that comes only with drill and indeed pride in the ship. The breeze off the land carried the sweet pungency of Jamaica — raw sugar and molasses, the salt tang of coastal marshes, and the deep, earthy scent of tropical growth wilting in the sun.

"All secure, sir," said Mr. Forester, touching his hat with a studied formality that marked their return to the disciplines of a fleet anchorage. The freedom of their six days at sea – where Forester might have added a remark, was now replaced by the rigid etiquette of a King's officer in port.

"Very good, Mr. Forester. Signal *San Isidro* to anchor a cable's length to leeward, if you please. Then, given the lack of a signal from the flag, I suspect we must prepare to receive the Admiral's flag officer. He will no doubt be with us directly – news of a prize travels faster than a midshipman to his dinner."

Indeed, before the *San Isidro* had finished fully furling her sails and coiling down, a twelve-oared barge was pulling smartly toward them from the flagship. Nicholas observed it through his glass, noting the gold lace gleaming on the lieutenant's hat in the early morning sun.

As the barge came alongside, the bosun's calls shrilled their piercing welcome, the notes hanging in the still morning air as the flag lieutenant was piped aboard with all the ceremony due his rank and function.

"Captain Cruwys," the young officer said, coming smartly to attention, his face glistening with perspiration despite the relative coolness of the hour. "Lieutenant Edward Humphries, sir, flag lieutenant to Vice Admiral Rowley. The admiral presents his compliments and requests the honor of your presence aboard *Princess Royal* at seven bells. I am further directed to convey his particular desire that you bring all dispatches and documents taken with the Spanish vessel."

"Thank you, Lieutenant Humphries. Please convey my respects to the admiral. I'll be aboard Princess Royal at the appointed hour, with the dispatches."

With the formal part of his mission complete, Humphries allowed his gaze to drift meaningfully around *Alert* and then toward the *San Isidro*, where the British colours flew above the captured Spanish ensign. "A handsome prize, Captain. The talk at the Admiral's table last evening was of nothing else, after word reached us from the signal station that you were approaching. They say she carries specie?"

"She does," Nicholas confirmed, offering nothing more. Prize business was delicate, and loose talk had been the undoing of many a promising capture before the slow-grinding wheels of the Prize Court had completed their necessary revolutions.

Humphries waited a moment for elaboration that did not come, then nodded with professional understanding. "I shall inform the Admiral to expect you at three bells, then. Good day to you, Captain."

As Humphries departed with the same ceremony that had marked his arrival, Nicholas turned his attention to his Spanish passengers. Doña Elena had emerged from his cabin, where she had spent most of the voyage in a state of dignified seclusion. She stood now by the larboard rail, her dark hair caught in the gentle morning breeze, her figure outlined against the rising sun in a way that caused several of the hands to find sudden reasons to be working nearby until ordered forward by the bosun.

"We have arrived in Jamaica, Captain," she observed in her perfect, accented English. "I presume my uncle and I will now be transferred to more appropriate accommodation ashore?"

"Indeed, Doña Elena," Nicholas replied, acutely conscious of the need to maintain proper distance now they had returned to the scrutiny of port. The six days at sea had created between them a familiarity that would be dangerous to acknowledge in the gossip-filled society of Kingston. "I shall make arrangements for suitable quarters for you and Don Francisco today, after I have attended upon Admiral Rawley. Lieutenant Forester will see to your immediate needs until then."

She regarded him with those remarkable eyes – as deep and dangerous as the waters of the Mona Passage – and inclined her head slightly. "You have been most... accommodating, Captain Cruwys. I shall not forget your courtesy during our voyage."

Something in her tone caused Nicholas to glance sharply at her face, but her expression remained unreadable, a perfect mask of aristocratic composure. He became suddenly aware of Maxwell, the surgeon, watching their exchange with interest from his position by the mainmast.

"It was my duty and pleasure to ensure your comfort, madam," Nicholas replied, retreating into the formal language of a naval officer addressing a lady of quality. "Now, if you will excuse me, I must prepare for my meeting with the Admiral."

In his cramped cabin, Nicholas found his servant had already laid out his best uniform coat – the bright blue superfine with the gilt buttons that had cost him nearly a month's pay in Antigua. The white breeches and waistcoat had been sponged clean of the inevitable shipboard grime, and his best silk stockings had been discovered from the depths of his sea chest. As he dressed with care, he reflected on the strangeness of naval life. A man might pass from the desperate violence of a cutting-out expedition to the rigid formality of an Admiral's reception in the space of a week.

The Jamaica sunlight struck him with physical force as he emerged on deck. It held none of the gentle qualities of the morning light that had greeted their arrival; by just past seven it had become a palpable presence, pressing down with mallet-like insistence upon every exposed surface. The wooden decks were already hot enough to feel through the thin soles of his dress shoes, and the previously pleasant harbour smells had intensified to a miasmic ripeness that caught in the back of his throat.

Waiting by the entry-port was his gig, manned by six of his best hands in clean white duck trousers and checked shirts, with Midshipman Parker sitting stiffly in the stern sheets next to the coxswain. The boy had proved himself during the cutting-out of the *San Isidro*, displaying a coolness under fire that belied his sixteen years. Nicholas had determined to reward him with the duty of accompanying him to the flagship – valuable experience for a young officer with aspirations.

"The charts and documents are secured, sir," Parker reported as Nicholas descended into the boat. "Mr. Forester had them placed in the dispatches box along with your reports."

"Very good, Mr. Parker," Nicholas replied, settling himself in the stern. "Coxswain, carry on."

The gig pulled away from *Alert*'s side, the oars rising and falling in perfect unison as the coxswain steered them toward the three-decker flagship. Nicholas took a moment to observe his ship from this exterior vantage, something a captain rarely had an opportunity to do. *Alert* sat well in the water, her trim lines showing to advantage even at anchor. He felt a twinge of pride in her graceful form. She presented the very image of a swift vessel in perfect fighting trim.

His gaze moved to the *San Isidro*, anchored nearby. She also was a handsome vessel, no question, with the sleek lines of her Havana-built hull promising speed under canvas. If the Admiral bought her into the service, as seemed likely, she would make a valuable addition to His Majesty's fleet, perhaps as a fast dispatch vessel or a small sloop of war.

Looking around the naval anchorage, he noted two 74-gun third rates and two frigates, and beyond them a large fully rigged ship sloop.

The boat kissed the high side of the flagship, and to the sound of pipes and stomp of marines boots he went aboard, followed by Parker. He saluted the quarterdeck, was welcomed aboard by the *Princess Royal*'s first lieutenant, and turned to find a familiar figure standing next to Flag Lieutenant Humphries.

"Cruwys, you dog!" Commander Harrington said as he stepped forward, abandoning naval formality in his evident pleasure. "When I heard *Alert* had brought in a Spanish prize, I should have known it would be you. Some men have all the luck in the service."

Smiling at Harrington's enthusiastic greeting and with pleasure at this unexpected reunion. "Luck had precious little to do with it, Commander Harrington. Hard information and harder work, rather."

They laughed and Harrington clasped his hand warmly. Their acquaintance had begun aboard the *Lynx* during Nicholas's return from the Pacific, where Harrington—the son of Viscount Westborne—had initially regarded him with skepticism due to his unconventional background. That skepticism had gradually transformed into professional respect and then friendship, especially during their time in London where Harrington had generously offered Nicholas accommodation at his family's Grosvenor Square house and guided him through the intricacies of society that his years in the Pacific had left him ill-prepared to navigate.

"So they all say, but we know better, don't we?" Harrington laughed again, his aristocratic features animated with genuine pleasure at their reunion.

"So that large sloop is your *Falcon*? I should have guessed when I saw her figurehead."

"Indeed she is," Harrington said proudly, glancing across the harbour at the sleek three masted 18-gun ship with a black hull, buff strakes between the gunports, the figurehead a bird of prey picked out in fresh paint, with gilt carving at the bow and stern—almost a small frigate in fact. "We arrived with a convoy two weeks ago."

Nicholas smiled. "She's a beauty, and you must tell me all about her over a coffee or punch later. I must beg your pardon now, Admiral Rawley is expecting me."

"Then I shall not delay you, but come across to *Falcon* when you are finished here."

Nicholas composed himself for the coming interview, as he turned to follow Humphries aft. Vice Admiral Rawley's reputation in the service was formidable. He was said to be honorable, diligent, and competent. A "safe pair of hands" during uncertain times, and not player of naval politics, but rather a career officer with a focus on duty and service. His questions would be penetrating, his assessment of Nicholas's conduct during the capture of the *San Isidro* rigorous. The prize was valuable enough to attract attention from the highest levels of the Admiralty, and Rawley would want every detail correct for his reports to London. The dispatch box felt suddenly heavy under his arm, its contents potentially significant for the ongoing war effort, and for his own career prospects.

Admiral Rawley received him in his spacious day cabin whose windows commanded a magnificent view of Kingston Harbour and unsurprisingly reminded him of those of *Formidable* and *Barfleur*, for she was their sistership, a second rate of 90 guns. The room struck a careful balance between naval functionality and splendor, charts and dispatches sharing space with fine mahogany furniture and a portrait of the King in full regalia.

"Commander Cruwys," Rowley greeted him, rising from behind a broad mahogany desk, its surface neat but well-worn. He was a man of about eight-and-forty, with the sun-browned complexion of long service and the comfortably solid frame of a senior officer who had spent rather too many months ashore amid the indulgences of Jamaca's planters. His eye retained a piercing quality that had made him a formidable captain during the Seven Years' War. His methodical approach to command was legendary in the service, a man who left nothing to chance and whose ships were always in perfect fighting order.

"Sir." Nicholas bowed, placing the dispatch box on the desk between them. "I have brought the documents recovered from the Spanish vessel, as requested, along with my reports."

"Be seated. We have much to discuss." As Nicholas complied, the Admiral broke the seal on the box and began to examine its contents with methodical care, occasionally adjusting his spectacles or making a marginal note with a silver pencil. The only sounds in the room were the rustling of papers, and the distant cries of gulls from the harbour beyond the open stern windows.

"Most interesting," Rawley murmured after several minutes. "Most interesting indeed. Admiral Hood's dispatch mentioned the possibility of intelligence value, but these"—he tapped a sheaf of coded documents—"may prove more significant than anticipated." He looked up, studying Nicholas with renewed attention. "I'm sure your written report is comprehensive, Commander, but I wish to hear the particulars from your own mouth. The *San Isidro*—speak freely."

Nicholas began to recount the capture, his verbal account matching his official report but enriched with the subtle nuances of personal observation. He described the nighttime approach to Aguadilla, the careful reconnaissance, the moment of detection, and the swift, brutal boarding action.

Rawley listened intently, occasionally making a marginal note, his sharp eyes otherwise never leaving Nicholas's face. "You lost how many men in this action?"

"None killed in the taking of the *San Isidro*, sir," Nicholas replied. "Though we sustained a few minor wounds during the boarding."

The admiral nodded, understanding the significance of a bloodless capture. "And the crew and passengers?"

Nicholas stated that the Spanish captain and his two lieutenants had been killed, along with six others and ten wounded. He then described Don Francisco Valdés and his niece, Doña Elena—their demeanor during capture and subsequent voyage, the delicate diplomatic situation they represented.

"I see," said the Admiral, rising from his chair to peer through the stern windows at the harbour beyond. He was silent for a long moment, studying the arrangement of vessels in the anchorage. "Hood's orders for you to proceed directly to England, most interesting. Particularly with Admiral Pigot having taken the most of the fleet north so early."

Rawley turned back, a knowing gleam in his eye. "You understand what Admiral Hood is about, don't you, Cruwys? These papers are important, yes, but their journey to the Admiralty could have been entrusted to any number of vessels. Admiral Pigot would certainly take an interest in both your prize and your command, were he here to exercise his authority."

"Sir?" Nicholas replied, careful not to presume.

"Hood and I have been acquainted since the late '50s," Rowley remarked, his tone measured. "Our paths crossed during the war with France, though we served in different theaters. He is not one to frequently concern himself with the careers of junior officers, yet he mentioned you with notable specificity in his correspondence. It seems he perceives qualities in you worth nurturing, beyond the unpredictable tides of naval politics."

Nicholas inclined his head slightly, acknowledging the implied meaning. "Admiral Hood has been most generous in his assessment of my service."

"Indeed," Rawley said, settling back into his chair. "And I shall not interfere with his designs. You will prepare *Alert* for sea as quickly as possible. You will sail three days following the Prize Court's ruling. That should see you well away before any... complications might arise. I shall inform the dockyard that your requirements take precedence over all but the most urgent repairs to the squadron."

As his gig pulled away from *Princess Royal*, Nicholas ordered the coxswain to pull for the *Falcon*. Harrington's command rode gracefully at anchor, her eighteen ports open to the fresh air, her new canvas neatly furled, brass gleaming in the fierce Jamaican sun. A model of naval efficiency that spoke well of her commander.

The side party was ready as Nicholas came aboard, the pipes offering their shrill welcome as he gained the deck. Harrington waited, resplendent in his uniform coat despite the heat.

"Nicholas, at last!" he exclaimed, shaking Nicholas's hand with genuine warmth once the formalities had been observed. "Come below where it's cooler, and we shall have something wet. This infernal heat makes a man's uniform stick to him like sailcloth to a yard in the doldrums."

Harrington's cabin was a study in naval elegance—not ostentatious, but revealing his aristocratic background in a dozen subtle ways: the silver-framed miniature of his family's estate in Hampshire, the leather-bound volumes neatly arranged in a brass-fitted bookcase, the fine linen napkins on the dining table. A servant appeared with a pitcher of cooling punch, disappearing just as silently once glasses had been poured.

"To your prize," Harrington said, raising his glass. "A neat piece of work, by all accounts. The talk at the Admiral's table last evening was of nothing else."

"You exaggerate," Nicholas replied, though pleased nevertheless. "*San Isidro* is a handsome vessel, but hardly remarkable in herself."

"Perhaps not, but her cargo certainly is." Harrington sipped his punch with evident appreciation. "They say she carries specie?"

"She does," Nicholas confirmed, offering nothing more.

"Well, you must tell me about the cutting-out action. I've heard fragments, but nothing complete."

They spent the next two hours comparing their recent experiences, the qualities of their respective commands, the merits of different sailing techniques, and catching up on the war and political news. Nicholas admired the *Falcon*'s clean lines and the ingenious modifications Harrington had made to her rigging and sail plan—an additional stay here, a reshaped yard there, all contributing to improved performance.

"She's weatherly as a gull," Harrington said proudly as they stood on the quarterdeck. "Points higher than any comparable sloop I know of. We took a French privateer five weeks ago on the crossing. Caught him trailing the convoy ten miles astern and ran him down in less than four hours."

It was past noon when Nicholas prepared to depart. "I must get back to *Alert*. Admiral Rawley wants us ready to sail in three days after the Prize Court ruling, and there's much to be done."

"So soon?" Harrington raised an eyebrow. "The Admiral must be eager to have those dispatches on their way to London."

"There are considerations beyond mere paperwork," Nicholas replied carefully.

"Ah." Harrington's expression showed immediate understanding. "Pigot's shadow looms large, even in his absence. Hood has always kept an eye out for promising officers, by all accounts."

Nicholas smiled slightly. "I remain grateful for the Admiral's good opinion, however expressed."

"As you should be," Harrington said, adjusting his hat against the sun. "Now, before you disappear, you must promise to join me at the Hargrove plantation tonight. All the Navy interest will be there, and Mrs. Hargrove has particular reason to welcome the officer who captured Don Francisco and his niece."

Nicholas raised an eyebrow. "Indeed? I was not aware of any connection."

"Mrs. Hargrove is cousin to Lady Portland, whose husband has considerable Spanish investments. The war has placed them in a delicate position, and intelligence from a gentleman of Don Francisco's standing might prove valuable. Besides," Harrington added with a knowing smile that reminded Nicholas of their many conversations about women in London society, "Doña Elena is said to be a beauty, and Mrs. Hargrove never misses an opportunity to enliven her gatherings with new faces, particularly those attached to substantial fortunes."

They had reached the quarterdeck, and Harrington's officers moved respectfully to the leeward side, such as it was at anchor. Nicholas paused, "You seem remarkably well-informed about my passengers, Harrington."

His friend laughed with the easy confidence that had always characterized him. "My dear Cruwys, this is Jamaica – half a day in port and the entire island knows your business. Now, will you dine at Hargrove's? Mrs. Hargrove was most particular that I should secure your attendance."

Nicholas hesitated, but the prospect seeing Doña Elena, and of an evening in society, with Harrington's familiar company and ready wit to guide him through the complexities of colonial social hierarchies, held undeniable appeal. The memory of his friend's impeccable navigation of London's drawing rooms and clubs came vividly to mind, how Harrington had introduced him to proper tailors, secured his invitation the membership in the Anchor and Crown, and generally eased his reintegration into English society after years in the Pacific.

"Very well," he conceded.

"Excellent!" Harrington exclaimed. "Eight o'clock, then. The Hargrove plantation is two miles east of Kingston proper – any driver will know it. I shall alert Mrs. Hargrove to expect you." His tone suggested he was already calculating how to position Nicholas advantageously within the evening's social currents, much as he had done during their time in London.

The Hargrove plantation stood upon rising ground two miles east of Kingston, its white-columned mansion commanding views across the distant harbour where the naval vessels rode at anchor. The carriage bearing Nicholas wound up the crushed-shell drive as the last traces of sunset faded from the sky, the mansion's windows already aglow with dozens of candles. The evening air carried the mingled scents of tropical flowers and roasting fish and meat, punctuated by occasional bursts of laughter from the open verandah where guests had gathered to escape the lingering heat of the main rooms.

Harrington awaited him at the entrance, resplendent in his best uniform. "Nicholas you have arrived! Mrs. Hargrove has been quite beside herself awaiting your arrival. The hero of the hour must not be kept waiting, you know."

Nicholas, uncomfortable with such characterization, merely smiled as they passed into the house. The main drawing room buzzed with conversation—naval officers in their blue and white, army officers and marines in scarlet, colonial officials in formal black, merchants in silks revealing their prosperity, and ladies whose gowns somehow managed to combine London fashion with concessions to the tropical climate. At one end of the room stood Don Francisco, engaged in earnest conversation with the Governor, while nearby, somewhat separate from the main English gathering, stood Doña Elena.

She wore a gown of ivory silk with subtle Spanish embroidery at the bodice, her thick dark hair arranged in a style that navigated the narrow channel between Madrid formality and colonial practicality. As Nicholas approached, he noted how the other guests gave her a certain space, as though her nationality created an invisible barrier that even colonial hospitality could not entirely breach.

"Commander Cruwys," she acknowledged as Harrington performed the introduction with practiced ease. "How curious that we should meet again in such different circumstances."

"Indeed, Doña Elena," Nicholas replied with a formal bow. "I trust your accommodations ashore prove more comfortable than my cabin aboard *Alert*."

"Considerably more spacious," she conceded with the hint of a smile, "though perhaps lacking in certain interesting elements of motion."

Harrington's eyebrows rose fractionally at this exchange, though his aristocratic breeding prevented any more obvious reaction. "I shall leave you to become reacquainted," he murmured, already scanning the room for his next social obligation. "Mrs. Hargrove beckons from across the room, and I have learned never to keep our hostess waiting."

As Harrington departed, Elena regarded Nicholas with those remarkable eyes that had first caught his attention aboard *Alert*. "I understand your ship sails within three days of the Prize Court providing its ruling. Admiral Rawley appears eager to have his dispatches on their way to London."

Nicholas was surprised by her knowledge of naval movements. "You are remarkably well-informed, Doña Elena."

"Kingston harbors few secrets, Commander. My uncle's position necessitates awareness of such matters." She drew her fan from its ribbon, opening it with a practiced flick of her wrist. The simple action transformed her from captive to aristocrat with startling completeness. "It seems such a brief time."

"The Admiralty values prompt execution of orders, particularly in wartime," Nicholas replied, aware of curious glances from nearby guests.

"So I imagine." She regarded him over the edge of her fan, her expression suddenly more thoughtful. "Though I wonder if diplomatic considerations might occasionally supersede naval schedules. My uncle has found your insights regarding the circumstances of our capture most illuminating. He remarked only this morning that further consultation with you might prove valuable to his discussions with the Governor."

The suggestion caught Nicholas by surprise—was she hinting at some scheme to delay his departure? Before he could formulate a proper response, dinner was announced, and the assembled company began moving toward the dining room in couples and small groups.

"Perhaps you would be so kind as to escort me," Elena suggested, offering her arm with formal correctness. "As my uncle appears deeply engaged with the Governor."

Nicholas complied, acutely conscious of the curious glances that followed them. The Spanish diplomat's niece and the officer who had captured her vessel, their appearance together created precisely the sort of colonial gossip that enlivened Kingston society. Yet as they moved toward the dining room, he found himself considering her words with growing interest. The prospect of an extended stay in Jamaica, initially unwelcome when set against Hood's urgent orders, had suddenly acquired an unexpected appeal.

The Prize Court convened two days later, in a high-ceilinged chamber above the Customs House that overlooked the harbour. The room, with its dark mahogany paneling and portraits of previous admiralty judges staring down from smoke-darkened canvases, carried all the solemn weight of English law transported to the tropics. Despite the early hour, the heat already pressed down upon the assembled company, causing the attorneys' formal wigs to sit uncomfortably on perspiring brows, and the spectators to fan themselves with increasing vigor as the morning wore on.

Nicholas sat beside Harrington in the section reserved for naval officers, his formal uniform coat unbearably hot but necessary for the proceedings. Before them, Mr. Willoughby, the admiralty proctor, methodically laid out the case for declaring the *San Isidro* a lawful prize, his nasal voice cutting through the torpid air with surprising clarity.

"The vessel was engaged in commerce contrary to the established blockade, carrying specie that would undoubtedly have been employed in support of Spain's military efforts in the Caribbean theater. Furthermore, her resistance to lawful boarding constitutes clear hostile action against His Majesty's forces."

The Spanish consul, a dyspeptic gentleman with an unfortunate tendency to mop his brow with alarming frequency, offered counterarguments regarding the diplomatic nature of Don Francisco's mission. These were meticulously recorded by the court clerk, though the judge's expression suggested they would carry little weight in his final determination.

"The documents recovered from the master's cabin," Willoughby continued, producing the logbook and manifest that Nicholas had personally delivered to the Admiralty agent upon arrival, "clearly establish the vessel's trading purpose, regardless of any passengers she might have carried. Don Francisco's presence, while acknowledged, does not convert a merchantman into a diplomatic vessel."

Nicholas found the proceedings simultaneously tedious and fascinating—the legal machinery of prize adjudication operating with a curious blend of formality and pragmatism that characterized British naval administration at its most efficient. While attorneys argued points of international maritime law, the practical outcome was never truly in doubt. The *San Isidro* would be condemned as a prize, her value assessed, and the resulting sum distributed according to the established formula: one-eighth to Rear Admiral Hood under whose orders *Alert* was operating, two-eighths to Nicholas as capturing commander, one-eighth divided among his lieutenants, one-eighth among the warrant officers, and the remaining three-eighths distributed among *Alert*'s crew.

"Commander Cruwys," the judge inquired during the second day of proceedings, "pray describe the precise circumstances of the boarding action."

Nicholas rose, conscious of Doña Elena and Don Francisco observing from the gallery set aside for interested parties. "Your Honor, having identified the *San Isidro* as a vessel subject to capture under the terms of the blockade, I dispatched boats under cover of darkness. Upon approaching the vessel, we were fired upon by her crew. The boarding party, under my direct command, secured the vessel after a brief action. Resistance ceased upon the capture of the quarterdeck."

The court's final determination came the next day, nearly unheard of swiftness for the court, a fact attributed by many to Admiral Rawley's desire to expedite proceedings for a favored officer. The *San Isidro* was declared a lawful prize, her value and that of her cargo assessed at £12,000—a substantial sum that would transform the fortunes of many among *Alert*'s crew. Nicholas's share, approximately £3,000, represented more wealth than he had ever imagined accumulating so early, over fifteen years of his current pay. As the sole lieutenant, Forester would see almost £1,500, and he seemed dazed when he rose from his seat, as though he had never really believed it would happen.

As the court adjourned, Don Francisco approached with formal correctness. "Commander, while I naturally regret the court's decision regarding our vessel, I cannot fault the legal reasoning. The *San Isidro* was, indeed, engaged in commercial activity despite her secondary diplomatic function."

"You are most gracious, Don Francisco," Nicholas replied, surprised by this magnanimity.

"Not at all. The realities of war make such encounters inevitable." The Spanish diplomat glanced toward Elena, who stood conversing with the Governor's wife some distance away. "My niece and I have been most courteously treated since our arrival, a fact I attribute largely to your own conduct during our capture and subsequent voyage. Such consideration deserves recognition, regardless of our opposing national interests."

This unexpected acknowledgment, delivered with aristocratic dignity, reinforced Nicholas's growing respect for the Spaniard. Whatever Don Francisco's official mission might have been, he carried himself with a personal honor that transcended mere diplomatic posturing.

The conclusion of the Prize Court proceedings removed the legal cloud hanging over the *San Isidro*, allowing final preparations for Nicholas's departure Three days after the prize court finished, Admiral Rawley had indicated, three days before the tide and wind would carry them away from Jamaica and whatever possibilities it might hold.

That same afternoon, Nicholas was summoned once again to Admiral Rawley's flagship. He found the Admiral reviewing documents at his desk, with a freshly broken seal indicating recent delivery.

"Ah, Commander. I've received a rather unusual request from Don Francisco." Rawley tapped the document before him. "He has formally asked that your departure be delayed by a fortnight to assist with certain aspects of the neutrality negotiations. He believes your firsthand knowledge of the *San Isidro*'s capture and her contents would prove valuable in establishing the precise circumstances under which his mission was interrupted."

Nicholas maintained a carefully neutral expression, though a sudden warmth in his chest betrayed his inner reaction. The request could only have come through Elena's influence with her uncle. "I am, of course, at your disposal, Admiral. Though I understood Admiral Hood's orders regarding our return to England were rather pressing."

"Indeed they are," Rawley agreed, studying Nicholas with shrewd assessment, "but diplomatic considerations occasionally take precedence over even the most urgent naval matters. The Spanish negotiations may significantly impact our operations throughout the Caribbean. A delay of two weeks should not materially affect the value of your dispatches, while Don Francisco has indicated that your assistance could substantially expedite his discussions with the Governor."

Nicholas recognized that the Admiral was offering a plausible diplomatic fiction that would satisfy all parties while allowing ample flexibility in its execution. "Very good, sir. I shall make myself available to Don Francisco as required."

"Excellent. I shall inform Don Francisco that you will attend him at his convenience."

As Nicholas departed, he found himself confronting a curious mixture of emotions—professional concern at the delay in executing Hood's orders balanced against an undeniable anticipation of extended time in Elena's company. The diplomatic pretext, flimsy though it might be to discerning eyes, offered a fortnight's reprieve from separation that he had not dared hope for.

Nicholas and Elena's interactions over the next week had been carefully choreographed—meetings ostensibly about diplomatic matters, conversations always conducted in public spaces, always with at least minimal supervision. But something had been building. Elena was no passive captive. She moved through Kingston's social circles with a grace that belied her technical status as a detainee, her uncle's diplomatic connections providing her a degree of freedom unusual for a captured noblewoman.

Their private meetings began innocently enough, discussions of books and philosophy in the botanical gardens, chance encounters at the harbour's edge where they exchanged observations on Jamaica's natural splendors within sight of watchful eyes. But the formality that had characterized their early interactions aboard *Alert* gradually gave way to something more intimate, a connection that transcended intellectual exchange.

Seven days after their arrival in Kingston, the tension between Nicholas and Elena had become unbearable. The Governor's ball that night marked the official celebration of Don Francisco's provisional agreement with the colonial authorities—a complex arrangement of mutual non-interference that stopped short of formal neutrality yet provided valuable breathing space for both Spanish and British interests in the region. The ballroom of Government House had been transformed for the occasion, softened by palms in massive Chinese pots, hundreds of beeswax candles in crystal sconces, and garlands of tropical flowers whose heavy perfume hung in the warm evening air.

Nicholas arrived in full dress uniform, conscious that this would likely be his final formal appearance in Kingston society before *Alert* sailed for England. The diplomatic pretext for his continued presence in Jamaica was rapidly approaching its natural conclusion, even if a few more days would be needed to settle all details.

Harrington found him near the entrance, a glass of punch already in hand. "A triumphant evening for you, Nicholas," he said with a dry smile. He laughed quietly, then leaned in, his tone laced with amused irony.

"I'm told you've passed many industrious hours in her company. I daresay you'll be the talk of Kingston before the night is out."

"Her education is remarkably broad for a Spanish lady," Nicholas replied, measured. "We've discovered a shared interest in certain philosophical questions."

"I've no doubt you have," Harrington murmured. He lifted his glass in subtle salute.

"Ah — and here she is now. A vision in Spanish lace, no less. Prepare yourself, my friend; every eye in the room will be weighing your fortune."

Elena entered on her uncle's arm, her gown a deep crimson that stood in striking contrast to the pale pastels favored by the English ladies. The Spanish cut, with its close-fitting bodice, narrow waist, and elaborate lacework, did little to conceal the contours of her figure. On the contrary, it seemed designed to celebrate them, particularly the high, gracefully rounded swell of her bosom, which the fine lace framed like a deliberate flourish.

At her throat, a delicate choker of jet and gold rested just above the hollow between her collarbones, its dark gleam drawing the eye to the skin it adorned. A single drop-shaped ruby hung from its center, poised just above the rise of her breasts, like a punctuation mark chosen for effect. Matching earrings swayed with each measured step, catching the candlelight and casting brief, flickering sparks. The interplay of silk, lace, and jewels gave the impression not of excess, but of beauty worn with unshakable confidence. She was poised, richly feminine, and unmistakably aware of the effect she created — drawing appreciative glances from more than a few officers, and thin-lipped stares from their wives and other women.

Nicholas felt something shift in his chest, a quiet breath stolen before he knew it had gone. She was beautiful, yes, but it was not merely the color or cut of the gown that held him. It was the ease with which she wore it, the quiet command of every turn of her head, the subtle intelligence behind the glint in her eyes. The memory of their long conversation that afternoon stirred, not her words precisely, but the warmth of her laughter and the way her fingers had paused over the edge of a book, as though marking not the page, but the moment.

Don Francisco guided her through the formal courtesies with the Governor and his lady before releasing her to circulate freely, a liberty that hinted at his unorthodox views on female independence.

Nicholas followed her movement without meaning to, his gaze drawn by the whisper of silk and the shimmer of lace. He noted the sway of her skirts, the gleam of candlelight on the ruby at her throat, the faint, polite smile she offered a passing officer — unhurried, but coolly detached. It took a beat too long for him to remember he still held his glass.

"You're staring," Harrington murmured at his elbow, not turning his head. "Which is understandable, of course. But still — staring."

Nicholas cleared his throat, shifted his stance, and raised the glass to his lips in a too-obvious feint at nonchalance.

"Was I?"

"As a cat might stare at cream just out of reach." Harrington said dryly. "It's always the second look that gives a man away."

Nicholas attempted a smile, but the corners of his mouth betrayed him, too tightly drawn, too full of the effort to seem at ease. The awareness of being seen settled on his shoulders like a coat too suddenly heavy.

Across the room, Admiral Rowley stood among a knot of gentlemen, his hands folded lightly behind his back, his eyes moving with the slow, practiced calm of a man who had seen a great many things and drawn hasty conclusions about none of them. He was not looking at Nicholas, not directly, but in his direction, the way a seasoned sailor watches the wind: quietly, methodically, judging its nature before it shifts.

Then, just briefly, his lips curled at the corner. A flicker passed through his expression — not judgment, but memory. He had been a young officer once, too, among these seemingly exotic islands.

He turned back to the conversation at hand, saying nothing, his features once again composed. But for a moment, there was a softness in the set of his shoulders, as though he had just been reminded of something worth keeping.

It was during the third dance that Nicholas and Elena found themselves momentarily isolated at the edge of the ballroom, the complex figures of the dance having brought them together then left them briefly unattended by the other participants.

"I understand your ship sails within the week," Elena said, her voice pitched low enough that nearby dancers could not overhear. "My uncle's business concludes, and your Admiral's patience undoubtedly wears thin."

"That is likely," Nicholas confirmed.

She nodded, her expression revealing nothing to casual observers. "The botanical gardens are particularly fine this time of year. The night-blooming cereus is said to be flowering near the eastern pavilion. Tomorrow afternoon, perhaps?"

Nicholas understood precisely what was being proposed. "I have heard the same. Though I understand the best specimens can be observed only in the late afternoon, when the gardeners have retired for their meal."

"Indeed." Her fan opened with a decisive snap, concealing the lower portion of her face from potential observers. "Four o'clock, then. For botanical observations of a scientific nature."

The remainder of the ball passed in a blur of formal dances, polite conversation, and increasingly tedious toasts to Anglo-Spanish cooperation.

The following day Don Francisco had gone to Spanish Town for diplomatic meetings that would occupy him until the following afternoon. With careful planning that reflected both their temperaments, Nicholas and Elena had confirmed their arrangement to meet at a small pavilion on the grounds of the Hargrove estate, which Commander Harrington had made available through discreet arrangement, no questions asked – the code among gentlemen extending even to matters that might, in stricter interpretation, border on treasonous.

"My dear Cruwys," Harrington had said when Nicholas approached him the morning after the ball with a carefully phrased request, "I've arranged similar accommodations for distinguished officers since my first posting to the West Indies. The pavilion offers perfect privacy—the gardeners never venture there on Wednesdays, and the sight lines from the main house are conveniently blocked by the magnolia grove." His aristocratic features had shown neither judgment nor surprise, merely the same practical acceptance of human nature that had characterized their discussions about society.

Nicholas arrived first, in civilian clothes that would attract less attention than his naval uniform. The pavilion stood in a secluded part of the estate's extensive gardens, built in the classical style with white columns supporting a domed roof that offered shelter from both tropical sun and occasional rain.

He found himself recalling Harrington's advice from their London days regarding discreet liaisons: "The appearance of propriety matters more than the substance, my dear Cruwys. Society forgives much if it occurs beyond direct observation. It's flagrancy, not indiscretion itself, that invites censure." The memory brought a wry smile. Harrington had been counseling him on navigating certain social waters in Mayfair, not anticipating involvement with Spanish aristocrats captured aboard prizes of war. Yet the principle remained sound.

She came on foot from the main path, wearing a simple gown of pale yellow that seemed to capture the afternoon sunlight. No duenna accompanied her – a breach of Spanish propriety that signaled her intentions more clearly than words could have done. Her hair was arranged more simply than court fashion demanded, falling in loose waves confined only by a single ribbon. She carried a small volume, Rousseau's Social Contract, the pretense for their meeting should anyone question it.

"I feared you might not come, Elena" Nicholas said as she approached, the formality of their public encounters falling away.

"Did you Nicholas?" Her smile held both warmth and challenge. "Then you understand me less than I believed." She stepped into the pavilion, moving with the fluid grace that had first caught his attention aboard *Alert*. "We are past pretense, I think, Nicholas. We have both considered the consequences of what we contemplate, and yet here we are."

"Here we are," he agreed, closing the distance between them with deliberate steps. "Though I confess my naval training provided little preparation for... privateering of this nature."

Elena laughed, the sound both musical and liberating. "What poor metaphors you sailors employ. Is that how you see this, as a form of licensed piracy?"

"Not licensed," Nicholas corrected, reaching for her hand, which she gave without hesitation. "And therefore considerably more dangerous."

Their first kiss contained none of the hesitant exploration that often marks initial intimacy. Instead, it reflected the weeks of tension that had built between them—passionate, decisive, a mutual claiming rather than tentative request. Elena's arms circled his neck with surprising strength, pulling him closer as though the physical connection might compensate for the constraints that had limited them until this moment.

The pavilion's stone bench proved an inadequate setting for what followed. By mutual, wordless agreement, they moved to the small anteroom behind the main structure—a space intended for storage of gardening tools but which Harrington, with remarkable foresight that reminded Nicholas of his friend's similar arrangements during their London days, had furnished with a daybed and simple linens. The practicality of the arrangement might have seemed crude in other circumstances, but in the heat of the moment, it represented nothing less than salvation.

Their coupling was a study in contrasts—Elena's composed assurance meeting Nicholas's measured restraint, both giving way to something less controlled as the moment deepened. She moved with the confidence of experience, but there was a kind of reverence in the way she received him—a quiet intensity that spoke not of novelty, but of something rare. Nicholas, attuned to the shifts in her breathing and the tension in her body, matched her with a care that became urgency, then release.

Afterward, as they lay tangled in the simple linens, a light breeze from the open window providing blessed relief from the tropical heat, Elena traced the scar on his shoulder—a souvenir from the boarding of the *San Isidro*.

"This is the price of your duty," she observed, her fingers following the jagged line where splinter had torn flesh.

"One of many," Nicholas replied, catching her hand and raising it to his lips. "Each mark has its own history."

She shifted slightly, her touch drifting across his collarbone and then, without warning, to the patterned lines inked along his left shoulder. Her fingers stilled.

"This is not from battle," she said, softly.

He did not answer at once. The tattoo—its geometric precision stark against his skin—had been inked during the mourning rites on Bora Bora, a permanent emblem of loss and belonging, of the life he had lived in the wake of Atea's death. It was not something he had expected to explain.

"No," he said finally. "It's from another life. One I carry forward."

Her expression was unreadable—curiosity, perhaps, but without intrusion. She bent and placed a kiss just at the edge of the tattoo, light and deliberate, not as a question but as an acknowledgement.

"You wear your profession on your skin," she said, her hand moving to his chest, where no visible marks marred the surface. "And what marks will I leave, I wonder? None so obvious, perhaps."

"Does that concern you?" Nicholas asked, his voice quieter now. "That our connection leaves no visible trace?"

"On the contrary." Her dark eyes held his with characteristic directness. "The most profound influences often leave no external mark. Like philosophical ideas that reshape a mind while leaving the body unchanged."

"A comfortable rationalization," Nicholas suggested, though without criticism.

"Perhaps." She smiled, rising to retrieve her scattered clothing with unselfconscious grace. "But rationalization is the privilege of those who consciously transgress. We choose this knowing its impropriety, its danger. That requires a certain philosophical framework, does it not?"

Nicholas watched her dress, admiring the efficient economy of her movements – no wasted motion, no false modesty. "You've considered this more thoroughly than I," he admitted. "My justifications run more toward seizing rare opportunities when duty permits."

"A practical naval approach." She finished arranging her hair, achieving a semblance of its earlier order that would pass casual inspection. "We should not linger. Suspicion grows with duration, and while Harrington's discretion may be reliable, servants talk."

They departed separately, Elena first, carrying her volume of Rousseau as though returning from philosophical contemplation in the garden pavilion. Nicholas followed thirty minutes later, taking a circuitous route back to the harbour where his gig awaited to return him to *Alert*.

Their next meeting followed a similar pattern, carefully arranged, brief in duration, intense in content. The physical aspect of their relationship developed alongside their intellectual connection, each encounter adding layers of intimacy and understanding that transcended the limitations of their circumstances.

Their third meeting proved particularly significant. Held in a small cottage on the outskirts of Kingston that belonged to a retired naval lieutenant now conveniently visiting relatives in Spanish Town, it afforded them several hours of privacy – a luxury their previous encounters had lacked.

"We must speak of what follows," Elena said as they lay together in the cottage's single bedroom, the afternoon light filtering through partially closed shutters creating patterns across the tangled sheets. "You will depart for England soon – Rawley cannot delay further without raising questions. And I must eventually return to Spain."

Nicholas had been avoiding this particular conversation, preferring to exist in the diplomatic fiction that their connection might continue indefinitely. "Must we discuss this now?" he asked, tracing the curve of her shoulder with deliberate distraction.

"Yes." She captured his hand, forcing his attention to her words rather than the diversion he offered. "We are not children, Nicholas, to imagine that passion conquers practical reality. You have your commission, your ship, your duty to king and country. I remain a Spanish diplomat's niece with family responsibilities that will shortly take me far from Jamaica."

"You sound remarkably pragmatic about our separation," Nicholas observed, unable to keep a hint of resentment from his tone.

"Pragmatism is not the absence of feeling," Elena countered, her eyes holding his with characteristic directness. "It is the recognition that feeling alone cannot overcome the structures that govern our lives." She sat up, gathering the sheet around her with unconscious grace. "Do you imagine I expect you to abandon your naval career? To resign your commission and follow me to Spain? Or perhaps you think I might renounce my family, my position, my entire existence to become a naval officer's wife in England?"

Put so bluntly, both possibilities sounded absurd. "No," Nicholas admitted. "Though I confess the thought of never seeing you again after Jamaica holds little appeal."

"Then we must accept what this is, a rare alignment of circumstances that allowed two people who would normally never have met to discover a connection." She leaned forward, kissing him with unexpected tenderness. "The world will separate us, Nicholas. But that makes what we share now more precious, not less."

Her philosophical approach struck him as simultaneously admirable and frustrating – a rational framework that acknowledged reality while offering little comfort. Yet as they resumed their physical connection with renewed intensity, Nicholas found himself adopting her perspective. If their time together was inherently limited, then each encounter became more valuable, each moment worthy of complete presence rather than diluted by regret for what could not be.

Their affair might have concluded with this bittersweet understanding, a diplomatic disengagement to match their diplomatic initiation, had events not intervened in the form of Miguel Álvarez y Valdés – Elena's cousin, a captain in the Spanish Royal Guard who arrived unexpectedly in Kingston aboard a neutral Dutch merchantman from Havana, claiming diplomatic immunity.

Nicholas first learned of Miguel's arrival through Harrington, who brought the news to him aboard *Alert* two days before the ship was scheduled to finally depart for England.

"You have a complication, my friend," Harrington announced without preamble as he joined Nicholas in his cabin. "A Spanish officer arrived yesterday claiming familial connection to your lovely Doña Elena. Captain Miguel Álvarez y Valdés – and from what I gather, he's not merely a cousin but a rather possessive one."

Nicholas maintained a carefully neutral expression. "I fail to see how this concerns me. My official interaction with the Valdés family concluded with the Prize Court's adjudication."

Harrington's expression combined amusement and concern. "Come now, Cruwys. Your 'interaction' with Doña Elena has extended considerably beyond official capacity, a fact that appears not to have escaped her cousin's notice."

"How?" Nicholas asked, abandoning pretense with his oldest friend.

"The usual way – servants talk, someone observes a pattern of coincidental absences, suspicions form." Harrington shrugged. "In any case, Captain Valdés was making rather pointed inquiries about you. His manner suggested more than casual interest."

Nicholas absorbed this information with the focused calculation of a naval officer assessing tactical threat. "Has he approached Admiral Rawley?"

"Not yet, though that seems a likely next step. Rawley would be duty-bound to investigate any formal complaint, particularly one involving a British officer and a Spanish national while our countries remain technically at war."

The potential consequences unfolded in Nicholas's mind with professional clarity: investigation, possible court-martial, certainly the loss of *Alert*, perhaps his commission entirely. Beyond the professional impact lay the diplomatic complications. Don Francisco's neutrality negotiations would be compromised, Elena's reputation destroyed.

"I must see her," Nicholas decided. "Warn her of this development."

"Already arranged," Harrington replied with efficient pragmatism. "The cottage will be available this afternoon. I've sent word through channels that should reach her without attracting her cousin's attention."

Elena arrived at the cottage in a state of controlled agitation that manifested not in obvious distress but in a heightened precision of movement and speech, the same disciplined focus Nicholas had observed in her approach to intellectual debate.

"My cousin Miguel knows," she confirmed without preamble as she entered, removing her bonnet with efficient motions. "He came due to rumours about us from neutral shipping. Then yesterday, my maid, Luisa, revealed our meetings to him. Her loyalty to family honor apparently exceeds her loyalty to me personally."

"Then we have little time," Nicholas observed. "Your cousin will undoubtedly approach Admiral Rawley, and once formal mechanisms engage, events will move beyond our control."

"Miguel is not a man who immediately seeks official channels." Elena's expression combined concern with a kind of resigned understanding. "He considers family honor a personal responsibility rather than a matter for authorities. He will seek you directly first."

The implications were immediately clear to Nicholas. "A challenge, then."

"Almost certainly. He was trained in the Royal Academy in Madrid – swordsmanship is a particular pride." Elena's composure wavered momentarily. "Nicholas, you must understand Miguel's perspective. In Spanish society, matters of family honor require personal resolution. He believes he acts to protect not only my reputation but the dignity of our entire family."

"I understand the principle," Nicholas acknowledged. "Though I cannot say I fully subscribe to it."

"Yet you will accept if challenged." It was not a question but a statement of certainty.

"I can hardly refuse without confirming the very dishonor he alleges." Nicholas moved to the window, looking out toward Kingston harbour where *Alert* waited, symbolic of the duty and discipline that had defined his life until recent weeks. "Besides, a duel, properly conducted, establishes parameters for the dispute. Better a structured confrontation than informal accusation that might spread without containment."

Elena studied him with the penetrating gaze that had first drawn him to her aboard *Alert*. "You approach even matters of honor with tactical calculation. How very naval of you."

Despite the gravity of their situation, Nicholas smiled. "We rely on what training we possess when navigating unfamiliar waters."

Their discussion of Miguel's likely actions proved prophetic. The challenge arrived that very evening, delivered to *Alert* by Don Raphael Montoya. Later, the lamps were lit aboard *Falcon* when Nicholas arrived, boarding via the port side to avoid ceremony, the letter from Don Raphael Montoya folded neatly in his coat. The quartermaster passed him without challenge, and a marine at the companionway knocked once on the stern cabin door before ushering him inside.

Harrington looked up from his desk, coat in his shirtsleeves with the coat thrown over a nearby chair, a glass of port in hand.

"Nicholas. I wasn't expecting company."

"I've received a communication," Nicholas said, withdrawing the sealed note and handing it across. "From Don Raphael Montoya, on behalf of Valdés."

Harrington took it without comment and read the brief contents. When he finished, he set the paper beside his glass and leaned back slightly, considering.

"Entirely proper in tone," he said at last. "Civil, even — if that can be said of a request for violence." His expression was composed, but there was a faint tension in his jaw.

"Of course, a flagrant breach of the Articles of War. Were it ever officially acknowledged."

"Officially," Nicholas agreed with a flicker of a smile.

"And you mean to answer?"

"I do." He met Harrington's gaze squarely. "And I hoped you would stand for me."

"Naturally," Harrington replied without hesitation. He took another sip of port, then nodded to the chair opposite. "Sit, then. Let's consider the matter."

Nicholas sat.

"I haven't replied directly. I thought it best to leave the terms in your hands."

"Wise," Harrington said. "I'll call on his second tonight — likely Montoya himself — and settle the particulars." He paused, then added, "Any thoughts on the weapon?"

Nicholas was quiet a moment.

"Swords, if you think it acceptable."

Harrington raised a brow. "You surprise me. I've seen you shoot, and by reputation he's no mean hand with a blade."

"I know," Nicholas said. "All the more reason."

There was a pause.

"Pistols are... final," he went on. "Clean, yes—but fixed. I'm good, but at ten paces, it's a coin toss, and I don't care to kill a man over insult, however studied."

Harrington cocked his head. "Yes, swords allow for discretion."

"They allow for proportion. A wound may be enough. A warning, even."

Harrington regarded him a moment. "Very well. I'll make it swords—unless Montoya objects, which would surprise me. He's said to take pride in his blade, and appearances count with men like him."

Nicholas gave a faint smile. "Then we understand each other."

Harrington nodded slowly.

"A surgeon can patch up most sword wounds from a duel. A bullet through the spine is less forgiving."

"You've seen me with a blade," Nicholas said. "I'm not without preparation."

Harrington's expression turned briefly wry.

"I have. That day aboard *Lynx*, when you disarmed me in front of half the wardroom. Walsh called it 'decorative nonsense' until you made me miss."

He leaned back in his chair. "That Portuguese blade of yours, different balance, entirely un-English. But effective."

"Silva taught me things no English master would," Nicholas said. "But I imagine the code won't permit anything beyond a proper small-sword."

"No," Harrington confirmed. "Small-swords only. But the technique remains. Valdés will likely fight in the Spanish academy style — formal, geometric, precise. If you can disrupt his rhythm with something less conventional, you may unbalance him before he can assert control."

Nicholas nodded, thoughtful.

Harrington stood and reached for his coat.

"I'll speak with Montoya and arrange the details. Location, time, seconds. I'll also see to it that Dr. Maxwell is conveniently riding near wherever we agree to meet. These things are better done quietly."

Nicholas stood as well.

"Thank you, Henry. Truly."

Harrington gave him a steady look, dry, but not without affection.

"Let's make sure it's Valdés who needs stitching, not you. One duel may pass as youthful misjudgment. Two begins to look like character."

Nicholas gave a short, rueful laugh.

"I'll aim to stop at one."

The clearing selected for their meeting lay on abandoned plantation land two miles outside Kingston. Far enough from official scrutiny to avoid immediate discovery, yet accessible by discrete paths that allowed the participants to arrive without drawing undue attention. Nicholas and Harrington arrived first, as protocol dictated for the challenged party. The early morning light filtered through the surrounding trees, creating a dappled effect across the small open space.

Miguel arrived precisely at the appointed time, accompanied by Montoya. He was a striking figure – tall for a Spaniard, with the lean muscular build of a cavalry officer accustomed to physical demands. His uniform, though not officially appropriate for the occasion, conveyed his military identity – dark blue coat with red facings, gold epaulettes indicating his captain's rank in the Spanish Royal Guard.

The formal introductions proceeded with the rigid courtesy that governed such encounters. Miguel's English proved excellent, his aristocratic accent lending his words a precise, clipped quality.

"Commander Cruwys," he acknowledged with a minimal bow. "I regret that our meeting occurs under such circumstances."

"As do I, Captain Valdés," Nicholas replied with matching formality. "Though I must note that the offense you cite remains a matter of allegation rather than established fact."

Valdés' expression hardened slightly. "The honor of a Spanish lady is not subject to legal standards of evidence, Commander. Reasonable certainty is sufficient when family dignity is at stake."

Further discussion would serve no purpose. The seconds measured the ground – twelve paces. The rules established that first blood would constitute satisfaction, though as all present understood, such limitations often proved difficult to maintain once combat commenced.

They removed their coats, Valdés folding his uniform with military precision while Harrington assisted Nicholas. Both men wore simple white shirts, sleeves secured at the wrist to prevent entanglement. The swords – regulation small-swords of the type carried by officers of both countries—were inspected by the seconds to ensure equal quality and condition.

As they took their positions, Nicholas studied his opponent with professional assessment. Valdés' stance revealed his formal training – balanced, controlled, with the practiced ease of a man thoroughly comfortable with his weapon. By contrast, Nicholas's own training in recent years emphasized practical combat rather than formalized dueling. His experience came from boarding actions and the close quarters fighting of naval engagements, where survival rather than form determined success.

He felt the balance of the small-sword in his hand, lighter than his Portuguese blade. The morning air was heavy with dew, and the scent of crushed grass rose from beneath his feet as he settled into his stance. Somewhere in the surrounding trees, a bird called once, then fell silent, as if sensing the gravity of the human drama unfolding below.

"Ready, gentlemen," Montoya announced, stepping back to join Harrington at the edge of the clearing.

The initial engagement proceeded cautiously, each man testing the other's skill with probing attacks. Nicholas could hear Valdés' controlled breathing, could see the slight flare of his nostrils with each exhalation. The Spanish officer moved with the grace of a dancer, his feet barely disturbing the grass, while sweat had already begun to gather at Nicholas's collar despite the early hour's relative coolness.

Their blades met with a crystalline ring that seemed unnaturally loud in the morning stillness. Nicholas felt each contact through his arm, a shivering vibration that traveled from the steel up to his shoulder. Miguel's attacks grew more confident, more aggressive, driving Nicholas back across ground that grew slippery under his boots. A shaft of early sunlight broke through the trees, momentarily catching Miguel's blade and dazzling Nicholas's eyes. He blinked away the sudden glare, tasting salt as sweat ran down to the corner of his mouth.

Then came the moment that altered the engagement's trajectory. Miguel, pressing his advantage, executed a perfect lunge that by all conventional standards should have succeeded. Nicholas felt the disturbance in the air as the blade passed a hair's breadth from his side, heard the soft exhalation of triumph start to form on Miguel's lips. Then, with the sudden instinctive movement that had saved him in shipboard skirmishes, Nicholas executed the same unorthodox side-step and counter that had so surprised Harrington. His blade caught the morning light as it sliced across Miguel's extended arm, drawing first blood—a thin crimson line that beaded and then flowed in the sudden silence of the clearing.

"The matter is settled," Montoya declared, moving forward. "First blood has been achieved."

Valdés stared at the spreading red stain on his white sleeve, then at Nicholas. For a moment, it appeared he might reject the outcome and continue the engagement. Then, with visible effort, he regained his aristocratic composure.

"Satisfaction is received," he acknowledged stiffly, allowing Montoya to examine the wound – a clean slice across the outer forearm, painful but not debilitating.

Dr. Maxwell, appearing with suspiciously convenient timing from a nearby path, offered his services. The wound required several stitches, which he administered on site with professional efficiency while the seconds maintained a careful buffer between the principals.

As Maxwell completed his work, Valdés addressed Nicholas directly, his tone formal but no longer hostile. "You fight unlike any European officer I have encountered, Commander Cruwys."

"Naval service encourages practical solutions rather than established form," Nicholas replied, carefully avoiding any hint of superiority that might reignite the confrontation.

"Indeed." Miguel flexed his bandaged arm experimentally. "My cousin's... judgment in certain matters becomes more comprehensible, though not more acceptable." He turned to Montoya. "We are finished here."

As the Spaniards departed across the dew-heavy grass, Harrington clapped Nicholas on the shoulder. "Well handled, though entirely unorthodox. The same move you used against me aboard the *Lynx*," he observed with a shake of his head. The Viscount would have a fit of apoplexy if he witnessed such a display at the Westborne family armory. Of course, Admiral Rawley will certainly hear of this encounter, regardless of the participants' discretion."

Nicholas nodded, already calculating the likely consequences. "Then I should return to *Alert* without delay. I have preparations to complete if we are to sail with tomorrow morning's tide."

The carriage had just reached Kingston when a marine lieutenant intercepted them, delivering Admiral Rawley's requirement for Nicholas's immediate attendance on the flagship. The summons contained no explanation, but its timing left little doubt regarding its purpose.

Admiral Rawley received him alone in his day cabin.

"Commander Cruwys," Rawley greeted him, his weathered face revealing nothing of his thoughts. "I understand you engaged in extracurricular activities this morning. Activities expressly forbidden by Admiralty regulations."

"Sir." Nicholas neither confirmed nor denied, recognizing that the Admiral likely possessed specific information. He recalled Harrington's counsel years earlier about such situations: "When confronted by superior authority, neither lie nor volunteer, occupy the middle ground of minimal acknowledgment."

"Captain Valdés has not lodged a formal complaint," Rawley continued, studying Nicholas with penetrating assessment. "Nor, I suspect, will he. Spanish officers maintain their own code regarding such matters. But the fact remains that a British naval officer under my command engaged in forbidden conduct with a foreign national during time of war."

"Yes, sir." There was no point in evasion.

Rawley sighed, his formal demeanor softening slightly. "Sit down, Cruwys. This conversation need not be conducted at attention."

As Nicholas complied, the Admiral moved to a sideboard and poured two glasses of Madeira.

"Your relationship with Doña Elena is not unknown to me," Rawley said, offering one glass to Nicholas. "Kingston is too small for such matters to remain entirely discreet, particularly when they involve our respective nations during continuing hostilities."

Nicholas accepted the glass but did not immediately drink. "I understand, sir."

"Do you?" Rawley settled into the chair opposite, his expression combining resignation with a hint of what might have been sympathy. "I was young once, Commander. The combination of danger, exotic locations, and beautiful women with whom association is officially forbidden – I understand the appeal perfectly."

This unexpected acknowledgment caught Nicholas by surprise. Rawley continued, his tone reflective rather than condemning.

"The service demands certain sacrifices from its officers. Personal entanglements that conflict with duty represent a luxury few of us can afford, particularly during wartime." He paused, taking a sip of his Madeira thoughtfully. "Yet we remain men."

Nicholas waited, sensing the Admiral had more to say before response would be appropriate.

"I could, of course, initiate formal proceedings," Rawley observed. "The duel alone provides sufficient cause, without addressing the... precipitating circumstances. But such action serves no practical purpose at this juncture. The diplomatic negotiations with Don

Francisco have progressed to a point where embarrassment to his family would create more problems than it would solve."

"Then you intend no official response, sir?" Nicholas ventured cautiously.

"I did not say that." Rawley set down his glass with deliberate precision. "Tomorrow morning, *Alert* will depart for England as previously arranged. You will deliver Hood's dispatches and the intelligence recovered from the *San Isidro* directly to the Admiralty. Upon arrival, you will report directly to Lord Keppel regarding both the operational details of the capture and the intelligence implications of the documents recovered."

The instructions matched their previous arrangement, suggesting no punitive alteration. However, Rawley had not finished.

"Tonight, you will dine with me privately at Government House. No other guests will be present. Following dinner, you will be permitted thirty minutes of private conversation with Doña Elena to make your farewells. Her cousin has been persuaded to attend diplomatic functions elsewhere, and Don Francisco has indicated his understanding of the... complexities involved."

This unexpected arrangement left Nicholas momentarily speechless. Rawley's expression softened further into something approaching paternal understanding.

"We are at war, Commander Cruwys, but we need not be barbarians. A proper farewell, conducted with appropriate dignity, seems the least concession I can make to two young people caught in circumstances largely beyond their control." He raised a cautionary finger. "However, I must insist that following your departure tomorrow, all communication with the Valdés family ceases, at least until this war is over. For your own protection as much as theirs."

"I understand, sir. Thank you."

Rawley nodded, then added more quietly, "I was posted to Batavia as a young lieutenant—part of a naval escort for a trade delegation. The Dutch governor's niece... well, some stories are better left untold. Suffice it to say, I am not entirely without sympathy for your situation."

The dinner that evening proceeded with formal correctness, the conversation restricted to naval matters, Caribbean politics, and the broader context of Britain's global conflicts. Rawley proved an engaging host in this private setting, his decades of experience providing perspective that transcended immediate tactical concerns.

As coffee was served, the Admiral glanced at the clock and rose from the table. "I find myself required to review certain dispatches in my study for the next hour. I believe Doña Elena is taking air in the garden pavilion, should you wish to pay your respects before departing."

With this transparent fiction establishing deniability for all concerned, Rawley withdrew, leaving Nicholas to make his way through the garden paths to the now-familiar pavilion where Elena awaited.

She wore a gown of deep blue silk that emphasized the olive tones of her skin, her dark hair arranged in a simple style that required minimal attention to maintain. As Nicholas approached, he noted how perfectly composed she appeared – not a woman preparing for emotional farewell but a diplomat's niece fulfilling social obligation.

Only when he drew nearer did he observe the slight tension around her eyes, the barely perceptible tightness in her posture that betrayed the control she maintained over deeper emotions.

"Admiral Rawley arranged this meeting," she said as he entered the pavilion. "A kindness I did not expect from a British flag officer."

"He possesses more understanding than his official position might suggest," Nicholas replied, taking the seat beside her – close enough for private conversation, far enough to maintain nominal propriety should anyone observe them.

"As does my uncle." Elena's smile held a hint of irony. "He expressed disappointment in my 'indiscretion' but acknowledged that diplomatic rationality cannot always govern human connection. I believe his exact words were, 'The heart follows no national boundaries, nor respects declarations of war.'"

"A surprisingly poetic observation from a diplomat."

"Don Francisco has hidden depths." Her composure wavered briefly. "As do we all, I suppose."

They sat in silence for a moment, the garden dense with the scent of jasmine and night-blooming cereus, the air warm and close about them like a held breath. Beyond the hedge, a tree frog called once, then fell quiet. From the pavilion, they could see the scattered lights across Kingston Harbour, including those aboard *Alert*, where preparations for the morning's departure were already in motion.

"I regret the incident with Miguel," Elena said at last. "Luisa's loyalty to family tradition outweighed her affection for me. I should have foreseen her action."

"The matter is resolved," Nicholas said gently. "Your cousin conducted himself with honor, and the outcome satisfies the formalities of a gentleman's code."

"And now you sail for England," she murmured. Her voice was steady, but the tension in her clasped hands betrayed the effort behind it. "While I return to Spain, eventually. Different winds, carrying us toward different duties."

"We return to your philosophy in the end," Nicholas observed, half-smiling. "That feeling alone cannot overcome the structures that define our lives."

"Perhaps." She turned to face him fully, her dark eyes catching the lantern light. "But I find cold comfort in philosophy tonight."

Nicholas reached for her hand, and she gave it to him without hesitation.

"I've been instructed not to contact you or your family again—not until peace is concluded, that is. What would you have of me, Elena? That I abandon my commission? That you renounce your family? Neither path leads to happiness, only to different forms of regret."

"I would have exactly this," she said, her voice firm but thick with feeling. "These final minutes, undistracted by regret for what cannot be, or illusions about what may come. No promises. No lies. Just presence, honest and whole."

Her words struck him with particular force. Throughout his career, Nicholas had trained himself to be wholly present in critical moments—to focus utterly in the chaos of combat or the nuance of command. That same discipline now anchored him here, beside her, allowing him to feel the weight of each breath, each glance, each second slipping past.

"Then we shall have this," he said quietly, drawing her into his arms.

Their final embrace held all the intensity of their earlier meetings, but it was shaped now by something deeper, an understanding that this parting was not a failure, but a choice forced by circumstance. They had found a kind of truth together, however briefly, and it would remain with them.

When the agreed time had passed, they stood. Their farewell was conducted with formal restraint that belied the depth of feeling beneath. No oaths, no weeping, no impossible vows—only a quiet acknowledgment that something had passed between them that neither time nor distance would quite undo.

"Fair winds and following seas, Commander Cruwys," Elena said as they stood at the pavilion's edge.

"Vaya con Dios, Doña Elena," Nicholas replied, bowing over her hand one final time.

She held his gaze a moment longer.

"I may write once there is peace," she said, soft but deliberate. "No promises—only intention."

"Then I may reply," he said. "Without expectation, but not without hope."

They separated without another word, each turning toward the structured worlds that awaited them, he to *Alert* and the crossing ahead, she to diplomatic escort and the long road back to Spain once Don Francisco's negotiations concluded. As Nicholas walked through the darkened streets of Kingston toward the harbour where his gig waited, he carried with him not only memories of Elena but also a perspective he had not possessed before their meeting: an understanding that duty and desire need not always exist in perfect alignment, that the disciplined naval officer and the passionate man might coexist within the same individual without fatal contradiction.

The insight brought to mind something Harrington had told him during their time in London, when they had discussed the complexities of balancing naval duty with personal inclinations over brandy in the library of the Westborne townhouse: "The finest officers I've known have always been men of passion as well as duty. It's not the absence of desire that makes a commander effective, but rather how he channels such impulses. The totally dispassionate man lacks the fire needed when circumstances demand extraordinary measures."

Alert sailed with the morning tide, past Port Royal and into the open Caribbean. From the quarterdeck, Nicholas watched Jamaica's mountains recede into the distance, their peaks gradually dissolving into the haze of tropical humidity that marked the horizon.

Two days after leaving Jamaica, the sea lay broad and blue to the farthest rim of vision, stirred only by the long, slow breathing of the Gulf Stream and the fresh breeze blowing from the southwest. *Alert*, sailing north with the Stream and the wind three points free on the larboard tack, moved easily through the gentle swell, her taut canvas drawing full and silent. Her wake was a luminous seam in the water, flecked with foam and trailing like silk behind her raked transom.

The world was all sail and sea. No land. No sound but the wind and the murmurous hush of water sliding past the hull. The schooner heeled gracefully to the wind like a creature built for such motion — not burdened with it, but made whole by it. Her large fore and aft sails and all three jibs were set, as was her square top'sl, and the canvas glowed in the light of the setting sun.

Nicholas stood at the taffrail, hands easy at his back, watching the last light catch the curve of the mainsail and kindle along the brass of the binnacle. The air was warm still, touched with salt and sun-blanched wood, and faintly scented with pine tar and lemon peel from the deck seams. Somewhere forward, a bosun's mate hummed an air from Devon — low, tuneless, content — and the helmsman adjusted course slightly.

The ship lived beneath them in a manner that no landbound dwelling could ever emulate. Every stay and shroud resonated with its own note as the breeze played them like the strings of some vast marine instrument; each creak of spar and crack of canvas contributed to the complex symphony that only a sailor's ear could fully comprehend. Here, Nicholas reflected, was something approaching perfection—not ease, for the sea granted that to no man who ventured upon it—but rather that rare equilibrium where all elements stood in proper relation. A harmony of wind, of the sea streaming along the shapely hull, of seasoned timber flexing just enough but never too much, and of human hands making the minute adjustments that kept this intricate balance intact. It was, he thought, what landsmen could never understand and what kept sailors returning despite all hazards—this moment when man, vessel, and the great forces of nature achieved a brief but transcendent unity.

They would ride the stream north another day or two before turning for the Banks. For this rare, perfect evening, there existed only the ship, her people, and the measureless ocean.

CHAPTER SIX

The tide was making upriver, sluggish with seaweed and the fallen leaves of autumn, as *Alert* beat carefully along the broad grey reaches of the Thames toward Gravesend in the early morning of the 14th of October 1782.

It had been nearly eight weeks since she had cleared the Windward Passage between Cuba and Hispaniola, leaving Port Royal and the Caribbean astern—a long passage for a vessel of her qualities, the result of two separate gales in the north Atlantic, the first south of Sable Island. Now, at last, after weeks of nothing but the immensity of ocean and sky, the open sea had yielded first to the confined waters of the Channel, and now the narrowness of the river, bordered by the gentle contours of civilization. The Kentish hills sloped away from the southern shore, their flanks patched with the tawny brown of harvested wheat fields and segmented by the ancient network of weathered stone walls that had defined this landscape since Tudor times. The air hung cool and damp against the skin, carrying the mingled scents of salt marsh, river mud exposed by the ebbing tide, and the rich decay of leaf-mould from the wooded slopes beyond. A thin autumnal haze lay over the estuary like a gauze veil, not the acrid pall of coal smoke that would greet them farther upriver, but rather the gentle exhalation of the season itself—England breathing out the last warmth of summer and drawing in the first chill intimations of winter

Nicholas stood on the weather side of the quarterdeck, his coat collar turned up against the keen east wind that so often plagued the Thames approaches. His posture, hands clasped behind his back in the habitual stance of a naval officer, revealed nothing of his inner thoughts to the practiced eyes of his subordinates. But there existed nonetheless a certain tautness in the line of his jaw, a careful stillness in his grey-green eyes as they surveyed the familiar English shore, that suggested a man who approached his return to England with something less than unalloyed pleasure.

Shall we anchor here, sir?" asked Lieutenant Forester at his shoulder, speaking in that moderated tone that officers learn to use on the quarterdeck—not so loud as to be overheard by the hands manning the braces, yet clear enough to carry over the sound of wind in the rigging and water along the hull. His question was more than mere inquiry about their present station; it contained within it all the complex protocols of a King's ship returning to home waters after foreign service, the necessary formalities of customs inspection, health certification, and the formal reporting of their arrival to the Admiralty.

"Aye. Gravesend will do." Nicholas nodded, his voice equally measured. "Have the gig readied. I'll take the packet forward myself."

The best bower anchor splashed down from the cathead in a shower of foam, its cable rumbling through the hawse as the hands on deck braced the yards aback and clewed up the courses with practiced efficiency. *Alert*, her way gradually diminishing, swung her head into the tide as her canvas was gathered and furled to the booms, a ship handling evolution executed with the silent precision that spoke of a well-found vessel under proper discipline.

In his cabin he knelt beside the sea chest of japanned cedar that had accompanied him since his wanderings aboard a Portuguese trader in the Pacific. His hands moved with the methodical care of one accustomed to stowing and retrieving possessions in the perpetual motion of a sea-going vessel, gathering the essential items for his journey to the Admiralty: the dispatch case of red Morocco leather wrapped in tarred canvas against the river's damp, his sword, a pair of Henry Nock pistols, a small valise containing two shirts, a fresh neck-cloth, a second pair of stockings, and the few other necessities for what he hoped would be a brief sojourn in London. The maritime life, he reflected, had a remarkable way of reducing a man's material existence to its bare essentials. Unlike his landed counterparts with their households full of possessions, a sea officer's worldly goods must fit within a chest measuring forty inches by twenty-four, with a corresponding economy of attachment. He changed into his best uniform coat—a superfine of that particular deep blue that the Admiralty had specified in the '67 regulations, cut long in the tails as was the fashion, with white lapels and facings, and bearing just the modest gold braid at the cuffs appropriate to a commander rather than a post-captain. His silk neck-cloth was arranged with care but without ostentation, secured by a plain gold pin. His boots had been cleaned to a respectable if not brilliant shine, no easy accomplishment after weeks at sea, though the persistent crystals of salt still lingered in the welted seams, resistant to even the most diligent brushing.

A knock at the door by the marine sentry. "First Lieutenant, sir."

"Enter," Nicholas replied, securing the leather straps of his valise with a practiced movement.

Forester stepped inside, ducking slightly to clear the low overhead beams despite his only moderate height—one of those unconscious adaptations that all but the most newly commissioned officers developed after sufficient time at sea. His hat was tucked precisely under his left arm according to regulations, his expression that carefully composed blend of formality and familiarity appropriate to a first lieutenant reporting to his commander while they were alone.

'There's a Trinity House pilot aboard the coal hoy lying a cable's length off our starboard quarter, sir,' he said, 'who rowed across specifically to pass the news. He comes direct from Woolwich and says they've been speaking peace in Paris these three weeks past. No formal articles signed as yet, but the negotiations have advanced considerably. He says the Admiralty has already begun the cull.' He hesitated fractionally before adding, 'Officers without interest or particular distinction are being turned out like lanterns after the morning watch, scores of them already on half-pay, and more to follow when the preliminaries are signed."

Nicholas gave a slow, deliberate nod. "Expected, given what we heard from that Dutch East Indiaman we spoke in the Channel three days since," he said, recalling the portly master of the Zeeland vessel who had hailed them off the North Foreland with news already old at Amsterdam. "The Shelburne ministry can ill afford to continue the war, not with the French fleet still powerful despite Rodney's victory, and the Treasury coffers depleted after these seven years of conflict. Peace may well be necessary, but it shall come at considerable cost to those who wear the King's coat without the good fortune of influential connections."

Their camaraderie had developed into something approaching friendship—insofar as the rigid hierarchies of naval service permitted such a relationship between commander and lieutenant. They had shared the confined quarters, immediate perils, and occasional triumphs that forge bonds stronger than those known to landsmen. Within the strict bounds of naval propriety, they had achieved that rare balance where formal address on deck gave way to Christian names in the privacy of the cabin, without any diminution of the respect essential to proper discipline. Nicholas turned to Forester, noting the slight creases of concern at the corners of the older man's eyes.

"You've your prize share at least, Michael," he said, "Near £1,500—a tidy sum for a lieutenant, even in these uncertain times."

"Yes, a veritable fortune by any lieutenant's reckoning," Forester acknowledged, with the air of a man who still couldn't quite believe his good fortune. "Sufficient, I dare say, to purchase a modest estate in the country. Or to live in considerable ease for five or six years in London. Longer still, with a prudent hand and some investment in the Funds, especially with half-pay between appointments. I know I'm vastly more fortunate than many, particularly those poor devils who've seen no prize action these past years in the Channel Fleet."

He straightened almost imperceptibly, a subtle shift that Nicholas recognized as the prelude to unwelcome news. "But there's more from our loquacious pilot. Sheerness Yard is filled to overflowing with vessels being decommissioned. Every available mooring and careening berth is occupied, with more ships arriving weekly as the squadrons are reduced." He hesitated fractionally. "The word among the dock officers is that *Alert* may not even be laid up in ordinary with the possibility of future recommission. They say she's to be sold outright at public auction—like so much surplus merchandise now that her usefulness to the service has ended."

Nicholas stared, losing his habitual composure. "Sold, by God!"

"Yes, sir. Quietly," Forester confirmed, his voice lowered though there was no one to overhear them."

The news struck him with unexpected force. There was a chance it was wrong, but rumors among pilots and other professionals along the waterfront rarely were.

Alert was no ordinary vessel to be lightly discarded at the convenient end of hostilities. She had been built with the uncommon skill that characterized the best American shipwrights, her frames and planking fashioned from seasoned live oak harvested from the southern forests that the Crown had once, in its imperial wisdom, reserved exclusively for Royal Navy construction—timber that now, ironically, served His Majesty after its brief service to rebellion.

Nicholas had come to cherish *Alert* with what he recognized as the particular, perhaps unreasonable affection, that a naval officer invariably feels for his first command. This despite her obvious limitations: her 'tween decks were so confined that he could not stand fully upright in his own cabin except directly beneath the small skylight where the deck-beams were notched to provide those extra three inches of clearance, while the gunrooom would accommodate no more than four officers at dinner, and even then they dined with their elbows pressed together like schoolboys rather than King's officers. Yet even with the peace negotiations advancing in Paris, it made remarkably little sense that the Lords of the Admiralty would so readily dispose of such a vessel. Small, fast schooners were perpetually in demand regardless of the formal state of hostilities, whether for carrying urgent dispatches, conducting inshore reconnaissance along hostile coastlines, or performing those particular services of a more discreet nature that an admiral on a foreign station might require.

Perhaps he could find the truth of it in London. The deeper purpose behind the Admiralty's haste to dispose of such a useful vessel might yet be divulged through careful inquiry in the proper quarters, though he held no great expectations on that score. The Lords seldom troubled themselves to explain their decisions to officers of his modest rank.

The chaise rattled through low mist and leaf-rot, the smell of harvest and coal smoke hanging in the air like a London fog transported to the countryside. Nicholas sat upright, sword at his boot, the dispatch packet secure beside him. His thoughts turned unbidden from the Gulf Stream, from sunlit rigging and the deep hush between ocean swells, and then, with unwelcome persistence, to the *San Isidro* and Elena.

The road into London was long and wet. The chaise clattered over rutted roads beneath a slate-coloured sky, the air thick with damp earth and chimney smoke, as though autumn and winter had conspired to present the least favourable aspect of England to a man too long in warmer climes. Nicholas passed the hours in silence, neither sleeping nor truly awake, recalling instead the feel of a canoe paddle in his hand, the taste of salt on the wind, the extraordinary clarity of South Pacific mornings that now seemed more imagined than lived.

He was shown into the Admiralty by a junior clerk with little ceremony and less interest, a balding potbellied man who regarded naval officers as merely one more species of petitioner to be managed with minimal effort. The waiting room was cold, lit by one guttering lamp whose oil had not been replenished since early morning. After nearly an hour, he was admitted not to the First Lord's chamber, nor even the outer committee room where captains of consequence might expect to be received, but to a minor office down a narrow hall, where a thin man with copper-rimmed spectacles accepted the package and his reports with no expression at all.

"Commander Cruwys?"

"Yes."

"This concerns the *San Isidro*?"

"It does. Taken under orders from Admiral Hood."

The man glanced at the seals without breaking them. "You are instructed to remain in London until further notice."

"No additional orders?"

"None at present."

"Am I to be informed—?"

"You will be contacted. Please provide an address to the clerk once you have one."

Nicholas left the building in silence. Behind him, a great brass clock ticked above a still hearth, its pendulum swinging with the same implacable regularity that governed Admiralty decisions, indifferent to the fates of the men who served beneath its roof.

He took a set of rooms at The Old White Horse, an inn just off Jermyn Street: private staircase, fire laid daily, decent plain fare. Though his prize money from the *San Isidro* and other captures would permit far grander accommodations, he chose this establishment for its unassuming character and the discrete habits of its proprietor. He dined on cold beef and small beer, then sat for a time by the bow window, looking over the street below where oil lamps cast pools of yellow light at intervals along the cobblestones, and link-boys with their flaming torches guided gentlemen from their carriages to doorways through the evening gloom.

If the rumor about *Alert* was correct, Nicholas had no ship now, no active patronage to counter what seemed a veiled displeasure, or certainly an indifference, of the Admiralty. Forester would vanish into the fleet lists, uncalled. Markham—if he was lucky—might find his way to a merchant quarterdeck. Parker, still green, might yet be shaped into a proper officer if he also was fortunate enough to find a ship.

The note arrived the next morning, its hand unmistakable in its decisive strokes and economical flourishes—the penmanship of a man accustomed to having his instructions obeyed without question or delay:

Commander Cruwys— I understand you are newly arrived. I would be pleased to receive you at my house this evening. We dine at six. —Westborne"

The house in Grosvenor Square was as he remembered it: the Turkish carpet in the entry was unchanged, its blues and crimsons subdued by English light. The silver was polished to warmth, not glitter, displaying the confidence of old wealth that required no ostentation. Morley, the butler, met him at the door with his usual economy, a man who had spent decades perfecting the art of presence without intrusion

"Commander Cruwys. Welcome home, sir."

"Thank you, Morley."

He was shown to the drawing room, where Viscount Westborne stood by the hearth in a coat of dark plum that spoke of wealth with the same quiet confidence as his house—rich fabric and perfect tailoring that required no embellishment or modern excess. A folio lay closed on the desk, its red leather binding suggesting state papers rather than personal correspondence.

"Nicholas."

"My lord."

Westborne smiled faintly. "None of that here. You are thinner."

"I've been better fed aboard than ashore."

"And salt preserves. In that case, let us proceed to dinner."

They moved toward the dining room in companionable silence, the subdued flicker of candlelight playing along the polished rails of the banister and gleaming faintly upon the brass finials. The air held the clean scent of beeswax and old books, and from some distant part of the house came the faint chime of a clock marking the quarter hour.

The dining room—known in the household simply as the blue salon—was as Nicholas remembered: dark paneled walls softened by tapestries in muted tones, silver laid with understated precision, and a long table set for three beneath a canopy of discreet candlelight. As they settled into their chairs, the double doors opened with a quiet grace, and Morley announced, "Rear Admiral Matthew Trevenen, my lord."

Nicholas rose, surprised despite himself, as Rear Admiral Trevenen entered with the composed step of a man accustomed to both ceremony and consequence. He had last seen his distant relation three years before, in Gibraltar, then a senior post captain. Now he wore the uniform of his new rank with the same quiet authority, the gold lace on his cuffs and the distinctive arrangement of buttons gleaming faintly in the candlelight. "Sir—I didn't know—my congratulations, of course."

Trevenen inclined his head. "It seemed an appropriate moment to see you again, Nicholas."

Trevenen took his seat without further explanation, his expression unreadable but not cold. Westborne, watching the exchange with faint amusement, sipped his wine and said, "Be seated, Nicholas."

Supper was well-paced: roast duck with bitter orange, celeriac, a tart of chestnut and mushroom. The claret had been decanted without comment. Trevenen ate sparingly, as ever. Westborne allowed the silence to hold until the second course had passed. Then, with his glass turning slowly between his fingers, he said, "The peace will be signed soon. At Paris, if not Madrid."

Trevenen gave a soft grunt. "Too soon, some would say. Rodney not least."

Nicholas looked between them. "He's written strongly against terms, sir. Claimed we win at sea and give it back on paper."

"Rodney wins at sea," said Trevenen. "But he is no diplomat. And the City is not inclined to pay for more victories."

Westborne added, "Nor is the Commons, now that the war has crossed its crest. Lord North's ministry collapsed last spring, and since Rockingham's premature death in July, Shelburne has spent the past months trying to settle the business. The Americans negotiate through Franklin, Adams, and Jay. Preliminary articles are expected to be signed before the end of the year."

Nicholas absorbed this. "Then it is done?"

"Nearly," said Westborne. "The formal treaty will take longer. Spain and France remain at table. But the direction is set."

"And the Navy, sir? Are we to be idle?"

Trevenen sipped. "We are to be lean. Squadrons will be reduced, many ships laid up in ordinary, crews dismissed."

Westborne studied his port. "Even those officers with fine records may find themselves on half-pay. Not disgrace—but no invitation either."

Nicholas inclined his head. "And those with enemies?"

"Wait longer," said Trevenen. There was a pause. The candles flickered faintly in the draft. Then Westborne said, without turning:

"I understand from Henry's letter you carried home that you stood in a duel. In Kingston. Over the Valdés woman, was it not?"

Nicholas felt his face grow unexpectedly warm. With all he had experienced since, gales, silence at the Admiralty, the strangeness of London, this mention struck deeper than he had thought it might.

"Yes," he said quietly. "Doña Elena Maria Valdés y Castellano."

Trevenen arched an eyebrow. "Over an insult?"

"Over her honour," Nicholas replied, his voice steady again. "An accusation—it touched on her reputation."

"Were you the challenger?"

"No, sir. I was challenged. Miguel Álvarez y Valdés—Elena's cousin. A captain in the Spanish Royal Guard. Nephew to Don Francisco."

"And Henry stood as your second?" Westborne asked.

Nicholas nodded. "He handled it with precision. Quietly."

"I was pleased with his letter," said Westborne. "No excess. No loose ends. And the outcome?"

"First blood. Small-swords. He pressed hard—high lines, classic Spanish form. I slipped the fifth pass and touched his forearm. Clean. Nothing serious. He stepped back. That was the end of it."

"Formal but fair," said Trevenen.

"Just so," said Nicholas.

Westborne nodded once. "I am glad Henry stood with you. And that you gave him no cause to regret it."

There was a pause, not awkward, but deliberate, as though each man were weighing what had just been said against what was still to come. The candles flickered slightly in the draught. Then Trevenen, his voice quieter now, said: "And Doña Elena? You've said little."

Nicholas looked toward the hearth, the glow of the coals catching faintly in the rim of his glass.

"She was composed. I believe she knew more than she allowed, and less than she feared. She had been placed in a difficult position—by her uncle, and by the Spanish crown's needs. But not unwillingly, I think. The ciphered packet came from her cabin. And several of the letters that bore the Viceroy's seal from La Habana. She did what was asked of her, as any loyal subject might."

He paused. "I've thought of writing to her. I may yet—when the peace is made."

"She travelled under her uncle's protection?" said Trevenen.

"Yes. Don Francisco Valdés claimed diplomatic status, but my orders, which were later confirmed by the Admiralty Court in Jamaica, were that *San Isidro* was also carrying out trade, and a legitimate target."

Westborne raised an eyebrow. "There are older ties. Don Francisco has operated out of Cádiz for over twenty years, often under diplomatic cover."

He glanced toward Trevenen. "And the girl's mother was a Mildmay."

Nicholas looked up, surprised. "I didn't know."

"No," Westborne said mildly. "You weren't meant to."

Nicholas frowned, then turned his eyes to the amber in his glass. "But her uncle—Don Francisco—he wasn't acting alone. There was a pattern to the transmissions in the documents I read: Lisbon, Bombay, a few routed through Trieste. It might be coincidence. But it looked coordinated, at least in part."

Westborne said nothing. But the glance he exchanged with Trevenen was sharp, and not at all casual.

"It's seldom only the foreign hand," Trevenen said. "Packets of that sort don't move halfway across the globe without a little help. Not unless someone ensures the gates are left unguarded."

Nicholas lifted his head. "You mean here."

"I mean precisely here," Trevenen said, his voice low. "In London. In the Ministry. Perhaps higher still."

Westborne turned his glass between his fingers. "The Mildmays have been threaded through the civil apparatus for a generation—Treasury, Board of Trade, even a cousin in Foreign Intelligence. It would not be the first time one of their number facilitated something inconvenient for the Admiralty, though that's a long step from treason in war."

He paused a beat, then added, "Lord Ashton is distantly tied to the Mildmays, through his mother's line. I believe she was a second cousin to the late Sir Peregrine."

Nicholas said nothing, but he felt himself tense.

"Which may mean nothing," Westborne went on, with a trace of irony. "But then again, it may not."

"Curious," said Trevenen, almost to himself, "how loyalty so often finds itself on the losing side of convenience."

Later, Westborne poured the brandy himself.

Trevenen took a sip, looked at Nicholas, his gaze steady but unreadable.

"*Alert* is gone," he said. "Not reassigned. Laid up at Sheerness. Likely to be sold."

Nicholas looked down into his glass. "*Pylades*."

Trevenen gave a faint nod. "Yes. Because you outsailed her before Hood's entire squadron off Barbados. Because you made a heavier, better-connected ship look slow. Because you were not supposed to win."

Nicholas said nothing for a moment. The silence in the room was not tense, precisely, but it held weight.

"Hood was satisfied," Trevenen continued. "He said as much. And meant it. But he's a fighting admiral, not a political one. And Fanshawe's family has a long reach."

"You're telling me I've given them a reason to remember my name—for the wrong reason."

A flicker of amusement touched Trevenen's mouth, for he recognized his own words to Nicholas when they last met. "Not precisely, Nicholas. I'm telling you that you are not under censure. But nor are you in favour. And in London, the absence of favour is often just as final."

Nicholas exhaled slowly. "That has the feel of instruction."

"It is," said Westborne.

They all rose in accord, the scrape of chairs soft against the carpet. They drank to the King.

Westborne extended a card between two fingers. "Mr. Levering will call on you tomorrow. Three addresses, all in Half Moon Street. Not too grand. Not too mean. You'll choose."

Nicholas took the card, turned it once in his hand. "Very good."

Westborne nodded. "A man who speaks little may be forgotten—or remembered, depending on who's listening."

Trevenen, standing near the hearth, glanced toward the curtained window. "Watch everything. Speak little. Someone will call."

As he stepped back into the damp London light, Nicholas felt not released, but repositioned. The clerk's indifference, the absence of formal instruction, the sealed packet received with no more ceremony than a butcher's bill, all bespoke a system that already knew what it intended of him, though had yet to admit it aloud.

And now *Alert*—not reassigned, not held in reserve, but to be *sold*. No explanation. The vessel he had brought through squalls and reef-strewn channels, whose rig and keel he had come to know as one knows the shape of thought, was to vanish from the lists without ceremony. Not for want of usefulness, for she was fast, responsive, and sound. But she had outsailed *Pylades*, and *Pylades* was a Fanshawe ship. That had not been forgotten.

Yet even the supposed sale rang hollow. Too quiet. Too soon. It had the feel of pretext, removing him from notice, appearing to discard him, while in truth keeping him close to hand. But not officially so.

There was something in the *San Isidro* affair that had travelled farther than cipher or silver. Something that had passed through Habana, yes, but reached back to London by channels less visible. He had known Westborne as Henry Harrington's father: patrician, distant, and influential in the way aristocrats are expected to be. But now it was clear the man was more than that. He was involved. And not merely as an observer. He and Trevenen had spoken in concert, like men who had rehearsed a part in which Nicholas was not the audience but the subject.

The names came too carefully now, shadowed but unmistakable, Ashton and the Mildmays. Bloodlines and influence, a web spun generations deep. He had not stumbled into this. He had been placed. Prepared. And now—perhaps—deployed.

Whatever this was, it no longer resembled war as he had known it. This was something colder, more deliberate. An old game, played in drawing rooms and chancelleries, by men who did not speak in orders but in implications. And it had the scent of betrayal, not shouted from a masthead, but written in careful hands, passed from fireside to dispatch box, unspoken.

The door latched softly behind Nicholas, and silence settled like dust in the stillness that followed. Only the fire moved, its light playing across the brass work and the pale sea-chart tacked above the hearth.

Trevenen remained by the mantel, glass in hand, his stance easy but watchful.

"He's changed," he said, not as observation but as fact.

Westborne, now returned to his chair, nodded once. "Since Gibraltar?"

"Markedly. He was already accomplished then—Cook's best assistant surveyor, a real seaman, steady under pressure. He'd killed, yes. Fought with his hands. But the shape of him was still forming. There was honour, but not weight."

"And now?"

Trevenen studied the fire a moment. "Now I see a line in the jaw. A man who's been tested hard and not found wanting. He's been in a fleet action and done well, seen much blood spilled at close quarters. He's fought and killed—more than once now. And he bears it."

Westborne offered nothing, but poured a little more brandy into Trevenen's glass with the quiet precision of an old habit.

"He was always capable," Trevenen went on, "but now he's—how do you say it—stripped to weight. No vanity. No fret. He's become what he was meant to be."

"*Alert* did that," Westborne murmured. "And Hood."

"Aye." Trevenen swirled the brandy once. "And the girl."

Westborne glanced toward the empty chair Nicholas had just vacated. "Doña Elena."

Trevenen's mouth tightened—not in disapproval, exactly, but in the weary recognition of a pattern well known. "He would not have crossed swords unless it mattered."

"No," said Westborne. "He wouldn't. But she was not innocent of intrigue. Don Francisco and the Spanish made good use of her."

"He knows that. Knows it now, at least."

"And still considers writing to her," Westborne added softly, almost to himself.

The fire snapped sharply in the grate.

After a moment, Trevenen said, "Thornhill will want him."

"He already does. Asked if I had a name. I told him I might. But he'll need your leave."

"My leave or my silence?"

Westborne raised one brow.

Trevenen exhaled through his nose, long and slow. "He's a naval officer, James. That's what he is. You set him adrift among shadows, he may not know which way's up."

"He'll learn. He already has. And there are things moving below the waterline now—things we cannot address through a ship's broadside or a court-martial."

"He's not trained for that work."

"No," Westborne said. "But he is willing to see what most men choose to ignore. And—" here he leaned back slightly in his chair "—he has already proved that he knows how to keep his own counsel."

Trevenen said nothing for a time. Then, without looking up: "His bearing's altered, but his sense of proportion remains. That's rare."

"I would not send him if it weren't."

Another pause. The clock ticked faintly in the corner.

Finally, Trevenen spoke. "Then speak to Thornhill. I'll not stand in the way. But he doesn't go blind into it—not like the others. He's owed the truth, or something near it."

Westborne nodded once. "Thank you, Matthew. He'll have it. Or as much as any of us do."

They drank without toasting. The coals hissed down in the grate. Outside, the fog pressed close against the glass, and a night-watchman's rattle passed faintly on the street below.

CHAPTER SEVEN

Nicholas Cruwys stood in the upper chamber of a house in Half Moon Street, watching a coal fire take its first breath.

The match had been struck with deliberate care, and the paper caught with a whisper, drawing flame into the kindling and stacked coals beneath. The smell was London itself: smoke, brass, and boiled flannel, with the faintest undertone of lavender from the hearth brush.

The room was taller than it was wide, with a ceiling that had once been white but was now the colour of damp chalk. A Turkey carpet in deep red and gold covered the centre of the floor, its pattern softened by years and boot heels. Two wing chairs stood either side of the hearth, upholstered in faded blue wool, their arms worn smooth by unknown hands. A low mahogany table stood between them, flanked by a writing desk of modest size but elegant build—its surface of green tooled leather, its drawers lined in paper flecked with rust.

The west-facing sash window let in a wash of late afternoon light, pale and clean. On the sill sat a ship's glass and a battered volume of Robertson's Elements. Outside, the street moved at a measured rhythm: carriage wheels, boot heels, the occasional cry of an orange girl from Piccadilly.

It was the third property Levering had shown him that day, and by far the least flamboyant. The first had been oppressively furnished, with porcelain spaniels, watercolours of Venice, a rug stiff with lavender. The second, on Cork Street, had windows too large and too low, and a faint but unshakable smell of cats. This, by contrast, was quiet. Well-kept. Dry underfoot. The sort of place where a man might live invisibly, yet comfortably.

He had moved in that morning.

The agent, Mr. Levering, had been precise in both manner and tone—mid-fifties, neither tall nor short, with a style of dress that hovered between valet and chaplain. He had spoken very little, but with weight when he did.

"Her ladyship lived here until last Christmas," he had said, as they ascended the final stair. "Quiet woman. Bookish. No guests. Passed in the chair, by all accounts."

Nicholas had nodded.

"I am instructed," Levering had continued, "to offer these rooms on favourable terms, and without advertising. The house is in the name of Mrs. Dalley, a widow of the cloth. You will find she does not inquire."

They had stepped into the sitting room then, and Nicholas had known at once.

"This one."

The bedchamber was smaller, set back, with a wardrobe of polished walnut, a proper basin stand with Delft jug and bowl, and a looking glass that bore the faint speckling of age around its edges. A narrow fireplace was flanked by two candle sconces; a half-curtained window looked east toward the mews.

He unpacked with the quiet efficiency of the sea: sea chest into the press, spare boots beneath the bed, small books laid out in order—*Falconer*, *Guthrie's Naval Biography*, *Dampier*, *Don Quixote* in an older binding.

From his account at Coutts, he had drawn a modest sum for living expenses, enough to furnish the rooms properly, lay in coal, and pay for linen service without extravagance. The remainder of his prize money from *San Isidro*—just under £3,000—had been invested in the Funds, at the advice of Mr. Lawrence, the bank's senior partner and a man who had once fought a financial duel with a Spanish privateer over rum futures.

Nicholas had no immediate use for a fortune. What he needed was position, and time.

His days assumed the tempo of discretion.

On the first day he woke early, as he had aboard ship, shaved with care, and walked west—across the Park, beneath the limes of Green Street, and along the colonnades where merchants arranged their wares. He visited the Anchor and Crown most afternoons, where officers with sharp coats and dull eyes read the *Gazette* beneath portraits of Anson, Rodney, and Hawke. The club steward recognised him at once, admitted him without comment, and set him up with the *Naval Chronicle*, a cut-glass tumbler, and a chair by the fire.

The talk was quiet. The faces, measured. Peace was coming, it seemed. And with it, the attrition of commissions.

One week into his new routine, Nicholas opened the *London Gazette* brought by the steward with the afternoon post and laid it out with quiet precision, alongside a decanter of Madeira and a plate of roast mutton, sliced thin and served with a dab of sharp mustard.

Nicholas turned the pages absently—Parliamentary proceedings, trade movements, a letter from Vienna—until a familiar name caught his eye.

> *Admiralty Office, 12th of October, 1782*
> *A letter has been received from Captain Henry Walsh, commanding His Majesty's Ship Triton, dated the fifth of September, off Martinique:*

> *Sir,*
>
> *I have the honour to inform you that on the 1st of this month, at dawn, the frigate under my command, while cruising in latitude 14° 43' N, Martinique bearing SW approximately three leagues, sighted a sail bearing NNW, which upon approach was identified as the French frigate Hébé, of 36 guns, chiefly eighteen-pounders.*
>
> *The enemy stood toward us, and we bore up to engage. At approximately two o'clock in the afternoon, Triton, having the advantage of the wind, manœuvred such that we raked the enemy twice from stern quarters, and then closed within pistol-shot and exchanged broadsides.*
>
> *The action was spirited and lasted fifty-five minutes, during which the superior steadiness and execution of our fire proved decisive. The Hébé, having suffered considerable damage and the loss of her mainmast, struck her colours at three o'clock. Our own casualties amounted to five seamen killed and fifteen wounded. The conduct of the officers and crew, particularly at the guns, was exemplary throughout.*
>
> *I have the honour to be, Sir, your most obedient and humble servant,*
>
> *H. Walsh, Captain.*

Nicholas read it through again, more slowly. He could picture it—the deep blue of the Atlantic sea off the northeastern shore of Martinique, Walsh standing at the break of the quarterdeck with that stillness he always wore in a fight, never raising his voice, never needing to. The well-trained crew allowing *Triton* to manoeuvre for effect, the guns laid true.

There was no self-congratulation in the letter, but Nicholas knew what it meant. A 28-gun frigate, armed with nine pounders, had taken a heavier opponent cleanly. The account was characteristic of Walsh: precise, unembellished, and free of vanity.

Recalling their last meeting, Nicholas remembered Walsh's counsel and the quiet confidence he had instilled. The successful action and capture of a superior French frigate underscored the merit of Walsh's command.

He folded the paper with care, set it aside, and sat back, eyes on the fire. The tides and winds were shifting. And not all fortunes rose on the same wind.

A week later, the next *Gazette* brought the expected sequel:

Admiralty Office, 19th of October 1782
Captain H. Walsh, late of His Majesty's Frigate Triton, has been appointed to Fortunée, 40-guns, for Channel service.

Nicholas nodded once. *Fortunée*—a fast, powerful ship by all accounts. Originally a French frigate, taken four years earlier off Grenada, and now one of the most formidable on the list. A plum, and rightly earned. Walsh was a fighting officer, and yet perhaps there was more to his connections than Nicholas had guessed.

No new orders arrived. But on the twelfth morning, Mrs. Dalley handed him an envelope with her usual deference.

"It was placed upon the hall table, sir. I did not see the hand."

The note was folded twice. No seal. No name.

You are being watched. But not, yet, asked. Be patient. The wind shifts soon.

The hand was narrow, deliberate, unfamiliar—the writing of someone accustomed to discretion rather than display. Nicholas burned it in the grate that evening after supper, watching the wax blacken and fall inward upon itself, the paper curling to ash with a faint blue flame at its edges. He stirred the embers once with the brass poker until no trace remained, then resumed his seat by the window, where the last light of day had faded to the peculiar luminous dusk of London, neither fully dark nor properly lit, like the uncertain state of his affairs.

Two days later, he glimpsed her for the first time. Not in full view, not with certainty, but in the shifting crowd along Jermyn Street— near a print-seller's window where patriotic engravings of Gibraltar and Dominica were displayed between portraits of celebrated admirals, he saw a figure in dove-grey silk, a familiar profile but one which he could not place, the angle of a head held with particular composure. By the time he turned fully, she had vanished into the press of sedan chairs and coal wagons, leaving only the impression of movement rather than its confirmation.

He said nothing of it to anyone, though he found himself paying closer attention to the streets as he walked them, noting faces that appeared more than once, the occasional hackney that seemed to maintain pace with his own progress, the small signs of observation that his years at sea had trained him to detect. Subtle disturbances in the natural flow of things that indicated purpose rather than chance.

On the afternoon of the fourteenth day he again went to the Anchor and Crown. Taking a chair near the hearth in the reading room, he nodded to the steward, and turned the page of a printed debate from the previous week — *House Enquiry on the Portuguese Trade Bill* — and read no more than two lines before closing it again.

The fire offered no heat. He sat with his hands folded, watching the coals collapse by degree.

"Cruwys."

He looked up.

Captain Henry Walsh stood before him, hat in hand, his best uniform coat of navy blue broadcloth darker than it had been in the islands, the gold braid on the cuff newly relaid though with a certain economy. He looked well, though leaner, and more still.

"Captain," Nicholas said, rising, and they shook hands briefly, without ceremony, the clasp of men who had shared a weather deck in a blow.

"I heard you were promoted commander by Hood. Well-deserved I'm sure." Walsh said, eyes taking in Nicholas's civilian attire with the merest flicker. "Though I didn't expect you here, at a club in London."

"Nor I," Nicholas said. "But here I am. And, sir, my hearty congratulations on your action and appointment to *Fortunée*. I read your dispatch in the *Gazette* and the service was still talking of it when I first arrived."

Walsh nodded, "My crew fought well, and in the end superior gunnery told."

They sat, two chairs angled toward the fire, which hissed occasionally as a drop of rain found its way down the chimney. Nicholas leaned closer to the warmth, a habit he had developed since his return to England. The perpetual chill of London had settled in his bones in a way the fiercest gale at sea never had. Each morning he woke with a profound longing for the brilliant light of Jamaica, for the warm Trade winds that had once filled his lungs and sails alike.

The silence between them had no awkwardness, punctuated only by the ticking of the longcase clock and the distant sound of glasses from the card room.

"You've no ship." Walsh said, not a question but a statement of the obvious, in the naval way.

"None offered. My sloop *Alert* was ordered to Sheerness as soon as we returned from the Islands."

Walsh nodded, "I heard about her . . . and indeed something about wiping the eye of a frigate also from Hood's squadron commanded by one of the Fanshawes." He looked at Nicholas thoughtfully. "I've been at the Admiralty this week. Briefings, courtesies. Tea served in those damned shallow cups, and tall chairs designed by some landsman who never learned to sit with a deck moving under him."

"And?" Nicholas leaned forward slightly.

"They're cleaning house," Walsh said, lowering his voice though no one sat near. "Or rearranging it. The preliminaries are signed in Paris, or soon will be. Those without titles or a fighting interest in Parliament are advised to keep their voices low and their expectations lower."

Nicholas said nothing. The darkness of these shortening London days as October turned to November oppressed him more than he cared to admit—grudging daylight under leaden skies, so unlike the vivid splendor of the South Pacific he had known as a midshipman in his youth. For more than eighteen months he had lived and loved among the natives of the Society Islands of Tahiti and Bora Bora. There, even the storms had a certain glory, but it was if memories of that paradise he found at age seventeen were fading like a receding tide. He was only twenty-two, but at times he felt older. Here, the gloom seemed to extend from the skies to the Admiralty corridors to the very soul of the city. A young man might bear it easily enough, but he had seen too much of blue waters and unspoiled shores to reconcile himself to this gray purgatory.

"You'll not like this city," Walsh added, after a moment, glancing at the rain-spattered window. "Too much hurry and scheming, and not enough horizon."

"I don't intend to stay long. Just until matters are settled."

"That," said Walsh, taking a pinch of snuff from a silver box that had once belonged to a French captain, "is a good instinct. London has a way of making a sailor forget his proper element."

They sat a little longer. Walsh refused the steward's offer of tea with a sailor's preference for stronger drink or none. Nicholas declined a second glass of Madeira.

When Walsh rose, he offered his hand again, and Nicholas noted the fresh scar across the knuckles, still pink and new.

"If they do offer you something," he said, "you'll have to take it. The best peacetime commissions go to those with interest. But mind you look carefully at the orders. Just be sure the flag behind it is still flying and not being struck."

Walsh gave a thin smile that didn't reach the weather-lines around his eyes. "Some days I wonder if we haven't fought these seven years only to surrender at the table what we won at sea."

And then he was gone, leaving behind only the faint scent of tobacco and the distant tropical sun that seemed to cling still to men returned from the West Indies.

Nicholas left the Anchor and Crown in the early evening. The lamps in the lower windows along King Street were already being lit, and the clerks from the offices were walking faster, their coats pulled high and their boots ringing harder on the paving stones.

On the sixteenth day, Westborne called.

Not a note this time, nor a messenger. The man himself appeared in a travelling coat of dark drab, hat square upon his brow, gloves of seal-brown leather folded in one hand. Despite the casual nature of his appearance, there was a profound intentionality to it, as though even his apparent informality had been calculated to achieve a specific effect.

"I thought I'd walk," he said by way of greeting, "Too much time in carriages, and one begins to believe the world comes to you rather than the reverse. A damned poor attitude for any man with responsibilities beyond his own comfort."

Nicholas opened the door fully. "You're always welcome, my lord."

"I know."

He stepped inside, looked about the room with the swift, comprehensive glance of a man accustomed to assessing situations at a glance, and nodded with evident satisfaction.

"This will do. This is very good. The carpet's worn enough not to attract envy. The chairs are deep enough to sit and think. And no pianoforte—those wretched instruments that seem designed expressly to prevent conversation of any consequence."

Nicholas smiled. "I've never owned one."

Westborne sat without invitation, a privilege of his rank and their acquaintance. His posture remained erect despite the depth of the chair, as though decades of attendance at the Lords had rendered him incapable of true relaxation.

"Trevenen is watching carefully," he said without preamble. "There is motion at the Admiralty—more than mere gossip or the usual shifting of favor that accompanies a change in ministry. Your name has been mentioned in certain chambers. You are not forgotten."

"I don't feel remembered," Nicholas said, moving to stand by the hearth rather than sitting opposite his visitor.

"You are marked. That is entirely different." Westborne's voice carried the particular cadence of a man accustomed to making distinctions that others might miss but which contained, to his mind, the very essence of understanding.

He leaned back, inspecting the fire with a gaze that seemed to penetrate beyond the mere physical flames, as though reading portents in their movement. The coal settled with a soft hiss.

"When I was a younger man," he said after a contemplative silence, "I once saw an East Indiaman refitted for war—the *Marlborough*, fifty-four guns, a beautiful vessel converted from Company service. She went out for convoy duty under a retired commander, and within a month was back with her foremast gone. When they asked the man what he had done wrong, he said, 'I was ready before they needed me.'"

Nicholas waited, sensing the weight of the anecdote's intended application to his own circumstances.

Westborne looked up, his grey eyes carrying the calm certainty of a chess player who has plotted several moves ahead.

"Do not be too ready. That's all."

And with that cryptic counsel, he rose, nodded once with aristocratic economy of movement, and let himself out with no further ceremony or explanation, leaving Nicholas to consider the precise implications of his words in the lengthening shadows of late afternoon.

Nicholas poured himself a half-measure of the Martinique rum he had carried back from the West Indies—liquid gold in the glass, the color of sunlight through shallow water, and sat in the far chair, where the light fell soft across the desk. The city moved on outside, untroubled by his silence or his thoughts. But the air had changed, as it does before a storm while still far from land, when only a practiced eye can detect the first subtle signs of alteration.

He could feel it. Something was shifting.

The next day the fire had sunk low by the time Nicholas returned to Half Moon Street, after a supper at the Anchor and Crown where naval officers spoke in low tones of ships laid up and commissions withdrawn. Its last heat was drawn into the coals like breath withheld, the grate offering more shadow than warmth. He did not call for fresh light, nor stir the room to wakefulness.

He drew off his gloves and coat with the methodical precision born of shipboard habit, laid them over the back of the nearer chair with a sailor's instinct for order even in darkness, and stood a long while at the window. The glass was weeping slightly, thin trails of condensation drawn down by the cooling of the pane in the winter chill. Outside, the street was muffled by damp and distance: a single carriage lamp moving past in shadow, the brief clatter of iron-clad wheels swallowed by wet stone, a solitary watchman with pike and lantern moving with the slow certainty of a man paid by the hour rather than the mile.

He lit one of the wax tapers from the hearth's dying embers and sat at the writing desk beneath the window. He drew out a sheet of heavy laid paper, pale cream with the subtle watermark of a Dutch mill, and laid it square before him with a precision that brooked no compromise.

He took up his pen, dipped it with care, and wrote:

My dear Elena—

He stopped. The words, when written, seemed both immediate and impossibly remote, as though belonging to a different life or a different man. He watched the ink soak and settle into the fibres, growing less black as it dried. His hand remained still above the page, the nib slightly angled, ready to write more. But no second line came. The gap between intention and expression seemed suddenly unbridgeable, the Atlantic itself no wider than the distance between what he wished to say and what propriety, circumstance, and his own nature would permit.

Admiral Rawley's order, when given those months ago in Jamaica, had been unambiguous: no correspondence, no signal, no contact with the Valdés family until peace was formal and ratified. Not from him. Not from anyone connected to the *San Isidro*. The matter had been judged too delicate—too politically charged, too laden with inference both diplomatic and personal—to permit even the most innocent communication.

And yet he had written the first line.

He folded the page once, left it unsealed like a door neither opened nor properly closed, and slipped it into the drawer beside the copy of *Falconer's Marine Dictionary* and a sheaf of unread *Gazettes*, whose columns studiously avoided any mention of certain negotiations now proceeding in Paris. The drawer closed with a soft click that seemed to echo in the stillness—the sound of something put away but not resolved.

From the hallway came the soft shift of boards: Mrs. Dalley drawing the bolt at the front door, the coal-scuttle replaced near the kitchen hearth with the small domestic sounds that marked the transition from one day to its successor. The house settled into itself, quiet as a tomb but for the occasional creak of timbers contracting in the night's increasing cold.

He rose early.

The morning came on heavy, the kind of London damp that did not fall but simply was: soaked into the mortar, the cloth of one's coat, the back of the throat. The street outside lay under a low weight of sky, the soot of countless chimneys smearing the light into a muted cream, neither daylight nor its absence but the peculiar half-state that made London winters so oppressive to a man accustomed to the clarities of tropical skies.

He walked west through Green Park beneath the remaining plane trees, their leaves turned the colour of old brass. Boots crushed them to paste against stone still wet from overnight mist. A horse passed at a trot along Piccadilly, its hooves clicking hollow on the stone despite the damp. Somewhere behind, a sweep was whistling off-key—not a tune precisely, but a sequence of notes particular to his kind, the sound rising and falling above the smoke from a hundred morning fires.

At the corner of St. James's, he paused.

She was there again. The same figure—grey coat of foreign cut, precise silhouette, hat drawn low over features too fine for complete concealment—standing near the print shop, her posture calm, almost studied. She made no pretense of browsing the window or of being engaged in any particular business. She was not waiting. Nor was she trying not to be seen. Rather, she stood with the peculiar stillness of a person who has selected their position with deliberate care, like a piece correctly placed on a chess board.

He crossed the street. Not hastily, but without wandering, his path as direct as the geometry of London streets would allow.

When he reached the shop, she was gone.

The bell above the door still swayed faintly, its clapper ticking once against the brass like the final increment of time before a fresh accounting. The glass panes held only his own reflection, indistinct against printed scenes of naval glory and the muted outlines of passers-by.

He stepped inside. The room smelled of dust and ink and the faint metallic sharpness of old type. The scent of knowledge preserved and multiplied. Naval prints were pinned along the far wall with the studied randomness of a curator who understands that apparent disorder may increase a customer's sense of discovery: Rodney off Dominica, his ships breaking the French line; The Saints, where British seamanship had prevailed against superior numbers; The Surrender at Savannah, with its delicate suggestion of colonial rebellion suppressed. A caricature of Fox and Shelburne in debate hung near the window, each figure holding a cracked globe, their argument threatening to shatter what little of the world remained intact.

But the woman had left nothing behind—no note, no signal, no dropped handkerchief as in some romantic intrigue from the novels that filled the lending libraries and the imaginations of young ladies who had never encountered actual danger. Only a scent—faint, not floral: orris root and something sharper. Not perfume, precisely. Not English.

He stepped back into the street. A brewer's dray was rumbling past, pulled by three heavy horses, their flanks steaming in the chill air, the wagon's iron-bound wheels striking sparks from the cobblestones in the places where damp had not yet penetrated. A costermonger's barrow was parked half-up on the kerb, its cargo of winter apples arranged in precarious pyramids. The air held the complex, contradictory smells of the city—horse dung and coal fires, fresh bread and river mud, tobacco and wet wool. There was no sign of her.

He walked back the long way, taking the sweep of the Mall, the rhythm of his boots against stone counting out the distance like a glass marking half-hours at sea. His thoughts moved with similar precision: calculation, assessment, the careful arrangement of observed facts into some semblance of order. Her appearance twice now could not be coincidence. Her manner suggested purpose rather than chance. Her departure, timed to the moment of his arrival, implied communication rather than concealment.

It was just past noon when Mrs. Dalley knocked once and entered without comment, as was her habit, a woman who understood that service consisted largely in anticipating needs rather than responding to them.

"A letter, sir. It was left on the hall table."

The envelope was of rough stock, the kind used for business rather than social correspondence, the seal plain red wax—no crest, no marking. Nicholas took it with a slight inclination of his head that served for thanks.

"Was there anyone seen, Mrs. Dalley?"

"None that I observed, sir. Though I was in the kitchen these past two hours."

Nicholas waited until she had withdrawn before opening it at the desk, using the same small ivory letter-knife that had served him aboard *Alert*—for despatches, and the occasional orange when they touched at Mediterranean ports.

There was no salutation. No signature.

> *Do not mention the San Isidro in writing. Do not speak Holloway's name aloud. There is more than one traitor.*

The paper was unwatermarked, the kind used in any counting house in the city. The hand was narrow, deliberate, anonymous. A script trained not to speak of its writer.

He read it twice. Then again. The last line struck hardest—not as warning, but confirmation. *There is more than one traitor.*

He turned to the cipher fragment still on the desk—the one from Don Francisco's despatches: *A. sails east*

He had marked it idly before, but now the line seemed to rise off the page.

A.

Not a vessel. Not a consignment. A person. A name left unnamed. One that did not appear in any captured paper.

He thought of Elena's uncle, of his mannered evasions, of the routes traced through false ports and names.

And yet. The mind circled, unwilling.

He had loved Caroline. Had accepted her choice—had respected it, even, in a way. But Ashton's name had always carried weight in his thoughts, not for what he had done, but for what he had been allowed to be. The husband. The peer. The shield.

He stared at the cipher. At the silent room.

What if it was nothing? What if *A.* stood for another man entirely? What if he was merely shaping suspicion to match a wound he had never quite confessed?

But then he remembered Trevenen's words. Westborne's silence. The note's flat certainty.

He picked up his pen, hesitated.

Then wrote:

Ashton.

The line sat beneath the cipher like a dropped anchor. He stared at it for a long time.

Then he added, smaller, in the corner of the page:

—or is it only that I want it to be him?

He crossed to the hearth, raked the coals apart with the iron poker until they glowed red at their centers, and laid the paper carefully across the embers. The flame took slowly, curling the paper from the corners inward, the letters paling to gold, then grey, then nothing as the substance that held them dissolved into ash. He stirred it once more with the poker, ensuring no fragment survived intact, then returned to the desk.

He looked at the drawer, but did not open it.

Instead, he pulled the *Gazette* from that morning and began to read, one hand turning the pages, the other steady on the table. Near the center column, beneath the formalities of Parliamentary addresses, a dispatch confirmed what rumors had already begun to suggest: Admiral Howe had successfully relieved Gibraltar, landing supplies under the guns of the Franco-Spanish fleet, and had engaged the enemy off Cape Spartel in an action deemed "spirited and well-conducted." No decisive outcome had been claimed, but the *Gazette*'s tone carried the quiet satisfaction of a strategic success, thinly veiled beneath official understatement.

Nicholas's expression remained neutral, betraying nothing of the thoughts that moved beneath the surface like currents under a calm sea. His eyes moved across the page, but his attention was not on the printed columns with their careful reports of events already past, but on the unfolding present and its uncertain course.

Two nights later, on Friday the 8th of November, over three weeks after arriving in London, Nicholas attended a chamber concert at Hickford's Rooms on Brewer Street—Corelli and a new quartet by Haydn, played with more enthusiasm than precision by a group whose technical limitations were somewhat masked by the room's favorable acoustics. The room was long and low-beamed, filled with the warm hush of candles and the muted creak of well-polished boots on ancient floorboards. He stood at the back, declining the chair reserved for him by a naval acquaintance whose name he barely recalled, a lieutenant from the Channel Fleet whose conversation ran almost exclusively to promotions gained and denied. It was the sort of evening where nothing was expected of him but silence, and even that, for once, he welcomed.

London beyond the windows was muffled in wet wool and horses' breath, the streets glistening under occasional lanterns like a black mirror shattered and imperfectly reassembled. When he stepped back out into the air, it felt heavier than before, as though the very atmosphere had been compressed under the weight of the low clouds. He knew with quiet certainty that he would never truly adapt to London's damp, enclosing dark. There was a kind of shadow in it, he thought, that a man might carry inside without knowing, like a contagion that spreads without symptoms until suddenly it manifests in ways that cannot be ignored.

Nicholas returned later than usual, the fog low and clinging, curling against the lamplight in oily halos that distorted perception and rendered familiar landmarks strange. The stones of Half Moon Street were slick underfoot, glistening with coal soot and fine rain that had never properly fallen but rather consolidated out of the saturated air.

He let himself in with the key from his coat pocket. Mrs. Dalley had already turned down the lamp in the hall and drawn the bolts for the night. The silence of the house was complete—brick, brass, coal, and stillness, as though the building itself were holding its breath.

He opened the door to his sitting room.

And stopped.

She was standing by the hearth, one hand resting lightly on the mantel, the other holding a glass of brandy he had not poured. She did not turn immediately—let him see her in profile first: the clean line of her cheekbone in firelight, the pale sweep of her hair caught behind with an unadorned jet comb that spoke of function, not ornament.

Her hair had changed. Once dark—he remembered that distinctly—it was now ash-blonde, nearly silver in the flicker of the coals. Looser than fashion allowed, and more uneven than any London modiste would permit. As though she had cut it herself, with surgical calm and no thought of approval. It lent her a new quality—a readiness, a certain asymmetry that made her seem less like a woman returned than a memory reassembled.

The coat was navy wool, sharply cut, fastened with a single clasp high at the collar in the style of certain continental officers. Beneath it, a pale blouse—foreign weave, open at the throat—caught just enough shadow to suggest shape rather than declare it. Her boots, narrow and black, turned slightly out at the toe, as though she had been standing there for some time, not waiting, but observing: the fire, the room, or him.

Then her eyes met his—still that strange, inward green that seemed to absorb light rather than reflect it—and her mouth curved very slightly. Not a smile. Not quite. An acknowledgment.

He knew her at once: Catherine Holloway, the woman last seen in Hood's quarters, ostensibly bound for custody. And yet—here, with that fair hair, that stillness—she was also someone else. A glimmer of Caroline Carlisle moved through her, like a figure glimpsed behind gauze. Same colouring, same silence, same pull. Not the same woman. But not wholly different either.

"I thought you were dead," he said.

"You weren't the only one."

Nicholas remained by the door, unmoving. "I turned you over to Hood. To Thornhill. His report said—he told me you'd likely end up in a cell. Or the ground."

"Yes," she said softly. "That was the idea. I might be. And if Ashton has his way, I still will be. But some people"—her eyes met his—"find second uses for broken tools. Even those marked for disposal."

She drank slowly, without haste. The fire caught her fully now: the curve of her hip traced through the fall of her coat, the taut line of her waist. Not voluptuous—there was nothing ornamental about her—but each line precise, honed. She was built like a weapon, and carried herself like one.

"How are you here?" he asked.

"Quietly," she replied. "As ever."

She stepped forward—not quickly, but with that same precise stillness, as if movement were a choice she calibrated by degrees. It reminded him she could vanish again, without hesitation, if she wished.

He said nothing.

She stopped a pace away. "You're thinner," she said. "Tired. Your eyes show it."

"I've been at sea. And London is not my town."

"I know." Her hand rose—ungloved, small, pale—and touched his lapel with two fingers. Light. Brief. Deliberate. Then she withdrew.

"I should report this," he said.

"To whom?" Her voice was soft, cool. "Thornhill? He already knows. Westborne?" A faint lift of her brow. "He prefers not to."

Nicholas did not reply. He didn't need to. Her touch had already answered the question she hadn't asked.

"You're not here by chance," he said at last.

"No," she said. "But not by order, either. I chose this."

She reached into the inner pocket of her coat and withdrew a folded folio wrapped in plain linen—no seal, no ribbon. She offered it across the narrow space between them.

"I copied it in Lisbon. Donnelly's books. A ship that doesn't exist. A shipment that never sailed. Payments routed through Ashton's firm: Spanish and French coin for cargo disguised as Company freight, shipped through Lisbon."

Nicholas opened the folio and read without a word. His thumb moved slowly down the ledger entries. *Santa Marguerite*. Dyewood and Jesuit bark, bound for Lisbon. Two matching sums—one in *reales*, one in *livres*—processed through separate fronts under the same cargo mark.

No ship. No cargo. Only money, moving quietly beneath Portuguese neutral cover.

He looked up. "He's taking payment from France. And from Spain. Using Company charter codes."

Catherine didn't answer. She only watched him. Something in her face shifted, very slightly. Not regret. Not triumph. Perhaps simply recognition.

He turned the final page of the folio, the name *Santa Marguerite* written in neat copperplate: a ship that never sailed, a fiction made ledger-born. He looked up.

"It's not fraud," he said. "It's treason. Payments for information." A pause. "Why give this to me? You could have passed it to someone in government."

"They already have pieces of it," she said. "But not enough. This shows movement—Spanish coin to French hands, masked by Company freight. It's structure, not intent. They'll need more. The correspondents, the ciphers, the pattern of signals passed. That's what burns them. Ashton. And Everett."

He stilled. "Everett?"

"James Everett. Principal Secretary to the Treasury. He recruited Ashton years ago—quietly, without paper. He's behind the shell firms, the misfiled manifests, the manipulated posting lists. Every convoy routed wrong, every delay that cost lives—it traces back to him."

She met his eyes fully now. "But he's protected. You don't accuse a man like Everett. Not a Secretary. Not a peer like Ashton. Not unless you've got it all, in hand. Inked. Undeniable."

Nicholas was silent a moment, a foreboding growing in him. "It's Caroline, isn't it? She's the rest of the evidence."

Catherine nodded. "Yes I came back to England to warn her, and she refused to leave. Insisted she would find the evidence. But now I can't reach her."

"Where is she?"

On the estate. Or was, last I knew. Not locked in a room, but not free either. Watched. Managed. Letters don't reach her. Her movements are reported. Even Thornhill can't get close without setting off every bell in the house."

"You think she's a prisoner?"

"She wouldn't call it that. But yes."

He closed the folio gently. "And you want me to reach her."

"I want you to try."

He studied her face. "Why would she trust me?"

Catherine's voice was quiet. "She trusted you before all this. She never said it, not plainly, but I knew. That final week in Luanda, you remember?"

Nicholas nodded once. "The convoy was preparing to sail in a few days, then *Lynx* was ordered to sail the next day alone to Gibraltar."

"You met to say farewell along the quay that morning you sailed."

Nicholas looked up again, not with surprise, but with something quieter—acceptance, maybe, or sorrow.

"She was going to write," he said. "She never did. Instead after they reached England her father explained she was marrying Ashton."

"I know." Catherine's eyes softened. "She wrote the first page. And then her father spoke. Then came the arrangements. And Ashton."

There was no accusation in her tone—only clarity.

"She regrets it now. She told me so. Not in those words, but clear enough. She was ready, Nicholas. Ready to love a man. Not just have an arrangement. You know, even now she's never been with a man, never with Ashton. It was part of what was agreed."

He breathed out once, very softly. "And you?"

Catherine's eyes shifted—just briefly. Not evasive, but as though registering a memory before deciding it needn't be defended.

"There was something between us. Bombay. Brief. But close. And kind." A pause. "But as I say—she's past that now."

"No," Catherine agreed. "But she painted that island, didn't she? Bora Bora, from your charts. She gave it to you when you sailed. And that was her answer."

He nodded, folding the papers with slow precision. "And if I fail?"

"Then she stays in that house. And we lose everything we haven't already lost."

He paused. "And if she's already gone?"

"Then she hasn't told me." Catherine's voice was quiet. She crossed to the table and set down the brandy with a soft, deliberate click.

"I know about her," she said, in a different tone, not looking back.

"Elena," he said quietly.

"She's far away," Holloway said. "Untouched. Clean." She turned then, facing him fully. "I'm not. But I'm here."

A pause—half a breath—and then she crossed the space between them.

"You don't have to want me," she said, voice low and even. "You just have to need me. For a moment."

Nicholas inhaled. Her scent was subtle. Perfume? Her breath touched his cheek like the edge of a match before it strikes.

Then her mouth was on his.

She undressed with the same clarity she used to kill a lie. No rustle of silk, no dramatic sweep—just motion and intention. Her body in firelight was pale and spare: hips narrow, back long, thighs marked with faint pressure-lines from the road. No lace. No perfume. Only skin. And choice.

What followed was not gentle. It was not affectionate. But it was powerful, practiced, and precise—like everything else she did. She moved over him like someone born to command. She did not ask what pleased him. She showed him.

He had known women before—tender, skilled, elegant. With Silva in the east, he had learned discretion. In Batavia, there had been ceremony in a lacquered room above the spice docks; in Makassar, a courtesan had whispered poetry in Malay against his throat. In Samarinda, one woman had lit a pipe for him afterward and rested against his chest like they'd made a pact not to speak.

But none of them had done what Holloway did.

What she offered was not delight, but revelation. And Nicholas, to his quiet astonishment, received it without resistance.

She moved with the certainty of someone used to making decisions others obeyed. What passed between them had nothing to do with surrender, and everything to do with precision—two elements, volatile and rare, briefly made to balance.

There was no violence in her. But there was no mercy either.

She dressed with that particular economy which spoke of both habit and purpose, pinning her hair precisely with the same black comb she had worn upon her arrival. The transformation was immediate and complete—not merely a woman resuming her attire, but an agent returning to form, the private moment sealed away as though it had never occurred.

At the threshold she paused. "I shall not return," she said, her voice carrying neither regret nor promise. "Not unless you ask it."

Then she was gone, her departure marked by neither sound nor lingering trace—vanishing with the same efficiency with which she had arrived. As complete in its finality as a word spoken once and then deliberately forgotten.

Still later Nicholas sat at the desk, clothed again, the brandy untouched. The smaller lamp burned beside him, the one with the narrow shade, and its pale circle of light lay tight upon the leather blotter, leaving the corners of the room in shadow.

He had not written. He had not slept.

He had tried.

The pen sat ready. The name—*Elena*—waited at the top of the page like a sail never raised. But he had not touched it to paper.

He thought of Atea—her breath in the dawn, the way she watched him read without interruption. Of Helena Montague, who had said nothing the night he left Calcutta, only placed her fingers at his temple and let them fall. Of Elena's voice in Jamaica—first in the garden, and later, in the cottage. Low. Grave. Very far away.

They had given him something. Each of them.

But Catherine had taken, without pretense. For all his prior experience—brothels, courtesans, the elegant choreography of women trained to flatter or conform—nothing, certainly not Atea or Elena, had prepared him for the reversal of position. Helena Montague had come closest in feeling, perhaps, but not in physical fact. Catherine Holloway simply was, and he found himself unready.

He realised Silva would have laughed. Harrington, with that maddening half-smile, might have called it a lesson overdue.

And as Nicholas sat, clothed, sober, and unsleeping, he understood: this was not romance. It was something else entirely. And at last, he was old enough to name it without reaching for poetry.

It was experience. And that was all.

CHAPTER EIGHT

The note arrived just past seven the next morning, delivered by a boy in plain livery bearing a letter sealed with red wax, unadorned but firm.

Nicholas opened it at the writing desk beneath the window.

Admiralty House, 9th of November 1782
St. James's, London

Commander Cruwys,

I hope this finds you well. If your engagements permit, I would be pleased to receive you for breakfast this morning at Boodle's, eight o'clock.

With all due regard,
— M. Trevenen

Boodle's presented itself with the sort of modest permanence that needed no architectural flourish. It stood soberly on St. James's Street, neither ostentatious nor obscure, its brick darkened by decades of London soot, its white lintels scrubbed each Thursday. The knocker had been freshly polished. The foot-scraper cleaned. It smelled faintly of waxed wood, coal smoke, and excellent restraint.

Nicholas arrived precisely at the time appointed in the note, dressed with exacting care: dark blue superfine coat, pale waistcoat with small silver buttons, buff breeches, and black boots he had polished himself that morning. His hat—a black felt tricorn of modest brim—he carried under his arm, as custom required indoors. He passed beneath the small fanlight, etched not with a name, but the simple numeral *49,* and into the hush within.

The club was quiet, but not empty. A few members read the *Gazette* behind barricades of coffee and toast racks; others nodded above half-finished letters, their quills drying beside silver sand pots. A steward moved softly among them, bearing a salver with a pot of chocolate and a narrow copy of the *Courier*. The floorboards beneath the Persian runner had been swept and oiled. The hush was not enforced. It was understood—an institution built on the principle that power need not raise its voice.

A young footman in pale blue livery led him down the inner corridor, past oil-dark portraits of patrons and ministers to one of the inner breakfast parlours, rarely spoken of and never listed on the members' floor plan. Its walls were panelled in ancient oak the colour of tobacco. There were no windows—only a high fan of frosted glass above the door to admit what light was necessary. A fire burned low in the grate. A table had been set with care: Wedgwood, polished silver, linen crisp from the mangle. Covered dishes waited beneath domes that did not steam, and the scent of deviled kidneys and egg cress hung faint in the warmth.

Rear Admiral Trevenen sat at the head of the table, posture straight as ever. He nodded, but did not rise.

Across from him, already seated, was Martin Thornhill.

Nicholas registered the face at once—Hood's secretary, methodical and alert, never quite of the quarterdeck but never beneath it either. He remembered Thornhill's voice during the Holloway briefings aboard *Barfleur*: measured, exact, always a half-step ahead of the officers around him.

He had not expected to see him here. Not because Thornhill lacked importance, but because importance, in his case, had always worn its weight lightly. To find him seated in Boodle's inner parlour, beside a flag officer and without a folio in hand, suggested he no longer merely reported intelligence.

He directed it.

"Commander Cruwys," Thornhill said.

Nicholas inclined his head. "Mr. Thornhill."

"Sit down, Nicholas," Trevenen said. "The eggs are first-rate."

Nicholas took the open chair. A steward entered at once and poured coffee without being asked. The silver gleamed. The linen was stiff with starch. The fire snapped softly in the grate. No one spoke as they began to eat.

They ate in the manner of men accustomed to balancing consequence with ceremony—precisely, efficiently, without haste. Nicholas took a measured portion. Trevenen spread mustard on cold beef with the confidence of a man who had breakfasted in gunrooms. Thornhill helped himself to a single kidney and a cut of roll, which he ate with slow economy, as though food and thought required the same precision.

After a time, Trevenen set down his cup and looked across the table. "You will not be made post."

Nicholas set down his knife. "I see."

"There is no available ship. No appetite for expansion. And certain names," Trevenen said, "draw comment in the wrong rooms."

Nicholas nodded once, as though registering a wind shift. "That is clear."

Trevenen stood and adjusted his coat with a flat sweep. "I brought you here because I was asked to. The rest is not mine to speak."

As Nicholas and Thornhill rose, Trevenen paused at the door, his hand resting on the polished brass handle.

"Nicholas," he said quietly, "a captain stands on his quarterdeck in full view of all, his conduct governed by the rules of war—and of gentlemen." He glanced at Thornhill, then back. "There are those who serve differently. In waters where no chart shows the shoals."

A shadow passed across his face.

"I had hoped to see you with your own ship again. Even without promotion. Not…" He stopped, then continued. "You've always understood honour in the clearest terms. Remember that clarity—even when the lights are dim."

He looked to Thornhill. "This is not official."

And with that, he walked out.

The door clicked shut behind Trevenen with the soft precision of its well-fitted hinges and latch. A moment passed as both men listened to the admiral's footsteps recede down the corridor, fading until only the quiet tick of the mantel clock remained. Then Thornhill gestured to the table.

Nicholas settled back into his chair, the wood creaking softly beneath him.

"You understand," Thornhill said at last, "that what I am about to discuss exists in no Admiralty record, no ship's log, no official dispatch. It was advised, in multiple quarters, that you not be involved further."

Nicholas said nothing.

"One man dissented. He pointed out that while you had thus far acted only as a fighting captain in intercepting and procuring information with *Alert*, you had shown initiative, and an understanding of what was found. And you are not thought to be anything more than another officer in London, quietly seeking a new command. That was enough."

Thornhill drew a narrow folder from his coat and laid it flat on the table. It bore no crest or cipher. It had been folded, carried, opened, and folded again. Nicholas glanced at it once but did not touch it. Instead, he looked across the table, noting the faint tightening at the corners of Thornhill's eyes.

"You knew Holloway was in London," he said.

Thornhill didn't blink. "We did."

"She came to my rooms last night," Nicholas said. "Unannounced. She said she wasn't under orders. That she returned on her own."

"She did," Thornhill replied. "Her departure from Lisbon was not sanctioned. We were aware of her presence. We let it be."

Nicholas reached into his coat and drew out the linen-wrapped folio, laying it beside the unopened folder. "She gave me this. Said it was copied from Donnelly's books in Lisbon. A ship called *Santa Marguerite*, supposedly carrying dyewood and Jesuit bark to Lisbon. But the ship never sailed. The cargo was never loaded."

Thornhill didn't reach for the folio. He glanced at it once, then back to Nicholas.

"We've seen that route before," he said. "Lisbon to Le Havre. Sometimes Genoa to Barcelona. Always neutral ports. Always ghost cargo. Ashton's signature appears at the authorisation stage—but under his commercial alias, not his name. 'H. Ashmere,' typically. The seal matches Company records. After that, he vanishes. The funds move. Nothing else does."

Nicholas gave a slight nod. "She said it wasn't commerce. It was payment. Wrapped in neutral ink."

"It is," Thornhill said. "Silver and gold from Spain and France, routed through Portuguese or Genoise accounts. The ledger entries are real. The ships are not." He tapped the folder with one finger. "She was never our agent. Not in the formal sense. But she operated in La Habana for over a year—under our knowledge, if not always our direction."

Nicholas said nothing. His face was impassive, but his eyes had narrowed a shade.

"She moved in diplomatic circles via Don Francisco Valdés," Thornhill continued. "He believed she was there on private American business—linked to the Valdés trading house. In truth, she was gathering intelligence on French payments moving through Spanish colonial accounts."

Nicholas's voice was quiet. "So when she boarded *Liberty*—"

"She was trying to vanish. Whether for her sake or someone else's, we still don't know. Our orders were to intercept *Liberty* for her capture and any documentation aboard. That intelligence helped open the Ashton trail. But Holloway's return to England? That wasn't part of the plan."

Thornhill reached for his coffee cup, found it empty, and set it down with the care of a man used to weighing his actions. "She's effective. But she's never been reliable. She passed us what we needed in La Habana—but not always when asked. She works to her own clock. Her own tolerances."

Nicholas said nothing.

"There are people who serve the Crown by commission," Thornhill said, "and others who serve by opportunity. She's the latter. And she has appetites—political, personal, otherwise—that don't lend themselves to predictable loyalty."

He stirred his spoon once in the cold cup, then set it down with care, the kind of care that comes when small gestures conceal larger meanings.

"She gives what she means to—documents, intelligence, herself. That doesn't mean you were misled. Only that she decided you were part of the message."

Nicholas didn't answer. He sat still, letting the last words settle like lead shot in still water. Then: "So you were watching me—why?"

"We thought it best not to knock twice," Thornhill said. "Holloway returned on her own terms. She wasn't under orders. And if she wanted contact, she'd choose who and when. We wanted you in

London to see who might react. And sure enough, she sought you out. What else did she tell you?"

"That she came back to warn Lady Ashton. That Lady Ashton refused to leave and instead determined to find the needed proof herself. And that now she's lost contact, but hopes I might reestablish it."

Nicholas paused, his hand drifting toward his waistcoat pocket, where a miniature once rested.

"Caroline—Lady Ashton—and I became acquainted in Bombay. And later on the voyage home, before my ship separated and left Luanda for Gibraltar."

"We surmised as much," Thornhill said. His tone carried neither surprise nor interest, though his eyes remained on Nicholas's face.

Nicholas returned the look. "And you believe Holloway? That she came back to protect Lady Ashton?"

Thornhill frowned. "Possibly. They knew each other. India, some years back. When Lady Ashton was unmarried, living under her father's roof in Calcutta. Holloway was moving through Company circles then. Quietly."

His mouth tightened a fraction. "She's always had a way of getting into places no one invited her."

Nicholas absorbed that. The implication settled like ash across the page.

"You think she renewed the connection."

"I think," Thornhill said, placing his spoon precisely beside the saucer, "she used what she had. And Lady Ashton may be the only person in London she still trusted to listen."

Nicholas's voice was level. "Do you believe Lady Ashton is involved?"

Thornhill shook his head once. "No. And not because I wish otherwise. We've traced her husband's accounts through three false fronts—Lavington, Varnier, a short-lived Dutch house out of Rotterdam. Her name doesn't appear. Her funds aren't touched. Everything we've seen suggests she's unwitting."

He turned a page with deliberate care. "But Ashton—that's different. There's a trading house listed under *Ashmere & Co.*, quiet as a tomb. Registered in Bishopsgate, no signage, no clerk with a name worth noting. The correspondence is managed through agents in Madras and Genoa, sometimes Lisbon. But the instructions come from here. From him."

Nicholas frowned. "He's *already* the Earl. What use has he for aliases and freight ledgers?"

Thornhill looked up, the fire catching faint in his eye. "Because influence in daylight can be challenged. But power in the dark? That answers to no one. Ashton trades for more than coin—he trades for *silence*, for access, for knowing things before the rest of us even realise they're moving."

He leaned back slightly. "He's not building wealth. He's building *position*. Not the kind Parliament grants, but the kind you use when governments fall."

After a moment, Nicholas reached for the folder Thornhill had laid down earlier. It was narrow, well-handled, the edges softened by repetition. No seal, no cipher, no official mark. Just a scrap of twine binding it closed, knotted as neatly as a signal halyard.

He untied it and opened the cover.

Inside: a ledger of ship movements—East India Company and otherwise—annotated in two hands.

"Look at the routing marks," Thornhill said quietly, leaning forward just enough to indicate the page without touching it. "Start in column three."

Nicholas traced them with a finger—Lisbon, Genoa, Leghorn, Calais. Always ports under neutral flags, or compromised ones. The shipments were marked as Company-chartered, but the cargos repeated with unnatural regularity: ballast metals, wax, paper. Low-value, easily excused, rarely inspected.

But the payment sums didn't match. Not wildly, but enough to catch the eye of a man long used to reading prize manifests.

"These aren't trade goods," Nicholas said, his voice taking on the clarity it held when issuing orders in difficult weather. "They're disguises. The money's the point, not the manifest."

Thornhill nodded once—the gesture of a man confirming, not discovering. "That ledger came out of Calais by way of a clerk who died three days later. A fever, supposedly. He didn't know what he had. But the handwriting matches Donnelly's. And the authorising signature on four of those entries is Ashton's."

Nicholas stared at the column for a long moment, then turned the page and found the signature again—same ink, same angular hand, signed without flourish. The authorisation bore no formal crest, but the script was unmistakable. The signature read 'H. Ashmere,'

There was a particular coldness in seeing treason written in a gentleman's hand—precise, efficient, as clean as a merchant's bill of lading.

Nicholas looked down. "And yet she married into it."

"She did," Thornhill said. "And whether by design or misfortune, that puts her near the heart of it. If Ashton suspects she's noticed anything, he won't trust her."

Thornhill's fingers tapped once on the table—the first visible sign of unease. "She's not simple. She's not sentimental. She won't panic. But she's likely seen more than she understands. She may already be collecting the edges of it, without knowing what she's holding. Based on what Holloway told you, she may have gone far beyond that."

He looked up. "Admirable—but it makes her dangerous. To herself. And to our ability to expose the rest. Not because she'll act, but because someone may decide she *might*. And then..."

"Because none of them would reach her," he said at last.

"And if they did, they wouldn't be believed," Thornhill replied.

"Lady Ashton isn't a fool." The last word was spoken with a certain inflection, the kind used by men who had seen what came of underestimating intelligent women.

"She's not even a typical Company director's daughter. Since her mother's death, her father's raised her inside the Company's *core*, not its drawing rooms. She grew up listening to how things are said—and watching what isn't written down."

"You send a man she doesn't know," he continued, "she'll see it. The posture. The questions. The silences. She won't say anything that matters. And then we lose the only clean thread we've still got."

He paused, adjusting his cuff with the precision of a man accustomed to perfect order.

"And we have reason to think she may already be watched."

Nicholas met his gaze. "What about Carlisle?"

"We considered him," Thornhill said. "And dismissed it. He's not touched. He's a merchant of the older school—India first, now turning to China. One of the senior directors of the Company." Thornhill's fingers spread momentarily on the table, like a man flattening a chart against a sudden gust. "He has enemies, but none who question his ledgers. Or his judgment. He's clean, as I said. No question there. But if he's seen to be asking questions—or meeting with the wrong people, even about his daughter—Ashton's allies will notice. Some of those allies may be in Whitehall. And we don't yet know which desks are safe."

He leaned back, the chair creaking softly with the shift of weight. "That's why I'm not asking you to bring her in. I'm asking you to speak with her. See if she knows. See if she's frightened. If she has something—names, paper, even just a sense—take it. Quietly. No confrontations. No declarations. Just enough to get her clear."

Nicholas considered this. When he did speak, his voice was level. "So I'm to walk in without authority, without cover, and ask her what she knows?"

"No, indeed." Thornhill's voice took on the patient tone of a senior officer explaining a complex maneuver. "To most of London, you're just another commander waiting for a ship, if not promotion. Perhaps losing coin at cards while you wait. You don't appear on any list that matters. That gives you freedom. More than you think. You're to ask after her as an old acquaintance. She may hear of it and find you as someone she still trusts."

"You think she's waiting to be found?" Nicholas asked, his head inclining slightly, as if taking a bearing off an uncertain coast.

"I don't know," Thornhill said. "And if she means to speak—if she has something to pass—she'll choose who receives it. If she's unwilling to speak, give her what you've seen. The ledger."

Nicholas sat silent, his expression that of a man studying a chart with uncertain soundings.

Thornhill reached into his coat and produced a single slip of folded paper, with the practiced motion of a man accustomed to handling documents that never officially existed. "This is the address Holloway gave when she returned from Lisbon. Rented under a false name. But the handwriting matched a prior file. She's used that script before."

He placed the slip on the table. "If you've heard nothing more after making inquiries about Lady Ashton, I suggest you use it to find Holloway again. If she thinks you can reach Lady Ashton, she may help you do it."

Nicholas folded the slip and placed it inside his coat. He didn't speak. There was nothing to confirm. No formal order. No acknowledgement to sign.

Thornhill glanced at the coffee again, left it where it was. "If this scandal comes to light," he said, "it will cross two ministries and burn half a dozen reputations."

He paused. His gaze met Nicholas's with the clarity of a signal lantern on a moonless night. "But if this conspiracy isn't stopped, it grows. Quietly. And the Crown's interests suffer."

"You're not required to do this," he said, more softly now, his voice dropping to the confidential register of a quarterdeck conversation, beyond the hearing of the common hands. "There's no commission. No sanction. If you walk away, there's no dishonour in that. But if you don't—then you'll go alone."

Nicholas stood. "That seems to be the pattern."

Thornhill rose as well, and drew a smaller card from his coat. "One thing more. From Admiral Trevenen. He asked that I give you this, if you agreed to proceed."

Nicholas took it without opening it, recognizing the weight and finish of a gentleman's card.

"Manton's," Thornhill said. "You'll find it quiet. And discreet."

They shook hands, briefly. Thornhill's grip was dry and exact, like the pressure of a practiced helmsman on a well-balanced tiller.

CHAPTER NINE

Outside, the air had chilled. Fog rolled along the gutters like spilled milk, curling around bootheels and drainpipes. The bells from St. James's rang a flat hour—neither late nor early, only grey.

Nicholas turned east and began to walk.

He left Boodle's with the folder pressed close against his ribs, the sky now veiled with high, soft cloud and the wind shifting east. The walk along St. James's felt steeper than usual—not in grade, but in tone. The streets, glistening from the earlier rain, bore the smell of wet brick and dung and the faint iron tang of spent coal smoke.

Just past the corner at Albemarle, he paused beneath a low awning to read the folded note Thornhill had slipped to him with the plain efficiency of a clerk passing a bill.

> *This is to be delivered if the Commander accepts further work. You will find Manton in Dover Street. Ask for the elder brother. The suggestion comes by way of Westborne. No more need be said.*
> — M.T.

There was no signature, no seal—only those few lines, written in Admiral Trevenen's spare hand.

Nicholas turned down toward Dover.

Manton's stood quiet beneath its modest signage—*Gunsmith & Lock-Maker*, etched in gilt over weathered green-black paint. The shop was narrow, its windows half-shuttered despite the hour. No goods were displayed, only the dull glint of dark walnut and steel behind rippled glass.

Nicholas stepped inside.

The bell gave a discreet chime overhead. The air within was dry and precise, with the faint tang of iron filings, charred cloth, and linseed oil. A long counter of English walnut ran the width of the room. Behind it, a glass-fronted cabinet held a dozen long arms resting against baize—military and civilian, flint and percussion, each one presented without fuss or flourish.

To one side, narrow shelves bore powder flasks, cap boxes, mainsprings, and turn-screws arranged with the kind of precision that did not announce itself. Everything was in its place. Nothing bore a price.

A moment later, a man emerged from the rear—compact, broad through the chest, his grey hair tied short. He wore a plain brown coat under a clean linen apron. His manner was quiet, self-contained.

Nicholas removed his gloves. "I was referred by Admiral Trevenen. I require something discreet. Reliable. It must be concealable, and it must fire without remark."

The man inclined his head. "Very good, sir. Then I suggest not too short in the barrel. You'll want steadiness. And less flash. Short barrels throw loud and dirty."

He reached beneath the counter and drew out a long tray lined in faded green baize. Inside, five pistols were fitted to shaped compartments.

"This," he said, tapping the first, "is a coat pistol. London pattern. Walnut stock. Belt hook filed smooth. Single shot. Easy to hide—but light, and the barrel's short. Loud in the room. Muzzle flash is broader. You don't want that if you're trying to leave quietly."

He moved to the second. "This is mine. Flattened double-barrel, over-under. Locks recessed. Triggers curled under the guard. Walnut, French oil finish. Steel mounts drawn down, no shine. Built to ride flat in a gentleman's coat."

Nicholas lifted it. The balance was excellent. The weight sat close to the wrist. The barrels were just long enough to give steadiness; the over-under arrangement kept the frame narrow. It would lie flat beneath a wool coat. It would not catch.

"It draws smooth," Manton said. "And won't foul with damp. I've tightened the pin. Load it right, and it'll fire twice without complaint. Won't print under cloth."

He moved down the tray. "This is a pepperbox. French. Three barrels. Fires well, if it feels like it. Cap's moody in the cold."

The fourth: "One of a matched pair. Maple grip. Silver mount. Never fired. Not for pockets. But it will strike a feather off a hat at sixty paces."

And the last: "Turn-over piece for saddle or chaise. Loud. Good in an open road. Less so in a quiet room."

"I'll take the double."

He paused. "Is there a way to try it?"

Manton gave a short nod. "Of course."

He led Nicholas behind the counter and through a narrow door into a low-ceilinged chamber at the rear of the shop. The walls were exposed brick, blackened in patches, and the floor was thick with trodden sawdust. A short target board stood ten paces off, its surface flecked with powder burns and pocked by years of quiet use. An oil-lamp burned behind thick glass, trimmed low.

The room smelled of burnt powder, oiled steel, scorched wadding, and something faintly bitter beneath it—charred cotton, perhaps, or old lead.

Manton looked carefully at the pistol, checked the springs once, then loaded the first barrel—powder, patch, and ball—with steady precision. The second followed just as cleanly. He tamped both charges, primed the pans, and tapped the frizzens closed. Then he passed the weapon to Nicholas, butt-first, with the muzzle turned down.

Nicholas took it, cocked the first barrel, and fired.

The shot cracked flat and sharp in the confined room, the sound smothered by the brick but no less serious for it. A bloom of smoke drifted slowly toward the far wall. The ball struck the target just right of centre.

He cocked the second barrel and fired again. The second report was more contained, the smoke folding back into itself. The second ball landed close beside the first.

Manton didn't speak until the echoes had settled.

"Trigger's light," he said. "She favours the off hand a hair. But she'll tell true if your coat doesn't pull."

Nicholas nodded, tested the balance once more, and set the weapon carefully back on the bench.

Manton turned to the leather case on the side table. It was compact with no ornament, lined with green baize, stitched at the corners. Into it he packed two spare flints, a turnscrew, a powder flask, and a simple bullet mould. He placed the pistol wrapped in cloth beside it without comment.

Nicholas reached for the pistol again. "I'll load it myself."

Manton stepped aside.

Nicholas moved with quiet efficiency—checked the bore, measured the powder from the flask, seated the patched ball, and rammed it down with two even strokes. He primed the pans, tapped each flint into place, and set the hammer to half-cock with a quiet, metallic tick.

He folded a square of clean wool around the weapon, then tucked it—carefully, deliberately—into the inner pocket of his coat.

It was not how most men carried a live pistol. It was weighty. It pulled slightly at the line of the coat. But it was there.

Manton watched the motion, his expression unchanged save for the smallest lift of one brow.

"Most prefer the case," he said.

Nicholas met his eye. "I'm not most."

There was a pause. Then Manton gave a single nod—not approval, but recognition.

"Then you're ready, sir."

Nicholas drew out the guineas without ostentation—forty in all, several months pay, and the price for best London work and Manton's name besides.

He did not turn back toward Half Moon Street. Instead, he walked north toward Pall Mall, where the lamps burned brighter and the fog lifted slightly in deference to the firelight behind club windows. At the corner near Warwick House, he stepped through a narrow archway and into the low door of the Smyrna Coffee-House.

He had been there once before, years ago, in the company of Henry Harrington, shortly after returning from the Pacific. They had called on a man from the Navy Board, and afterward Harrington had brought him here for what he called *"a proper intelligence roast"*—not a term for coffee, but for the quiet habit of watching the right men say too little over a cup that said more.

It had not changed. The room was long, dimly lit by whale-oil sconces, and heavy with the layered scents of ink, cardamom, and old coats. The walls bore framed maps of the Levant, faded broadsheets in Greek and Arabic, and above the hearth, a Turkish scimitar mounted with faint ceremony—spotted with rust, but handsomely balanced.

Nicholas nodded to the steward, who offered neither greeting nor question, and selected a table near the rear where he could watch both door and street without obvious effort. A boy brought him coffee in a narrow-necked pot with the usual battered china cup, its rim chipped at the edge. It was bitter and thick with grounds—but hot. Nicholas drank half, then folded his gloves precisely before drawing a small notebook from his coat pocket.

On the page he had left blank for three days, he wrote:

Lady Caroline Ashton
Broxbourne Hall
daughter of Carlisle, East India Company

Below, in a smaller hand:

Unlikely to use post—prefers messages conveyed by word of mouth. Probable habits: rides about midday, walking in the garden. May yet confide in her father. Possibly reliant on household staff. Inquire after recent dismissals, alterations in routine, or letters unsent.

The pen scratched faintly as he wrote, and outside the window a coach rolled past, lamps bobbing, the horses' breath rising silver in the air. A few men came and went in the coffee room, their coats damp with fog. A pair of naval captains took up a table near the hearth and began speaking low over a folded *Chronicle*. Nicholas caught a name—*Fanshawe*—and marked it without comment.

He returned to his work.

He made no inquiry of the steward. Not here. But a glance at the noticeboard near the stairwell yielded something useful: several visiting cards pinned beside the ledger of correspondence. One, newly tacked, bore the name *Mrs. T. Ellis, Milliner of Mount Street, late in service to Lady Ashton.* It had been added within the week.

Nicholas closed the notebook, left a shilling on the table—far more than required—and slipped back out into the damp mid-afternoon. He made his way to Mount Street.

The shop was modest, set slightly back from the pavement beneath a painted sign that read *Mrs. T. Ellis, Milliner.* The window displayed a pair of bonnets, one in dove grey with Indian muslin trim, the other navy with a cluster of jet beads at the crown. Neither was remarkable, which was likely the point.

Inside, the air smelled faintly of starch, pressed wool, and dried lavender. A girl of perhaps sixteen looked up from a sewing frame as he entered, but said nothing. Moments later, a door behind the counter opened and a woman emerged—compact, mid-forties, with a face shaped by London air and close work.

"Commander Cruwys," Nicholas said, offering his card.

Her eyes flicked to it, then back to his face. She hesitated, then gave a slight nod. "Yes. I remember you."

Nicholas held her gaze. "From Bombay?"

"From the *Ocean*, more likely. You came aboard more than once during the convoy. Lady Ashton—Miss Carlisle then—spoke of you." She glanced at the card again. "Come in."

She led him into a small rear room with a fire already laid. She did not offer refreshment, but she did not stand on ceremony either.

"You served in her household," Nicholas said.

"I did," Mrs. Ellis replied. "I left at her request. Three weeks ago."

"Request—or dismissal?"

"A bit of both. She gave notice, and a full quarter's pay. Said she would no longer require my services, and that she would be leaving Broxbourne herself. Quietly."

"Alone?"

"No. Escorted. But not by her father's men, I'd wager. And not by her husband's."

"Do you know where she went?"

"No," Mrs. Ellis said. "But I believe she meant to vanish. Carefully. And on her own terms."

She studied him for a moment, then added, "I wouldn't have said a word to another man asking these questions—not with the world being what it is. But I know who you are. I know you were kind to her, when she had few people who were."

Nicholas said nothing.

"She never said it plainly," Ellis continued. "But I watched her closely. I think she trusted you. Or wanted to."

He inclined his head. "And you think she left to escape her husband?"

"I think," said Mrs. Ellis, "she left to stop being managed. She said, the night before I went—'It's time I did one thing for myself. Just one.'" Her voice softened. "And I think she trusted someone would come looking."

Nicholas nodded once.

That was all she would say. And all she needed to.

The next morning, a Sunday, Nicholas rose early, as he always did. The city was still wrapped in grey, the windows of Half Moon Street weeping condensation in slow trails that caught the first grainy light. He shaved by habit, dressed with care—black superfine coat, dove-grey waistcoat, gloves of modest grey kid. He had chosen these not for mourning, but for visibility.

He did not expect to see Caroline. That would be too simple. But he had learned in the tropics, and in war, that there were ways of being seen that did not require proximity. Presence mattered. Placement mattered.

And London had its own ways of whispering.

At the small writing table beneath the window, he folded a visiting card—his name engraved in copperplate, *Commander N. Cruwys, R.N.*—and placed it in a pale blue envelope, the kind carried by shop messengers and club stewards. No address. Only the initials *C.A.* on the front.

He left it just inside the front door for Mrs. Dalley, with a sovereign beneath.

"Should anyone inquire," he said. "Let this be passed discreetly."

Nicholas left Half Moon Street just after eight. The fog still lingered low along the paving stones, softening the outlines of passing carts and early foot traffic. The city was beginning to stir, though not yet fully awake. Chimney smoke curled into the damp air; the bell of a dustman's cart echoed faintly from the west.

He walked west by way of Shepherd Market, keeping to the edge of Piccadilly, where the shops were only half-open and the tavern doors still closed to trade. The streets were quiet in a way that reminded him of early watches aboard ship—clean, expectant, a city before its pulse returned.

At the Anchor and Crown, the steward admitted him without question and directed him to the smaller breakfast room, where the hearth was already laid and the linens still crisp from the press.

He took a table near the window and ordered simply: coffee, a dish of eggs, a small cut of ham. Nothing extravagant. But enough to place him.

He did not read the *Gazette*. He let the other men do that, two at the far table, one in a faded lieutenant's uniform, the other in a civilian coat cut too fine for a true gentleman, both murmuring over the latest dispatch from the Indies.

Nicholas sat in stillness, one hand resting lightly on the handle of his cup, his gaze distant, not idle, but focused inward.

He thought of Caroline—not Lady Ashton, but the woman he had first watched, then met, at a reception in Bombay. The dinner that followed—just the Carlisles and himself—had changed everything. Her questions had been pointed but never impolite. She had listened when no one else did. She had challenged him, gently, on the value of Pacific knowledge to East India strategy. She had known more than she let on.

During the convoy they'd seen more of each other. After he saved her father's life during the French attack on *Ocean*; over a dinner when the convoy was becalmed and Nicholas had joined the escort captains aboard *Ocean*; again at the Cape, at dinners both aboard her father's ship and in his own borrowed cabin on *Growler*.

There had been a shift. For Lord Ashton had been returning from India on another vessel in the convoy, and his pursuit of Caroline had become evident. Her father, Carlisle, had been ambivalent.

And then Luanda.

The end had come quickly, with the arrival of an admiral and reinforcements. His temporary command of *Growler* as prize captain was stripped from him by patronage, and he had reverted to third lieutenant aboard *Lynx*, ordered to sail at once for Gibraltar. No time to make arrangements. Barely time to take his leave.

But Caroline had arranged to meet him at first light.

She was composed when she arrived. But the moment she reached him, her face changed. They stepped into a quiet alley for privacy, and there—without hesitation—she kissed him. Fiercely. Without reserve.

It had not felt like farewell.

It had felt like a beginning.

When he tried to speak, she pressed her fingers to his lips.

"Not now, Nicholas. Not yet."

She had handed him a parcel, small and precisely wrapped. He opened it at sea, as she had asked: a small silver case—oval, finely worked, the surface engraved with a subtle geometric pattern.

Inside, along the inner rim, a narrow band of inlaid ivory framed the miniature beneath its glass: a watercolor of *Bora Bora*. The island's high peak rose above the lagoon, rendered in delicate, confident strokes. He recognized the view at once—from one of his own sketches, given to her father during that dinner aboard *Growler*.

Inside the lid, engraved in small, careful script:

Islands of memory anchor us through life's storms.
C.C. July 1780

He had known, even then, that there were parts of her he did not understand. Attachments that lay outside convention. Silences that held more than decorum. She had not lied. But she had withheld—not from cruelty, but from necessity.

Yet she had understood him. Perhaps more than she meant to. And perhaps more than he'd allowed himself to say.

He had never spoken of it.

And he had never thrown it away.

Even when he later heard of her marriage to Ashton.

He thought of Elena, too—of the garden in Kingston, and the cottage, and the duel. What they'd shared had felt like clarity. But it had been born of pressure, of proximity and blood, and the impossibility of any lasting peace.

Caroline had never offered that kind of clarity. Only questions left unasked.

And now she was married to a man suspected of treason. And, if Holloway and Thornhill were right, perhaps in danger herself.

At ten forty-five, he rose, nodded once to the steward, who returned it without expression, and collected his gloves from the chair.

Outside, the bells of St. George's had just begun to sound.

He crossed Hanover Square on foot, boots muffled against the damp flagstones, passing a cluster of hired carriages and one or two footmen waiting with folded arms. The autumn air was sharp but not cold, the kind of morning that seemed to hold its breath just before the turn of season.

At the church, a silver coin to the beadle secured him entrance to the upper gallery, where gentlemen without family pews sat in mild seclusion. From there, he had a clear view of the nave below, and of those who might be watching from the other direction.

He did not expect Caroline to appear. That would have been too simple. But if she were in London, and if any message had reached her, this was a place she might reasonably look.

The church filled as the prelude began—organ and strings weaving into a slow, rising line. The scent of stone and wool and old cedar polish hung in the air. Nicholas took his seat with unhurried precision, glancing once across the nave—and saw Lord Ashton.

Two rows from the chancel, in the Ashton family pew, Ashton sat alone.

His coat was flawless. His linen, crisp. The cane beside him bore a silver wolf's-head cap—a new affectation, perhaps, or a piece meant to reassure. But the pose was too composed. Too considered. And from above, Nicholas could see what those beside him could not: Ashton's right hand, resting on his knee, clenched once before slowly unfurling.

His hair had thinned slightly since Luanda. The skin beneath his eyes held faint shadows. Not haggard. Not disgraced. But weathered. Like a man whose hold on events was no longer absolute.

Nicholas remembered him at the Governor's reception: cool, affable, decisive. Already laying polite claim to Caroline with the entitlement of a man who never expected refusal. He had circled her like a captain eyeing a captured vessel, inspecting for flaws, measuring her lines, confident the purchase would be made.

Now, seated alone in London with no wife at his side, Ashton looked… alert. And perhaps uneasy.

As the sermon began, Ashton shifted. Not dramatically, but just enough to scan the pews behind him.

His gaze passed slowly across the rows. Deliberate. Calm. A reflex, perhaps—the instinct of a man who felt he might be watched.

But he did not look up.

Nicholas, still and unreadable in the gallery, did not move.

The sermon—a well-meant exposition on order and the virtues of temperance—drifted past. Nicholas listened only to the cadence of the words, not their meaning.

When the final blessing was given, Ashton bowed his head. Then, rising with slow precision, he gathered his gloves and left the church in silence, the pew doors closing gently behind him.

Nicholas waited a full five minutes before rising in turn.

He stepped out into the square as the last murmurs of the benediction faded. The crowd dispersed quietly, silk and wool rustling against the low ring of carriage wheels on stone. He walked down the hill and across St. James's Park, cutting along the northern path beside the water, the grass underfoot wet from last night's rain. The limes were yellowing at the tips, and a faint scattering of leaves marked the path in gold. Chestnuts had fallen in their prickled husks. The breeze carried the faintest scent of turned earth and the resinous undertone of coal smoke rising toward evening.

He walked without haste, boots soft on gravel, posture composed. He was not looking for anyone. But he allowed himself to be seen.

By half past three, the light already thinning, and the crowds in the park. By four, the lamp-lighters had begun their rounds, poles in hand, coaxing fire into the glass globes along Pall Mall.the gas-men had begun to strike their tapers, and the city was folding into dusk." The wind picked up from the west, tugging lightly at the corners of Nicholas's coat. He stood for a long moment at the top of the gravel path, watching the sun slip behind the chimneys beyond the Horse Guards, then turned northward along Pall Mall. At Hatchard's—the narrow bookshop with its scarred windows and heavy brass bell—he stepped inside without conscious intent.

The shop was warm with the smell of paper and wool, and the iron tang of burnt oil from a lamp near the till. He moved past the expected volumes—*Dampier, Anson, Hawke's Instructions*—and stopped at a case marked *Philosophie et Histoire*.

After thirty minutes or so of browsing, he saw, in clean gilt and rough cloth:

> *Rousseau – Du Contrat Social (The Social Contract)*
> *London, 1781. Translated with Notes and Preface.*

He turned a few pages.

> *"The strongest is never strong enough to be always the master, unless he transforms strength into right, and obedience into duty..."*

He bought the book without comment, slid it into his coat, and stepped back into the wind.

He walked the five minutes south along St. James's Street, past the club doors and stewards brushing soot from the steps, then turned left onto King Street, where the streetlamps had begun to glimmer against the dusk.

At quarter past five, he reached Wilkes's, a quiet dining house set back from the street. The fire in the front room had been lit, and the steward, who knew Nicholas by name, if not conversation, showed him to a table near the wainscoting.

He ordered deliberately: grilled sole in anchovy butter; marrow bones with parsley and toast; braised greens in lemon oil; a bottle of Bordeaux—Lafitte, '77. The wine, poured with quiet care, gleamed like garnet in the lamplight—good wine, not ostentatious, and better than he strictly required. And for after: Stilton, walnuts, and a glass of Old East India port.

When the fish came, he opened Rousseau and read between courses, one hand resting lightly on the edge of the page.

The ideas—so clean, so confident in their claim that political legitimacy must come from the governed, echoed uncomfortably against his memory of Luanda, where slaves had been examined like livestock and marched across the square in iron collars. He remembered the merchant's voice, light and reasonable: *"They live because of our trade."*

And in Jamaica: the quiet labour on the docks, the empty stares of men whose names had been bought and lost twice over.

"Man is born free," Rousseau had written, *"and everywhere he is in chains."*

Nicholas closed the book for a moment, letting the stem of the port glass rest cool against his thumb. The cheese had been brought. A proper cut of Stilton, moist and blue-veined, set beside fresh walnut halves and a spoon of quince preserve.

The port was exquisite. Dark and full-bodied, it carried a warmth that seemed to settle between the ribs. He drank it slowly, listening to the muffled clink of plates in the kitchen and the creak of a chair settling across the room.

He was not part of the world Rousseau described, where revolution fermented in cafés and salons, but he had seen where such thoughts would land if men continued to be bought and sold by ledger.

He finished the port.

Folded down the corner of the page.

Left a tip too generous for the silence he'd been given.

Then walked home, alone.

The fog had returned by dawn, low and pale, moving in folds over the rooftops. Nicholas rose early, the fire in his room long since guttered out. He deliberately did not shave, but dressed in his bottle-green superfine and the grey waistcoat with mother-of-pearl buttons—modest, but well cut. His boots he polished himself. Again. He took no breakfast.

He left Half Moon Street just after seven, the city still half-dreaming. A boy ran post with a folded sheet under one arm. A fishmonger's cart rattled north toward Mayfair. The scent of coal smoke drifted low over the stones.

He entered Rawthmell's a little past eight. The room was warm with pipe smoke and boiled chicory, already half-full of men whose loyalties could be guessed by the thickness of their eyebrows and the angle at which they held their newspapers. He took a table near the window, ordered black coffee—no milk, no sugar—and unfolded the *Morning Chronicle*.

Midway down the second page:

DUTCH POSITION CONFIRMS AMERICAN STATUS IN PARIS TALKS

The States General of the United Provinces, having earlier in the year acknowledged the independence of the American colonies, are said to have reiterated their position in recent communications with the American plenipotentiary, Mr. John Adams, presently residing at The Hague.

Sources close to the French delegation suggest that this renewed alignment strengthens the American footing in the ongoing peace deliberations at Paris, where the outlines of a general settlement are said to be under preliminary discussion. It is further reported that Dutch representatives have expressed willingness to enter separate talks with His Majesty's government upon satisfactory conclusion of the American articles.

No formal response has yet been issued by Lord Shelburne's Cabinet. However, it is believed the Ministry views the development with cautious concern, as Dutch concurrence may encourage further intransigence among the French and Spanish commissioners regarding territorial adjustments and maritime provisions.

Nicholas read it twice, then set the paper down.

He was not given to abstractions. He had fought the war as ordered. He had enforced blockade, seized Spanish coin. But this—recognition—was something else. Not retreat. Not surrender. Something quieter. Something permanent.

He did not pretend sympathy with rebellion. But he understood now that change, once loosed, did not always declare itself with noise. It moved beneath the surface, like current under glass—quiet, steady, reshaping everything in time.

He folded the *Chronicle* neatly, drained the last of his coffee, and left the paper untouched on the table—precise, as if he had never been there.

At Tobyn's, two blocks west, the lamps still burned low and the fire in the grate gave off a gentle snap. The barber said nothing as he took Nicholas's coat, nor when he drew the cloth across his shoulders and began to strop the blade.

The shave was clean. The towel, hot. The air carried the sharp green scent of rosemary and bay. In the next chair, a Guards officer read the *London Gazette* aloud to himself, muttering lines about Rodney's displeasure and a "dispute over American fisheries" that had rattled the ministry.

Nicholas said nothing. The razor passed cleanly beneath his jaw.

When it was done, he declined cologne, paid without comment, and stepped back into the street—the fog now lifting in slow ribbons toward the rooftops.

He turned south, without real intent.

There were errands he might have invented—an inquiry at the map-seller's, a parcel never truly expected—but instead, his feet took him downhill toward Haymarket.

Nicholas returned to Half Moon Street as evening descended. Rain had begun again, that persistent London drizzle which penetrated wool and resolve with equal efficiency. He had walked the long way from Foster's, through St. James's Park and along Piccadilly, letting his thoughts settle like disturbed sediment in still water.

Mrs. Dalley had left a cold supper on the sideboard: sliced beef, bread, a pot of mustard, and a decanter of claret. No note accompanied it. None was needed. The quiet presumption of service lent the rooms a sense of permanence he had not felt since first taking them.

He removed his coat and gloves with practiced economy, laying them over the back of a chair with a sailor's instinct for order—even in darkness. The room was cold, the fire long since burned low.

Nicholas knelt at the hearth, building the fire not as a servant might, but as a midshipman learns aboard ship, where such tasks are never beneath one's station. Tinder, kindling, then coal—each element properly laid, each serving its purpose. The fire caught, wavered, then drew steadily into itself, casting amber patterns across the worn carpet.

He poured a glass of claret and settled by the window. The street below was muffled by damp and distance: a single carriage lamp moving past in shadow, the brief clatter of iron-shod wheels swallowed by wet stone, a solitary watchman with pike and lantern moving with the slow certainty of a man paid by the hour rather than the mile.

From the valise beside his writing desk, Nicholas withdrew a small leather portfolio. Inside lay papers he had not examined since leaving the Indies: his commission to *Alert*, Hood's letter of commendation after the *San Isidro* action, and his last orders returning him to England. Each document marked a transition—a step in a career that now seemed suddenly in abeyance.

He held Caroline's miniature to the firelight, studying not the image but the brushwork itself—each stroke evidence of her presence, of choices made with deliberate care. She had shaped the island as it appeared from the eastern approach, with the same precision she brought to her correspondence and her silences—as though geography itself were a kind of language, to be read and spoken rightly.

His thoughts turned, unbidden, to Elena in Jamaica: the quality of evening light against whitewashed walls, the scent of jasmine, the weight of obligations left unsettled between them. She had met him without illusion, and their parting had left no wound—only the trace of something once cleanly understood. That clarity now felt distant. Not diminished, exactly. But complete.

Then to Catherine Holloway—recent, precise, unreadable. What Holloway had offered had not been connection. It had been something rarer: a clear exchange in a world built on misdirection. He found he neither regretted it nor misunderstood it.

On the morrow, he resolved, he would seek her out. He would learn what purpose had truly drawn her back across the Atlantic—what message she had returned to deliver.

He ate without awareness: the food merely sustenance, the wine merely warmth. His thoughts had turned forward, leaving reminiscence behind like a coast falling away beyond the horizon. Thornhill's intimations, Westborne's cryptic guidance, Trevenen's careful distance—all suggested currents moving beneath the visible surface of events.

At the writing desk, he laid out a single sheet of paper and dipped his pen.

My dear Elena—

But again no further words came. The gap between what could be expressed and what must be felt remained unbridgeable. He realized, with quiet certainty, that no letter would be sent. Not out of coldness, but because there was nothing more to ask, and nothing more to give.

Nicholas examined the priming of the Manton pistol with practiced care, a habit acquired in warmer latitudes, where vigilance is not excess but necessity. He laid the weapon within easy reach beside the bed.

He undressed with the methodical economy of a man long accustomed to the confined quarters of a King's ship, where both space and privacy are closely rationed commodities. As weariness claimed him, his mind summoned the precise sound of water passing cleanly along a well-formed hull—that hushed cadence which marks the marriage of perfect design with its intended purpose.

Tomorrow would bring what it would. Tonight, sleep came with the certainty of a tide following its appointed course.

Nicholas woke early, and for a moment he lay still, listening to the different silences of Half Moon Street: no creak of timbers working against a swell, no snap of canvas overhead. Only the distant rattle of an early cart and the soft hiss of moisture dripping from the eaves.

He rose and went to the window. The street below lay wrapped in the peculiar half-light of a London late autumn morning, neither properly illuminated nor genuinely dark. A solitary link-boy trudged homeward, his torch extinguished, shoulders hunched against the damp. In the distance, church bells marked the hour with muffled precision.

Three days had passed since his breakfast at Boodle's with Thornhill, three days of careful inquiries about Caroline that had yielded nothing. He had visited the places Thornhill suggested, asked the right questions with calculated casualness, and watched the usual points of intelligence exchange for any sign of her. Nothing. It was as if Caroline had simply vanished, or was being kept so carefully isolated that no word of her could escape whatever walls now surrounded her.

Only yesterday had he learned from Mrs. Ellis that Caroline had left Broxbourne of her own accord. Not dragged. Not dismissed. Escorted, but not by those whose names appeared on the household's ledgers.

Which left Catherine Holloway.

He had resisted seeking her out directly—partly from caution, partly from a deeper reluctance he chose not to examine too closely. But with each day of silence regarding Caroline, the calculation shifted. Whatever complications existed between Holloway and himself, she remained the thread most likely to lead to Caroline and to the truth behind Ashton's activities.

Nicholas rang for Mrs. Dalley and requested hot water. While waiting, he took out the slip of paper Thornhill had given him at Boodle's: *Newman Street, No. 17.* His decision was made. After three days of fruitless searching, he would call on Holloway later that morning.

He studied the address again, and looked at a map of London he had purchased along with the Rousseau. Newman Street lay just north of Oxford Street, respectable but not fashionable, the sort of street where a woman of means but modest position might take rooms without attracting undue notice. The location itself revealed something of Holloway's nature: not hiding in the rookeries, nor displaying herself in Mayfair, but positioned where she could observe both worlds with equal facility.

Mrs. Dalley knocked and entered with a copper can of steaming water, followed by a boy carrying a second, larger vessel. "Will you be taking breakfast, sir?" she asked, her voice pitched with that particular inflection of London servants, neither deferential nor familiar, but precisely calibrated to the status of the establishment.

"No," Nicholas said. "I'll be going out directly."

She nodded once and withdrew, closing the door with practiced quietness. Nicholas poured the steaming water into the hip bath that had been positioned before the hearth the previous evening. He bathed methodically, the ritual familiar from years at sea, where water was rationed and every movement economized. Even with the luxury of a private room and ample hot water, he retained the habits of a naval officer: thorough, quick, purposeful.

After bathing, he shaved with equal precision, the razor's edge gliding over his jaw with the same studied attention he brought to every task involving steel. He dressed with care: clean linen, a fresh neck-cloth arranged with simple economy, buff waistcoat, and trousers of dark grey wool.

From the wardrobe he selected his best civilian coat—a deep blue superfine that, while not precisely a naval uniform, carried the unmistakable cut and bearing of a King's officer. He had commissioned it from a tailor in Half Moon Passage after his return from the Indies, a quiet compromise between his naval identity and his current ambiguous status. The cloth itself spoke of quality without ostentation. The buttons were plain gilt—no crest, no anchor. It was the coat of a man who did not require insignia to mark his profession.

He checked the Manton, verifying that both charges remained properly seated and the flint securely fixed. The weight of it felt right in his palm—not excessive, but substantial enough to remind its holder of consequences. He slipped it into the inner pocket of his coat, where the wool's thickness would conceal its outline.

He buckled on his sword, adjusting the frog so that the weapon hung at the precise angle for a smooth draw. Unlike the pistol, the sword made no attempt at concealment. Not a small-sword to be sure, and unusual for a man in civilian dress in London, but not unknown.

Nicholas paused at the writing desk before leaving. The unfinished letters to Elena still lay in the drawer where he had placed them, the last the night before. He considered briefly, then closed the drawer without adding a word.

He took his hat and gloves from the stand by the door. No greatcoat, despite the morning chill. The weight of it would hamper movement, if needed.

The street had come more fully to life by the time he descended. A maid scrubbed the steps of the house opposite, her breath visible in the cool air. A tradesman's boy hurried past with a covered basket.

From somewhere nearby came the clatter of shutters being thrown open.

Nicholas considered walking but decided against it. He signaled a passing hackney, its driver hunched against the morning chill.

"The Duke's Head," he said, stepping inside.

It was a modest establishment on Sackville Street he had discovered during his first week back in London—quiet enough for contemplation, but not so exclusive as to draw attention.

The proprietor, a retired bosun from the Channel Fleet who had invested his prize money in pewter and porter, greeted him with a nod rather than words. Nicholas settled at a corner table and ordered a proper breakfast: eggs, thick rashers of bacon, fresh bread with butter still glistening from the churn. The coffee came black and bitter, needing neither sugar nor milk to assert its purpose.

He ate deliberately, with the measured pace of a man accustomed to shipboard routine but no longer constrained by the turning of a glass. Through the window, he watched London's commercial machinery engage its gears: clerks hurrying toward counting houses, porters hauling goods from river wharves, women with baskets negotiating with stallholders. The metronome of the city's heartbeat, steady and indifferent to individual concerns.

His thoughts turned again to Holloway. Their last encounter had been precise, deliberate, and unfinished. Beneath her control, he had sensed a single, unguarded emotion: concern for Caroline.

No accusations, he decided. No questions about their encounter. Only the ones that mattered: Where was Caroline now? Was she truly in danger—or simply moving in ways the world was not built to recognize?

After breakfast, Nicholas walked through the gradually filling streets, letting his thoughts settle like disturbed sediment in still water. He found himself at the mappery off Haymarket, where cartographers bent over tables of scraped vellum, rendering coasts and soundings into navigable certainty. For nearly an hour, he studied new charts of the West Indies, not from need, but from instinct.

The bell of St. James's struck ten as he emerged. The clouds had thickened, and a few drops struck the cobblestones with audible presence. Nicholas purchased a copy of the *Morning Chronicle* from a boy with smudged fingers and took shelter in a coffeehouse near Leicester Square, where the compressed air carried the mingled scents of rain-dampened wool, tobacco, and arabica.

He read without hurry, absorbing the rhythms of London's concerns—Parliamentary debate, market prices, shipping news, society's small vanities. Beneath the printed columns lay the real movement of power: the peace negotiations in Paris, naval dispositions, and the quiet dealings between men whose names rarely appeared in public print.

At half past eleven, he paid his reckoning and stepped into the rain of neither storm nor mist.

Nicholas hailed a second hackney, settled his hat, and composed his thoughts for the conversation ahead.

"Newman Street," he said. "Number seventeen."

The vehicle moved off with a jolt, its wheels cutting through puddles left by the night's rain. Nicholas settled back against the worn leather seat, feeling the familiar weight of the pistol against his ribs and the sword at his hip. The gentle sway of the carriage was nothing like the motion of a ship, yet there was comfort in movement itself, in the sense of purpose restored after days of careful waiting.

Through the small window, London passed in fragments: a pie seller arranging his wares, clerks hurrying toward counting houses, a lamplighter making his rounds to extinguish the street flames. The city lived by its own rhythms, as complex and demanding as any ocean current.

The hackney turned onto Oxford Street, joining the steady flow of commerce that served as London's main artery. Carts laden with goods, carriages bearing the well-to-do, shop boys hurrying on errands—all moved in their appointed courses, like ships navigating by established routes. Nicholas watched it all with the detached attention of a man accustomed to observing without being observed.

As they turned north onto Newman Street, he noted the change in character—narrower, quieter, its houses of uniform brick with polished brass knockers and modest curtains. A street of the respectable middle sort, where a woman of Holloway's particular talents might blend without disappearing entirely.

"Here, sir," the driver called, drawing up before number seventeen.

Nicholas paid the fare, adding a coin for the earliness of the hour, and stepped down to the pavement. The house rose four stories, plain brick, its windows shuttered against the morning chill. A narrow fan of glass above the door showed no light within.

He mounted the steps, his hand moving briefly to check the pistol in his coat. The sword shifted with him, not burdensome, but present.

He knocked once.

Nothing.

He waited, then knocked again—firmer this time, though not loud. The sound fell flat against the wood, swallowed by fog.

Still nothing.

He tried the latch. It gave. The door creaked inward on a well-oiled hinge. But with a chill he saw the splintering around the lock. It had been forced.

Nicholas stepped into the vestibule and closed the door quietly behind him. The air inside was colder than expected—still, but not stale. A narrow passage led to the stair, unlit. There were no voices. No footsteps overhead. The silence was not the stillness of sleep.

It was the wrong kind of silence.

He drew the pistol from his coat and eased the hammers to full cock. The weight in his hand steadied him, though it did not comfort. The flints were seated. The pans primed.

He moved forward with care.

The coat by the door stopped him.

Grey, lightly cut. The right shoulder softened by wear. Rain-darkened at the hem. He had seen it last in Half Moon Street, when she stood by the hearth with a glass in her hand and the map of everything unspoken in her eyes.

She had come back. That much was certain. She had come back—and had not gone again.

Nicholas continued up the stairs, his tread slow and deliberate. He kept the pistol close, muzzle low, finger outside the guard. His breathing had flattened. The silence in the house had thickened.

He reached the landing and paused outside the door.

A sliver of light escaped from within—not candlelight, but daylight: grey and cold, filtering through a curtain pulled imperfectly closed.

He nudged the door open with the back of his knuckles.

The room was still.

A single chair had been overturned near the hearth. A tea cup sat on the table, rim dark with a half-inch of untouched liquid.

And Catherine Holloway lay half-curled beside the bed, one arm outstretched toward the door.

Her dress had slipped open at the collar. The muslin at her throat had fallen open, the fastening undone—whether in haste or violence, he could not tell. The blood had spread from beneath her throat in a wide, uneven pool, thickening where it met the floorboards. A clean cut—but not delicate. Not ritual. Done quickly—from behind, or while she was held. He gagged, once, without warning. He had seen death in battle, and in the brutal accidents of sea-life. But this was different. This was a woman.

Nicholas crouched slowly. Her fingers were curled, and there was blood beneath two nails—one broken back to the quick. On the corner of the side table, a sharp smear that hadn't been cleaned. She had reached for something, or struck at someone. He followed the line of the wound and saw the dark stain on the edge of the hearth rug where she had fallen.

He placed two fingers at her throat, though he knew what he would find. No warmth. No pulse. Just stillness.

There had been more than one man. That much was clear.

They had not stayed long. The room was quiet, ordered. Not ransacked. No personal papers. No folios. Drawers open but not emptied in haste. Efficient men. Professional. Sent to finish, not to question.

He was thankful for that. There was no sign she been questioned, or had suffered beyond the moment itself.

They had worked quickly. Struck, searched, left. The desk had been emptied. The wardrobe pulled apart and closed again. Even the underside of the hearth had been cleared of ash. Whoever they were, they were good.

He stood and scanned the room again, not for sentiment, but for omission. Not what had been taken. What had been missed.

A draft stirred near the window. He moved toward it—then paused. A small black comb lay on the floor, a few feet from the body. Her hair had come loose in the struggle. She had worn it tight before. Or had she been trying to do something with it when she heard them at the front door? *Her hair – and how she used it to conceal and change her identity.*

He stepped closer.

The braid was mostly intact—except one section, slightly thicker, pulled to the underside and bound with a length of dark thread. And somehow less neat, out of symmetry.

He crouched again, drew out his penknife, and slid it beneath the cord. A single knot. Neatly tied.

The braid fell open. Inside was a ring.

Gold, thin and smooth. The setting was flush—a dark green emerald, square-cut, no prongs, polished flat. The stone caught the light faintly, like her eyes had, the last time she had looked at him after their encounter.

He turned it once. There was no inscription. No letters. No symbol. No numbers.

But it had not been left. It had been carefully and cooly hidden, perhaps in those last moments as she heard the front door forced and footsteps on the stairs. The way Catherine Holloway did everything.

Nicholas pocketed it without a word.

He rose, pistol still in hand, and stepped to the door, and went down the stairs.

Without pause, he slipped into the fog and pulled the front door closed behind him.

The street was silent. A few oil lamps still guttered along the wall-brackets, their flames dulled by soot and mist, halos drawn in tight. The fog had thickened while he'd been inside—now it pooled at ankle-height and hung low around the windows like smoke that had forgotten where it came from.

He walked slowly. Twenty yards. No more.

Then he heard it—a footfall where there shouldn't be one. A soft scrape of leather on wet stone. Another. Closer. Two men. Pacing with him.

He pivoted left, raising the pistol in one smooth motion. Sight focused. Balance perfect.

The first man broke from the shadow by the rail.

Shot one.

The ball took him just below the right eye. He fell forward without a sound, a burst of red spattering the brick behind him. His coat was clean, tailored—dark wool, no brass. Boots polished. Not a street cutthroat. A professional.

The second came in fast from the right.

Younger. Quicker. The blade in his hand was short, curved inward—meant for gutting, not duelling. Brutal. Practical.

Nicholas swung, retracting the pistol and firing more by instinct than aim.

Shot two.

The second barrel cracked flat and deep. The ball struck center chest. The man staggered, gave a single sharp breath, and dropped.

Nicholas stood still, breathing through his nose. No sound but the quiet ringing in his ears.

He thought of Silva—of the drills at São Gabriel, the chalked paper targets, the stillness before the shot. He thought of *Ocean*, of the moment his pistol cracked and Carlisle lived. And others—men fallen with sword and ball, in places far less quiet than this.

He stepped forward, crouched over the second man. Still alive. Breathing raggedly. Blood soaking through his coat near the heart. The knife lay beside him, blade slick, curved like a butcher's hook.

This was the blade that had cut Holloway's throat.

No rage. Just recognition.

Nicholas searched the coat—quick, one-handed. A paper packet, oilskin-wrapped. No time to check it. He pocketed it.

The first man was beyond reach. Blood pooling beneath the rail.

Voices now—closer. A woman's gasp from a window above. A child's cry farther down the lane.

Nicholas turned. He didn't run. Just walked swiftly away.

CHAPTER TEN

He moved westward, keeping to the darker edges of the street where the inadequate lamplight failed to reach. His boots made little sound on the damp cobbles; he had developed a sailor's tread, placing each foot deliberately, testing the surface before committing his weight.

Two streets on, he found the hackney stand—three carriages waiting, their drivers hunched against the chill, sharing a flask of something that steamed in the cold air. Nicholas approached the nearest, a solid-looking vehicle with a driver whose face bore the weathered lines of decades on the London streets.

"Where to, sir?" the man asked, tucking away his flask.

Nicholas considered. Half Moon Street was now denied him. The Anchor and Crown would be watched as well.

"Bishops Coffee House."

The journey through fog-wrapped London took longer than it should have, the driver forced to proceed at a walking pace in many streets where visibility extended no more than a few yards ahead. In the privacy of the carriage, he reloaded the pistol by feel—powder, patch, and ball, the old rhythm returning like a familiar verse. He primed both pans and set the hammer back to half-cock before tucking the piece once more inside his coat. Finally, the carriage stopped across from a hanging sign that creaked gently in the morning air: *Bishop's Coffee House – Gentlemen's Letters Conveyed, Freights Discussed, News Received Daily.*

The interior was long and low-beamed, panelled in dark oak that had darkened further with the seasons. A pair of coal fires glowed low in opposing hearths. The floorboards, sanded clean and swept with lye, bore the faint sheen of decades of boots and spills. The ceiling was hung with iron hooks from an earlier century, now pressed into service for nothing more than shawls and damp hats.

The room smelled of roast beans, damp wool, and scorched sugar — not unpleasantly. A narrow counter ran along one wall, stacked with clay cups, a tin pot of cream gone to gloss, and a chipped tray of nutmeg in its shell. A boy in a patched waistcoat moved briskly between the tables with a kind of nautical economy, weaving, balancing, vanishing again.

Nicholas paid and took a place near the rear, where the wall met a recessed alcove set with a narrow bench. He sat with his back to the panelling and his eyes on the room.

The cup, when it came, was chipped at the rim and thick as a musket ball. But the coffee was real: strong, hot, faintly smoky, with no sign of chicory or barley to stretch it. He drank half of it without thought, feeling the warmth settle through his chest.

The room was half full. At the table nearest the hearth sat two Company clerks with shipping ledgers and a map spread between them, whispering over tonnage marks. A man who looked like a retired purser, or an actor doing a poor imitation of one, sat beside the window with a printed sheet folded four times and a twist of salt beef on waxed paper.

He felt the tension slowly draining away, his mind replaying what had just happened, even as he continued to watch the door.

After a moment he unwrapped the packet taken from the second man with care. Inside was a single folded sheet, creased from long concealment. It bore no heading—just a list of names and dates, each rendered in a narrow, practiced hand. *Holloway* appeared halfway down, beside a date two days before. *Cruwys* stood lower, uncrossed, with no date at all.

He thought about his time with Catherine in his rooms just four nights before. They watchers had been that close.

He thought of her admission about Caroline had come when they were dressing, the words offered without emotion or apology.

"Why risk yourself for her?" he had asked, watching as she fastened the tiny pearl buttons at her wrist.

"We knew each other in Calcutta, as I said," she had replied, her gaze steady. "More intimately than her father would care to know. Such connections forge loyalties that transcend conventional arrangements."

"And yet you knew of Ashton," Nicholas had observed.

A shadow had crossed Catherine's face then. "I facilitated an introduction. The marriage was her father's doing, and her own choice, made before she understood what Ashton truly was." Her fingers had stilled momentarily. "I have debts to repay."

Now, Nicholas considered what lay beneath those words. Catherine Holloway was a woman of calculated moves, of carefully weighed advantages. Yet in this, he had sensed something different. Not sentiment, precisely. But perhaps the nearest thing to genuine concern she had ever allowed herself to show.

He drew the ring from his pocket and placed it on the table before him, shielded from view behind the heavy coffee mug.

It was finely made. The band was gold, the emerald was set flush against the metal and caught what little light filtered through the coffeehouse windows, glinting with a deep, steady green that reminded him of Catherine's eyes.

Where was Caroline?

He turned the ring over slowly, feeling the smooth edge, the hidden weight of it. On impulse, he held it up to the light, the emerald between his eye and the window.

Through the stone, faint but unmistakable, he saw numbers etched into the inner surface of the band:

17–4–5

A code. An address. A meeting place. He wasn't sure. But it was no mere keepsake. Not a token of grief or loyalty. It had been left, or hidden, with intention.

Nicholas set the ring down again, beside the mug. He did not touch the coffee.

The room had quieted behind him. The clerks had packed their ledgers. The purser—real or false—had left his paper folded beside a half-eaten twist of beef.

There were others he might speak to. Thornhill. Even Westborne. But each step upward would cast a longer shadow. And this—whatever it was—had not been meant for committee.

He looked down at the ring again.

Carlisle.

They had spoken last in London, just before Nicholas joined Hood's staff. The man had been measured, dignified—but not unkind. He had shared more than Nicholas had expected: Caroline's brilliance, her complexities, even her choices. He had spoken not as a merchant arranging a marriage, but as a father attempting, within the limits of his world, to protect a daughter whose life would never be simple.

Nicholas had not written. And Caroline's promised correspondence had never come.

To contact Carlisle now was not just a step toward information. It was a return to a door that had been closed deliberately, though not locked. The ring might mean nothing. It might mean everything. But it had been left for him. And there was no one else who might know what it meant.

He drew a slow breath.

Then he beckoned the boy and asked for pen and paper.

He wrote a short note to Carlisle, stating that he was writing on an urgent matter requiring discretion and, if agreeable, a brief audience that day. He sent it by express runner to Ocean House, Portland Place.

The reply came within the hour:

> *Mr. Carlisle will be pleased to receive Commander Cruwys at two o'clock. Please use the side entrance, as the front door is being painted.*

Nicholas paid for his coffee and left, the ring still warm in his coat pocket, the scent of scorched sugar and damp wool clinging to the cloth.

The coffee had helped, but he was beginning to feel the strain of the day's events. It had started to rain again—persistent now, fine and chill. At the corner, he hailed an empty hackney, its driver hunched in oilskins. The man nodded and opened the door without comment. Nicholas stepped gratefully inside, the damp rising off his coat like steam.

"Portland Place. Ocean House."

The carriage moved off with a lurch, its wheels hissing over wet cobbles. Nicholas leaned back and closed his eyes briefly, the scent of damp leather and the steady rattle of the rain setting his thoughts in motion again. The city moved outside in blurred silhouettes and lamplight. His thoughts moved faster.

It was near two.

Ocean House emerged at last through a curtain of drizzle and coal smoke: a handsome Portland stone facade of three storeys, its windows tall and well-proportioned, the brass plate beside the door polished to a soft gleam that spoke of attention rather than ostentation.

Nicholas dismissed the chaise and paid the fare without comment. For a moment he stood at the foot of the steps, rain spattering across his hat brim, observing the house. A light burned in the first-floor window—Carlisle's study, if he recalled correctly from his last visit the night before leaving for Portsmouth and sailing for the West Indies.

He ascended with measured tread, avoiding the shallow pools that had gathered along the flagstones. A manservant of middle years—

Winters, he remembered—admitted him through the side entrance, as the note had instructed.

The air inside was markedly warmer than the damp chill outside. It carried the scent of a house where matters of consequence occurred: beeswax and leather, tobacco and polished brass. The atmosphere stirred memory, not just of his earlier visit, but of the quiet clarity with which Carlisle had once spoken to him about Caroline.

That meeting, framed as congratulations on Nicholas's new appointment, had in fact been an explanation. Caroline, Carlisle had said with careful directness, would marry Ashton—not for love, nor with illusions, but with an understanding suited to their station. Ashton required a wife who could maintain appearances and permit private accommodations that would never pass in polite society.

Nicholas had accepted it, perhaps more than he should have. But now, with Ashton revealed as something darker than a man of flexible virtue, Nicholas found himself asking again: what had the marriage really served? And what did Caroline know?

The study into which he was shown bore the unmistakable signature of its occupant. A substantial walnut desk bore the marks of genuine use—ink stains and faint scratches across the grain. Shelves of books lined the walls, their spines slightly faded and some cracked from handling. Several charts hung behind the desk—not decorative, but practical—annotated in pencil, marked by the eye of a man who calculated distances and returns in the same breath.

A large map of the Coromandel coast lay open across the desk. Along the mantel stood a line of carved ivory cranes—delicate Chinese work Nicholas remembered from his last visit. Their wings seemed to shiver faintly in the fire's flicker, as though waiting.

Edward Carlisle stood by the hearth, where a coal fire burned with steady purpose beneath a dark marble mantel. He was dressed plainly but well: a coat of fine, sober blue cloth, buff waistcoat without embroidery, no rings save the heavy gold signet that had been his father's. His face bore the weathering of years spent in tropical climes, but his eyes remained clear and assessing. He took in Nicholas's rain-damp appearance with a single, comprehensive glance.

"Commander Cruwys," he said, extending his hand. "You look tired. Come—sit by the fire. The roads must be foul in this weather."

"Mr. Carlisle." They shook hands—neither warmly nor coolly, but with the precise pressure of men who understood the gravity of present circumstances. Nicholas was indeed tired, with the kind of bone-deep weariness born of sustained vigilance rather than physical exertion. The events at Newman Street had left him drained, though little of it showed.

"The roads are tolerable. It is the purpose that weighs."

Carlisle gestured to a chair opposite his own, placed to catch the fire's warmth. He moved to a sideboard, where a decanter stood beside several glasses.

"You'll take Madeira?" he asked, already pouring.

"You have something of importance, your note suggested," Carlisle said as he handed over the glass. His tone was measured, gaze steady—the attentiveness of a man who negotiated not merely with figures, but with consequences.

Nicholas accepted the glass, the cut rim cool against his fingertips. He sipped—it was good Madeira, Nicholas noted, of an older vintage—slightly dry, with a trace of resin beneath the sweetness. A merchant's choice: refined, unostentatious, and meant to convey quiet discernment.

The fire crackled softly behind him.

Carlisle continued, settling into his chair. "I confess your appearance in London comes as a surprise, Commander. The last I was aware placed you still in the West Indies."

There was a question in it, though framed too delicately to be a direct inquiry.

Nicholas exhaled once—slowly—then nodded. "I sailed from the Islands several weeks ago with dispatches taken from a captured Spanish aviso." He paused, letting the words settle between them. The heat of the fire pressed against his back; the weariness behind his eyes did not ease.

Then, more quietly: "Mr. Carlisle—what I'm about to say concerns your son-in-law, Lord Ashton."

That changed the air between them. Carlisle said nothing, but his stillness sharpened.

"There is strong evidence he's been engaged in activities contrary to both Crown and Company interests. Diverting shipments. Falsifying manifests. Passing intelligence to foreign powers."

Carlisle's expression did not shift, but the stillness in the room grew heavier.

"These matters came to light through an investigation undertaken by certain offices within the Admiralty," Nicholas continued. "One of the investigators—an unofficial agent, highly placed—was Catherine Holloway."

That caught him. Not a visible start, but a tightening of the shoulders. A fractional narrowing of the eyes.

"I believe you knew her. From Calcutta. She spoke of it to me."

Carlisle said nothing, but his silence had the shape of recognition.

"Yesterday," Nicholas said evenly, "I found her murdered."

He reached into his coat and drew out the ring, placing it on the small table between them.

"It was concealed in her hair. Hidden deliberately—as a final message."

Carlisle's reaction was immediate and profound. The practiced neutrality of a seasoned merchant fell away in an instant. His complexion paled beneath its sun-weathering; the muscles along his jaw tightened. He looked, Nicholas thought, older than he had two years ago, even two minutes ago.

He reached for the ring with a hand that trembled slightly.

"This was Caroline's," he said, his voice low. "A gift on her seventeenth birthday. It was her grandmother's—my mother's—before that."

He turned the ring slowly between his fingers, examining it with studied precision. Then, in a gesture Nicholas found oddly moving, he held it up to the light, squinting through the emerald.

"There are numbers," he murmured. "Beneath the setting. Visible only through the stone."

He passed the ring back. "17–4–5. Caroline had that added years ago.

Nicholas watched without speaking.

"I encouraged that match," Carlisle said suddenly. He set his glass down hard; a splash of Madeira stained the polished table. He seemed not to notice.

"Believed in it. To an extent, for all the usual reasons—position, access, the bridge between merchant and noble. He offered her a world I could never buy her into. And I thought she..."

He broke off, collected himself.

"As I told you when we last spoke here—before you sailed—Caroline is exceptional. But she's not protected by convention. She sees things others don't. Desires things others wouldn't admit. Ashton offered her autonomy, or said he did."

His eyes met Nicholas's then, and there was a cold fury in them, aimed as much at himself as anyone else.

"Now I think I may have brought a viper into my own house."

Still Nicholas said nothing.

"I do not yet know whether Ashton acted from ideology or appetite," Carlisle continued, his composure returning by degrees. "But I noticed peculiarities. Funds moving through Company accounts that matched no shipments. Names in the registers I couldn't trace. A Bombay clerk suddenly maintaining a style far above his salary. Ashton's own firm—too clean. Too quiet."

He shook his head. "I assumed embezzlement. Or speculation. But you suggest something worse."

"Not theft," Nicholas said quietly. "Payment. According to what Catherine uncovered, Ashton has been receiving Spanish and French payments, indirectly—for shipping schedules, naval movements, diplomatic reports. The anomalies you noticed were simply the mechanism. The coin passed through false cargo manifests."

He paused, allowing the words to settle.

"Treason pays better than legitimate trade, it seems."

Carlisle's face had grown ashen. He picked up the ring again, studying the emerald as if it might yield further truths.

"You didn't know your daughter had given this to Holloway?"

"No," Carlisle said after a moment. "Though indeed they were... close. In Calcutta, some years ago. More than acquaintances."

He met Nicholas's gaze directly.

"My daughter has never conformed. Her mind is too independent, her questions too pointed. In Catherine Holloway, she found someone similarly unbound by expectation. I knew they were friends. But not the depth of it."

He exhaled slowly.

"If Caroline gave her this ring, it was with purpose."

Nicholas inclined his head.

"Do you recognize the meaning of the numbers? 17–4–5?"

Carlisle frowned, studying the ring again with narrowed eyes.

"It's familiar. Caroline and I established several private references over the years—signals, phrases, fallback arrangements. This one... I should have a record somewhere."

He rose abruptly and crossed to a cabinet inlaid with tortoiseshell. From within, he withdrew a small ledger bound in red Morocco leather.

"When she began accompanying me on Company business," he said as he leafed through it, "we established certain precautions. The East India trade is not without its hazards. I insisted she have means of reaching safety should we ever be separated, even in London."

His fingers stopped at a page marked with a ribbon.

"Here."

He studied the entry. "Yes. Now I remember. Lincoln's Inn—building seventeen, fourth floor, fifth chamber. A barrister's rooms. Caroline had me record it as a place where messages might be left, or shelter taken, if the need arose. The code on the ring matches the entry exactly."

He closed the ledger with care.

"Caroline must have sent her the ring. Likely just before her death. She knew Catherine would pass it on if she could—or, failing that, hide it where someone might."

Nicholas sat back slightly. "Then the ring itself was the message. Not just the numbers—but the fact of it being passed on at all."

Carlisle nodded. "If found by the wrong hands, the code appears meaningless. Just a family heirloom. But to Caroline, and to Catherine, it meant only one thing: that she had gone to ground."

His voice softened. "She would not have given it away lightly. And Catherine would not have failed her."

Nicholas rose. "Then I must go. Before Ashton's men guess what she meant to say."

"I'll accompany you," Carlisle said at once, rising with him.

"With respect, sir," Nicholas replied, his tone quiet, "it's better if you remain. If you come, they'll know something's afoot. But from here, you can still move the pieces—if anything goes wrong."

Carlisle hesitated, his mouth tightening slightly. Then he crossed to the window and stood for a moment, looking into the misted pane.

He gave a single nod—not quite to Nicholas, not quite to himself.

"Very well," he said. "I'll send men with you. Discreet men. Well equipped."

"You saved my life once. On *Ocean*. I never forgot."

He turned.

"I am entrusting you with something far dearer."

"I understand," Nicholas said.

Carlisle hesitated.

"And if I've already lost her—"

"You haven't," Nicholas said, with more certainty than he felt. "Catherine wouldn't have risked the ring unless she believed Caroline still lived."

For a moment, something moved in Carlisle's face—grief, perhaps, or a flicker of hope. Then it was gone.

"Go then," he said. "And may God speed you."

CHAPTER ELEVEN

Nicholas departed Ocean House with two men Carlisle had vouched for—Simmons and Clark, both former Company security officers who had served in the East under Carlisle's direct authority. Simmons was the elder of the pair, a square-built man of perhaps fifty with a scar that ran from temple to jaw on the left side of his face. He spoke little, but moved with the balanced readiness of one accustomed to hazardous situations. Clark was younger, leaner, with close-cropped hair and the bearing of a man who had seen military service. They had been joined, at Clark's insistence, by a third man—Fraser, a hard-faced Scot who had served as Carlisle's chief of security in Bombay during the troubled months of '79.

At Nicholas' inquiry, all three indicated how they were armed—discreetly but thoroughly, Nicholas noted with approval. Simmons carried a short-bladed hanger beneath his coat, the hilt bound in cord rather than metal to avoid a tell-tale glint, and a small Queen Anne-style flintlock tucked into the deep inner pocket of his riding jacket. Clark favored precision over weight: a fine-bodied pistol of East India pattern sat holstered against the small of his back, barely visible unless he turned sharply, and a narrow stabbing dirk rode sheath-bound inside his boot. Fraser carried his weapons with the casual confidence of a man who had used them often—a cavalry pistol inside his coat and a kukri knife, its curved blade marked with notches, concealed beneath his greatcoat. None bore the look of men who wished for a fight—but all moved with the calm inevitability of those who had survived many.

They took a hackney from Portland Place to Chancery Lane, alighting some distance from Lincoln's Inn to avoid direct approach. The rain and fog had thickened further, wrapping London's buildings in a gray shroud that reduced visibility to mere yards. It was, Nicholas reflected, both hindrance and help—concealing their movements, but also potentially masking any watchers who might be stationed near their destination.

"We'll circle the perimeter first," Nicholas instructed as they neared the venerable complex of buildings that comprised the Inn. "Look for anyone paying too much attention to the entrances. Any carriages waiting without obvious purpose. Anything that suggests surveillance."

The men nodded, separating slightly as they moved through the fog-laden streets. Nicholas kept his right hand near but not upon the butt of the pistol within his coat, his senses alert to the movements around them. Lawyers and clerks hurried past, collars turned up against the damp, faces hidden beneath hats and the occasional umbrella. A link-boy called his services from a corner; a chairman shouted for passage through a narrow turning. The normal commerce of London continued unabated, indifferent to the purpose that drove Nicholas and his companions through its familiar choreography.

"Nothing obvious," Clark reported, his voice pitched low. "Usual traffic. No watchers I could detect."

"Agreed," said Simmons. "Though in this fog, a regiment could be waiting and we'd not see them till we walked into their bayonets."

Fraser merely nodded, his eyes never still.

Nicholas considered the layout again, then glanced to each man in turn.

"Simmons, you and Fraser will remain below in the main courtyard—one at each entrance. Clark, you'll come with me as far as the third floor, but wait at the stairhead. I'll take the last flight approach the chambers alone. Lady Ashton is likely to be wary, and the sight of armed men might provoke an unfortunate reaction."

"Questions? Comments?"

Clark spoke. "One thought, sir. If Simmons or Fraser see anything—anything at all—they should come up to the fourth-floor landing and wait just out of sight. That way there's no delay. And I'll see them. No need for signals in this muck."

Nicholas hesitated a beat. The suggestion was sound. Even so, it shifted the weight of their reaction upward—toward him, and maybe Caroline.

But Clark's tone was calm, his logic unassailable.

"Very well. Do that."

All three nodded. They required no further detail.

"On my signal," Nicholas said, checking the pistol's priming one last time. He nodded to Simmons and Fraser, who vanished into the mist with practiced efficiency.

He adjusted his hat, checked the hang of his sword, and with Clark shadowing at a discreet distance, stepped into the main courtyard of Lincoln's Inn.

The fog seemed to grow thicker within the confines of the ancient buildings, pooling in corners and doorways like a living thing seeking shelter. Nicholas moved purposefully, consulting a small pocket watch as though late for an appointment, his gaze constantly scanning for movement or irregularity.

He located building seventeen without difficulty—a substantial structure of Portland stone with the same somber dignity that characterized the Inn as a whole. At the entrance, he nodded to Clark, who took up position at the foot of the main staircase, his bearing shifting subtly to that of a man waiting for a barrister to conclude business.

Inside, the air was warmer but still damp, smelling of old books, ink, and the peculiar mustiness of legal chambers. A porter sat at a small desk near the entrance, an elderly man more interested in the newspaper spread before him than in the comings and goings of visitors. Nicholas nodded to him as he passed, receiving the briefest acknowledgment in return.

The staircase rose in a broad spiral, its wooden treads worn into shallow depressions by centuries of ascending and descending feet. As he climbed, he glanced back once to confirm that Clark had now moved to the stairhead as instructed, watching both the entrance and the second-floor landing.

He climbed steadily, passing the second and third floors without incident. The building grew quieter as he ascended, the sounds of quills scratching on parchment and muted legal consultations giving way to an almost complete silence broken only by the occasional creak of the ancient timber frame settling against itself.

At the fourth-floor landing, Nicholas paused momentarily, listening with the practiced attention of a man accustomed to discerning changes in wind by the altered note of rigging. Satisfied, he proceeded along the corridor lined with oak-paneled doors, each bearing a small brass plaque engraved with a name and legal specialty. He moved quietly now, counting until he reached the fifth door on the right.

The plaque read simply: *J. Bowles, Esq. – By Appointment Only.* There was no light visible beneath the door, no sound from within.

Nicholas stood to one side, his back against the wall, and knocked softly—three measured raps that seemed unnaturally loud in the hushed corridor, like the first drops of rain on a calm sea.

Silence.

He knocked again, slightly harder.

Still no response from within. The silence now felt deliberate rather than empty—a silence of suppression rather than absence.

With careful movements, Nicholas tried the handle. It turned smoothly, but the door itself was secured from within. He withdrew the small case of picks he had carried since his midshipman days—insurance against locked cabinets and private sea-chests when searching for papers aboard a prize—and selected a slender implement. The lock was well-made but not complex; it yielded to his efforts after less than a minute's work, the tumblers settling into place with a precision that reminded him of correctly aligned rigging blocks.

Nicholas eased the door open a fraction, alert for any sound or movement from within. The room beyond was dim, illuminated only by what little daylight penetrated the fog-shrouded windows. He could make out the shapes of furniture—a desk, several chairs, bookshelves along one wall—but no immediate sign of occupancy.

His practiced eye noted the signs of habitation: a small spirit stove pushed beneath the desk, a portmanteau half-hidden behind a screen, several bottles of wine ordered in a neat row alongside bread wrapped in linen and sealed containers of the kind used for potted meats and preserves. A kettle sat cold upon the small hearth, and beside it a basin with soap and folded linen—the careful arrangements of someone prepared to remain hidden for some time, yet maintaining the standards of a person accustomed to better circumstances.

A sudden movement from the shadows to his right—a figure rising from behind the desk, followed by the unmistakable sound of a pistol being cocked.

"Who are you?" demanded a woman's voice—low, clear, and steady, though tension edged its control.

Nicholas froze. He knew that voice. Even altered by fear and fatigue, its precision remained—the unmistakable cadence of Caroline Carlisle. She had always spoken like that: carefully measured, never rushed, as if each word were an instrument laid precisely in place.

"Step forward where I can see you," she said.

He obeyed slowly, his hands visible at his sides.

"Caroline," he said. "It's Nicholas."

There was the briefest intake of breath. Not a cry—just a soft, involuntary gasp.

She didn't lower the pistol. But something in her posture eased—a taut line slackening, ever so slightly.

"I thought it might be," she said. Her voice remained composed, but it carried a new texture now—recognition, and something just short of relief. "But I still want proof."

Nicholas nodded. He understood.

"Your father sent me," he said. "I have Catherine's ring."

She remained in shadow. "Show me."

He noted the precise stillness in her stance—the way she neither wasted movement nor invited it. The small travelling desk beside her was open, papers laid in meticulous order. A half-filled cup of tea, cold, sat forgotten at the edge. Even in hiding, she had continued to work.

Nicholas reached into his coat and withdrew the emerald ring. He held it up so the light caught its facets.

"Seventeen, four, five," he said. "Lincoln's Inn. Your arrangement with Catherine. In case of emergency."

There was a pause.

Then, the quiet click of the pistol being uncocked.

Caroline stepped into the light.

She was more beautiful than he remembered—even here, in the still hush of that shadowed room.

The fabric of her dress clung just enough to trace the lean curve of her hips, and the bodice lay smooth across the full rise of her breasts, the wool shifting gently with each breath. Her face bore the subtle marks of a person who had been alert too long—a faint tightness around the eyes, a vigilant stillness in the shoulders—yet she carried herself with the quiet composure of someone who had drawn strength, not desperation, from solitude.

Her fair hair was pulled back with simple economy, revealing the fine structure of her features: the arch of her brow, the line of her cheek, the understated curve of her mouth. But it was her eyes that stopped him—deep green, clear and watchful, with that same quick intelligence he remembered. Older now. Sharper. But still hers.

She moved with the same fluid grace, though something in it had deepened—less uncertainty, more command. There was nothing fragile in her bearing. Even in fatigue—and he could see it now, in the set of her jaw, in the careful control of her breath—she stood like a woman who knew the power of her body, and wore it as other women wore jewels.

A single candle stood ready but unlit in a silver holder near her writing case, suggesting her careful rationing even of light.

He had forgotten.

Or rather, he had tried to forget—had folded her away like a letter placed too precisely. But now, with no warning, she was before him again, and he understood, with quiet astonishment, that even Elena had never quite measured against her—neither in form nor in spirit.

The realization came without drama, but with the inescapable certainty of a correctly plotted bearing.

"Nicholas," she said—her voice low and velvet-rich, as though they had spoken only yesterday, not two years ago. "You found her, then."

It was not a question, but he answered nonetheless. "Yes. At her lodgings in Newman Street. She had been killed—efficiently, professionally. The house was searched."

He watched how Caroline received this news—the momentary stillness, followed by a small, deliberate exhalation. Not surprise. Confirmation.

She closed her eyes briefly—not in shock, but in sorrow. When she looked up again, her gaze was steady. Composed not by nature, but by long practice.

"I always knew something was wrong," she said. "Not just secrets—anyone in his world keeps those—but something colder. There were patterns I couldn't explain. Catherine helped me see the shape of it."

She moved to a small portable writing desk, fitted with brass corners and a lock that showed signs of recent attention—oiled, maintained, the key on a slender chain at her wrist. The action of a woman who understood that information required protection.

She had arranged the chamber with the particular economy of someone accustomed to rapid departures—the writing table placed where the morning light would fall across it, yet positioned to observe both the door and the casement. A second pistol lay beneath a folded handkerchief on the sill, and her modest effects stood packed and corded in a valise near the threshold. These were the preparations of a person who understood that circumstances might admit no leisurely withdrawal.

Her hand moved to a satchel resting on the chair, fingers brushing the worn leather.

"I found the records five days ago—hidden in the pier glass in Ashton's dressing room. It was custom work. The frame was built with a concealed catch set into the lower moulding. If you pressed just so, the back panel slid free. The mirror had been sent out for 'restoration' the year before—I remember because the absence left an odd space on the wall. And afterward, it chimed slightly when touched, as if something inside had shifted."

Her description had the precision of a navigator's log—each detail recorded not for its emotion, but for its potential significance.

She met his gaze now, her voice calm, but edged with something quieter and sharper.

"The compartment was dry and narrow—built to hold documents flat between the backing and the glass. He could slide them in and out easily. Change names. Add letters. Work from it. It wasn't a vault. It was a desk no one else could see."

She paused, then opened the desk with practiced efficiency, withdrawing several papers and placing them into the satchel. A small writing case of red Morocco leather lay open beside it, the pages inside filled with her own neat hand—copies, he realized. Duplicates of the evidence. She had planned for failure. The work of a methodical mind leaving nothing to chance.

"If they killed Catherine," she said, "it wasn't to question her. It was to silence her. And to leave me no one."

Her eyes were clear now—not afraid, but alive with the terrible certainty that comes after fear has passed.

"I gave her the ring. I told her where I would be, if it ever came to that. It was my room. My safe place—not hers. I couldn't save her. But I can finish what she began."

She straightened another stack of papers with a single, practiced motion, aligning the edges with quick precision. The gesture of someone converting emotion into action. She added them to the satchel, along with the duplicates.

"The ring was hidden," Nicholas said quietly. "Sewn into her hair. They missed it. Your father explained it to me."

"She would have ensured that," Caroline said softly. "She was always meticulous about what must be preserved."

A fleeting expression crossed her face—something between grief and a deeper, more private emotion—before it vanished again behind her composed facade.

"You've come to take me to my father."

"If that can be done safely," Nicholas confirmed. "I have three men with me—Simmons, Clark, and Fraser. Your father vouched for their discretion."

Caroline shook her head slightly. "I know Simmons. He was in Calcutta when—"

She stopped, then changed direction. "I don't know this Clark or Fraser. Are they new to my father's service?"

"I couldn't say," Nicholas replied. "They seemed competent enough."

Her expression changed—a tightening around the eyes, a slight paling of her already fair complexion.

"Nicholas," she said quietly, "I know all of my father's confidential agents. There is no Clark or Fraser among them."

The implication settled between them like a physical weight.

"We need to leave," Nicholas said at once. "By a different route than the main stair, if possible."

"There's a service stair at the far end of the corridor," Caroline replied. "Clerks use it to bring documents up from the archive. It leads to a small courtyard with access to Carey Street."

Nicholas drew his pistol and checked the priming again. "Take only what's essential. We may need to move quickly."

"This," she said, securing the satchel with practiced speed, "contains everything—the complete evidence against Ashton and Everett. Their correspondence, false shipping records, payments routed through dummy companies."

She stepped to the window, lifted the handkerchief, and retrieved the pistol that lay beneath. It was the one Nicholas had seen earlier on the sill—compact, steel-barrelled, no ornament. She checked the flint, then slipped it into her coat.

"I'm ready."

They moved to the door. Nicholas checked the corridor before allowing her to step through. It was empty. The only sound came from a door closing somewhere below—distant, hollow, but real.

They moved toward the service stair, Nicholas slightly ahead, senses taut.

The stairwell was narrow, dim, and descended in tight switchbacks. They had just reached the second landing when voices rose from below—male, confident, moving with purpose.

"Back," Nicholas whispered, drawing her upward again. "We'll try another way."

They retraced their steps toward the main corridor, but had scarcely reached it when the regular staircase at the opposite end disgorged two figures into the hallway.

One was Simmons—but something was wrong. His movements were constrained, his expression tight with distress.

Behind him came the man called Clark. It was immediately clear he was directing rather than following. One hand remained inside his coat, in a manner that suggested a weapon pressed against Simmons's back.

"Commander Cruwys," Clark called, his voice cordial, but edged with something colder. "I was growing concerned for your safety. Mr. Simmons here was just about to help me find you."

Nicholas shifted his stance slightly, positioning himself before Caroline, shielding her from a clear line of sight. A fool, he thought—Clark was still speaking. If their positions had been reversed, Nicholas would have acted first and spoken, if at all, only after.

But every word was time.

"It seems I misunderstood your relationship to Mr. Carlisle," Nicholas replied, keeping his tone conversational despite the tension crackling beneath it.

"A common enough error," Clark said with a thin smile. "Mr. Carlisle believes I serve his interests. In truth, my loyalty lies elsewhere—as does Mr. Simmons's, now that certain arrangements have been explained to him."

He gave Simmons a prod forward.

"Isn't that right?"

Simmons's face was a study in conflicting emotions—anger, shame, resignation. He looked at Nicholas.

"I'm sorry, sir. They have my daughter. In Gravesend. I had no choice."

"There's always a choice," Clark said mildly. "Yours was simply... constrained by circumstance."

Then his gaze shifted to Caroline.

"Lady Ashton. Your husband has been most distressed by your absence. He'll be relieved to know you're safe."

"I doubt that very much," she said. Her voice was calm, precise. "My husband's concern is for what I know, not for my welfare."

"Perhaps both," Clark suggested, with mock solicitude. "But in either case, you'll be coming with us now."

He gestured with his free hand toward the staircase.

"After you, if you please. There's a carriage waiting below."

Nicholas assessed their position with the cool detachment born of combat. Clark had Simmons as hostage and partial shield. But the man was still talking when he ought to have acted.

From the service stair behind them came the unmistakable sound of boots ascending—measured, deliberate. Fraser, most likely, returning from below.

The trap was closing.

But not as tightly as it should have.

Nicholas didn't hesitate.

He raised his pistol in one smooth, swift motion and fired.

The shot cracked through the confined space. Clark's head snapped back, a red mist blooming where his right eye had been. He collapsed without a sound, his own unfired pistol falling from suddenly lifeless fingers.

"Down!" Nicholas shouted.

Simmons dropped instantly.

Nicholas pivoted toward Caroline. "The door—now!"

She was already moving, her reactions matching his intent without need for elaboration. The door swung open beneath her hand and closed firmly behind her.

Nicholas drew his sword in a single, practiced motion, the blade clearing the scabbard like the old friend it had been ever since Silva's gift.

A shout from the service stair—Fraser, appearing at the landing twenty feet away, sword drawn, his face twisting from confusion to fury as he took in the scene.

He charged without hesitation, blade extended in a killing thrust.

Nicholas raised the pistol and squeezed the trigger on the second barrel. The shot echoed sharply, but Fraser had already veered—moving too fast. The ball struck the paneling inches from his shoulder in a spray of splinters.

Steel met steel with a ringing clash that echoed down the corridor.

Fraser fought with the compact fury of a man trained for close quarters—no wasted movement, every strike aimed to kill. He lacked finesse, but his raw power forced Nicholas back toward the wall with relentless pressure.

Nicholas parried a thrust that would have skewered his throat, the blades grinding together until they locked at the hilts. Where Fraser's edge wavered under pressure, Nicholas's held firm.

For a moment they stood chest to chest, muscles straining, breath mingling. Fraser's face contorted with effort, yellowed teeth bared in a clenched snarl.

With a sudden shift of weight, Nicholas broke the bind and stepped aside, letting Fraser's momentum carry him forward.

As the man stumbled, Nicholas's blade found the opening—driving in just below the shoulder blade, deep and clean.

Fraser gave a wet, choking sound. His sword fell with a clatter as his body went rigid—then slack.

"Go," Nicholas ordered, grabbing Simmons by the shoulder. "Get to the street. Find a hackney. Wait for us at the corner of Carey and Portugal."

Nicholas turned back to the door where Caroline had taken refuge. Breathing hard, he said, "Caroline, let me in."

The lock clicked, and the door opened just enough to admit him before closing firmly behind.

The room was similar to the one she had occupied—a barrister's chambers, though somewhat smaller, with the same arrangement of desk, chairs, and bookshelves. Caroline stood by the window, her pistol still in hand, her face composed but alert.

"Are you hurt?" she asked immediately.

"No," Nicholas replied, wiping his sword clean on a handkerchief—the blade unmarred, still glinting razor-sharp. It slid home into its scabbard with the same precision with which it had killed moments earlier. "But we must move quickly. Fraser was likely not alone."

Caroline nodded, already reaching for her satchel.

"There's another stair—through there." She indicated a door at the rear of the chamber. "It leads down to the library, and from there to a small courtyard with access to Serle Street."

"Good," Nicholas said. "Simmons will meet us near Carey Street. If we're separated, send word to your father. He's expecting us, but may be under watch."

They moved through the indicated door and down a narrow, winding stair that smelled of old leather and the peculiar dust of seldom-used passages. The library below was deserted at this hour, its high shelves casting long shadows in the fading afternoon light.

"This way," Caroline whispered, leading him between rows of leather-bound volumes to a small door half-concealed behind a shelf of ancient folios. She opened it cautiously, revealing a compact courtyard enclosed by high walls.

"The gate to Serle Street is just opposite."

Nicholas scanned the courtyard with practiced vigilance. Empty—save for a few rain barrels and a dry winter fountain. The high walls offered both security and constraint: protection from view, but only one exit.

They crossed quickly, keeping to the shadows beneath a leafless linden tree, its bare branches forming a delicate lattice against the dusk. Caroline moved with remarkable assurance, her steps quiet and exact—no hesitation, no excess motion. It struck Nicholas that she had prepared for this moment—had studied this route with the same methodical attention she once gave her father's ledgers.

At the gate, Nicholas paused and signaled Caroline to remain in cover. Serle Street lay just beyond—narrow, often quiet, but potentially watched. He listened. Nothing but the distant rumble of wheels on Chancery Lane and the soft patter of rain returning after its brief pause.

He opened the gate a fraction, scanned the street, then beckoned her forward.

They slipped through and turned north, keeping close to the buildings where the shadows lay deepest. The rain had intensified, plastering Caroline's hair to her temples and darkening her cloak to near-black. Nicholas kept one hand near his sword, eyes scanning ceaselessly for movement.

Simmons was waiting as arranged, a hackney drawn up beside him. The driver hunched under his sodden hat, reins slack in his hands. The horses stood quietly, steam rising from their flanks in the chill air.

"Any sign of pursuit?" Nicholas asked.

Simmons shook his head, his expression still drawn with the weight of betrayal and aftermath.

"None, sir. Streets are quiet. Too wet for most folk." He hesitated. "My daughter—"

"She'll be seen to," Nicholas said. "Your service today won't be forgotten. Mr. Carlisle will ensure her safety."

Caroline stepped into the hackney first, her movements economical despite the weight of wet skirts and the satchel clutched at her side. Nicholas followed, taking the forward-facing seat.

"Nicholas," she said quietly, "you're right—we can't go to my father's. Not directly. Clark knew who I am. If he knew that much…"

"He knew more," Nicholas said. He leaned forward and opened the hatch. "Covent Garden," he told the driver, then turned back to her. "First, a safe place to think. Then we send word to those who can help."

The hackney moved off into the rain-swept streets, its iron-rimmed wheels throwing up sheets of water from the puddles that had formed between the cobblestones. Caroline and Simmons watched as, with sure practice, Nicholas reloaded both barrels of the Manton gun.

Then they sat in silence.

The close air held the mingled scents of wet wool, leather, and the faint metallic trace of blood that still clung to Nicholas's cuff despite his efforts to clean it. Caroline sat opposite, her hands folded atop the satchel in her lap, her gaze direct and unwavering.

The satchel, Nicholas knew, contained more than enough to destroy both Everett and Ashton. But the knowledge it held would burn other hands as well—reaching into ministries, counting houses, and perhaps even the Board of the Admiralty itself.

"He'll have men searching," she said quietly. "Not just for me. For the papers."

"Yes," Nicholas agreed. "Which is why we must place them beyond his reach as quickly as possible."

The carriage turned down a narrow lane near Covent Garden, the familiar bustle of the market dimmed by rain and the hour. They stopped beneath the awning of a modest coffee house—*The Sextant*—its leaded windows glowing amber against the grey evening.

"Take a seat just inside the entrance and watch," Nicholas instructed Simmons.

Inside, *The Sextant* offered the particular anonymity of establishments frequented by naval officers of middling rank—men with enough consequence to be left undisturbed, but not so much as to attract attention. The room was half full, its patrons murmuring over papers and small plates, their conversations forming a low hum beneath the hiss of the fire.

Nicholas selected a table in the rear alcove, partially screened by a worn tapestry depicting a naval engagement of the previous century. He ordered coffee and bread for both of them, then drew a folded sheet of paper from an inner pocket.

"I'll write to Admiral Trevenen at his house—the hour is late enough," he said, dipping a pen into the inkwell provided by the establishment. "He can arrange a secure meeting without alerting any of Ashton's allies."

Caroline watched him write, her expression thoughtful.

"You trust him that much?"

"With my life," Nicholas replied. "And with matters of greater importance."

He finished the note—brief, direct, with a coded reference drawn from naval signal flags—and sealed it with a wafer from the case beside him.

A boy was summoned—one of those quick-footed, sharp-eyed messengers who made their living carrying private letters through the rain of London—and dispatched to Audley Street with the sealed note and a silver coin to ensure both speed and discretion.

They waited in the relative safety of the coffee house, speaking little but watching the door with measured attention. Simmons remained near the entrance, pretending to read a broadsheet while his eyes moved steadily across the room.

Nicholas relaxed fractionally. Caroline's hands, despite their steadiness, occasionally tightened around the satchel in her lap—a gesture that spoke less of fear than of resolve.

The messenger returned within the hour, rain dripping from his cap and shoulders. He delivered a folded note sealed with plain wax, then vanished back into the wet night with another coin for his trouble.

Nicholas broke the seal and read the few lines within.

"Trevenen has arranged for us to meet with Thornhill. Not at the Admiralty—a private residence in Bloomsbury. He believes it safer."

Caroline nodded, gathering her things. "And my father?"

"He'll be notified once we're secure. Trevenen thinks it best that no one knows our location except those directly involved."

Nicholas sent Simmons to secure a hackney. They exited by a side door when he returned. The rain had intensified to a steady downpour, cloaking the city in sheets of water that transformed the streets into rivers of reflection. Perfect weather, Nicholas thought, for moving unseen.

"Russell Square," he told the driver. "By way of Great Queen Street and Montague."

The longer route would let them detect any tail, though in weather like this, he doubted anyone could follow them effectively.

The journey through rain-blackened London seemed endless. The horses picked their way carefully through deepening puddles, now ponded at every intersection. Caroline sat in silence, her gaze turned to the streaming window. Nicholas doubted she saw much beyond the rain and her own thoughts.

They entered Russell Square, which—even in downpour—maintained its air of respectable prosperity. The houses stood back from the street, their brick facades regular and orderly, presenting a united front of gentility against the disarray of the night.

The hackney drew up before a modest townhouse midway along the eastern side—not ostentatious, but of that particular sort suggesting its occupant valued competence above display. A single light burned behind curtained windows on the ground floor.

"Wait here," Nicholas told Simmons as they alighted beneath the narrow shelter of the entryway. "If there's any sign of trouble, leave at once and make for Admiral Trevenen's house."

Simmons nodded. His face still showed the strain of the day's events, but his bearing remained firm.

"Understood, sir. I'll watch the street."

Nicholas knocked at the door—three deliberate raps followed by two lighter ones, as specified in Trevenen's note. There was a brief silence, then the sound of a bolt being drawn back. The door opened to reveal not a servant, but Thornhill himself, dressed with his usual precision despite the hour.

"Commander Cruwys," he said with a slight nod. "Lady Ashton. Please come in quickly." He stepped aside to admit them, then secured the door with the same swift efficiency with which he managed all matters. "I've been expecting you. Admiral Trevenen's note indicated the situation has escalated considerably."

The entrance hall was modestly appointed but immaculate—polished floorboards covered with a Turkish carpet in subdued blues and reds, a hall table of dark mahogany bearing a single lamp and a brass tray for calling cards, a hat stand of bent cherrywood. Nothing ostentatious, nothing neglected. Two men in unremarkable clothes resumed their seats in chairs, their discretion not totally concealing the butts of pistols tucked in their belts.

Thornhill led them into a small parlor where a fire burned steadily in the grate, dispelling the chill of the rain. The room was furnished for function rather than show—two comfortable chairs flanking the hearth, a table between them bearing a decanter and glasses, a small writing desk positioned to catch the light from the window during daylight hours, and bookshelves filled with neatly arranged volumes whose bindings showed signs of actual use rather than mere display.

"Please," Thornhill said, indicating the chairs. "You must be cold after your journey. May I offer you something? Brandy, perhaps, or tea?"

"Brandy, thank you," Caroline said, her voice composed despite what Nicholas recognized as the beginning of reaction now that they had reached momentary safety. Thornhill's presence, his familiar efficiency, the ordered calm of the room—all combined to create a space where the events of the day might finally register fully.

Thornhill poured three measures with the precise economy Nicholas had observed in all his movements, then took up a position near the desk, his back straight, his attention focused.

"I understand there was violence at Lincoln's Inn," he said without preamble.

"Yes," Nicholas confirmed. "Clark revealed himself as Ashton's man. He had forced Simmons's cooperation through threats against his family. When confronted, he left us no choice."

Thornhill absorbed this with a slight nod. "And Fraser?"

"Also dead," Nicholas said. "He came up the stairs to support Clark and attacked. I was forced to defend myself."

"I see." Thornhill's expression revealed nothing beyond professional assessment. "And the documents Lady Ashton has been gathering?"

Caroline opened the satchel and withdrew a leather portfolio bound with silk cord. "Everything I could assemble—the ledgers showing payments through false shipping manifests, correspondence with agents in Calais and Madrid, instructions to his brokers regarding the disposition of funds through accounts that exist on no Company register." She hesitated, then added, "And this, which I found only yesterday."

From a hidden inner pocket of the satchel, she drew a folded paper sealed with a broken red wax seal bearing the impression of the Treasury. "I believe it's a copy of instructions meant for our negotiators in Paris. How it came to be in my husband's possession, I cannot say—but its presence among his private papers suggests connections that extend well beyond what I knew of his role in Government."

Thornhill took the document, weighing it in his hand as though its physical presence might reveal its significance, and read through it quickly. "This confirms our worst suspicions," he said quietly. "What began as an investigation into irregular shipping manifests and espionage of what we might call the somewhat usual sort has led us to something far more consequential." He looked up, his gaze moving between them. "The situation has grown more urgent. I believe we shall shortly secure Everett, but Lord Ashton has fled London."

"When?" Nicholas asked sharply.

"Two hours ago, according to our sources at the docks. Aboard a French merchant vessel bound for Calais. Intelligence suggests he carries with him additional documents—not only those related to his own activities, but other sensitive materials concerning our negotiating positions with both France and Spain—perhaps indeed copies of this," he said, tapping the packet.

Caroline set her glass down carefully. "He means to sell the information, or exchange it for safe harbour."

"Precisely," Thornhill confirmed. "To parties who would use it to extract greater concessions from us at the peace table." He paused, then, speaking carefully: "You have both done a great service, and as soon as you've rested and refreshed yourselves, a carriage will be provided to take you to Ocean House and Lady Ashton's father—once we have confirmed it is safe."

Caroline nodded, but said, "Please—it is Miss Carlisle. The other name has no meaning." She turned to Nicholas. "And it never did."

Nicholas nodded, and Thornhill, watching the exchange, merely said, "I understand." Then, with a rare flicker of something that might have been warmth: "This house is secure. Please—relax. I must see to matters." He rose, bowed slightly, and left, closing an inner door softly behind him.

The fire crackled softly in the grate as rain continued to lash against the windows, transforming London beyond into little more than suggestions of light and shadow.

CHAPTER TWELVE

The rain had not ceased for three days, transforming London's streets into mirrors of leaden sky. However, in the late afternoon of Friday, 18th of October 1782, inside the private library of Lord Howe's Grafton Street residence, a fire burned with steady purpose, and candles in sconces helped disperse the gloom, casting shadows across the map table where three men stood in silence.

Admiral Lord Howe leaned forward, his substantial frame casting a broader shadow than the others. At fifty-six, newly ennobled for his successful relief of Gibraltar and still in command of the Channel Fleet, he carried himself with the particular gravity of a man accustomed to directing the movements of entire fleets. His face—weathered by decades at sea and broad across the brow—commanded attention without effort. His remarkable deep-set eyes were pools of watchful intelligence beneath heavy lids, giving him the aspect of a man perpetually considering matters beyond the immediate horizon. His nose was prominent but well-proportioned, his mouth set in that familiar firm line that had discouraged impertinence from generations of subordinates. The powder on his hair, applied with naval precision rather than fashionable excess, emphasized the natural dignity of his bearing. Though his figure had thickened somewhat since his more active days commanding the North American Station, there remained about him that indefinable quality of contained power—a man who had weathered storms both meteorological and political without yielding his essential composure. His large, capable hands moved across the chart with deliberate purpose, betraying nothing as his fingers traced the French coast from Calais to Cherbourg.

"He has crossed to Calais, then," Howe said, his voice pitched low despite the room's privacy. "Our man in the port confirmed it two days past. Traveling under the name Harville, with Spanish papers."

The library was precisely what one might expect of a senior naval officer who was also a peer of the realm—handsome without ostentation, functional yet befitting his station. Shelves of leather-bound volumes lined three walls, many bearing the gilt titles of naval histories and maritime charts. The fourth wall featured a substantial fireplace of grey Portland stone, above which hung a fine portrait of the King in his naval uniform, a reminder of His Majesty's particular fondness for the senior service. A ship model—*HMS Eagle*, Howe's flagship during the American campaign—rested in a glass case near the window, its exquisite detail suggesting it had been presented to him by his officers.

Across the table, Vice Admiral Sir Samuel Hood nodded once. He was the leaner of the two, with a face more angular than Howe's, etched with the permanent vigilance of a commander who had spent decades anticipating the movements of enemies on distant seas. Where portraits showed Howe as imposing and substantial, Hood appeared as precision incarnate—his features chiseled rather than molded, with high cheekbones that caught the light and cast subtle shadows beneath. His eyes, keen and assessing beneath arched brows, possessed that particular sharpness of a man accustomed to discerning enemy intentions from intuition, patterns of intelligence, and strategic sense. Though now in his early sixties, he maintained the erect carriage and contained energy of a much younger officer, his slender frame betraying none of the softness that often accompanied advancement in rank and years. His hands, when they moved, did so with an economy that mirrored his tactical approach—no wasted motion, no unnecessary gesture. His reputation for tactical brilliance had been cemented off the Chesapeake and reinforced at the Saints, though the glory there had ultimately gone to Rodney—a fact that those who knew him well could occasionally detect in the momentary tightening around his eyes when that campaign was mentioned.

"And the intelligence concerning his next movement is reliable?" Hood asked, the with a slight Dorset inflection in his speech.

Between them, Thornhill looked somehow diminished, though not in stature or presence. It was rather that the combined weight of these two admirals—men who had commanded squadrons and indeed fleets of ships of the line in the greatest battles of the age—rendered even the Admiralty's deputy head of naval intelligence momentarily secondary.

The choice of venue was no accident. What they discussed could not take place at the Admiralty, where Viscount Keppel as First Lord might encounter them. The political implications would be explosive—a direct channel from the King to naval officers, circumventing the cabinet and the First Lord himself. Keppel, as a Rockingham Whig sympathetic to peace with America, would be duty-bound to inform the cabinet of any operation that might affect the delicate negotiations in Paris.

"As reliable as any we receive from Brest, Sir Samuel," Thornhill replied. "Our source has served us well these three years. Ashton will take passage aboard *Le Furet*, twenty guns, six-pounders, probably 120 crew, and rumored to be one of the fastest of the new corvettes. She's to sail as soon as eight days hence, to deliver him to Bilbao, with Santander as an alternative heavy weather port, and he will take a fast post chaise from there to Madrid. He has with him documents detailing our negotiating positions—naval strengths, colonial concessions, trading rights in the Indies."

Howe's mouth tightened almost imperceptibly. "Documents prepared by Everett."

"Yes, my lord," Thornhill confirmed. "The Spanish will use this intelligence to extract greater concessions in the peace talks. If they believe our position weaker than it is—"

"We are well aware of the consequences, Mr. Thornhill," Hood interrupted, though without heat. "What concerns me is why this matter comes to us at all. The government has indicated its intention to settle this business quickly. Shelburne's ministry cannot afford another winter of war. Fox and North grow stronger by the day."

Hood's eyes met Howe's in a rare moment of political alignment. Both men understood that the Whig ministry's desperation for peace had rendered certain operations... politically inconvenient.

"That is precisely why it comes to us, Admiral," said a new voice from the doorway.

All three men turned as the fourth figure entered—smaller than the admirals, and indeed than Thornhill, yet instantly commanding the room's attention. Philip Stephens, Secretary to the Board of Admiralty, closed the door behind him with a quiet precision that bespoke decades of handling the nation's most sensitive communications. Though nearly sixty, he moved with the methodical efficiency that had made him indispensable to a succession of First Lords for twenty years. His neat, almost ascetic appearance—thin face with prominent nose, careful wig with minimal powder, and sober attire that spoke of function rather than display—belied the political acumen that had kept him in office through multiple administrations. He had perfected the art of navigating between the King's wishes and the Board's formal authority, understanding which matters required full disclosure and which were better handled through careful omission. While Viscount Keppel as First Lord might suspect something was afoot, Stephens had ensured the operation remained sufficiently compartmentalized that no direct questions need be answered—a delicate balance of loyalty to the Crown while maintaining the proper administrative forms.

Howe nodded and turned to the others with a gravity that suggested matters of great significance. "Now that Mr. Stephens has joined us, before we proceed further I should inform you that, as Mr. Thornhill is aware, the King has been fully briefed on this treason. I have had a private audience with His Majesty this morning." He paused, allowing the weight of this statement to settle. "His Majesty has expressed—in terms I found quite unmistakable—his particular concern that Ashton's activities might adversely affect certain royal priorities in the negotiations."

The implications were clear. George III's bitterness over the loss of the American colonies was an open secret in government circles. That the King should involve himself in an operation to prevent further erosion of British standing, even as his ministers pursued peace at nearly any cost, required no elaborate explanation.

"Did His Majesty indicate any specific wishes?" Hood asked carefully.

Howe met his gaze directly. "His Majesty observed that should Lord Ashton's vessel meet with some misfortune before reaching Spanish waters, he would consider it a service to the Crown not easily forgotten." He straightened his cuff with precise movements. "I believe the His Majesty's meaning was quite transparent, despite the necessarily oblique nature of the conversation."

Hood's eyebrow rose fractionally. The implication was clear enough. With the government's attention fixed on the peace negotiations, the Admiralty would soon undergo significant changes. Howe's name had already been mentioned as a potential First Lord when the ministry was reshuffled.

"The difficulty," Thornhill observed, returning to the matter at hand, "is that we cannot simply dispatch a frigate with official orders. Any documented pursuit would compromise the government's position in Paris—and raise uncomfortable questions about Everett's involvement, which certain parties remain keen to obscure."

"Then we require something less official," Howe said. "A privateer, perhaps."

"Too unreliable, my lord" Hood countered. "And too easily disavowed by the Spanish should they capture her. This requires a King's ship—but one that appears on no current commissioning list."

Thornhill and Stephens exchanged a meaningful glance. "There is the matter of *Alert*."

Howe and Hood both looked up sharply. Howe said, "The topsail schooner taken off Jamaica? That American-built privateer? "

"Yes, my lord" Stephens confirmed. "She is docked at Sheerness, officially struck from the list to be sold due to certain . . . political considerations. But in fact she was not struck from the list, nor will she be placed in ordinary." He glanced at Hood, whose face was expressionless, and continued, "Yet no crew is assigned, no orders issued. She's remained there these three weeks and more, ostensibly awaiting sale."

"A remarkable little vessel, by all reports," Howe said, not missing the interplay between Stephens and Hood.

Hood broke in, "Narrow hull, raked masts set at fifteen degrees, capable of sailing closer to the wind than anything we've captured. Fast on a reach, weatherly, shallow draft. Fourteen guns, ten six-pounders, two quarterdeck twelve-pounder carronades and two rather unusual long nine pounders chase guns, procured in fact by her former commander, who is currently in London." Hood added. "One who knows her capabilities intimately."

Howe's expression remained neutral, though his fingers drummed once on the chart—the sailor's unconscious habit of marking time against tide. His mouth formed a thin smile. "Ah yes, the officer who so thoroughly embarrassed young Fanshawe off Barbados, I believe. One can hardly fault his seamanship, whatever the political consequences. The Fanshawes have grown too comfortable with their influence at the Board, he grumbled almost in an aside."

Thornhill spoke up, "Yes my lord, Commander Cruwys, the man I mentioned in my recent report to the Committee."

Understanding dawned, and Howe asked, "Indeed, the same officer who was involved in the Holloway affair? And the matter at Lincoln's Inn?"

Thornhill nodded, and Howe said, "One of yours, I take it, Sir Samuel?"

Hood merely nodded.

"Thornhill continued, "He has proven discreet, capable of unconventional thinking, and effective. More importantly, he has personal reasons to see Ashton removed. Lady Ashton was previously known to him—before her marriage."

An understanding passed between the men—the unspoken recognition that personal motivation often proved more reliable than formal duty in matters requiring absolute commitment.

"Cruwys is sound?" Howe asked Hood directly.

"Entirely," Hood replied without hesitation. "He served under my flag in the West Indies. *Alert* was his first permanent command—an appointment and promotion that he earned at the Saints and for his work on my staff. He intercepted both the *Liberty* and the *San Isidro* with dispatches meant for Havana. He handles a small ship well, and he understands discretion. He's not a political creature, my lord. He simply does what's necessary."

Howe straightened to his full height, decision made. "Very well. Bring Commander Cruwys here," Howe said. "Tonight. I wish to take his measure myself." He paused, his gaze moving between Hood, Stephens and Thornhill.

"Gentlemen, I need not emphasize that this conversation has not occurred. Should *Alert* fail to intercept *Le Furet*—or worse, should she be taken—neither the Admiralty nor the Crown can acknowledge any connection to her mission."

"Understood, my lord," Hood replied. "And should she succeed?"

Howe's expression softened fractionally. "Then perhaps Commander Cruwys might find himself made post after all, once sufficient time has passed. The Navy will need good captains when this peace inevitably gives way to the next war. Let us turn for now to other matters."

An hour later, the men turned as a soft knock came at the door. A young lieutenant entered, rain still beading on his cloak.

"Begging your pardon, my lords," he said. "Commander Cruwys has arrived as requested."

Howe nodded once. "Show him in, Lieutenant. And see that we're not disturbed."

Thornhill and Stephens exchanged glances. The wheels were now in motion—unofficially, deniably, but irrevocably.

Nicholas entered with the measured step of a man accustomed to maintaining dignity regardless of circumstance. His blue coat, while not new, was impeccably brushed; his boots polished to a reasonable sheen despite London's inclement weather.

If he was surprised to find himself in the personal study of Admiral Lord Richard Howe—the legendary "Black Dick"—he concealed it well. Nicholas had never served directly under Howe, though the admiral's reputation was known throughout the service: taciturn, formidable in action, fiercely protective of his officers yet demanding absolute competence. The man who had commanded the American station through the most difficult years of the war, and who—some whispered—had approached his duties there with a certain reluctance, having more sympathy for the colonists' position than most of his contemporaries would admit.

Nicholas's eyes took in the gathering with a swift, comprehensive glance that missed nothing—his old commander, now promoted from Rear Admiral to Vice Admiral Sir Samuel Hood, Secretary Stephens who he had met before joining Hood's staff, and less surprisingly, Thornhill. He noted the chart of the French and Spanish coasts laid open on the table, the brandy glasses set out but untouched, the fire built higher than mere comfort would require for men accustomed to sea-watches in all weather.

"Commander Cruwys," Hood said, gesturing to the other men present. "You know Mr. Stephens and Mr. Thornhill, I believe, and this is Admiral Lord Howe."

Nicholas inclined his head to each man in turn, lingering slightly longer when acknowledging Howe. " My Lord Howe, Mr. Stephens, Mr. Thornhill."

Howe's deep-set eyes studied Nicholas with the particular intensity that had unnerved many a young officer over the decades, that had made him both admired and feared throughout the service — searching not for deference, which any naval man could feign, but for that particular quality of steady competence that could not be falsified. "Commander. Admiral Hood speaks well of your service in the West Indies."

"We have been discussing a matter of some delicacy," Hood said, "A matter which, I understand, touches upon your recent activities in London."

"I am at your lordships' disposal," Nicholas replied simply.

Howe stepped forward, his substantial frame seeming to fill more space than it physically occupied—a quality that had served him well both on quarterdecks and in the House of Lords. "Commander," he said, his voice pitched low but carrying that particular weight that made men listen, "what we are about to discuss exists nowhere in the Admiralty records. There will be no written orders, no official dispatches, no log entries that connect to this conversation."

Nicholas's expression remained composed, though something in his eyes sharpened. "I understand, my lord."

"Lord Ashton has fled to France," Hood said without further ceremony. "He carries with him intelligence that would materially damage British interests in the peace negotiations—particularly regarding our position in the Indies and our naval strength in the Mediterranean. He will take passage aboard the French corvette *Le Furet*, sailing from Brest bound ostensibly for Bilbao, or to Santander in the event of heavy weather."

Nicholas absorbed this, his posture unchanged. "I see."

"The government," Thornhill interjected carefully, "is not officially aware of this development. Nor can it be, given the delicate state of the negotiations in Paris. Ashton's activities—and those of his co-conspirator Everett—represent an embarrassment that certain parties would prefer to see... resolved... without public acknowledgment."

"What is required," Howe said, his tone making it clear he had taken command of the conversation, "is a ship and commander capable of intercepting Ashton's vessel before she reaches Spanish waters, ideally soon after she leaves France. A ship that appears on no active list, operating under no official orders, yet manned by King's officers who understand what is necessary."

Nicholas's gaze shifted to the chart on the table, then back to Howe. "*Alert*," he said quietly.

Howe nodded, something almost like approval in his weathered features. "*Alert*. Currently laid up at Sheerness, awaiting sale. She could be made ready within two days—provisioned, armed, crewed by men of your choosing, though they must understand the unofficial nature of the service."

"My former first lieutenant Forester is available," Nicholas said. "As is my master Markham. Both would serve without requiring explanations beyond what is necessary."

"Good," Howe said. "Because explanations are in short supply in this matter, Commander. What we require is action. *Le Furet* sails in eight days from Brest. She is a twenty-gun corvette, with a reputation for speed. *Alert*, with her fore-and-aft rig, should be able to match her in most conditions, and certainly outpoint her, though you'll have fewer men and fewer guns. This must be a matter of seamanship, not merely gunnery."

"I understand, my lord," Nicholas said.

Stephens spoke for the first time, his voice carrying the quiet authority of a man who had drafted countless secret orders over decades of service. "Should you accept this commission, Commander, you would be operating outside the protection of the Articles of War. Should you be captured, the Admiralty would be forced to disavow any knowledge of your mission. Should you decline, you will leave this room and speak of it to no one."

"And should I succeed?"

Hood and Howe exchanged glances.

"Then after a suitable interval," Howe said, "arrangements might be made to regularize your status. The peace will not last forever, Commander Cruwys. When the next war comes—as it inevitably shall—the Navy will require captains with proven ability to act decisively without the comfort of explicit orders."

Nicholas recognized the offer implicit in Howe's words: succeed in this mission, and a post-captaincy might follow. In the Navy's rigid hierarchy, that single step would change everything—permanent rank, better ships, the possibility of flag rank itself in time.

"There is also the matter of Lady Ashton," Thornhill said quietly. "Her situation remains... complicated... so long as her husband lives. Should he meet with misfortune at sea, however, her future would be considerably less constrained."

Nicholas gave no visible reaction to this, though Thornhill, who had observed him closely since the Holloway affair, noted the slight tension in his jaw.

"When would *Alert* sail?" Nicholas asked, his voice level.

"Dawn, on Monday, three days hence," Howe replied. "The tide will be favorable for clearing the Thames. You'll proceed directly to Brest, maintaining distance from the port itself but positioning *Alert* to intercept *Le Furet* once she clears the approaches."

"And my orders regarding the French corvette?"

Howe's expression remained impassive, though something in his eyes—a certain reflective quality that had led some to believe he harbored complicated views on the colonial rebellion—suggested a man who measured the moral weight of his words. "You have no orders, Commander. You have no ship. This conversation has not occurred." He paused. "But were I in your position, I would ensure that neither *Le Furet* nor its particularly valuable passenger reached their destination."

He let the silence hang for a moment, then added with characteristic directness: "We send you not as an executioner, Commander, but as the instrument of necessity. This is not vengeance—it is surgery. The body politic requires the removal of a diseased element that threatens the whole."

Nicholas understood perfectly. No quarter was to be offered. No prisoners taken. *Le Furet*, with Ashton aboard, was to be sent to the bottom.

"There is a further consideration," Thornhill added quietly. "The attack must not appear to be the work of a British vessel. If *Le Furet* is seen to be attacked by a King's ship, it would constitute an act of war against a diplomatic vessel. The peace negotiations could well collapse immediately."

"What are you suggesting, sir?" Nicholas asked.

"That *Alert* must not be identifiable as a British vessel," Thornhill said. "No colors, no recognizable features. As far as any survivors or witnesses are concerned, you might be privateers, pirates, or rogue Americans—anything but the Royal Navy."

The enormity of what they were asking settled on Nicholas like a physical weight. Not only was he to attack a ship under diplomatic protection, but he was to do so under false or no colors—an act that would indeed make him a pirate in the eyes of maritime law.

"May I select my own crew?" he asked.

"Within reason," Stephens confirmed. "I have prepared a list of reliable men recently discharged who might be approached, as well as of your former crew still known to be available in Sheerness. But choose carefully. Every man must understand that no record of this voyage will ever appear in the Admiralty files."

Nicholas calculated quickly. He felt the gaze of the others on him, and then said, "The list will help, sir, but I'll need more than discharged hands." He looked at Howe, "With your permission, my lord, I'd like to request that Captain Walsh transfer up to one hundred men from *Fortunée* to Alert at Sheerness. Trained gunners and topmen who already understand naval discipline; men trained by Captain Walsh, who was my commanding officer in *Lynx*." He paused. "And of course the men can be returned to him once the mission is complete."

Howe exchanged glances with the other men. "I recall well his action in taking the French frigate *Hébé*. Most credible indeed. Captain Walsh is sound?"

All three nodded. "Entirely, my lord, one of our most reliable captains," Stephens confirmed, glancing thoughtfully at Nicholas, "And, *Fortunée* so happens to be at Portsmouth. She could be ordered up channel."

"Very well," Howe decided. "*Fortunée* will be ordered to Sheerness for 'maintenance inspection.' The transfer of men can be accomplished there, away from prying eyes."

He straightened to his full height, the interview clearly concluding. "Commander Cruwys, the service you are about to render cannot be acknowledged. But it will not be forgotten by those who matter."

Howe's gaze met Nicholas's directly, admiral to commander, but with the peculiar equality that sometimes exists between men who understand the difference between orders and necessity. In that moment, Nicholas glimpsed something of what had made Richard

Howe both respected and controversial throughout his career—a commander who weighed his obligations to the Crown against a deeper, more personal sense of justice. A man who could order deaths when necessary, but never without understanding the full weight of such decisions.

"I understand, my lord."

Nicholas then turned to Hood, who regarded him with measured gravity. "*Alert* has served you well, Commander, and you know her merits—and her flaws—as well as any man. But do not take your quarry lightly. This is no privateer, but a French naval corvette, attached to the Brest squadron under Vice-Admiral Pierre-Claude Haudeneau de Breugnon—who held firm at Rhode Island and Grenada, and who is not a man known to suffer fools. You may expect a steady hand in your opponent, and a ship well handled."

As Nicholas departed, Stephens moved to the sideboard and at last poured the brandy that had stood waiting throughout the interview. He handed glasses to each of the others, then raised his own in a silent toast.

They drank without speaking, four men who had just set in motion an operation that would never be recorded in any official history, yet which might significantly alter the shape of the peace to come.

"He'll do it," Hood said after a moment. "And he'll succeed."

"For King and country?" Thornhill asked quietly.

Hood smiled faintly. "For those, certainly. But also for the woman. And for himself." He set down his glass. "The best officers always find their own reasons to exceed their orders or convention, Mr. Thornhill. It's what separates mere obedience from true service."

Howe was already studying the chart again, his mind moving beyond this night to the broader naval considerations that might soon fall under his direct authority. After decades at sea, he had developed the habit of seeing beyond the immediate horizon—a quality that had frustrated his political opponents and sometimes even the King himself.

"*Alert* sails in three days with the morning tide, then. God speed her—and damn Ashton to the depths he deserves."

CHAPTER THIRTEEN

After leaving Howe's residence, Nicholas was conveyed back to the townhouse on South Audley Street. The staff had already drawn the fire, laid fresh coals in the hearth. A valet he did not recognize handed him a sealed note from Thornhill, unopened. The note was clear: stay in place, speak to no one, and wait.

He bathed, shaved, and packed methodically—spare uniforms, instruments, his sword, his Nock fighting pistols and the Manton gun, and his personal logbook from *Alert*. By nine o'clock, the chest was closed, the straps buckled, and his uniform laid out for the morning. The clock in the hall struck ten with a low, deliberate chime just as the knocker sounded.

Thornhill entered without removing his coat. His gloves were dry, but his face carried the look of a man who had walked through the fog regardless.

"A cutter sails at dawn," he said. "A fast one, handpicked crew. She carries sealed instructions for the admiral off Brest."

Nicholas said nothing, waiting.

"The orders are specific. No interference with the French vessel. They've already received guidance not to impede her approach—she was towed into the outer roadstead two days ago, despite the wind. The admiral's endorsement will be affixed before sailing."

Thornhill paused.

"The cutter will then make for the inshore squadron to repeat the order—same seal, same authority. Neither force will act. They are not to interfere, engage, or question."

Still, Nicholas said nothing.

"Whatever happens," Thornhill continued, "you are to rendezvous with the cutter at Dartmouth. It's quiet and out of the way, and she will bring you direct to London. A carriage will take you down to Sheerness overnight. It's stands outside when you are ready."

Nicholas gave a single nod.

Thornhill didn't linger. He stepped back to the door, then turned.

"Good luck, Commander."

The words were simple. Not formal. Not rehearsed. But they carried weight—because Thornhill was not a man given to sentiment, and Nicholas understood what they meant.

He gave a slight nod. Thornhill closed the door behind him with quiet finality.

Nicholas turned back to the fire. The room was silent, and nothing moved but the coals settling in the grate.

The carriage jolted over the rutted road to Sheerness, and Nicholas looked out at the clear morning light breaking through the early mist. He felt rested and alert, having managed to sleep several hours in the well-appointed and quiet carriage since they left London around midnight.

The events since Lincoln's Inn played through his mind.

He thought back to the safehouse in Russell Square. They had been there no more than an hour when Thornhill had knocked and entered without ceremony, his usual composure slightly disrupted—not by alarm, but by satisfaction.

"Everett has been taken," he had announced without preamble, removing his gloves with practiced economy. "At his club on King Street. No resistance, just surprise—and then resignation. Certain papers seized in his desk drawer match some of those you secured, Miss Carlisle." He had specifically avoided the name Ashton, Nicholas recalled, noting the courtesy in the act.

Caroline's face had shown no triumph, merely a quiet vindication. "And Lord Ashton?"

"No trace yet, but we're watching the ports," Thornhill had replied. "It appears safe now for you to return to Ocean House. Your father has been informed of your recovery and is expecting you. I've arranged for several men to maintain watch over the premises as a precaution."

The reunion at Ocean House remained vivid in Nicholas's memory. Carlisle had been waiting at the door when they arrived, his usual merchant's composure abandoned as he embraced his daughter with wordless intensity. Caroline had yielded to his embrace with a visible release of the tension she had maintained through their escape and the aftermath—her shoulders softening, her head resting briefly against her father's as though the burden of vigilance could finally be set down.

"My dearest girl," Carlisle had murmured, drawing back to study her face with paternal scrutiny. "When I think what might have—"

"But it didn't," she had interrupted gently, her hand on his arm. "Thanks to Nicholas."

Carlisle had turned to him then, extending his hand with a grip that conveyed more than words could manage. "Commander Cruwys – Nicholas – I find myself once again in your debt. It seems to be becoming a habit."

"Not at all, sir," Nicholas had replied, acutely aware of Caroline's gaze upon him. "Any officer would have done the same."

"No," Caroline had said quietly. "Not any officer."

That night, Nicholas had stayed as Carlisle's guest. Dinner had been served with the quiet elegance that characterized Ocean House, the conversation deliberately light, as though all three understood the need for respite after the day's tensions. They had spoken of inconsequential matters—the shifting fashions of London, the merits of various Bordeaux vintages, the surprising quality of a recent concert at Hickford's Rooms. Not once had Ashton's name been mentioned.

In the stillness of that night, Nicholas had lain awake for some time in the well-appointed guest chamber, listening to the house settle around him. The room was far more comfortable than his quarters at Half Moon Street—a fine feather mattress, Belgian linen, substantial furniture of polished mahogany. When sleep finally approached, he had heard the faint click of his door latch.

Caroline had entered without a word, closing the door silently behind her. Moonlight caught the edge of her profile as she moved toward him.

"I meant what I said at Lincoln's Inn," she had whispered, her voice steady despite the weight of her words. "I have never been with a man. Not with Ashton, not with anyone. That was part of our arrangement—a marriage of appearance only." Her hands had found his in the darkness. "I need you to know that."

He had understood then the significance of her presence. His response had been gentle at first, mindful of her inexperience yet guided by her clarity, her eyes widening briefly at the unfamiliar sensation before determination overcame initial discomfort. That gentleness had gradually yielded to a deeper passion as she met him with an honesty that surprised them both.

"I never thought," she had said afterward, her voice soft against his chest, "that I could feel this way with a man. But it's not just any man, is it? It's you, Nicholas. It has always been you."

What had begun with tenderness had transformed into something neither had fully anticipated—an understanding that required no words, only the truth of touch and breath and shared discovery. In that quiet room, they had found a language beyond convention or arrangement, one written in the certainty of bodies that recognized each other despite all barriers of time and circumstance.

Later, as she lay beside him in the darkness, her head resting against his shoulder, she had spoken with quiet conviction. "This isn't just choice," she had said, her voice barely above a whisper." This is how we were always meant to be. Starting in Bombay. In Luanda. This is truth, Nicholas."

The significance of what had passed between them lay beyond words. What had begun years before on distant shores and been interrupted by circumstance had finally found its completion.

"I know," he had replied simply.

Whether this moment would lead to some enduring arrangement between them—whether it could accommodate the complexities of her nature and his duty—remained for a future neither could yet see clearly. But in that night, such questions had seemed distant, overwhelmed by the simple rightness of their union.

She had left before dawn, silent as her arrival, leaving only the faint impression of her body on the sheets and the lingering scent of lavender.

The carriage hit a deeper rut, jolting Nicholas back to the present. Outside, the muddy roads leading to Sheerness continued to unspool beneath brightening skies. His mind shifted to the final meeting with Thornhill and the task ahead. There would be time later to consider what lay between himself and Caroline—what had begun years ago in Bombay, interrupted by circumstance, and now consummated in a way neither could have foreseen. First, Ashton must be stopped.

The following morning, Thornhill had arrived with instructions for Nicholas to move to a new residence—a handsome townhouse in South Audley Street off Grosvenor Square, far more elegant than his previous rooms. His possessions from Half Moon Street had already been transferred there, arranged with meticulous care. The house came complete with a discreet staff—a butler of military bearing, a cook whose skills rivaled those of many noble households, and two footmen who moved like shadows.

"Security and comfort both matter in times like these," Thornhill had explained as Nicholas surveyed the library stocked with volumes he had only dreamed of owning. "The Crown appreciates the importance of your service."

Over an exceptional dinner that night—roast pheasant with bread sauce and chestnuts, braised endive, and a claret that spoke of serious cellaring—Thornhill had briefed him further on the developing situation. Later, over Stilton and walnuts with a glass of old port, the conversation turned to names.

"Everett is being questioned, but quietly. Both his and Ashton's properties are being searched without fanfare. We must contain this before rumors spread too widely."

Two evenings later a messenger had arrived with a note from Thornhill: he had 10 minutes to prepare and then a carriage parked outside of the house would take him to a meeting at Admiral Lord Howe's private residence.

He thought of Howe's words in the library just yesterday: *"You have no orders, Commander. You have no ship. This conversation has not occurred. But were I in your position, I would ensure that neither Le Furet nor its particularly valuable passenger reached their destination."*

After what he had learned of Ashton's betrayal, Nicholas found no conflict in his duty. As a naval officer, he had taken lives before—in battle, at close quarters, with sword and pistol—always in service to king and country. This would be no different, despite its unusual nature.

And yet, as the carriage neared the naval yard where *Alert* waited, he acknowledged to himself that there was another dimension to his resolve. It was not vengeance, precisely. But when he thought of Caroline—her quiet strength, her composed intelligence, her capacity to endure—he felt a clarity of purpose that transcended mere orders.

Alert would sail on the next morning's tide. And Nicholas Cruwys would due his utmost to fulfill his duty—to the Admiralty, to England, and perhaps, though he would not admit it aloud, to the woman who had once painted an island from his charts, and who had now, against all probability, become truly his.

The boatman brought the cutter up under *Fortunée's* larboard quarter, steering her close in under bare canvas with no colour shown. The tide was ebbing gently now, pulling the frigate's stern downriver in slow pulses. A single midshipman waited at the rail above, composed and silent, offering a crisp salute as Nicholas came aboard.

"Commander Cruwys, sir. The captain's expecting you."

Nicholas inclined his head. "Take me aft, if you please."

They crossed the deck without ceremony. The morning sun caught at the brass work on the wheel and threw pale lines across the planks, but the ship was quiet—working trim, not parade polish. At the captain's door stood a marine came to attention the instant Nicholas approached, musket grounded with the clean stamp of the butt on deck.

The midshipman knocked once—sharp, correct. "Commander Cruwys, sir."

"Send him in."

Nicholas stepped into the cabin.

Walsh stood behind the table, coat off, sleeves rolled, the light from the stern windows gilding the edges of the papers beside him. His face was unreadable.

"Commander."

"Sir."

"I received a note from the Port Admiral this morning," Walsh said. "I'm to comply with any request you make—for men, stores, assistance—without delay."

"Yes, sir."

Walsh studied him for a beat. "So—what am I complying with?"

"I've come to borrow men, sir."

Walsh's brow lifted faintly, though his voice remained mild. "How many?"

"Eighty."

That word landed in the silence like a dropped cannonball.

"I see," Walsh said, after a moment. "And this borrowing—how permanent do you suppose it might become?"

Nicholas kept his tone measured. "Only for the duration, sir. We sail tomorrow morning."

"You'll have them working her today, then?"

"Yes, sir. Down in pairs. Quietly. Entered on the yard books as assisting with hull inspection. Some stores movement. The idea is no one will notice."

Walsh exhaled through his nose and stepped to the chart case. "You've got others?"

"My premier Forester's scraped up twenty—some old *Alert* hands, a few off the half-pay lists. But they're patchwork. I need a spine, sir. And I need men trained to your standard."

"You know what you're asking."

"Yes, sir."

Another pause.

"You'll name the target?"

"No, sir."

"But something."

Nicholas gave the faintest nod. "She's a ship-rigged corvette. Twenty guns—eighteen six-pounders, with bow chasers. Fast by reputation."

He added, "We won't catch her unless we carry every stitch and take the wind in our teeth."

Walsh looked at him, long and steady. Both men knew Nicholas had probably said more than he should. While he hadn't named her any knowledgeable captain would be almost certain he was talking about a modern French corvette.

"You'll not say where she's bound."

"No, sir."

"Nor who's aboard."

"No, sir."

Walsh let the silence draw out, then said, "I seem to recall advising you at the club to take the first command offered."

"You did, sir."

"I didn't mean this one."

"No, sir."

The faintest curl of a smile touched one corner of Walsh's mouth, but it passed quickly.

"You'll have Hart as Master Gunner, and Maitland as Quartermaster. Pemble from the tops. Jesmond—God help us—if he's sober. Rutley to bosun. I'll send them down by twos. My best gun crews and topmen. I'll have a full list made up by the hour. God preserve me if I'm ordered to sea."

"Thank you, sir."

"You'll have no support if she fails," Walsh said softly. "No flag, no recognition. No one to claim you."

"I know that, sir."

"And if she's lost?"

"Then I am, too."

Walsh considered this, then stepped forward and extended his hand.

"Godspeed, Commander."

Nicholas took it, firm and brief. "Thank you, sir."

He turned and stepped out, the marine sentry snapping once more to attention as he passed. The deck was brighter now, the tide dropping faster, gulls wheeling in a high, cold sky.

Down past the timber slips and the smoke-streaked chimneys, lying low in the water and silent as a ruin, *Alert* waited.

She would not wait long.

The wind had shifted east by the time Nicholas's cutter approached *Alert*. She lay moored against the far pier at Sheerness, her hull dark against the pale timbers, her deck showing signs of recent activity despite the weeks in ordinary. The lethal grace that had first caught his eye in Port Royal remained undiminished—that particular deadly elegance unique among His Majesty's vessels. Her raked masts still carried that cant from the perpendicular that made landsmen uneasy and sailors stare. He noted with satisfaction that her copper showed clean along the waterline; the yard had kept to Hood's original instructions, maintaining her despite her uncertain status. She would need every advantage of speed and weatherliness in the days ahead.

Nicholas climbed the hull battens, gripping the manropes as he pulled himself over the side and onto the deck with the particular feeling of homecoming that only a captain knows upon returning to his first command. The familiar quarterdeck, the precise angle of the wheel, the way the stern rose and fell with the Thames's brackish pulse—all spoke to him as clearly as an old friend's voice. Forester was waiting, hat respectfully removed though he had complied with the note about no ceremony, his expression revealing both pleasure at the reunion and curiosity at its unexpected circumstances. Behind him stood Markham, the master, his weather-beaten face impassive save for a quick nod of acknowledgment.

"Captain," Forester said, "we both received orders to report aboard by messenger before dawn this morning; it appears the messengers rode through the night from London. Most unexpected, after hearing

Alert was bound for the auction block." The question hung unspoken between them, but Forester, ever discreet, merely added, "Markham and I have been aboard since early morning, taking stock of what needs attention. She's sound enough, but undermanned, of course. That said, about twenty of our old crew turned up this morning, apparently by order of the Port Admiral. Which was... unexpected."

Nicholas smiled and extended his hand. "Good to see you both. I have just come from London as well. We'll speak in the cabin." He turned toward the companionway, aware of the small crew watching from the waist—barely twenty men where a hundred would be needed. "Mr. Markham, I trust the yards haven't neglected her rigging?"

"No sir. Markham replied, "We've checked her over stem to stern. The yard did well enough—keeping her up. Rigging taut and blackened and slushed, copper clean on the waterline, and the guns are still aboard, though secured below in the hold rather than mounted. We've begun running them up, starting with the forward battery."

The three men descended to the small cabin that had been Nicholas's home for more than a year. Nothing had changed—the same narrow space, the desk fitted to the side and full standing room only beneath the skylight, the shelf with its few books still secured by the leather strap he had added. Someone—Forester, most likely—had lit the small lamp that hung from the deck beam, casting a warm glow.

"Gentlemen," Nicholas began, removing his hat and placing it on the desk, "we sail Monday with the morning tide." He paused, noting their lack of surprise. Both men were seasoned enough to know something unusual was afoot. "Our mission is not a regular naval assignment. We'll carry no orders, fly no colors, and officially, we will not exist. What I'm about to tell you cannot leave this cabin."

"This mission comes directly from Admiral Lord Howe and Vice Admiral Hood," Nicholas continued, his voice low despite the empty ship around them. "Our target is the French corvette *Le Furet*, twenty guns, departing Brest as soon as next Saturday, so we need to be off Brest by then, sooner if possible. She'll be making directly for Bilbao, with Santander as an alternate heavyweather port. She'll be sailing under diplomatic immunity. Her passenger is Lord Ashton—yes, Markham the same Ashton from our time in Luanda."

Markham's weathered face tightened at the name, his eyes flickering momentarily to Nicholas with a look of understanding. Though neither man had spoken of it openly, Markham had observed enough during the convoy voyage to understand something of what had passed between Nicholas and Caroline Carlisle before her marriage to Ashton. He merely nodded once, a gesture that acknowledged both the professional task and its personal dimensions.

"The Admirals believe Ashton carries dispatches that would compromise British interests," Nicholas continued, deliberately omitting details of treason that remained above their need to know. "Our mission is to intercept *Le Furet* before she reaches Spanish waters, and to ensure those papers never reach their destination. We will want to intercept her as early as possible after she sails given the proximity of Spanish waters and possible patrols. We'll operate without colors or identification—this cannot appear to be a Royal Navy action given her diplomatic status."

He unfolded a chart on the small table, weighted at the corners with the brass navigation tools. "*Le Furet* will clear Brest here, then set course southeast across Biscay toward the Spanish coast. Given her destination and the prevailing winds this season, she'll likely favor this direct passage, keeping off the lee shore." His finger traced a line past Ushant and into the Bay of Biscay. "I've secured eighty men from *Fortunée*, Captain Walsh's best hands. They'll be transferred to us throughout today in small groups. Once at sea, we'll begin gun drills and sail exercises, but not before. For anyone observing at Sheerness, we're merely being prepared for inspection prior to auction."

"Our advantages will be in maneuverability and surprise," Nicholas continued. "*Alert* can point higher into the wind than any square-rigged vessel. However, assuming the usual prevailing westerlies or southwesterlies, we may not have the conditions to take advantage of that, until we have her pinned down. We will attempt to pick her up south of the entrance to Brest, and most likely we'll need to close quickly before she can recognize our intentions. If we are delayed or have not seen her by the evening of Saturday the 26th, we sail as fast as possible direct to the Spanish coast and risk taking her in their waters.

"Eighteen six-pounders, plus two chasers, unknown weight." Nicholas replied. "She's built for speed more than battle, but she can strike hard enough if cornered. Her captain is likely to run rather than fight—particularly with a valuable passenger aboard. He straightened, meeting each man's gaze in turn. "I won't deceive you about the nature of this service. Should we be captured, the Admiralty will disavow all knowledge of our mission. We sail without protection of the Articles of War."

Markham and Forester exchanged a glance, but neither hesitated.

"You've brought us through worse," Forester said.

The master nodded in agreement, his weathered face steady—the look of a man who had come through too many storms to fear one more.

Nicholas felt the force of their loyalty—not to the mission alone, but to him. In a Navy governed by rank and regulation, such trust was rare. And not lightly earned.

"We'll carry more than enough powder and shot," Nicholas said, moving to another matter. "The yard's storekeepers have special instructions, without regard to *Alert*'s supposed imminent sale. We'll sail with a full complement of naval stores, including spare spars and cordage."

His fingers traced the jagged line of the French coast. "What concerns me most is *Le Furet*'s sailing qualities. If she was built in Lorient or Saint-Malo, she'll be sharp-lined and fast—especially on a reach. And if she gets clear of the coast before we sight her, she'll be damnably hard to catch. Particularly in weather."

"*Alert* won't let us down, sir," Markham said. "If the wind holds steady, we'll have her." His broad, calloused hands moved across the chart with the confidence of decades at sea. "She answers well, and we know how to push her without carrying away the rig."

Nicholas nodded, acknowledging the likely truth in Markham's assessment. "We'll need to work the crew hard once we're clear of Sheerness—sail drills by day, gunnery practice once we're far enough from observers. The hands from *Fortunée* will be well-trained, but unfamiliar with *Alert*'s peculiarities and her fore-and-aft rig."

He turned to Forester. "I want you to organise the gun crews as they come aboard. Choose your best for the bow and stern chasers—we may need to slow *Le Furet* at range, especially if she turns toward us. And see to the shot: we've taken on chain for both the nines and twelves. Every round—chain, bar, or solid—is to be sorted for trueness before stowage. I want no warped iron or castings that fly wide."

"Understood, sir," Forester replied. "And our rules of engagement? Are we to take prisoners?"

The question hung in the air, its implications clear. Nicholas met his lieutenant's gaze, knowing that his answer would set the tone for the entire operation.

"No prisoners," Nicholas said quietly. "Those are the terms. *Le Furet* must not reach a Spanish port—or any port—once she sails. Lord Ashton must not deliver his dispatches. We are to ensure both vessel and passenger meet with what was termed 'maritime misfortune,' with no evidence pointing to British involvement."

He held Forester's gaze. "Any man who finds this duty beyond his conscience may remain ashore without prejudice. I'll not force anyone to this service."

Forester nodded slowly, accepting the gravity of the mission. "The men will follow your orders, sir. Those who've sailed with you before know your judgment. As for Walsh's hands—they'll do their duty." His voice carried the quiet certainty of a man who understood naval discipline and the loyalties beneath it. "Will you inform them of the mission's nature once we're at sea?"

"Only what's necessary," Nicholas said. "That we're pursuing a French vessel carrying intelligence harmful to British interests, and that we do so without flying any flag. I expect they'll be spoken to further when this is over. They need not know the details of Ashton's betrayal—or the politics behind it."

He moved to the sideboard and poured three measures of brandy. "We sail into uncertain waters, gentlemen—literally and otherwise."

They drank without further discussion, each man contemplating the risk and responsibility they had accepted. From the deck above came the muffled sounds of *Alert* returning to life—the creak of blocks, the dull thump of stores being lowered below, voices calling measurements across the planking.

Nicholas felt the familiar stir that came before action—not excitement precisely, but a kind of focused clarity, as though the world were distilling to its essential parts. He had commanded *Alert* before in the service of the Crown. Now he would command her beyond its protection, in that grey territory where duty and necessity met without the comfort of written orders.

After Forester and Markham had gone to their preparations, Nicholas remained with the charts. A knock came several minutes later, and Forester reappeared, dispatch case in hand.

"The first group from *Fortunée* has arrived, sir. Twenty men, including Rutley and Pemble. They're being assigned quarters now."

He placed the leather case on the table. "Captain Walsh sent this—charts for the Bay of Biscay and the Spanish coast, newly corrected last month. He said you might find them useful."

Nicholas opened the case: several carefully folded charts and a packet of sealed papers. The topmost sheet bore Walsh's hand—*Notes on French naval dispositions off Brest, current as of October 5th.* Below it lay another: *Le Furet sailed from Toulon three weeks past. Reported sighted off Finisterre on the 7th.*

Nicholas smiled faintly. Walsh had gleaned far more from their brief exchange than he'd let on—piecing together not only the mission's nature, but its target. A pencilled line traced *Le Furet*'s likely course from Brest southeast toward Bilbao, annotated with prevailing winds and currents.

"Good man," Nicholas murmured. "Have the bosun issue slops to any who need them. I want every man properly outfitted before we sail."

"One more thing, sir," Forester said, lowering his voice. "Lieutenant Adams is aboard. Came with the men from *Fortunée*. He asked to speak with you directly."

Nicholas raised an eyebrow.

"Signals specialist," Forester continued. "One of Walsh's. Apparently he thought Adams might be useful. And he sent his surgeon as well—Mr. Braitly."

Nicholas nodded. Walsh's foresight was exact. A signals man—capable of interpreting French flags, perhaps intercepting—and a trusted surgeon to calm the crew and patch what needed patching.

"Send Mr. Adams in," he said.

The debt to Walsh deepened. He had considered every angle.

The following Thursday morning the wind held steady from the southwest as *Alert* beat southward with Ushant one mile off her port bow, her sails taut, the morning haze lifting slowly from the sea. Five days at sea had transformed both vessel and crew—no longer the hastily assembled collection of hands that had slipped from Sheerness with the tide, but a ship coming into herself, her people finding their places within her. The men from *Fortunée* had adjusted to *Alert's* peculiarities with professional ease, adapting to her quicker motion and the demands of her fore-and-aft rig. Gun crews had drilled until they moved like parts of a single mechanism, running out the guns, loading, and simulating fire with increasing speed and precision, including with chain and bar, not just the usual round shot. The topmen had learned the specific tensions of her canvas, how to quickly execute sail changes and maneuvers through different points of sailing.

Two hours later, ahead and to larboard, a line of ships moved in deliberate formation—five ships of the line under full topsails, their hulls dark against the rising light. Gunports were closed. Sails trimmed flat. No challenge yet.

Adams lowered his glass. "That's *Robust* leading. And I make out *Valiant, Courageux,* and *Goliath* behind her. All seventy-fours. There's a fifth line-of-battleship half-concealed in haze. And two frigates—thirty-twos by the look."

As *Alert* held her course, the closest frigate—HMS *Minerva*—suddenly came up into the wind and turned towards them, turning cleanly onto a converging tack. Her intent was unmistakable. Within moments, signal flags were climbing her foremast—a standard challenge.

Nicholas turned slightly to watch, eyes on the flagship.

Even as *Minerva* heeled into the maneuver, a new hoist broke from the mizzen of *Robust*: Recall. Immediate. No further signal.

The order was crisp and unmistakable. *Minerva* checked her course—held it for only a heartbeat—then eased sheets and bore back to the line. Her colors were never dipped. The entire exchange had lasted barely three minutes.

"No challenge," Forester said, lowering the glass. "They're under instruction. They'll not interfere."

The next evening, the western horizon had begun to soften into dusk when Nicholas emerged onto *Alert*'s quarterdeck. The wind had held stubbornly from the southwest, blowing fresh all the way down the Channel, but *Alert* had worked to windward until they could finally ease sheets west of Ushant and crack off to the south. Now she sailed under easy canvas, six leagues southwest of the Pointe du Raz.

Nicholas stood at the leeward rail, glass extended, studying the faint suggestion of land off the larboard bow. Ushant lay nearly ten leagues to the north—well out of sight from deck level—the westernmost sentinel of the French coast. Between it and the Pointe du Raz, just visible from the masthead rising off the port quarter, lay Brest: harbor, arsenal, and home to a substantial portion of the French Atlantic fleet.

Somewhere in those protected waters—or perhaps already slipping out to sea—was *Le Furet*, with her dangerous passenger. The thought of Ashton—his arrogance, his betrayal, and above all, his treatment of Caroline—kindled a cold anger Nicholas kept carefully contained. This was not personal vengeance. It was duty. However unconventional.

"Mr. Forester, let's have the main and fore'sle reefed before full dark," he said, collapsing the glass with a practiced motion. "We'll stand off and on through the night, close enough to observe any ship leaving the port on a southerly course."

Forester nodded and moved off, calling orders that sent men aloft with the quick precision of a crew both disciplined and confident.

Nicholas had briefed them once they were well clear of the English coast—telling them only that they pursued a French corvette carrying intelligence harmful to British interests. Most had accepted this without question, understanding that some missions demanded discretion rather than explanation. A few had exchanged knowing glances—veterans who recognized the signs of an unusual commission.

Adams approached from the hatchway, logbook in hand. Like the rest of the crew, he had been told only the essential details of their quarry.

"Captain," he said, "we've practiced with the known French flags and signals. There should be no delay in answering—if they're still correct."

His tone was precise, professional—the report of a man who understood his duty without needing its broader context. Now a second lieutenant, Adams had proved a valuable addition, organizing the watch system with quiet efficiency under Forester's direction and implementing an enhanced rotation of lookouts with—though not usual practice—glasses for each man.

His gaze shifted forward, toward the deck where the bronze long nine-pounder rode its specialized carriage—a distinctive presence that set *Alert* apart from any vessel in His Majesty's Navy. Unlike her standard armament, this gun was Nicholas's personal property, acquired—along with its mate, the stern chaser—in Port Royal, during his first commission of *Alert*, when the dockyard had proved unwilling and he had been desperate to get her to sea.

The matched bronze nine-pounders had been taken from a captured American privateer and sold outside official channels—seventy guineas from Nicholas's own purse, with not too many questions asked. They were masterpieces of the Madrid foundry, their barrels elegantly cast with the Habsburg eagle, the metal gleaming with a subtle patina that spoke of age and exceptional craftsmanship.

The bow chaser sat on an ingenious sliding carriage—commissioned by Forester from a renegade Spanish gunner in Jamaica. Unlike conventional naval mounts, this carriage allowed the heavy piece to be stowed safely near the foremast when not in use, improving *Alert*'s trim and handling, especially in light air. When action threatened, the gun could be run forward on its brass-fitted slide onto a conventional carriage and fired through either the starboard or larboard bow port—giving the schooner remarkable flexibility in targeting.

Forester was on the forecastle now, along with Walsh's master gunner, Hart, and the selected gun crew—fussing over the piece and the garland of shot laid out beside it.

Hood had raised an eyebrow upon first seeing the modification during an inspection in Port Royal. "Unorthodox," the admiral had commented, studying the mechanism with professional interest. "But then, this is hardly an orthodox vessel." It had been as close to approval as Nicholas could expect from a flag officer regarding a private modification to a King's ship. The gun had more than proved its worth in the Caribbean, particularly during the interception of the *San Isidro*, when a precisely placed shot had shattered the Spanish vessel's rudder pintles. Today it stood ready to help ensure *Le Furet* and her treasonous passenger never reached Spanish waters.

Dawn on the 23rd of November broke clear over the Bay of Biscay, the eastern horizon faintly illuminated by the rising sun. *Alert* moved steadily northward on the larboard tack under a fresh breeze from the southwest, her decks cleared of all military appearance, her gun ports closed tight against both observation and spray. From the crosstrees some eighty feet above deck, the lookout's voice carried down: "Sail ho! Two points off the starboard bow, sir! Top's'ls and t'gallants."

Nicholas and Forester exchanged glances, both men instantly calculating. Not likely a merchant with such a spread of canvas. At that distance—perhaps twenty nautical miles, given the height of their mast and the curvature of the earth—they had just over an hour before the strange sail would show her hull. With *Alert* disguised as a merchantman, her officers in civilian dress, her seamen arranged in the typical disarray of a trader rather than with naval precision, they might yet achieve the surprise they sought. The previous evening, Nicholas had overseen the transformation himself: naval uniforms stowed in sea chests, weapons concealed beneath canvas, even the distinctive polish of the quarterdeck brass dulled with lamp black.

"Mr. Adams," Nicholas called to the second lieutenant, "take the glass aloft and tell me what you see." Adams, who had shed his lieutenant's coat for a worn pilot jacket, and with three days' growth of beard looked every inch the merchant officer, quickly ascended the ratlines. After a moment studying the horizon, he called down: "Ship-rigged, sir, running on the starboard tack—I can just make out her courses now." Nicholas raised his own glass, though the vessel remained little more than a suggestion of white against blue from deck level. Given the wind and their respective courses, *Alert* and the unknown ship were closing at a combined sixteen knots. If this was indeed *Le Furet*, they would be within gun range in less than two hours.

The next hour passed with calculated patience. Nicholas paced the quarterdeck with the deliberate, unhurried stride of a merchant captain, pausing occasionally to confer with Markham about their course as any trading vessel might. Below decks, gun crews waited in tense readiness, the six-pounders loaded with chain shot, slow-match burning silently in their tubs. Nicholas had briefed them thoroughly—no action until his direct command, and then a single devastating broadside aimed at Le Furet's rigging rather than her hull. They must cripple her ability to sail without sending her immediately to the bottom.

"Hull-up, sir," Adams called from aloft, his voice carrying clearly in the morning air. "I can make out the white flag with fleur-de-lis at her peak. 'Tis a royal ship, for certain." Ten minutes later Nicholas raised his glass again, and this time could discern the vessel's lines—the sleek hull of a corvette, her canvas drawing well as she reached across the wind on the starboard tack. *Le Furet* moved with purpose through the moderate sea, her course set southeast toward the Spanish coast, precisely as intelligence had suggested she would.

Forester observed quietly, noting the sudden activity visible aboard the distant vessel. "She's signaling, sir." Through his glass, Nicholas watched as bright bunting ascended *Le Furet's* signal halyard—the standard challenge demanding identification. At this distance—still nearly two miles—they had time yet before any response would be expected from a merchant vessel. "Let them wait," Nicholas replied. "We'll maintain course and continue as if bound north to round Pointe du Raz."

The distance closed steadily, and when they were within a mile Nicholas gave a nod to Forester. "Let us confuse them with our appearance, Mr. Forester. Run up the American ensign." Forester understood immediately, selecting a flag of the United States—thirteen stripes with a circle of stars—and having it raised smartly. This calculated deception might give them precious moments of advantage; the French, as allies of the Americans, would likely pay less attention to a vessel flying friendly colors, allowing *Alert* to close to effective gun range before revealing her true purpose.

Through his glass, Nicholas observed the French vessel maintain her course, apparently accepting the American identification without concern. *Le Furet* continued her southeasterly heading, making no move to intercept or evade *Alert*. "They've accepted our colors," Nicholas said quietly. "No change in course, no gun ports open. They expect to pass us without incident." He watched as a figure in a blue coat—not naval uniform—appeared on *Le Furet's* quarterdeck, studying *Alert* through a glass. Even at this distance, Nicholas recognized Ashton's distinctive bearing. The traitor was watching them, perhaps with some unease, but the French captain seemed unconcerned, maintaining his present course.

"We'll maintain our heading," Nicholas instructed. "When we're beam-on at six hundred yards, we strike the colors, open ports, and give them the starboard battery." He turned to Rutley, the square-built bosun borrowed from *Fortunée*. "Pass the word below. Gun crews to come up quietly and take stations on my command. Extra hands for the braces—we'll need to alter course sharply after firing." Rutley touched his forehead in acknowledgment, his scarred face betraying nothing of the tension all felt. "Aye, sir. They'll be ready," in a low growl.

The order came at exactly six hundred yards—"Strike colors! Open ports! Run out!" In an instant, *Alert's* deck transformed. Men who had been lounging about in apparent merchant idleness sprang to action with practiced naval discipline. The false American ensign came down with a single pull. Gun ports flew open along *Alert's* starboard side as the concealed six-pounders were run out with a concerted rumble. From below decks, additional gun crews swarmed up the ladders, taking their stations with the swift efficiency Walsh had drilled into them. Rutley's voice cut through the controlled chaos, directing men to braces and sheets in preparation for the maneuver that would follow the broadside. "Ready, sir!" Forester called, every gun now manned, every weapon trained on *Le Furet's* rigging.

"Fire as you bear!" Nicholas commanded, and *Alert's* broadside crashed out in disciplined sequence from bow to stern. Chain shot tore through the French ship's forward rigging with devastating effect. Splinters flew from the base of the bowsprit and it broke in half from the pressure of the flying and outer jibs, which went flailing off to leeward in the strong breeze held only by their halyards. As the ships swiftly passed each other, other shots went home and the spanker boom on the mizzen shattered at its base, bringing down the entire sail in a tangle of canvas and cordage. *Le Furet* had lost her ability to beat to windward and much of her maneuverability, but that was not the immediate concern. Nicholas swore under his breath. They had not crucially damaged her masts or square sails which with this wind would drive her towards Spain, or in any event the south coast of France.

Le Furet turned sharply to starboard, luffing up and presenting her own broadside to *Alert's* starboard quarter at a range now narrowed to less than four hundred yards. Orange flame and smoke blossomed along her side as nine six-pounders fired as one—a response so swift that Nicholas realized the French captain must have had his ship cleared for action behind the façade of peaceful sailing. Shot screamed across the water.

One ball shattered *Alert's* bulwark amidships; another smashed directly through a gun port, dismounting the piece and killing its crew in an explosion of wood splinters and bloodied flesh. A third struck lower, punching through the hull below the waterline. The deck shuddered beneath Nicholas's feet as men fell around him.

In that instant, Nicholas remembered Hood's warning: *"You may expect a steady hand in your opponent—and a ship well handled."*

Le Furet fell off again, coming back to her southeasterly course with the wind hard on her starboard beam. The maneuver was no act of strategy. It was necessity. Her spanker was destroyed, and only her inner jib flew from the half-shattered bowsprit. She steadied with effort, men swarming aloft to cut free the flying and outer jibs.

She had been crippled in her ability to maneuver—and forced downwind—but that was all. She still carried a full crew, and her hull and battery remained largely intact.

Adams, standing just forward of the mainmast, raised his glass and frowned.

"Sir—she's hoisted a white flag. Signal position on the mizzen. Plain cloth. The agreed convention for diplomatic passage during the peace negotiations."

Nicholas didn't move. "She's not going to Spain. Or France."

The words were quiet, almost dispassionate. Not a judgment—only a fact.

Adams hesitated, then gave a brief nod and turned back to his station. He said nothing more.

Nicholas stood at the rail, glass in hand, watching the French ship's rig.

Without turning, he said, "Put us directly in her wake, Mr. Markham. Let's take her forward. Mr. Forester, you have the stern chaser. Chain first. Then ball."

The long nine boomed from the taffrail, a deep report echoing across the wind. Smoke blew forward over the deck. The chain shot screamed aft and struck home from only three hundred yards—ripping through *Le Furet's* aft rigging. She responded with her two stern chasers, but the shots were poorly aimed: one went wide, the other fell short, a burst of spray showering *Alert's* quarterdeck.

The range opened—first in yards, then in hundreds.

"Carpenter reports shot hole plugged and one foot in the well, sir," Forester called.

Nicholas nodded. "Very well. We'll keep our angle. Switch to ball."

Another report from the stern chaser. The ball struck true at six hundred yards—smashing into *Le Furet's* taffrail and carrying splinters across her quarterdeck. Nearly a minute passed before the French guns replied again, both shots wide of the mark.

"Let us continue to open the range," Nicholas said. "She'll not touch us with those."

A few minutes later, Markham reported, "About nine hundred yards now, sir."

"Very well," Nicholas said. "Mr. Markham, we'll tack and pursue. Once round set the outer jib. Start the sheets as needed to hold the weather gauge. Mr. Forester—carry on. Aim for the base of her mizzen with the bow chaser."

Alert spun to starboard and brought the wind just forward of her beam, settling onto a parallel course. She answered the increase in canvas like a living thing. Her fore topmast leaned into the strain as the third headsail was sheeted home, and the schooner surged forward.

She slipped into the Frenchman's wake—not taunting, not fleeing, but climbing to weather like a gull rising on a thermal.

The first shot from the bow chaser went low and left, striking the port quarter gallery—splintering the timber in a spray of fragments visible even at that range. A cheer went up from the crew.

The firing continued—measured, cold, precise. The crew at the long nine worked in silence, Forester pacing behind them, correcting aim with small adjustments. Nicholas gave no further orders; there was no need.

Fifteen minutes passed. Two shots had missed, but others had struck hard, damaging her taffrail and tearing through the rigging about the mizzen. The gun had grown hot; the charge was reduced.

Le Furet began a turn to port, edging in toward the French coast, and the teeth of her port broadside began to bear.

"Bring her hard on the wind," Nicholas snapped.

The French broadside came, but it was mostly short and wide to port—their gunners caught unready by *Alert*'s sudden swing upwind. One ball skipped and struck the port quarter nettings. One of the helmsmen gave a short cry and fell, his arm nearly torn away by a large splinter. Markham, standing near the wheel, was struck with blood as he caught the man's weight and lent his own strength to the spokes.

Nicholas studied the Frenchman's course a moment longer. Her bows held steady to the ESE, sails straining against the damage. The mizzen sagged to port, but she was still making way.

"Cease fire," Nicholas ordered. "We'll close on her starboard quarter, then come off the wind and rake her at close range. Mr. Forester, double-shot the three remaining starboard guns with chain and ball. And the carronade—ball and canister."

The schooner responded with perfect balance—eating up the distance, angling out upwind of *Le Furet*, who couldn't follow her. Then, at three hundred yards, *Le Furet* again luffed up into the wind to bring her starboard broadside to bear and fired. Four of her shots smashed home, and there were screams along the deck as men fell. Nicholas felt a punch in his left leg and almost fell. There was a deep splinter-gash across his thigh, and blood was pouring down his leg. No pain—yet. Markham was at his side in a moment.

"Just bind it, Markham," Nicholas said, voice level. "Mr. Forester, hold your fire until we cross her stern and rake her. Aim for the base of her mizzen."

The distance closed rapidly now. At a nod from Nicholas, Markham began a turn to port, off the wind, tracking *Le Furet*'s stern as she continued downwind. *Alert*'s bow steadied on a course that would bring her directly across the French corvette's unprotected stern at perhaps twenty-five yards—point-blank range. And there was nothing the French captain could do to stop what was about to happen. His starboard battery no longer bore, and in any case, he hadn't time to reload.

Markham had timed it perfectly, and though muskets and other small arms were firing from both ships' tops, as the shadow from *Alert*'s masts fell across *Le Furet*'s quarterdeck, there seemed to be almost silence but for the waves and the wind in those final seconds. Nicholas could see the officers' expressions on her quarterdeck clearly. Of Ashton there was no sign—presumably below for safety, but the French captain was there, staring back at him. A broad-shouldered man of medium height in a blue coat with red trim and gold lace, a black tricorn hat with a white feather, and a smallsword—he looked every inch an officer of France's aristocracy. Nicholas stood stock-still as, with a look of obvious disdain, the French captain turned his back, as did his other officers. A moment later, Forester, standing at the forward six-pounder, yelled, "Fire!"—and the carronade and all three six-pounders went off almost as one.

The murderous effect of the double-shotted guns at such short range on the exposed stern was instantaneous. The corvette shuddered under the impact—timbers splintered, guns were flung from their carriages, and a red mist rose from her quarterdeck as men vanished in smoke and ruin. She paid off dead downwind with her helm shot away, and a moment later, as *Alert* swept past, the mizzen came down in a flurry of sail and the broken spar, collapsing forward into the mainmast and booms, tearing sails and cordage as it crashed down. Thin trails of blood ran down her port side aft.

All firing had stopped, and for perhaps ten seconds, as she dropped astern, Nicholas said nothing, still staring at her now-empty quarterdeck. He had her—but he knew what must come next.

Then he looked at Markham. "Bring her into the wind, tack, and prepare to cross her stern again—and we shall reduce sail. We'll rake her again with the port battery. Mr. Forester, double-shot the port guns with round shot, including the carronade. You will aim for the waterline."

Both men nodded and responded quietly, "Aye, sir."

A few minutes later, as *Alert*, within one hundred yards and closing, her intent clear, bore down again, there was motion at the shattered taffrail—frantic, uneven. A sheet, hastily raised on a broken spar, caught the wind like a torn flag. Men on her quarterdeck gestured upward with open hands. A white banner, of sorts—no ensign, but the meaning was unmistakable.

Forester lowered his glass. "They're trying to surrender, sir."

Adams came aft with his larger signals glass and said, "Captain—" he hesitated, then cleared his throat. "Sir, I see women aboard. Two, at least. Amidships, near the companion. Gowns. One is seated."

The words landed like a heavy weight. The cheer that had begun to rise along *Alert*'s deck died in men's throats. Nicholas said nothing for a moment—his face unreadable. Then he turned to the first lieutenant.

"Carry on, Mr. Forester. Prepare to fire as they bear. Broadside into the waterline, including the carronade. Let's finish this quickly."

"Sir—" Adams started again, his voice too loud in the silence.

"Belay that," Forester said, flat and final. "You have your station, Mr. Adams."

Nicholas remained motionless at the rail, eyes fixed on *Le Furet*. She lay low in the water, sails flapping slack, her deck fouled with the wreckage of spars and bloodied canvas. The makeshift white flag still fluttered from the jagged stump of her mizzen.

"Accept her surrender, sir?" Forester asked quietly.

Nicholas did not answer at once. His fingers tightened on the rail, knuckles white.

He had heard Trevenen's voice again in the silence, as clearly as if the man stood beside him.

> *"A captain stands on his quarterdeck in full view of all, his conduct governed by the rules of war—and of gentlemen. There are those who serve differently. In waters where no chart shows the shoals. You've always understood honour in the clearest terms. Remember that clarity—even when the lights are dim."*

And then, Howe's answer to his question: *"And my orders regarding the French corvette?"*

> *"You have no orders, Commander. You have no ship. This conversation has not occurred. But were I in your position, I would ensure that neither Le Furet nor its particularly valuable passenger reached their destination."*

No order. A suggestion of no quarter, perhaps. But no order.

Nicholas let the silence stretch until it nearly snapped.

The next broadside never came.

"Mr. Forester. Prepare a boarding party. Ten men only—including yourself and Mr. Markham. I'll lead the party. Minimum of talk aboard her, and no naval formality. Mr. Adams, you will take command and approach within hailing distance on my signal."

The boat bumped softly against *Le Furet*'s shattered hull. A rope was thrown down. Nicholas climbed first, boots scraping over charred planking as he hauled himself up.

The deck was a butcher's board—splinters, cordage, blood pooled in the scuppers. A section of bulwark hung by a single brace. Smoke still curled from the galley hatch. A gull wheeled above, crying once, then vanished into the wind.

A French lieutenant—young, pale, with blood down his face and one sleeve pinned hastily with a scrap of cloth—approached. He carried his sword reversed, but upright.

"You fired without colours," he said in French, voice tight with contempt. "On a diplomatic vessel."

Nicholas said nothing. He made no move to take the sword.

The Frenchman stared a moment longer, then let the blade fall point-first to the deck. It rang faintly and lay still.

Nicholas turned to Markham. "Find Ashton. Put him under guard in the stern cabin."

Markham nodded once and left.

Forester and the boarding party were already moving—quiet, efficient, wordless. The survivors were herded amidships: those who could walk, those who could not. Roughly seventy in all, with another twenty lying wounded or dazed where they'd fallen. One woman was dead. The other sat beside the injured, silent and dry-eyed, her travel cloak spotted with ash.

Every man and the woman was searched—thoroughly. Pockets turned out, boots removed, coats unstitched where lining might conceal. A few protested. Most did not.

Nicholas gave only one instruction: "Take any papers. Return everything else."

They found nothing of use. Not yet.

At his signal, *Alert* came within hailing distance. Boats were lowered, and the survivors—wounded first—were ferried out in silence. They were confined in the lower hold, along with the surgeon tending them and two guards posted with strict orders not to speak.

By the fourth trip, only Nicholas, Forester, Markham, and Petty Officer Dodge, standing guard on Ashton, remained aboard *Le Furet*. The last boat and its crew waited alongside.

"He's in the stern cabin," Markham said, coming aft. "Unharmed. Waiting."

Nicholas nodded once.

"Prepare a fuse to the magazine," he said. "Fifteen minutes' burn. I'll light it myself."

They didn't question it. Forester disappeared below, returning moments later with a coil of fine black powder line wrapped in canvas and sealed with pitch. It snaked aft, invisible beneath the shattered planks.

Markham looked up. "Instructions?"

Nicholas's tone was flat. "I'll send Dodge up. Everyone but me will wait in the boat. Fifty yards off. On my signal—return."

Forester glanced at the aft companionway, then at Nicholas. "Understood, sir."

The two men climbed down without another word.

Nicholas stood alone on the ruined deck of *Le Furet*, the ship creaking beneath him like something still alive. He picked up the sword the French officer had dropped on the deck.

He turned toward the shattered companionway.

The sea wind shifted, lifting the hem of his coat as he stepped inside.

The cabin was half-dark, stinking of smoke, scorched oak, and drying blood. One of the stern windows was gone entirely; the sea shone through the wreckage. The other was cracked, streaked with soot and salt. Ash drifted like snow through the fractured light.

Ashton sat alone in a surviving chair. The back was splintered, but he held himself with habitual poise—legs crossed, hands folded loosely, his spine erect as though still on display. His coat remained immaculate, though the cuffs were faintly smudged, the silver buttons dulled. The lace at his throat was still tied, but not precisely—creased at one edge, the knot slightly off-centre. A faint dusting of powder clung to his temple, gone damp in the heat. His powdered hair, once crisply set, now sagged slightly at the crown.

There was a tremor behind the pose—not fear, exactly, but strain. The corners of his mouth had set too tightly; his gaze flickered once to the door, then stilled.

Nicholas entered and shut the door.

"You're dismissed," he said quietly. "Get in the boat."

Dodge hesitated, then withdrew without a word. The door closed behind him with a soft click.

Ashton didn't look up at first.

"I assume," he said, "we're not to be exchanged."

Nicholas crossed the floor and lit the cabin lantern. The flare cast sharp lines across the warped beams and scorched furnishings.

"You were born," Nicholas said, "to one of the most powerful families in England. Your name opens doors in three ministries. Why betray your country?"

Ashton looked up. His face was handsome still, but tight—cheeks drawn, eyes bloodshot at the edges. He spoke with care, as though preserving breath.

"Because I saw further than the rest. Because I didn't think 'country' was worth dying for when it's already bankrupt in honour." He gestured toward the ruined stern. "Because London plays checkers while Madrid and Paris have already taken the board."

"You gave the names of our agents in Havana."

"I gave the future a better shape. You think I betrayed England. I corrected it."

Nicholas laid the French sword on the table—gently, deliberately.

"Take it. I'm giving you the chance to die with a blade in your hand—like a man."

Ashton looked at the sword. Then at Nicholas.

"No," he said. "I don't fight sailors."

Nicholas stood very still.

"The Cruwys of Cruwys Morchard have held land and title since before the Crown knew how to spell yours. Six hundred years of tenure—while your family's name was still wet in chancery ink, if it appeared at all. Your earldom's younger than most of our hedgerows. Don't talk to me of England."

Ashton tensed but did not rise. He didn't even look at him at first. Instead, he adjusted the fold of his cuff with studied care, then let his hand fall idle upon the armrest.

Then he looked up. His eyes were steady, cold. "Six hundred years of moss and debt, and you think it makes you England. You think it gives you the right."

He gave a small breath—half a laugh, more exhale than sound. "You want me to stand. I won't. You want a duel. But I've no need to play the gentleman for your conscience."

He leaned back slightly, the fire catching the edge of his collar. "So get on with it, Cruwys. Let's see what six centuries of breeding teaches you about killing a man in a chair."

"Stand up."

Ashton didn't move.

"Look at your fate. You sold men to their deaths. You betrayed your country for pride—and now you'd die seated, like a beaten dog."

Still nothing.

Nicholas's voice dropped, colder still.

"After the peace is signed, they'll name you. The King will see your letters. And every house in London will know what you were."

Ashton's composure cracked. "You think this earns you Caroline. It doesn't. You don't know her."

Nicholas's reply was calm and final.

"I do. And I know she never came to your bed. But she came to mine a week ago of her own will."

That struck. Ashton flinched—just once. His hands gripped the arms of the chair. For a moment, he looked as though he might rise.

He didn't.

Nicholas looked down at him.

"You've earned this. But I offered you a sword."

He raised the pistol, steady in both hands, and drew a breath. He did not aim for the head—that was too quick. Nor the gut—that was cruelty, not justice. He aimed squarely for the heart.

The flint struck. The hammer fell.

The shot cracked like a whip in the confined space, echoing off timber. Ashton jerked violently, the ball striking high in the chest just left of the sternum. His coat tore open in a dark star, blood blooming at once in a swift, arterial arc that spattered the chair back and wall behind.

He made no sound—only a sharp intake of breath, as if surprised. Then he convulsed once, struck the bulkhead with a dull, final thud, and crumpled sideways, his legs folding beneath him like a collapsing mast. Blood pooled swiftly on the deck, dark and viscous, catching the firelight in a dull sheen.

Nicholas did not move for a long moment. The smoke hung low, the bitter tang of powder filling the cabin like a second breath.

Ashton did not stir.

The pistol's barrel smoked faintly. Nicholas lowered it with care, set it on the table beside the untouched sword, and stood motionless, listening to the silence that followed a death.

Then he crossed and knelt. The body had slumped sideways, one arm twisted beneath it, the fingers curled unnaturally. The blood had spread in a wide fan across the deck planks, thick and dark and beginning already to congeal in the seams.

Nicholas searched him with methodical care—coat seams, waistcoat lining, inside the boots. There was a cut above the brow from the fall, seeping sluggishly into his hair. In the right-hand pocket of the inner coat, beneath a stitched flap, he found the packet—sealed, thick, the wax still unbroken. French, deep red, impressed with the fleur-de-lys and the formal cipher of the Bureau des Affaires Etrangères.

He slid it into his own coat.

The fuse was already laid—wound through the powder charges beneath the deck, thin as twine but soaked in saltpetre and resin. He struck the flint and touched it to the powder cord. It caught at once, the hiss low and steady, the fire dancing along it like a message written in heat.

Nicholas gave one last glance to the body on the floor—chest blackened, shirt scorched and stiff with blood—and stepped out into the wind.

Neither Forester nor Markham said anything as the boat pulled away from *Le Furet*. Markham watched not the brig, but Nicholas. The captain sat very still in the sternsheets, one hand resting on the gunwale. His face was expressionless. Not hard. Not cruel. Simply—absent. As though he had stepped inward, and shut a door behind him.

There was no satisfaction in him. No triumph. Only silence.

Markham alone had the memories of him as a young man—little more than a boy, really—living for over a year in the unearthly paradise of Tahiti and Bora Bora. In that life, a young Nicholas had known perfect love, perfect happiness, and peace. Before the blood, before the smoke. He had watched him fight with blade and pistol—on Silva's ship off Makassar, and later in the Caribbean. But this—this was different. This was colder. It was the full turn of the circle.

He understood the necessity. Understood the intelligence at stake, the danger of delay, the weight of the orders they had carried. But in that moment, watching Nicholas sit there with the salt wind tugging faintly at his collar, he wondered if something vital had been left behind—somewhere far from the sea.

Alert was standing off under easy canvas when *Le Furet* exploded.

The detonation began below, a deep-bellied thump that buckled her planks from within. A gout of fire erupted from the main hatch, hurling the half-charred skylight into the sky. Then came the magazine—swift, brutal, definitive. Her stern blew outward in a roar of flame and shattered timber. The mainmast leapt into the air like a javelin before crashing sideways into the sea. A shockwave reached them seconds later, thudding in the chest like a hard-spent round.

Black smoke rose in a great pillar, feathered with sparks.

Debris spread across the surface—splintered planks, twisted gratings, a yardarm stripped to bare wood, lengths of blackened rigging trailing ends like kelp. An arm surfaced briefly, pale to the elbow, then rolled and disappeared. A broken oar drifted with a woman's cloak caught fast in its rowlock, trailing like a streamer at half-mast.

Silence followed, vast and unnatural. Even the gulls kept distant.

Nicholas stood alone on the windward side of the quarterdeck, the wind pressing gently at his coat. Blood had begun to soak through the cloth around his thigh, the rough binding of rope and gun-wad already slackening with the weight of it. Still, he made no complaint.

His eyes remained fixed on the obscene swirl of debris where *Le Furet* had gone down.

At length, he turned to his officers and said in a quiet, level voice:

"Northwest by west. Make our course for home."

Chapter Nine

Alert made her approach to Dartmouth three hours past dawn, the morning sun casting long shadows across her deck as she beat into the wind on the final tack before the harbour entrance. The scars of battle showed plainly along her hull—the starboard bulwarks still a wreck despite the carpenter's best efforts, and the dark wooden plugs of shot holes visible in a ragged line down both sides where *Le Furet's* broadsides had struck home.

Five days had passed since the French corvette had gone down in the Bay of Biscay, and in that time no man aboard had spoken of it save in the most necessary terms. The log recorded only that they had engaged an enemy vessel, which had subsequently sunk—a sparse accounting that betrayed nothing of the complex, heavy silence that had settled over the ship.

Fifty-five prisoners had been taken: sailors, marines, a handful of warrant officers, and one woman, presumed to be a civilian passenger though no one had inquired too closely. Fifteen were wounded, several grievously so. Twelve had died on the voyage back—two from burns, one from fever, the others from wounds too deep to mend. Their bodies had been committed to the sea with brief ceremony, sewn into hammocks and slipped over the side at dawn or dusk, without priest or prayer.

The survivors were confined in the orlop aft of the magazine, under watch and without communication. Meals were passed through the scuttle in silence. There was no parole, no quarterdeck interviews, no questions. The prisoners were given water, bandages, and nothing else.

Nicholas stood at the quarterdeck rail, leaning heavily on a cane fashioned by the carpenter from a broken tiller—a necessity since the splinter from a French ball had torn a gash nearly an inch deep across his thigh. Mr. Braitly had stitched the wound with sailor's precision and insisted on redressing it twice daily, but the leg remained stiff and deeply painful, causing Nicholas to favour his right side as he moved about the ship.

His glass was trained on two vessels anchored off the harbour mouth: a cutter flying the White Ensign, and beyond her, the unmistakable silhouette of *Fortunée*.

"Mr. Forester," Nicholas said, lowering the glass, "it appears our rendezvous arrangements have been modified." His voice betrayed nothing of the weariness that had taken hold of him since their action against *Le Furet*—a fatigue that went beyond the physical demands of command or the pain of his injured leg. It was as though something essential had been spent in that final confrontation with Ashton, leaving behind a man who functioned with all his customary precision but whose inner light had been temporarily dimmed. The crew had responded to this change with a kind of protective quietness, performing their duties with exceptional care, as if the ship herself were convalescing alongside her captain.

Forester joined him at the rail, his own glass raised to study the waiting vessels. Like Nicholas, he had maintained a careful formality since the action, neither condemning nor explicitly approving the decision they had executed together in attacking a ship under diplomatic colours. "The cutter appears to be *Swallow*, sir. Eight guns. Lieutenant Meadows commanding, if I recall correctly." He paused, adjusting the focus slightly. "She's signalling: 'Welcome. Heave to. Captain to come aboard *Fortunée*.' Plain enough, I believe."

Nicholas acknowledged the signal with a nod. "Very well. Have the ship hove to once we're within proper distance." He turned to Adams, who stood nearby with the ship's log tucked beneath his arm. "Mr. Adams, you'll accompany me. Bring the log, but no other papers." The official account would be delivered, but the private annotations Nicholas had made in his own journal, documenting the full circumstances of their encounter with *Le Furet*, would remain secure in his sea chest.

Within the half-hour, *Alert* had been brought skillfully to windward of the waiting vessels, and the gig was lowered with the same quiet efficiency that had characterized all shipboard operations since the action. Nicholas descended the accommodation ladder with care, his injured leg causing him to favor his left side considerably, though he permitted no assistance. Adams followed, carrying the log book wrapped in oilskin against the spray. The crew of the gig—all veterans from *Fortunée*—maintained a respectful silence as they took up their oars, pulling with the measured strokes of men who understood the gravity of their return.

The sea beyond the harbour entrance rolled gently beneath a moderate breeze, the October sun casting a pale golden light across the water. Nicholas found his thoughts turning unbidden to Caroline—to the night at Ocean House before his departure, to the steady confidence with which she had sought him out, to the unspoken promise between them that now seemed simultaneously more distant and more essential than before. He pushed these reflections aside as they approached *Fortunée's* imposing hull, her long row of gunports and clean lines presenting the very image of naval authority. A side party waited at the entry port, bosun's calls ready—an unexpected formality for what had been, officially, a mission that never existed.

The pipes sounded the standard honors as Nicholas climbed somewhat painfully aboard with a cane. Captain Walsh stood at the entry port, his face composed in the particular neutrality that experienced officers developed when circumstances required discretion. "Commander Cruwys. Welcome aboard." He extended his hand, and in the brief clasp that followed, Nicholas detected both acknowledgment and something approaching concern. "You're injured, I see."

"A minor matter, sir. Mr. Braitly has been most attentive." Nicholas made no reference to the circumstances of the wound, nor did Walsh inquire. Instead, the captain merely nodded and gestured aft. "You are expected in my day cabin. Mr. Thornhill arrived yesterday aboard the cutter from London. He has been remarkably patient, by his standards." This last observation carried a hint of dry humour, quickly suppressed as Walsh led the way aft, Adams following at a respectful distance. The officers present maintained a studied focus on their various duties, deliberately affording Nicholas a passage unmarked by curious glances.

The stern cabin of *Fortunée* presented a marked contrast to *Alert's* cramped quarters. Stern windows admitted the morning light across a broad table where charts had been carefully arranged alongside dispatch cases and a silver coffee service that spoke of Walsh's particular refinement. Thornhill stood by the starboard bulkhead, dressed not in his usual civilian attire but in a coat that, while lacking formal insignia, bore the unmistakable cut of Admiralty service. He turned as they entered, his expression revealing nothing of his thoughts, though his gaze lingered briefly on Nicholas's left leg before meeting his eyes with that particular directness that brooked no evasion. "Commander Cruwys. Your presence in these waters suggests the completion of your task."

"It is complete, sir," Nicholas replied, matching Thornhill's circumspection while acknowledging the essential truth. He gestured to Adams, who stepped forward and placed the oilskin-wrapped log on the table. "The full account, insofar as any account was required." The careful phrasing maintained the fiction that had surrounded the entire enterprise—a mission that existed nowhere in Admiralty records, conducted by a ship that had been officially removed from the active list, pursuing objectives that could never be openly acknowledged. Walsh said, "Mr. Adams, please seek the hospitality of your fellow officers in the gunroom. Tell the sentry he is relieved until send for him."

When they were alone, Thornhill's posture eased fractionally. He poured coffee from the silver pot, adding with practiced precision the exact measure of sugar that Walsh evidently preferred, before preparing a cup for Nicholas and himself. This domestic gesture, performed without comment or consultation, suggested not only a longer acquaintance between Thornhill and Walsh than Nicholas had suspected, but also a mutual understanding of the complexities surrounding their present circumstance. "Captain Walsh is now fully informed of this matter, and you may speak without reservation. Admiral Lord Howe and Vice Admiral Sir Samuel Hood will be gratified to learn of your success," Thornhill said, seating himself at the table. "As will certain other parties whose interests were most directly concerned. Do please sit, I insist with that leg."

Nicholas eased himself gratefully into one of the chairs, but Walsh remained standing, positioning himself by the stern windows where the light caught the weather-lines of his face, rendering his expression both more austere and more human than his usual quarterdeck composure allowed. "Your officers and men performed admirably, I assume," he said, directing the statement to Nicholas while avoiding any specific reference to actions that might later prove inconvenient if recalled too precisely. There was a particular kindness in this approach—allowing Nicholas to acknowledge the service of his crew without requiring him to detail the specific nature of that service or its consequences.

"They did, sir" Nicholas said quietly. "The gunnery was precise and fast, and they learned to handler her well . Every order was carried out without hesitation." He paused. "Lieutenant Forester deserves mention. So do Lieutenant Adams and Master Markham. Mr. Braitly did well—four amputations. He lost one man on the table, but saved the others."

Walsh inclined his head without speaking, allowing the silence to fill with what was not said. After a moment, Nicholas added, "Eight killed outright. Ten wounded. We took one shot below the waterline just aft amidships, later plugged, and three more between wind and water, all starboard side. Two guns dismounted and the starboard bulwarks heavily damaged but repairs are underway. The Carpenter reports no structural damage beyond that."

"I saw your entry," Walsh said. "She answered her helm well." It was a statement of fact, but also quiet commendation—the words of a seaman who knew the difference between a ship limping into port and one arriving under command. "I also saw the damage. The engagement, please l just give me the bones of it."

"Aye, sir. We took position under easy canvas six leagues league southwest of the Pointe du Raz by last Friday morning." Anticipating a question he added, "We sighted the inshore blockading squadron, but the closest frigate—*Minerva*—was recalled by the flagship when she tried to close us." Thornhill nodded with satisfaction.

Nicholas went on. "*Le Furet* was sighted shortly after dawn on the 26th, and *Alert* closed under American colours. At six hundred yards, I hauled down the false colours, and engaged with a full broadside of chain into the French corvette's rigging," Nicholas said, his voice level. "We destroyed her spanker and most of her bowsprit, compromising her ability to maneuver to windward. However, she was more vigilant than I believed, and responded almost immediately with her starboard broadside of nine guns—six-pounders, but well handled. We took four killed and ten wounded, including a shot below the waterline and three more between wind and water. She hoisted the white diplomatic signal. We came into her wake and opened the distance, firing chain and ball into her with the stern chaser. I tacked around and opened with the bow chaser. She attempted to run for the coast. We closed by steering upwind on her starboard quarter. At three hundred yards she luffed to starboard and gave us her broadside, with four balls coming home." He paused, "At that point we came off the wind and raked her stern at close range, the guns double-shotted. Her mizzen went by the board, and our fire swept her quarterdeck clear."

He paused again, staring out through the stern windows. The sea beyond lay dull and heaving, a grey wash under a slate sky. Neither Walsh nor Thornhill spoke. The silence stretched, heavy with implication.

At length Nicholas continued, his voice flat, almost clinical.

"I would never have thought three six pounders and a twelve pounder carronade could do such execution. *Le Furet* struck her colours as we came about to rake her stern again. Our port broadside had already been run out. We hove to and sent over a boarding party."

He glanced down at his hands, then resumed.

"I went aboard personally with Lieutenant Forester and Mr. Markham, and eight men. There were fifty-five survivors out of a crew of ninety-seven. One junior officer, otherwise seamen and marines, and one woman passenger. A second woman was killed in the action. Fifteen injured, most badly: twelve died during the passage back. The surviving forty-three prisoners are confined below under guard, separated from our crew. No communication was permitted."

He shifted his weight in the chair slightly.

"Ashton was taken uninjured, without resistance, and held in the aft cabin. I sent the others to stand off in a boat. He said little. No protest, no justification."

There was a silence, thin as wire.

"I offered him a sword. He declined, remained seated. Said he did not fight sailors."

Another pause.

"So he died shot, sitting."

Nicholas continued, more quietly, "He carried the packet on his person. Inner pocket, right-hand side, beneath a stitched flap. Wax seal intact. Here it is."

He removed the packet from his pocket and gave it to Thornhill, who inclined his head slightly, saying nothing.

"We had laid charges and I touched off the fuse myself. She blew up ten minutes after I was back aboard. Main magazine. There wasn't much left."

Thornhill remained still, his hands clasped behind his back. Walsh's expression did not change, though he drew a slow breath through his nose, as if bracing against a wind.

Nicholas rose from the chair and straightened, his knuckles briefly white on the cane.

"We had orders to secure the packet, prevent intelligence reaching enemy hands, and to make no public show of prisoners. I have acted accordingly."

There was no reply at once. Only the faint creak of the hull and the distant murmur of water against the transom.

Walsh exhaled slowly through his nose, eyes steady on Nicholas. "A bitter business."

Nicholas said nothing.

"You were under orders," Thornhill said at last, his tone even,. "The destruction of *Le Furet* prevents any embarrassment to our allies or complications in the peace negotiations."

He paused, weighing his next words with care.

"As to the prisoners—well." He turned slightly toward the quarterdeck windows, hands loosely clasped. "Your orders did not specify what was to be done with survivors, should any be taken. Nor did they forbid it."

He turned back, gaze meeting Nicholas's with unblinking directness.

"War gives no prize for excess severity. And I do not believe His Majesty's government will ask too closely—provided the matter remains quiet," he said, adjusting a cuff with studied precision, "the prisoners alter things. But not in any way we cannot manage."

He turned away, speaking half to the air, half to himself.

"I had arranged for *Alert* to berth quietly at Dartmouth—brought in by a mate from *Fortunée*, with six hands uninvolved in the action. They're off to windward now, hove to in the cutter, waiting for the signal to board."

He paused. "The plan was to bring her into the yard under some tall tale of battle damage and rum cargo, and let her disappear into repair."

He turned back, voice tightening slightly.

"But with prisoners—particularly this number, and a woman among them—that plan no longer holds."

Nicholas said nothing. Walsh watched in silence.

Thornhill was already working the new shape of it aloud.

"She cannot make port. Not now. Not without questions. Instead—she sails for Spithead. I'll assign her a holding vessel off the Roads. The Transport Office can docket her as a civilian prize in transshipment—there's a packet service bound for the Indies in four days' time out of Portsmouth."

He stepped to the small writing table and flipped open his case, taking out a thin sheaf of documents already creased for use.

"I'll have the cutter bring the hands aboard with a marine detachment from *Fortunée*—ten men, disciplined, and unaware of the particulars. They'll provide guard. Is that acceptable, Captain Walsh?"

Walsh looked unhappy but merely nodded, and Thornhill continued, "Master Markham will command in place of the mate. Meals through the scuttle only. The woman will be listed separately—civilian custody under review, neutral foreign subject. I will have orders written for Markham to join the packet along with the hands and marines and join *Fortunée* in the Islands.

"I'll see to the papers tonight. *Alert* will put off before first light. By the time word reaches Whitehall, the prisoners will be bound for Trinidad, or Berbice, or Halifax if we must—anywhere quiet."

He gave a dry, unreadable smile.

"There are always ships. And always colonies."

Walsh made a low sound—perhaps disapproval, perhaps mere fatigue.

Thornhill met his eyes. "The essential thing is the packet, and the elimination of Ashton. The rest—" a brief pause, "—never happened."

Walsh gave a low grunt, not quite agreement. His arms were crossed, jaw set, eyes still on Nicholas.

"They'll know in the fleet," he said. "There are always tongues."

"Yes," said Thornhill, dryly. "But not many that speak twice."

He looked once more to Nicholas. "You did what was necessary. And you were discreet. Let that be your defence—if ever one is required."

Nicholas gave a single nod, not quite assent, not quite relief.

Thornhill moved to the windows, gazing out through the mist toward the faint outline of the cutter riding at anchor.

"There are whispers in town. About Ashton. About Everett. Not facts — not yet — but hints. Questions in the wrong rooms."

He turned back to them.

"We can't afford more questions. Not now. *Especially* not with a French corvette sunk with women aboard flying a diplomatic flag."

Nicholas gave a faint nod. "Then you've already decided."

"We have," Thornhill said. "Your crew will transfer to *Fortunée* before midday. Captain Walsh will carry them to the West Indies. Quiet orders. No attention."

Walsh added, "I'll see to them. Lieutenant Forester will replace my second lieutenant, who by happy coincidence was transferred ashore at my request two weeks ago. And I mind your long association with Master Markham—once he arrives in the packet I'll see him to a good new berth. I'm well with the Admiral in Antigua, and with the yellow jack there are always vacancies." He paused, "I'll tell you, it was no joke sailing here down Channel with most of my best hands gone, and I'm grateful to have them back."

Nicholas's gaze lingered on the table for a moment, then lifted. "And myself?"

"You and I will take the cutter. Straight to London." Thornhill's voice remained level. "No papers. No signals. No attention."

He paused, and when he continued, it was more softly spoken.

"You followed your instructions, Commander," Thornhill said. "What follows now is simply containment—ensuring the matter doesn't grow legs in a clerk's mouth or a backbencher's diary."

Walsh spoke next, low and firm. "You bore the point. It falls to us to see the haft doesn't splinter behind you."

Nicholas inclined his head, slow and grave. "My thanks."

Thornhill gave him a long look. "Make your farewells brief."

Nicholas made his way back to *Alert* with as much dignity as his injured leg would permit, the ship's gig rising and falling in the moderate swell. His mind was filled with the curious emptiness that follows the completion of a difficult duty—not satisfaction, certainly, but a kind of hollowed relief that the thing was done and could not be undone. The faces of his crew, lined up along the bulwarks as he came aboard for the final time, betrayed a similar complex of emotions: pride in their seamanship, certainly, but marked by a gravity that spoke of deeds best left unexamined too closely.

"Assemble the ship's company, if you please, Mr. Forester," Nicholas said, having climbed the ladder with perhaps more effort than he would have wished to display.

The hands gathered on the main deck, an uncommonly silent group of men who had faced death together and delivered it in equal measure. The morning sun slanted across their faces, illuminating weather-beaten features that had grown familiar to him in these weeks of shared purpose.

"Men," Nicholas began, his voice carrying clearly in the still air, "you have served with honor in circumstances that demanded the utmost. Within the hour, you will transfer to *Fortunée*, under Captain Walsh, for service in the West Indies. Lieutenant Forester will continue as your officer." He paused, studying their faces. "What we have done together will not be spoken of. Not now. Not ever. But know that those who matter understand its necessity."

A murmur passed through the assembly—not protest, but acknowledgment. Most were the hands originally lent from

Fortunée, and the others were not greenhands but seasoned mariners who understood the complexities of loyalty and service.

"It has been my privilege to command you," Nicholas concluded. "That is all."

He led Forester and Markham to his cabin.

Forester said, "It was well done, sir. Whatever's said or not said after." Forester hesitated, then extended his hand. Nicholas shook it, and turned to Markham, his weathered face set in its habitual stoicism, yet somehow softened.

"Mr. Markham, you will take command of *Alert* upon my departure and proceed to Spithead with hands now aboard the cutter and marines from the *Fortunée* to guard the prisoners. They will be transferred to a packet departing shortly for the West Indies, and you will sail with her to meet up with Captain Walsh, who will look to your further assignment.

"The islands have long memories, sir," Markahm said quietly, "And the sea keeps her own counsel. As shall we." He touched his forehead, the gesture containing all that would remain unspoken between men who had sailed together, first with Cook, then in Polynesia and among the Spice Islands, to this grey corner of the Channel.

"Aye, said "I have written a letter commending your service," Nicholas told him quietly. "Captain Walsh will see it properly delivered."

"No need for that, sir," Markham replied, his weathered face creasing into what might have been the suggestion of a smile. "I've sailed with you since Bombay Station. I know what was done and why. So does every man jack aboard."

"Even so."

Nicholas descended to the waiting gig for the short pull to *Swallow*, the cutter heaving gently at anchor a cable's length away. Nicholas did not look back at *Alert's* familiar silhouette, fixing his gaze instead on the vessel that would return him to London and whatever consequence awaited. Thornhill was already aboard, but nowhere to be seen.

"Welcome aboard, sir," the cutter's commander said as they mounted the side. "We have favorable winds for London. Mr. Thornhill has advised me that we should make all dispatch."

"Thank you, Lieutenant," Nicholas replied, noting the careful lack of inquiry in the officer's tone. Here was a man who had received orders he understood were best executed without elaboration.

Four days later, Nicholas stood at the window of the South Audley Street house, gazing out at the cold autumn rain that had fallen steadily since their return to London. The house seemed excessively large and uncomfortably elegant after the cramped simplicity of *Alert* and the even more confined quarters of the cutter. Thornhill had departed an hour earlier, after delivering unexpected instructions—Nicholas was to remain here, receive no visitors, and make no attempts to contact anyone, particularly not at Ocean House. "There will be a dinner tonight," Thornhill had said, his tone suggesting more significance than the words themselves conveyed. "You are to wear your best uniform. A carriage will collect you at six. The location," he had added, "need not concern you until your arrival."

Nicholas limped to the sideboard, his wounded leg still stiff though healing cleanly thanks to Braitly's ministrations, and more recently to a discreet physician who had tended him that afternoon. He poured a measure of brandy and carried it back to the chair by the hearth, where a fire burned with expensive indifference to the damp. The silence of the house pressed around him, broken only by the occasional crackle of coal and the persistent whisper of rain against the windowpanes.

His thoughts drifted back to the second night of their passage, when the weather had cleared briefly and a cold, brilliant moon had risen over the Channel. Unable to sleep, he had made his way on deck, finding it deserted save for the helmsman and the officer of the watch, both of whom had maintained a careful distance from the strange officer who they had been instructed was not to be remarked upon. Nicholas had stood at the taffrail, watching the cutter's wake spread like a silvered ribbon across the dark water, remembering another night on another deck.

The memory came with unforgiving clarity: the French officers on *Le Furet's* quarterdeck turning their backs in unison as *Alert* crossed their stern before that devastating broadside. It had been a final gesture of contempt for a man they believed had violated the laws of gentlemanly combat by attacking a vessel flying a diplomatic flag agreed to by each country. Even knowing what would follow, they had chosen to stand straight, to turn away rather than plead or cower. It was the gesture of men who understood what honor demanded and who would not dignify with so much as a glance one who had, in their eyes, abandoned it entirely.

Nicholas had said nothing of this to anyone, though he knew Forester had witnessed it too—had seen the coordinated movement, understood its meaning, and maintained the same silence afterward. It was a moment that belonged to them alone, a private weight to be carried alongside the more obvious burden of the dead woman's body, and of the execution of Ashton. He had justified his actions in the language of necessity: the mission's objectives, the intelligence at stake, the clear instructions from Admiral Lord Howe himself, acting with authority that circumvented the formal channels of the Admiralty Board. Yet those turned backs had spoken to something else—a judgment rendered by men of honor, even at the threshold of death.

There on the cutter's deck, with no witness but the moon and the indifferent sea, Nicholas had reached a decision. Without ceremony or hesitation, he had drawn Silva's sword—the blade that had served him since his time with Silva in the Pacific, the weapon that had taken lives in the close quarters of boarding actions from the Pacific to the Caribbean—and cast it from him in a single, fluid motion. The blade had caught the moonlight as it tumbled through the air, a brief silver arc that ended with a clean splash in the cutter's wake.

No one had seen. No one had questioned. The sword was simply gone, as if it had never been—consigned to the depths as was the wreck of *Le Furet* and the bodies of her crew and innocent passengers, if any there were. It was not repudiation, nor was it entirely atonement. It was simply an acknowledgment, made in silence and solitude, that some actions leave marks that cannot be scoured away by either duty or forgiveness.

Now, in the expensive silence of South Audley Street, Nicholas raised his glass in a private toast—to turned backs and sinking swords, to duty and its costs, and to the thin, fragile hope that whatever awaited him at this evening's mysterious dinner might offer, if not redemption, then at least a path forward that honored the sacrifice of all those lost beneath the indifferent waters of the Bay of Biscay.

The carriage bearing Nicholas to his mysterious appointment rolled to a stop before a substantial house in Upper Brook Street, its façade illuminated by a pair of flambeau torches that cast wavering light across dressed stone and polished brass fittings. A footman in the unmistakable Hood livery—blue with silver facings, far more subdued than the gaudy ostentation lately favored by certain admirals—stepped forward to open the carriage door and offer a steadying arm, which Nicholas declined with a slight shake of his head. The house itself spoke of quiet wealth rather than display: no marble columns or elaborate frontage, merely perfect proportion and the finest Portland stone, blackened at the edges by London's perpetual coal-smoke but meticulously maintained nonetheless. It was the dwelling of a man who understood power required no advertisement.

"Commander Cruwys, sir," the butler intoned as Nicholas was relieved of his boat cloak in the entrance hall, where a low fire of sea-coal burned in a grate of polished Purbeck marble, casting a gentle warmth that drove back the raw dampness of the October evening. "The Admiral is expecting you in the octagonal room." Nicholas followed the man up a shallow flight of stairs, the fine Turkey carpet beneath his boots absorbing all sound save the faint tap of his cane, which he had been obliged to retain due to his wound. The butler's candle threw elongated shadows along the wainscoting as they proceeded through a succession of chambers, each more elegant than the last, until they reached a pair of mahogany doors with brass fittings burnished to a subdued glow.

These opened upon a room whose form immediately explained its designation—a perfect octagon, with four of its walls pierced by tall windows now shuttered against the night, the others bearing portraits of naval engagements: the Battle of Quiberon Bay, Rodney defeating de Grasse at the Saints, and a fine depiction of Hood's own action off

Chesapeake Bay. At the center stood a round table of Spanish mahogany, its surface reflecting the light of two silver candelabra and a central astral lamp of exceptional workmanship. Three men rose as Nicholas entered, their blue coats gleaming with gold lace catching and holding the candlelight: Vice Admiral Hood himself, his weathered face composed in its habitual expression of contained authority; the broader, more physically imposing figure of Admiral Lord Howe; and to Nicholas's considerable surprise, Rear Admiral Trevenen, whose particular gaze met his with an intensity that suggested this gathering held significance beyond what he had anticipated.

Nicholas returned the gaze, not with challenge, but with a question plainly left unspoken.

"Commander Cruwys," said Admiral Hood, stepping forward with unusual warmth to take his hand, "your return is most welcome. We have followed your progress with particular interest." He gestured toward the table, where places had been laid with silver that caught the light with subdued elegance rather than ostentation. "You know Admiral Lord Howe, of course, and your relation Admiral Trevenen, who has been fully apprised of recent events." This last remark, delivered with studied casualness, revealed what Nicholas instantly recognized as a significant development—Trevenen, who had previously maintained a careful distance from the operation, allowing Nicholas's recruitment without directly involving himself, was now being deliberately included in their inner circle. The implications were clear: his relation's trustworthiness and their family connection had been deemed valuable enough to bring him fully into their confidence.

"My lords," he said, his voice quiet but even, "I did not expect this company—but I understand the honour it implies.

"Your health, sir," said Howe, raising his own glass in what might have been merely a conventional toast but which carried, in the particular circumstances, a deeper significance. "I understand your leg troubles you still. Captain Walsh sends his compliments and his assurance that your men have been well placed." The mention of Walsh brought an involuntary tension to Nicholas's shoulders—for if Walsh had communicated with these men since *Alert*'s return, what else might have been conveyed beyond the mere disposition of her crew? The admirals exchanged glances of such brevity and subtlety that a less observant man might have missed them entirely, but Nicholas, whose survival had often depended upon reading the unspoken, caught the momentary shift in atmosphere that suggested matters of consequence lay beneath the social forms.

"I am grateful to hear it, my lord," Nicholas replied, his voice steady despite the fatigue that had settled upon him like a physical weight since his return. "Lieutenant Forester and Master Markham are exceptional officers. They deserve every consideration." He sipped the madeira, its complex warmth spreading through his chest and easing, in some small measure, the tension within. Dinner was announced with quiet ceremony, and they seated themselves around the table—not, Nicholas noted, in the strict order of precedence that naval life dictated, but rather as men of equal purpose engaged in a matter that transcended conventional hierarchy.

The first course came and went with little conversation beyond the ordinary courtesies—observations on the excellence of the soup (a clear turtle of remarkable quality), discussion of the weather (persistently damp, even by London's dismal standards), and the expected movements of the Channel Fleet (which might or might not be reduced following the preliminary peace agreements, depending upon which faction prevailed in the ministerial deliberations). Throughout this exchange of apparent banalities, Nicholas remained acutely aware of the undercurrents flowing beneath—the careful avoidance of any reference to *Alert*, to *Le Furet*, or to Lord Ashton. It was only after the removes had been cleared and a saddle of mutton of exceptional tenderness had been carved and served that Hood, having dismissed the servants with a discreet gesture, turned the conversation to matters of consequence.

"You will have observed, Commander Cruwys, that of course there has been no public word or notice regarding the loss of the French corvette *Le Furet*," he said, his voice pitched low despite the privacy of their setting. "Nor has any official inquiry been lodged through diplomatic channels. This is not accidental." He paused, allowing the significance of this statement to register fully. "Mr. Thornhill has been most effective in managing certain delicate aspects of the affair. The preliminary articles were signed in Paris three days ago, and while the formal treaty remains to be concluded, the essential business has been settled on terms considerably more favorable to British interests than had been anticipated."

"To speak more plainly," Howe broke in gently, his deep-set eyes resting on Nicholas with a directness few men could sustain, "your service was essential to the outcome. The intelligence Ashton carried would have materially altered Spain's position at the negotiating table—particularly regarding the fisheries, Gibraltar, and our access to Honduras. Its loss has secured advantages that ships of the line could not have won." He reached for the decanter of claret—a Latour of the '59 vintage that even in these straightened times demonstrated Hood's cellar remained among the finest in London—and filled Nicholas's glass with his own hand, an extraordinary gesture from a man of his rank and station.

Howe went on, "You might have sunk her without quarter, you know. We gave you that latitude."

Nicholas looked at him, and said slowly, "I considered it, sir. God knows it would have been simpler. But they struck."

He paused, "As for the rest, I didn't want to be Ashton's judge, let alone as it turned out his executioner. I could have killed him at a distance, but at what price? Ordering my officers and crew to finish that ship at close range and all aboard after she surrendered, and have them live with that? Ashton wasn't worth such a cost, and so I handled it directly. And I gave Ashton more than he deserved, a choice. And he chose to die badly."

A stillness followed, then Howe nodded, "No, you did not choose the easy course. And it is the man who knows he must pull the trigger himself who remains a man. That is one reason why we invited you here."

"The influence of your action extends beyond mere diplomacy," Trevenen added, speaking for the first time since Nicholas's arrival, his voice carrying that particular measured quality that suggested each word had been carefully weighed before utterance. "Lord Ashton's disappearance has been attributed to private financial embarrassment rather than matters of state. Everett has been quietly removed to a property in Northumberland, where he will remain under what might be called protective confinement for the foreseeable future." He paused, his gaze meeting Nicholas's directly. "I feel I must acknowledge that I was initially reluctant to see you drawn into this affair. My reservations were not concerning your capabilities, but rather the peculiar burden such service places upon a man of conscience."

Nicholas returned his gaze. "I understand sir, and believe you were right to hesitate. It isn't the kind of duty a man should accept lightly. But I did accept it. And I have not found a way to wish I hadn't."

Hood's hand moved slightly toward the decanter, a gesture almost imperceptible yet charged with meaning in the context of naval etiquette. "Captain Walsh has written to me privately," he said, his tone deliberately conversational despite the gravity of the subject. "He mentioned a matter observed by Lieutenant Adams during your engagement with the French vessel—something concerning the conduct of her officers as you crossed her stern." There was a momentary stillness around the table, broken only by the faint crackle of coal settling in the grate. "It appears they turned their backs. A gesture of some significance among men who serve at sea." The words hung in the air, neither accusation nor absolution, merely the acknowledgment of what had passed between adversaries in that final moment.

Howe observed Nicholas with that particular intensity which had earned him his sobriquet "Black Dick" across a career spanning nearly five decades at sea. "We have also learned from Mr. Thornhill," he said, with the careful emphasis of a man accustomed to the precise deployment of information, "that during your return passage aboard the cutter, you were observed to dispose of a sword overboard. A personal weapon, I understand, and one of some significance to you." Nicholas felt a momentary chill that had nothing to do with the temperature of the room. Thornhill had seen that private act of renunciation, then—had witnessed what he had believed to be an entirely solitary gesture, and had evidently reported it. Yet there was no censure in Howe's tone; rather, a kind of grave understanding that spoke of decisions made and burdens shouldered across decades of command.

"The Navy has need of men who feel the weight of such actions," Hood said, breaking the silence that had fallen. "Not those who undertake them lightly, nor those who refuse them entirely from excess of scruple." He leaned forward slightly, the candlelight catching the silver at his temples and the fine network of lines that decades of squinting against tropical sun and North Atlantic gales had etched around his eyes. "What was done was necessary—unpleasant, perhaps even terrible, but necessary nonetheless. That you understand this necessity while still feeling its gravity marks you as the kind of officer this service requires, particularly in these uncertain times between war and peace."

As the port was served and began its measured circuit of the table, Lord Howe cleared his throat in that distinctive manner which invariably signaled a pronouncement of consequence. "There is one further matter, Commander," he said, producing a folded paper from his coat as the decanter paused momentarily before him. "His Majesty has been informed, in appropriately discreet terms, of the service rendered. He has commanded that a sword be commissioned for you from Bland & Foster, to your exact specifications. The Crown will bear all expenses." Nicholas was momentarily unable to conceal his surprise. Bland & Foster were not merely swordsmiths but artists whose blades were sought by admirals and princes; their waiting list was said to extend two years. The significance of such a gift—replacing the weapon he had consigned to the deep—was not lost on him, nor was the tacit acknowledgment it represented. "You need not respond at once," Hood added quietly, setting down his glass with practiced precision. "The craftsmen await your instructions whenever you are ready to provide them."

Nicholas understood it now. This was not honour in the usual sense, nor advancement by seniority. It was something quieter, more deliberate—a recognition that within the service there existed a duty beyond the signal book and the quarterdeck. These men—flag officers to the world, but stewards in truth, and stewards with the Crown's quiet backing—had long understood that the defence of Britain and its empire required more than broadsides and convoy lists. It required judgment where orders gave no guidance, and action where silence was the only possible report.

There would be no citation. Only a blade, commissioned in silence. A token not of elevation, but of trust, and from these men whose opinion carried the highest weight, an assurance of true honour. They had seen in him a willingness to act where others might pause, and to bear the consequences in full. That was the price. He had been accepted into the work.

And now, he understood what that meant.

He said, "Thank you my lord, I am honoured. And I will accept it with the seriousness it deserves."

Trevenen's eyes met Nicholas' briefly across the table—a glance containing both understanding and something else, a warning perhaps, that such royal notice carried obligations as surely as it bestowed honour.

Chapter Ten

For once it was a clear afternoon when two days after Hood's dinner Nicholas stepped off Haymarket and paused before a narrow door beneath a soot-darkened cornice. The appointment had been arranged with surprising dispatch given the establishment's customary waiting list. There was no display, no ornament. Just a polished brass plaque, engraved with the severity of purpose:

Bland & Foster

Sword Cutlers to His Majesty the King

By Appointment, Est. 1719

He stepped inside.

Mahogany panelled walls, burnished to a deep gloss that absorbed more light than it reflected. The floor laid in wide oak boards, waxed but unvarnished, each plank bearing the particular patina that comes only from decades of careful attention. A long walnut counter ran the length of the room, bare but for a leather blotter, a small sandglass, and a single lamp trimmed low. Behind it: cabinetry fitted with the precision of Swiss clockwork, and a glass-fronted case set into the far wall.

There was no bustle. No clerk. No scent of polish or lamp oil. The air held only the faint signature of charcoal, wax, and steel—the particular atmosphere of exacting work completed to the standard of men whose lives might depend upon it.

A tall man in a dark waistcoat stood behind the counter. His sleeves were rolled with mathematical precision. His hands bore the honorable stains of oil and pumice—the calloused hands of a craftsman who knew intimately the properties of metal and fire. He looked up when Nicholas entered and held his gaze with the steadiness of a man accustomed to measuring others against steel.

Nicholas removed his gloves, folding them with deliberate economy.

"I have an appointment; my name is Cruwys. I need a blade," he said. "Not for ceremony. Not for ornament. Something I can wear, and use."

The man gave a short nod, as definite as a compass point. Though Nicholas was not in uniform, he said, "Commander Cruwys, we were expecting you. My name is Foster, sir. My brother keeps the books. I keep the edge. We understand we are to make a blade to your specification of our finest quality, and that this commission is to move to the top of our list."

Nicholas said, "Yes that is so, but perhaps before we discuss my preferences, you could show me a selection of your work."

Foster nodded. He studied Nicholas for a moment longer, taking his measure with the practiced eye of a man who had fitted weapons to generations of officers and gentlemen. Then he moved to the case, unlocked it with a ring of small keys, and slid back the glass with a motion of practiced, unhurried precision.

He did not ask what Nicholas wanted to see. He simply began to lay out swords.

The first was a smallsword, light and faultless, the guard finely carved, the grip bound in silver wire over bone. A gentleman's weapon, made for duels behind closed doors, where honor might be satisfied without the inconvenience of death.

Nicholas turned it once in his hand, felt the flex, tested the stop. It was a beautiful blade, but it was for a different kind of decision, made in a different kind of world.

He set it back.

The second, a court sword—longer, heavier, with a stiffer blade, the guard flared and fluted, the scabbard lined in oxblood leather with a polished chape. An admiral or a senior captain's sword, meant for dinners, salons, the receiving line of command—for men whose authority was never questioned.

Nicholas gave it a glance, the way a veteran might regard the ceremonial armor in a country house. Nothing more.

The third blade—heavier still. A duelist's weapon: broad in the forte, deep shell guard, dark grip with a thumb recess and a narrow, cutting edge drawn full to the point. Built for single combat. Serious. But deliberate. A blade made for rules, for witnesses, for surgeons standing by.

He took it up. Drew it slow. Tested the flex. Then the return.

"This type and pattern?" Foster asked quietly, his voice carrying the particular inflection of a man accustomed to reading intentions through hands rather than words, who had seen how men hold weapons they truly mean to use.

"No," Nicholas said. "It's too much in its own mind."

Foster gave a small nod, the corner of his mouth tightening in what might have been approval. Said nothing.

Then, from the far right of the case, he lifted a fourth sword in a scabbard. He held it as he looked up and said, "This blade was not commissioned. I made it to see what could be done when nothing was hurried. Six weeks at the forge. I drew the temper slowly, with the patience of winter. Filed the edge myself, with stones finer than any ship's blacksmith would know how to use, much less possess. Not a grindstone within a league of this edge—such brutality would ruin the temper. The guard's mine, too—cold-drawn and polished."

He gestured to the double line. "That's not for show. It's just the mark where everything—hesitation, compromise, doubt—stopped."

He paused, "It had not been for sale before now." He did not place it with the others. He laid it directly before Nicholas, alone, with the particular reverence that men of true craft reserve for their finest work.

The scabbard was black leather, steel-throated, the chape drawn long and swept slightly back, giving it the subtle curve of a predatory bird's talon. The grip—dark horn, polished to a fine matte that would never betray a hand by glinting, wrapped in black sharkskin, bound with five turns of steel wire, tight and flat as a surgeon's sutures. The guard was a half-shell, shallow, blued steel, with no pierce work—nothing that might catch on sleeve or cuff in the critical instant. Along the inner curve, near the quillon, were two fine etched lines, curved like the signature pause in a perfect lunge.

Not decoration. Not signature. A gesture, as eloquent as a flag hoist on a clear day.

Nicholas took the handle and drew.

The blade whispered like a secret shared between equals.

Thirty-three inches of Solingen steel, in shape like an elegant long hanger, nearly straight, curved just enough to carry speed through the cut, achieving the precise balance between authority and swiftness. The fuller ran past the midpoint, light but true, lightening the draw, sharpening the return. The blade had no flaws, just a single pure line.

Nicholas brought it forward, turned once, low guard. It came back without resistance, as responsive as thought itself. He shifted his grip minutely, testing the balance with the sensitivity of a physician's fingers seeking a pulse. He executed a half-lunge, then a swift recovery, feeling how the blade's weight distributed itself through the motion. A quick moulinet, wrist circling in the economical gesture of a practiced swordsman, and the blade whispered through the air with neither flutter nor drag. Finally, he performed a complex cut—terza to seconda—watching how the edge maintained its plane throughout the movement.

Foster watched with the critical eye of a master craftsman surveying his finest work.

Nicholas said nothing. He brought the blade through again—wrist, elbow, shoulder. It asked nothing. It offered everything, with the reliable certainty of mathematical truth.

Nicholas lowered the blade.

"I'll wear it out."

Foster nodded once. "Left hip?"

"Standard draw."

The frog was fitted. The blade settled low and flat beneath the line of his coat. It didn't pull. It didn't swing.

It simply belonged, like a perfect theorem proven in steel, and like an extension of will, a final argument held in abeyance.

Foster disappeared briefly into the back room, returning with a small oilskin-wrapped parcel which he placed on the counter. "The blade will need these. Japanese water stones—three grades. The finest barely distinguishable from silk. A bottle of oil pressed from the roe of sturgeon—cleaner than whale or mineral oils. And a leather strop I've prepared with a particular compound." He looked directly at Nicholas. "No common stones or oils should ever touch it. The edge isn't merely sharp—it's architected. These will maintain its nature without compromise."

Nicholas nodded once himself, accepting the parcel with the same gravity with which he had accepted the sword. The tools of maintenance were inseparable from the weapon itself—each necessary to the other's purpose.

Ten days later, early winter had settled firmly upon London. The intervening period had passed with a particular tedium for Nicholas in the comfortable but increasingly confining safe house in South Audley Street. He had complied with Thornhill's request that he not circulate, and that he refrain even from writing to Caroline. Aside from reading extensively from the well-appointed library and receiving daily visits from the surgeon to attend his healing leg, his sole relief from confinement had been his appointment at Bland & Foster. It was therefore with considerable relief that he received Westborne's note early that morning requesting his presence "at the earliest convenience which your recovery permits."

Nicholas had arrived shortly before nine, and been conducted through the house by Morley with that particular quiet efficiency he recalled from his previous visits and indeed stays at the house, including with his friend and former shipmate, Commander Henry Harrington, Westborne's son. Yet he had never before been admitted to this inner sanctum of the Viscount's study.

Here was a space designed for sustained, private work rather than ceremonial occasion: walls lined with maps under glass, showing regions from around the globe; a substantial chart-table positioned to catch the northern light; shelves laden not with ornamental volumes, but with bound reports, navigation tables, and leather-cased journals whose worn spines suggested frequent consultation. Westborne stood by the hearth where a coal fire burned steadily against the November chill, and with him were Trevenen and Thornhill.

"May I offer you something, Nicholas?" Westborne asked, nodding toward a silver tray upon which rested a porcelain service—not the elaborate Chinese export ware fashionable in London drawing rooms, but rather the simpler, more elegant white porcelain that true connoisseurs preferred. "Coffee or tea? Both freshly arrived on the last India fleet." The casual reference to Company shipping struck Nicholas as deliberate, though he could not yet discern its significance.

"Coffee, thank you," Nicholas replied, accepting the cup that Westborne himself poured. The aroma rising from the dark liquid carried notes of cardamom and clove, suggesting beans from the Malabar Coast rather than the West Indies. He settled into the chair Westborne indicated, noting that the arrangement suggested a council of war rather than a social gathering.

"I trust your leg continues to improve," Trevenen observed, his manner carrying that particular combination of familial concern and professional assessment characteristic of him. "The surgeon reports favorably on your progress."

"It mends well enough, sir," Nicholas replied. "I can walk without the cane now, though not yet with complete comfort." This was perhaps slightly optimistic—the wound still troubled him considerably after extended movement—but conveyed the essential truth that he was fit for whatever service might be required.

"I believe the time has come," Westborne said in the pause that followed, "to speak somewhat more plainly about matters which have, until now, remained obscured by necessary discretion. You should know, Commander, that while I hold no official position within the current government, I serve as chairman of a particular committee that oversees certain aspects of naval intelligence of interest to the Crown." The admission was delivered with that careful precision which suggested not merely a revelation of fact, but an extension of trust. "Mr. Thornhill, as you have now likely surmised, operates under my direction in these matters, though he is also attached to the Admiralty in that department."

"Rear Admiral Trevenen," Westborne continued, "has graciously consented to serve as your direct connection to the Admiralty in any further matters requiring official naval sanction, yet are not within ordinary service."

Nicholas went still. The three others exchanged a glance, and Thornhill stepped forward with several documents that he arranged before them with methodical precision. "We have received intelligence," he said without preamble, "concerning a matter that may directly affect your position, Commander. Our agents in Brest report that the French Navy has opened an inquiry into the loss of *Le Furet*. It appears that the wreckage washed ashore near Lorient showing clear signs of cannon fire, and that a note was found wrapped in waxed silk, sealed in a corked bottle that was tied into a cabinet drawer. The note was found by fishermen and was written by a lady companion enroute to her mistress, the Vicomtesse de Monteil."

Nicholas felt a curious hollowness open within him. Thornhill continued, his voice maintaining that particular evenness that revealed nothing of the man behind the information. "The note reportedly describes a black ship flying no colors, with two distinctive raked masts, that fired upon them even after the hoisted a diplomatic flag of immunity. The French naval intelligence officers are examining records, seeking vessels matching this description."

"We have also," Thornhill continued with practiced smoothness, "been obliged to disseminate certain accounts regarding Mr. Everett. The official record now states that he died suddenly of a putrid fever contracted while examining waterworks near the Thames—a plausible enough tale given the miasmas that rise from that river, particularly in the warmer months." He sipped his coffee with the deliberate calm of a man accustomed to constructing and maintaining such fictions. "His papers have been secured, his estate placed under the administration of a trustee known to us, and his connection to Lord Ashton carefully obscured."

"What of Lady Ashton?" Nicholas asked, the question emerging before he could consider its wisdom. He had neither seen nor communicated with Caroline since before his departure on *Alert*, though thoughts of her had been a constant presence throughout the intervening weeks.

"Miss Carlisle," Westborne corrected gently, "has formally petitioned to relinquish all claims to her late husband's title and estate. Given the circumstances, and with certain discreet assistance from sympathetic quarters, this unusual request has been expedited through the proper channels. She has returned to her father's household and resumed her maiden name." He paused, studying Nicholas for a moment. "Ashton's title passes to a nephew—a country squire with little interest in politics and less in commerce. A convenient arrangement that allows the matter to quietly fade from society's attention."

Westborne set down his cup with deliberate precision. "The essential matter before us, Commander Cruwys, is how these various threads—the French inquiry, the local rumors, and the need to maintain our carefully constructed narrative—affect your position." He glanced toward Trevenen, suggesting a previously agreed division of responsibility in this conversation. "We have concluded that your continued presence in London or indeed England represents an unnecessary risk. Questions may arise, connections might be drawn, particularly given your previous command of *Alert*. Moreover, your recent injury would be difficult to explain in conventional terms."

Trevenen cleared his throat, "The Admiralty will issue orders placing you on extended leave for reasons of health—the wound to your leg providing sufficient justification without inviting scrutiny. You will not resign your commission; it will merely be held in abeyance until circumstances permit your formal return to naval service." The words were delivered with careful emphasis, suggesting both the official position and the unofficial truth beneath it. "However, this arrangement permits us considerable latitude regarding your actual employment during this interval."

Thornhill, who had been silently arranging further documents upon the table throughout this exchange, now placed before Nicholas what appeared to be a Company commission—the distinctive seal and elaborate letterhead unmistakable to anyone familiar with East India affairs. "This may prove of interest," he said with characteristic understatement. "It represents a possible solution to several problems simultaneously."

Before Nicholas could examine the document, Westborne rose and moved to the door, opening it himself rather than summoning a servant—an unusual action that emphasized the particular privacy of their gathering. "Captain Montague," he called softly, "pray join us now." A moment later, the door admitted a lean man of perhaps fifty, dressed in the plain blue coat and buff waistcoat of a senior Company official, though with none of the ornate buttons or excessive lacing that many such men affected. His face bore the distinctive weathering of decades in Eastern seas—the particular combination of sun-darkened skin across the forehead and cheeks, paired with the pale lines around the eyes that spoke of years squinting against the reflected glare of tropical waters.

"Commander Cruwys," Montague said, extending his hand with the particular directness of a man accustomed to the Company's blunt commercial culture rather than naval ceremony. "Your accomplishments have been recounted to me, though necessarily in the broadest terms." His accent carried a trace of something beyond standard English—perhaps Portuguese, or the particular inflection acquired by those who spend years speaking through Chinese and Malay interpreters. "I believe we face a situation that may require similar... discretion." This last word was delivered with a slight emphasis that conveyed mountains of meaning beneath the apparently innocuous surface. Nicholas noted the man's hands—brown and steady, with several small scars across the knuckles that suggested experience beyond mere mercantile navigation.

Montague took a seat at Westborne's gesture, his movements carrying that particular economy acquired by men long accustomed to the confines of shipboard life. "I have recently returned from Canton," he said, accepting the coffee Westborne offered him, "where I have spent the last two years as the Company's representative to the Hong merchants. My official capacity was purely commercial—securing favorable terms for tea, silk, and porcelain while managing our factory at Whampoa. My unofficial duties, however, extended somewhat beyond those parameters." He glanced toward Westborne, receiving a slight nod of permission to continue.

"During my final months in Canton," Montague continued, "we began to observe certain irregularities in the local trading patterns. French commercial agents have been unusually active among the Hong merchants, particularly those controlling the tea trade. They have been offering prices significantly above market value, apparently unconcerned with immediate profit." He sipped his coffee with the deliberation of a man ordering his thoughts. "More concerning still, we have identified unusual movements of silver—substantial quantities arriving aboard vessels flying Dutch colors but carrying French supercargoes. This silver is not being used merely for regular trade but appears to be financing something considerably more ambitious."

Nicholas studied the Company commission Thornhill had placed before him. It appointed him as master and commander of the East India Company ship *Ganges*, with full authority to "direct her course and operations in accordance with the particular instructions provided separately." The commission bore the signatures of three Company directors, including—Nicholas noted with immediate understanding—Edward Carlisle.

"What Mr. Montague has described," Thornhill said, drawing Nicholas's attention back to the conversation, "would be concerning enough as a purely commercial matter. However, during the interrogation of Everett we discovered references to a complex operation centered in Canton." He produced another document, this one bearing clear signs of having been hastily transcribed from a more formal original. "Ashton and Everett were not acting alone. Their operation extended far beyond merely providing naval intelligence to the French and Spanish. There exists a larger scheme, one involving deliberate undermining of British strategic interests in China."

"The Canton trade represents nearly one-quarter of the Company's annual revenue," Westborne observed, his tone conveying the particular gravity that accompanied discussions of matters where politics and commerce intersected. "Control of the tea routes alone gives us both commercial advantage and strategic leverage throughout the East. Any disruption to these arrangements would have profound consequences for the Treasury, particularly given the extraordinary expenditures required by seven years of war."

Montague leaned forward slightly. "We have reason to believe a French vessel departed Lorient three days ago bound for Canton via the Cape of Good Hope. She carrries not only silver but also certain specialized agents—men with knowledge of both Chinese customs and the particular vulnerabilities of our position in that region. Their purpose appears three-fold: to manipulate the tea and opium routes currently under British influence, to disrupt the Company monopoly positions secured through decades of careful negotiation, and to align Chinese coastal interests—particularly among the Hokkien merchants—with French commercial agents."

"This French vessel," Thornhill added, his voice carrying that particular flatness that suggested the information had been secured through means best left unspecified, "is believed to be a modified merchant ship, armed but flying civilian colors. She carries papers identifying her as the *Espérance*, though her true name may differ. We cannot intercept her in European waters—the peace negotiations remain too delicate to risk such a provocation. However, once she rounds the Cape..." He let the implication hang.

Nicholas looked down at the Company commission again, understanding now its full significance. "You propose that I take this vessel, the *Ganges*, and intercept the French ship before she reaches Canton."

"Precisely," Westborne confirmed. "Not as a King's officer, but as a Company commander operating under commercial authority. Should you succeed in locating and neutralizing this threat, you would do so without any official connection to the Admiralty. The Company would bear full responsibility for your actions, citing protection of its legitimate trade interests." He paused. "The legal standing is somewhat ambiguous, I grant you, but considerably less problematic than our recent arrangement with *Alert*."

Trevenen leaned forward slightly, his expression carrying that particular formality which indicated matters of substantial significance. "You would not be entirely unsupported, Nicholas. The Company maintains certain arrangements with elements of the Royal Navy operating in Eastern waters. Should circumstances prove particularly challenging, discreet assistance might be available—though any such support would necessarily remain unofficial." He exchanged glances with Westborne, the silent communication suggesting limits to what could be promised explicitly. "I should add that your acceptance of this commission would be viewed most favorably when circumstances permit your eventual return to regular naval service."

"The *Ganges*," Montague said, drawing a folded document from inside his coat, "is currently completing her refit at Blackwall. She was built four years ago at the Company yard in Bombay—teak planking on English oak frames, copper-bottomed last year. Three-masted, ship-rigged, approximately 650 tons. She carries twenty-four twelve-pounders on her gun deck, with six eighteen-pound carronades on the quarterdeck and forecastle, and two long nine bow chasers." He placed a ship's draft upon the table—professionally executed with the particular attention to detail that characterized Indian shipwrights trained in the English tradition. "She was designed primarily as a China trader, but with consideration for defense against pirates in the South China Sea. Her lines are sharper than most Indiamen, sacrificing some cargo capacity for speed and handling. She is in effect a cross between a larger Indiaman and a 32 gun frigate.

Thornhill added, "She has recently returned from Canton with a cargo of tea and silk. Rather than sending her back immediately with the general trade, the Company has agreed to place her at our disposal for this particular service." He did not elaborate on what persuasions might have been required to secure such an expensive asset, though Nicholas suspected Edward Carlisle's involvement extended beyond merely signing the commission. "She carries a crew of eighty, including lascars for the running rigging and European gunners. You would be permitted to select your own officers, subject to certain necessary conditions regarding Company protocol."

"The financial arrangements," Westborne said, addressing a matter which delicacy had heretofore left unmentioned, "include your commander's half-pay from the Navy, which will continue during your official leave. Additionally, the Company offers their standard captain's rate of £30 per month, with the customary privilege of private trade up to the value of thirty-eight tons of cargo space—a considerable sum if judiciously managed." This represented an income significantly exceeding what Nicholas might have expected even as post-captain in the Navy, where prize money rather than regular pay constituted the primary source of potential wealth. "There is also provision for a gratuity upon successful completion of the specific service, the details of which are outlined in the separate instructions."

Nicholas considered these propositions with the careful attention appropriate to a matter that would determine not merely his immediate future, but potentially the course of his entire career. The *Ganges* herself larger than anything he had yet commanded, as large as Montague had noted as frigate. Yet she was not in the end a naval vessel but rather just a well-armed merchant ship. Operating beyond the formal protection of the Royal Navy meant that should he be captured or his actions questioned, he could expect little official support. Yet the alternative was apparently some kind travel away from England with no purpose, and likely the tedium of enforced idleness while his leg healed.

"There is one further consideration," Montague said, breaking the silence that had fallen. "I have been authorized to accompany you as the Company's official representative. My knowledge of Canton, the Hong merchants, and their trading practices may prove useful in identifying the full extent of the French operation." His tone suggested this arrangement was not merely a suggestion. "I should add that while my formal position would be that of supercargo, responsible for commercial matters, I have some experience in operations of a more... vigorous nature." The faint smile that accompanied these words gave particular emphasis to the scars across his knuckles, which Nicholas had previously noted.

Westborne watched Nicholas closely, his expression revealing nothing of his own views regarding the appropriate response. "The *Ganges* can be ready to sail within a fortnight. So *Espérance* has a considerable head start, but not an insurmountable one given the lengthy passage to the East. The matter requires decision relatively promptly, though I would not press you for an immediate answer." He paused. "Perhaps you might wish to consult with those whose counsel you value before committing yourself to such an extended absence from England."

"I would be grateful for a day to consider the matter," Nicholas said after a moment's reflection. "The opportunity is not one to be declined lightly, yet neither should it be accepted without proper consideration." He folded the commission with careful precision, his movements betraying nothing of the complex calculations taking place behind his composed expression. The prospect of extended service in the East held particular resonance for him—it had been in those distant waters that he had first learned his profession as a surveyor under Cook, and later sailed among the Spice Islands with Silva. To return there now, under such unusual circumstances, represented a confluence of past and present that merited thoughtful examination.

"By all means," Westborne replied with the particular courtesy reserved for requests he had anticipated. "We shall reconvene tomorrow afternoon, if that proves suitable. Mr. Thornhill will have prepared the detailed instructions by then, and Captain Montague can answer any specific questions regarding the vessel or the situation in Canton." He rose, signaling the conclusion of the formal portion of their discussion. "I believe Sir Edward Carlisle mentioned he would welcome a visit from you, when circumstances permitted. Perhaps this interval might provide such an opportunity."

Nicholas did not miss the deliberate neutrality with which Westborne delivered this final observation—a masterpiece of suggestion without explicit statement. The reference to Caroline's father contained within it the unstated permission to see Caroline herself, yet framed in terms that maintained the proprieties. "I shall call upon him this afternoon," Nicholas replied with matching care, "to convey my respects and inquire after his family's welfare." Trevenen's expression remained carefully neutral, though a certain quality in his gaze suggested both understanding and caution—the silent communication between relations who comprehend matters requiring discretion.

A light rain had begun to fall as Nicholas's hackney made its way through London's crowded streets toward Portland Place and Ocean House. The weather matched his reflections—neither stormy nor clear, but that particular intermediate state that demanded patience and careful navigation. The proposition laid before him represented both opportunity and significant risk. To command a well-found East Indiaman with a specific objective appealed strongly to his nature; yet to operate in that ambiguous territory between naval and commercial service, without the clear chain of command and defined responsibilities that had governed his professional life, required careful consideration.

The familiar brass plate of Ocean House gleamed dully through the rain as the hackney drew up before the entrance. Nicholas paid the driver well but with the careful economy of a man who remained conscious of expenditure, notwithstanding his prize money from the *San Isidro*. The house itself appeared unchanged since his last visit—the Portland stone façade maintaining its dignified aspect, neither ostentatiously grand nor merely respectable but occupying that precise interval between which signified substantial mercantile success. The brass knocker yielded a firm, measured sound beneath his hand.

Winters, Carlisle's butler, admitted him with a bow that suggested both recognition and a certain private acknowledgment of circumstances better left unspoken. "Sir Edward is in his study, sir. He has left instructions that you are to be shown in directly." The entrance hall retained that particular quality Nicholas remembered—the scent of beeswax and good leather, the gleam of polished oak, the sense of a household managed with the same precise attention that had built Carlisle's commercial empire. As he followed Winters through the passage toward the study, Nicholas detected subtle changes since his last visit—the addition of a fine Chinese screen in the side parlor, a new arrangement of miniatures in the corridor, suggesting that Caroline's influence had already begun to reshape her father's household following her return.

Edward Carlisle rose from his desk as Nicholas was announced, extending his hand with genuine warmth. The merchant's face showed signs of the strain recent events had placed upon him—new lines at the corners of his eyes, a certain tightness around the mouth—yet his bearing remained that of a man accustomed to weathering commercial and personal storms with equal composure. "Commander Cruwys," he said, his voice carrying that particular richness Nicholas remembered from their first meeting in Bombay years before. "Your visit is most welcome." He gestured toward a comfortable chair positioned near the hearth, where a coal fire provided gentle warmth against the November chill. "May I offer you brandy? I've recently received a shipment of particularly fine Cognac that arrived under somewhat unorthodox circumstances—a small benefit of uncertain times in the Channel."

"Thank you, sir," Nicholas replied, accepting both the seat and the offered glass. The study had changed little since their last meeting—charts of trade routes still adorned the walls, ledgers bound in red Morocco leather occupied their accustomed places upon the shelves, and the scent of Carlisle's particular tobacco blend lingered pleasantly in the air. Yet here too there were subtle shifts—a woman's touch evident in the arrangement of fresh flowers upon the side table, a new set of watercolors depicting tropical scenes hanging in place of the formal naval engravings that had previously occupied the space. "I understand you've been consulted regarding a certain proposition that has been placed before me," Nicholas continued, once Winters had withdrawn and closed the door behind him.

"Indeed," Carlisle confirmed, settling into his own chair with a slight stiffness that betrayed his true age despite his vigorous appearance. "The Company directors were surprisingly amenable to the arrangement, particularly after certain financial considerations were properly aligned. The *Ganges* is a fine vessel—I sailed in her myself from Madras to Canton during her maiden voyage." He studied Nicholas over the rim of his glass, his merchant's eye making its habitual assessment. "This would be no small commitment, you understand. A voyage to Canton and back requires at minimum eighteen months, often considerably longer given the vagaries of weather, politics, and commerce in those waters."

Carlisle studied him for a moment, his expression softening slightly. "My daughter has shown remarkable resilience in these difficult circumstances. She has resumed her previous interests—particularly her work with the Company accounts and correspondence, where her particular acuity for patterns and discrepancies has proven valuable." He set down his glass with deliberate precision. "She is, I believe, in the garden pavilion at present. Her custom each afternoon, weather permitting, is to spend an hour there with her watercolors and journals." He rose and moved to the window, gazing out toward the rear of the property where the pavilion stood partially visible among carefully tended shrubbery. "Perhaps you might wish to take some air before you depart? The rain appears to have lessened considerably."

The garden pavilion stood at the far end of the property, a small classical structure of Portland stone positioned to catch the afternoon light. The path leading to it had been recently graveled, the wet stones crunching softly beneath Nicholas's boots as he approached. Rain still clung to the box hedges bordering the walkway, their scent sharp and clean in the damp air. His leg ached dully as he walked, the lingering reminder of *Le Furet's* broadside, but the discomfort seemed distant now, secondary to the quickening of his pulse as the pavilion drew nearer. Through its open doorway, he caught a glimpse of movement—the shifting of a pale blue dress, the turning of a page.

Nicholas paused at the entrance, suddenly conscious of the significance of this moment. His last sight of Caroline had been in the quiet hour before dawn at Ocean House, as she had left his bed chamber with that particular grace she possessed—deliberate, dignified, yet carrying an undeniable warmth. That had been before *Alert*, before the Bay of Biscay, before the deaths that now lay between them like a shadow. He cleared his throat softly, a gentleman's warning of approach rather than a disruption. "Caroline," he said, the name still slightly unfamiliar after years of thinking of her under her married title. "I hope I do not intrude upon your solitude."

Caroline looked up from her sketchbook, her composure betraying only the slightest alteration as she recognized him—a momentary widening of her eyes, a faint heightening of color in her cheeks. "Nicholas," she replied, her voice carrying that particular quality he remembered so well from Bombay and Luanda—clear, measured, yet with an undercurrent of feeling carefully contained. "You are most welcome." She closed her sketchbook with deliberate movements, setting aside her pencils on the small table beside her. She wore a gown of pale blue muslin, modest in cut yet becoming in its simplicity, her hair arranged without elaborate ornament in a style that suggested practical elegance rather than fashionable excess. "Please," she added, indicating the stone bench opposite her own seat, "will you join me?"

"I had hoped to call sooner," he said, the simple words carrying the weight of all that had transpired in the intervening weeks. The light filtering through the rain-washed air cast her features in a gentle clarity that emphasized both her composure and the subtle signs of strain beneath it—the slight shadow beneath her eyes, the particular tension in her posture that spoke of burdens borne with dignity rather than ease. "There were matters requiring resolution before I could properly express..." He paused, searching for words adequate to the complex reality between them. "Before I could properly speak with you about what passed between us."

Caroline studied him with that direct gaze he had first noted in Bombay—unflinching, appraising, yet not unkind. "You need not explain, Nicholas. I understand duty, and the necessary discretion such service demands." Her hands rested lightly upon the closed sketchbook, the absence of rings on her fingers a visible reminder of her deliberate return to unmarried status. "My father has mentioned something of the circumstances, though naturally without details. I gather you have been offered a position that would take you far from England, and for a considerable time." The statement contained no accusation, no resentment—merely the calm acknowledgment of a probability long considered.

Nicholas recognized the particular quality in her tone—not resignation, but rather the realistic assessment of a woman who had never expected conventional arrangements. "The East India Company has offered me command of the *Ganges*, bound for

Canton," he confirmed. "Ostensibly a regular trading voyage, but with certain additional responsibilities of a more discreet nature." He hesitated, then continued with careful directness. "The undertaking would require my absence for at least eighteen months, quite possibly longer depending on circumstances in the East." The admission hung between them, its implications extending far beyond mere separation by distance or time.

"I see," Caroline replied, her expression revealing nothing beyond thoughtful consideration. Then, after a moment: "You intend to accept." It was not a question but a recognition, spoken without surprise or recrimination. She had always possessed that rare ability to see clearly the necessities that governed his choices, just as he had understood the particular independence that defined her nature. "It is the appropriate decision, under the circumstances."

"I believe it is," Nicholas agreed, watching her carefully. "There are practical considerations—the rumors concerning *Alert*, the delicacy of recent events. But there is also..." He paused, formulating the thought with precision. "There is also the matter of what might exist between us, Caroline. I would not leave without some understanding, some clarity regarding expectations—yours and mine." This directness represented a departure from conventional courtship, but their circumstances had never been conventional, from their first meeting in Bombay to the night she had sought him out at Ocean House.

Caroline's gaze met his directly, a slight flush rising in her cheeks—not from embarrassment, but from the particular intensity that accompanied complete honesty. "I have never been one for traditional arrangements, Nicholas. You know this about me. My... affections have never been constrained by ordinary expectations." Her words, though carefully chosen, acknowledged without explicit statement her past relationship with Catherine Holloway and the unconventional nature of her brief marriage to Ashton. "What passed between us at Ocean House was neither impulsive nor regretted, at least not on my part. Yet I would not bind you with promises or demands that might prove... impractical... given the distance and time your service requires."

Nicholas leaned forward slightly, drawn by her candor. "We find ourselves in unusual circumstances," he said, his voice carrying that particular quietness reserved for matters of profound significance. "I would not presume to ask for promises that might prove difficult to honor across such distances and uncertainties. Yet I find myself..." he paused, searching for words adequate to express a sentiment both deeply felt and carefully measured, "unwilling to depart without some understanding between us. Not chains or obligations, Caroline, but a recognition of what exists."

"What exists," she repeated softly, her gaze falling momentarily to her sketchbook, where Nicholas glimpsed the edge of a drawing—the clean line of a ship's hull rendered with the precise understanding of one who had studied such vessels with genuine comprehension. When she looked up again, her expression held a clarity that reminded him of certain moments at sea, when cloud and horizon merged in perfect definition. "I will not pretend to conventional expectations, Nicholas. My life has never followed such paths, nor would I wish it to. While you are gone, I shall continue my work with the Company ledgers, assist my father as his health permits, and perhaps resume certain studies in natural philosophy that marriage interrupted."

She hesitated, then added with characteristic directness, "I shall make no claim on your behavior in distant ports—history suggests that naval officers face particular... circumstances... during extended voyages." Her eyes met his with unflinching honesty. "Similarly, I would ask that you understand the nature of my friendships with certain women. Such connections sustain me in ways different from what exists between us, yet they need not diminish it. I shall form no attachment to any man during your absence, but I would not have you demand a complete solitude of me either."

Nicholas considered her words carefully, recognizing both the practical wisdom and the emotional honesty they contained. Long separations created their own realities, as every naval wife and every sailor knew, though such matters were rarely discussed with such forthright clarity. "I understand," he replied after a moment. "What passed between us at Ocean House was neither casual nor incidental to me, Caroline. I would return to England with the hope—though I dare not call it expectation—of finding that essential connection between us unchanged." He paused, choosing his next words with precision. "The particulars of how we each endure eighteen months of separation matter less than the understanding we maintain. I ask only for honesty, not impossible standards."

This deliberate exchange, offered without dramatic declaration or excessive sentiment, represented the most they could properly express under the circumstances—a commitment substantial in its pragmatic recognition of reality, unadorned by false promises or romantic excess. He was a naval officer contemplating an extended and potentially hazardous mission; she was a woman newly freed from a disastrous marriage and possessed of uncommon independence. Neither conventional engagement nor mere understanding would adequately define what lay between them, but they had found their own balance of truth and commitment that suited their particular circumstances.

Caroline's face softened, the smile that transformed her features appearing briefly. "Then we have an understanding, Nicholas—not binding like formal betrothal, yet more substantial than mere possibility." She reached across the space between them and placed her hand briefly upon his. "I shall expect letters when opportunity permits, though I understand the uncertainties of communication across such distances. And I shall write as well, directing my correspondence through the Company offices in Canton." She withdrew her hand with. "Now tell me of this vessel, the *Ganges*. Is she well-found? Are her sailing qualities adequate to the service intended?"

Nicholas recognized and appreciated this shift toward practical matters—it was characteristic of her to move from emotional understanding to concrete detail without artificial transition. "She is reputed to be exceptionally well-constructed," he replied, grateful for the opportunity to discuss a subject where his expertise stood on firm ground. "Built of Malabar teak on English oak frames at the Company yard in Bombay, copper-bottomed last year. Twenty-four nine-pounders on her gun deck, with six eighteen-pound carronades on the quarterdeck and forecastle, and two chase guns." He paused, considering the specific attributes that would matter most for their intended purpose. "Her lines are reportedly sharper than most Indiamen, sacrificing some cargo capacity for speed and handling, a quality that may prove valuable given certain aspects of our mission."

"My father spoke of her with particular approval after his voyage to Madras," Caroline observed. "He mentioned her weatherly qualities, especially her ability to point higher into the wind than most vessels of comparable size. A characteristic that might prove advantageous should you be required to intercept another ship." The comment revealed both her understanding of maritime matters and her awareness that his mission likely extended beyond mere trade. Her perception had always been one of her most remarkable qualities—the ability to discern unstated realities without requiring explicit confirmation. "Will you be permitted to select your own officers?" she inquired, shifting to another practical concern that would significantly affect both his comfort and chances of success during the extended voyage.

"Within certain constraints," Nicholas confirmed. "The Company naturally insists upon a properly qualified supercargo—Captain Montague, who has recently returned from Canton and possesses particular knowledge of conditions there. And there are established protocols regarding the position of chief mate." He hesitated, weighing how much to reveal about Montague's dual role as both commercial representative and intelligence agent. "Markham would have made an ideal sailing master, but he has been sent to the West Indies. I shall likely have to accept a Company nominee for that position, though I believe I might successfully request one or two junior officers from naval service."

"Will you call upon any of your former officers before your departure?" Caroline asked, her question carrying the particular astuteness that had always characterized her understanding of naval connections. "Having trusted men would seem essential for such an extended undertaking, particularly given the... ambiguous nature of your position."

"I had thought to request one or two junior officers with whom I've previously served," Nicholas replied, acknowledging the perspicacity of her observation. "Though with Forester sailing to the Caribbean with Walsh and Markham also dispatched to the Indies, my options are somewhat limited." He considered the matter further, weighing the practicalities against the benefits of securing trusted officers. "Perhaps a request through Admiral Trevenen might expedite matters, though I hesitate to impose upon his good offices for personal preference rather than operational necessity." This last remark carried a certain irony, given that the entire arrangement represented an extraordinary exercise of influence outside normal naval channels.

Caroline's gaze swept the garden, not with anxiety but with the natural awareness of her surroundings that was characteristic of her observant nature. "Come," she said with sudden decision, rising in a smooth motion, the pale blue of her gown catching the filtered afternoon light. "There is a place behind the pavilion where the shrubbery forms a complete screen. My father had it planted to shield his meditation bench from the kitchen windows." The suggestion carried no coquetry, only the practical desire for a moment of privacy between them.

Once within this green enclosure, Caroline turned to him with that particular directness which had first drawn him to her in Bombay.

"My father has mentioned hosting a small dinner the evening before your departure, which I understand to be the 29th. He wishes to discuss certain commercial matters regarding Canton, but I suspect he also intends it as a proper farewell, "she said, her hands reaching naturally for his. "But before that now that you are free to visit, he asks that you spend Christmas with us, and stay at the house both on Christmas Eve and Christmas Day."

A slight smile touched her lips. "He has suggested that the house has ample guest chambers, should you wish to remain for those nights rather than returning to South Audley Street. I believe he understands our... situation... better than either of us might have expected."

Nicholas said nothing at first. The air between them held a December clarity—bare branches overhead, the faint scent of earth and box hedge.

"Christmas at Ocean House," he said at last, as if testing the phrase for soundness. "It would be quiet."

She tilted her head slightly. "Not empty."

He looked at her then—not with surprise, but with the long, careful recognition that follows when two people step past pretense at last.

"If your father truly does not object..."

She gave a short, amused breath. "He has not objected for some time. I believe he considers the matter settled—if unofficial."

Nicholas nodded once. "Then I'll bring a change of coat, and something fit to pass for cheer."

They walked on in silence a few paces more. From the house, the faint chime of a clock marked the hour. The holly at the garden's edge gleamed with frost.

"Your father has always shown remarkable perception," Nicholas replied, drawing her closer with the easy familiarity of established intimacy. "And an equally remarkable discretion." Edward Carlisle's tacit approval of their relationship—unorthodox though it might appear to conventional society—represented the particular wisdom of a man who valued genuine happiness above rigid adherence to social forms. "I should be honored to accept his invitation," Nicholas added, his hands finding her waist with remembered certainty.

Their kiss held nothing of tentative exploration—they had moved beyond such preliminaries during those quiet hours before, instead it carried the particular quality of connection between two people who had discovered in each other something both unexpected and essential. Her lips were warm against his, neither yielding nor demanding but meeting with equal presence. The scent of jasmine in her hair, the pressure of her fingers at the nape of his neck, the slight yielding of her body against his—these sensations held both the immediacy of the present moment and the promise of continuity across the separation to come.

When they finally drew apart, Caroline's expression carried that particular blend of composure and warmth that had always been uniquely hers. "I shall not burden our farewell with excessive sentiment when the time comes," she said, her hands still resting lightly upon his shoulders. "But I would ask one thing of you, Nicholas. Write when you can—not merely reports of position and progress, but something of your thoughts. I shall do the same." The request was delivered without melodrama yet carried a depth of feeling that required no elaborate declaration. "My father maintains secure Company communications to Canton. Our letters may be delayed, but they will find their destinations."

"I shall write," he promised, the simple words carrying the weight of genuine commitment. "And I shall return when the service is completed." He did not add unnecessary assurances regarding safety or timeframe; both understood too well the hazards of extended voyages and the particular dangers his mission might entail. "We shall have time before my departure," he added, "to speak further of arrangements. For now, it is enough to know that we understand one another."

Caroline nodded, her practical nature reasserting itself. "Let us return to the house," she suggested. "My father will be expecting some report of our conversation, though naturally not in its entirety." Her smile returned, carrying a hint of mischief rarely revealed to those who knew her only in her more formal aspect. "We should not disappoint him by remaining absent overlong, however understanding his nature might be."

The next day, Nicholas stood in Westborne's study once more, the charts of Eastern waters now spread fully across the table rather than partially concealed beneath other documents. His questions regarding the mission had been specific and thorough—the precise specifications of the *Espérance*, her commander's reputation and history, her expected route and sailing qualities. Captain Montague had provided what intelligence existed: "She is commanded by one Antoine Deschamps, formerly of the French Navy, a frigate captain until '78, then resigned under circumstances not entirely clear. The vessel appears to be a modified East Indiaman, approximately 750 tons, with renovations to improve her speed rather than cargo capacity. She carries twenty-four twelve-pounders and reportedly sails remarkably well on a reach, though she falls off considerably close-hauled."

"I shall require additional men," Nicholas said, his tone conveying not demand but professional assessment. "Eighty hands may suffice for a routine trading voyage, but for a vessel that may be required to chase and engage another ship of comparable size, I would need at least one hundred ninety men. Particularly European seamen for the guns—lascars are excellent on running rigging, but less practiced at the discipline required for effective gunnery." He traced a finger along the projected course of the *Espérance* as she would round the Cape of Good Hope and enter the Indian Ocean. "And I should prefer British warrant officers if possible—gunner, carpenter, bosun—men accustomed to naval standards rather than merely commercial efficiency."

Thornhill made notations on a small memorandum book as Nicholas spoke, while Westborne and Trevenen exchanged glances of quiet approval. "The additional manning can be arranged," Westborne confirmed after a brief consultation, "though with certain economies elsewhere to balance the Company accounts." It was the practiced response of a man who understood that bureaucratic constraints could be navigated given sufficient motivation. Nicholas's careful attention to operational details had confirmed their assessment of his suitability for the task.

"Given these arrangements and the information you've provided regarding the *Espérance* and her commander," Nicholas said with deliberate formality, "I accept the commission and will undertake this service to the best of my abilities." The words, simple yet weighted with significance, marked his formal commitment to a mission that would take him halfway around the world into circumstances of considerable uncertainty and potential danger. Trevenen nodded once with subtle approval, while Westborne's expression reflected the particular satisfaction of a man who has successfully aligned multiple interests toward a single purpose.

The Christmas days passed quietly at Ocean House, observed with that particular blend of reserve and intention that marked Edward Carlisle's household in all things. The dinner on Christmas Eve was modest by London standards—partridge, oysters, and a bottle of excellent port from the cellars—but it was served with form and grace, and no guest mistook its significance. Conversation turned easily from Canton to West Indian trade, then to naval transport rates..

That night, he did not return to the guest chamber that had been set aside for him. No remark was made; no explanation required.

Christmas morning at Ocean House unfolded with quiet precision. A fire was already lit in the smaller parlour, and the heavy curtains drawn back to admit what light the grey London sky allowed. After breakfast—served without fanfare but with evident care—they gathered briefly before the drawing room fire, where a modest arrangement of parcels had been laid out. It was not ceremony so much as intention: the marking of time with gestures that carried weight beyond the paper they were wrapped in.

Caroline handed Nicholas a narrow box, its lid inlaid with rosewood and ivory. Inside, on a bed of green velvet, lay a silver watch—slim, perfectly balanced, the face engraved with the four stars of the Southern Cross. He opened the inner lid to find a miniature: her likeness, finely rendered on ivory, tucked beneath the crystal in a setting of mother-of-pearl and gold. "So that you may keep something of the Pacific," she said, "and someone of London."

His gift to her was in a small hinged case of red Morocco leather. Inside lay a necklace of seed pearls and turquoise, the central pendant formed in the shape of a knot, bound with a ribbon of enamelled gold. The design was Neapolitan, delicate but strong—no overt symbolism, yet its message was clear enough. "To be worn," he said quietly, "if you wish to be remembered. Or even if not."

Caroline's fingers traced the clasp for a moment before she looked up. "I shall wear it when I write," she said.

Carlisle's gift was practical, as expected. A chest of a select private stores already packed for the ship: two cases of claret, a cask of preserved fruits, three pounds of chocolate, a jar of anchovies, and carefully packed jars of coffee beans.

Later that night, Nicholas did not return to the guest chamber that had been set aside for him. No comment was made; no adjustment required.

Outside of the holiday, the two weeks that followed passed in a blur of activity—*Ganges* in her final stages of fitting out at Blackwall Yard, where the East India Company maintained their substantial facilities for building and refitting their vessels. Her decks crowded with riggers and stevedores, her hold gradually filling with Company cargo according to the official manifest.

Walking forward on the main deck his first day aboard during the fitting out, he paused as he caught sight of the bow chasers—they were his own long nines, the Spanish brass pieces he had purchased in Jamaica at no small cost, now gleaming on their new carriages. For a moment he stared, then understood; Admiral Trevenen, it seemed, had arranged the transfer without a word.

The officers assembled gradually. The chief mate, Henry Rathbone, was a Company fixture—a broad-shouldered Yorkshireman of perhaps forty, whose face bore the particular weathering of three complete voyages to Canton and back. He met Nicholas with careful deference appropriate to the unusual circumstance of a naval officer assuming command of an Indiaman, yet with the quiet confidence of a man secure in his professional expertise. "She pulls slightly to starboard on the quarter-wave in a following sea," he remarked during their first tour of the deck together, the kind of detail that spoke volumes about his attention to the vessel's handling. "But she'll carry her topgallants in winds that would have most ships down to topsails alone."

By particular arrangement with Admiralty, facilitated through Trevenen's discreet intervention, two junior naval lieutenants were assigned to *Ganges*—William Parker, a serious young man who had served under Nicholas first as a midshipman aboard *Alert*, and who had recently been made lieutenant, and Thomas Petford from *Triumphant*, a seasoned officer with experience in Eastern waters. Their indicated temporary reassignment to "special survey duties," a convenient fiction that would allow them to serve aboard a Company vessel while maintaining their naval rank and seniority.

The warrant officers proved more difficult to secure, though eventually a gunner from the Marine Artillery, a carpenter who had served in frigates before transferring to merchant service, and a sailing master recently returned from the East Indies were all persuaded through some combination of appeal to duty and substantial financial inducement.

The 28th of December 1782, the final day before departure, dawned bright and clear with London's perpetual coal-smoke haze temporarily lifted by a brisk northerly breeze that brought with it a hint of frost. Nicholas spent the morning aboard *Ganges*, reviewing final stores and confirming that the Company's official cargo had been properly stowed and secured for sea. The crew was now complete—one hundred ninety men in total, including twenty-four former Royal Navy gunners who had been quietly approached and offered terms significantly more generous than standard Company rates. At midday he returned to South Audley Street, where his sea chest and personal effects were loaded onto a Company cart for transport to Blackwall.

As arranged, Nicholas arrived at Ocean House as the winter sun was setting, the last light casting long shadows across the Portland stone façade.

"Nicholas," Carlisle said, taking his hand with genuine feeling, "you are most welcome. The house is yours for this final evening before your departure."

Carlisle had arranged a small dinner—himself, Caroline, Nicholas, Rear Admiral Trevenen, and, somewhat unexpectedly, Thornhill, who arrived precisely at the appointed hour bearing a sealed packet that he placed on the side table with a significant glance toward Nicholas.

It was Trevenen's first meeting with Caroline, and for the better part of an hour he said almost nothing—not from reserve, but from the unmistakable stillness of a man momentarily caught without a frame of reference. Nicholas had seen that look before, though rarely in Trevenen: not confusion, precisely, but the kind of surprise that comes when elegance and intellect appear in equal force, and neither gives way to the other. Trevenen, who was largely immune to beauty and allergic to pretense, listened with an attention bordering on reverence—until, at the turn of the wine, he leaned slightly toward Nicholas and murmured, "I now understand things clearly. You are a fortunate man."

The meal passed with that particular quality of occasions laden with unspoken significance—conversation flowing naturally enough between practical matters regarding Canton, the peculiarities of dealing with Hong merchants, and the expected seasonal weather patterns along the intended route. Caroline, dressed in a gown of deep blue silk that caught the light with subtle richness, participated fully in these discussions, her knowledge of Company affairs revealing the extent to which she had resumed her role in her father's commercial enterprises.

Afterward, in the drawing room, Trevenen, Thornhill and Carlisle spoke quietly near the hearth; Nicholas and Caroline remained by the window, watching the frost gather on the glass.

He left the house just after four. The coach stood ready in the square, lanterns already lit, the horses shifting in the cold. She had helped him dress by lamplight, wordless, her hands steady at his collar, then his coat. Their parting upstairs had been no less final for its quiet. Her nightgown had fallen open at one shoulder; the candlelight caught the line of her neck, the rise and fall of breath. He had kissed her there, then lower. There had been time, even then, for passion. But they had made it slow, and nothing had been said until the end.

"Write," she had said, as he took his hat.

"Every landfall," he had answered.

And that had been enough.

Later, he stood a moment at the break in the rail, the winter sun just above the horizon and the tide making slow eddies in the black water below. *Ganges* lay quiet around him, her spars bare, her decks freshly holystoned, the faint hiss of rope on wood the only sound. The city behind him pressed no harder than fog.

He reflected on the pattern. Something French. Something faintly out of bounds. A vessel no one could name aloud, a mission no one would claim if it failed. They called it discretion, and they valued it more than loyalty.

He touched the rail once, lightly, and turned aft. Below, the lanterns glowed faint behind the quarterdeck windows, and the watch waited to be called.

Eastward, the tide was already turning.

The End.

Author's Note

This book continues the course first set in *Soundings Edge*. It follows Nicholas Cruwys not in a careerist ascent, but through a sequence of postings, silences, and consequences that shape the life of a capable man in an indifferent system.

Though the war is real—its admirals, its ships, its politics—the concern here is not with the panoramic, but with the particular: what it meant to serve amid uncertainty, to know more than one kind of loyalty.

The events surrounding Admirals Hood and Rodney's campaign in the Caribbean are drawn directly from the historical record. The tensions between Rodney and Hood, the tactical debate over line-breaking, and the political friction that followed victory were real, and consequential. Britain won the battle, but not the peace. By year's end, commissions were rescinded, prize courts slowed, and ships were quietly sold off.

Nicholas's agreement at the end of this book to command the *Ganges* East Indiaman while temporarily outside of the Royal Navy marks not his redemption, but a reassignment into ambiguity. The ship is real; the mission is credible. Vessels of her type—East Indiamen with heavier armament—were often employed in postwar service for tasks neither purely naval nor purely commercial: part convoy, part intelligence-gathering, part diplomatic presence at a distance from home.

This book is not a tale of triumph, nor of disgrace. It is a record of professional survival: of a man trusted to act, but not to be seen too clearly. The war recedes; the Empire recalibrates. And in that silence, certain names are remembered—for usefulness, not favour.

Any errors or omissions are mine alone.

— *The Author*

Printed in Dunstable, United Kingdom